YOUR FRED

Michael Rex

VIKING

VIKING
An imprint of Penguin Random House LLC, New York

First published in the United States of America by Viking,
an imprint of Penguin Random House LLC, 2022

Copyright © 2022 by Michael Rex

Visit us online at penguinrandomhouse.com.

Library of Congress Cataloging-in-Publication Data is available.

Manufactured in China

ISBN 9780593206324 (hardcover)
ISBN 9780593206331 (paperback)

1 3 5 7 9 10 8 6 4 2

TOPL

Design by Kate Renner
Text set in Out of Line BB

The artwork in this book was created in Photoshop.

To my father, who was, above all, kind.

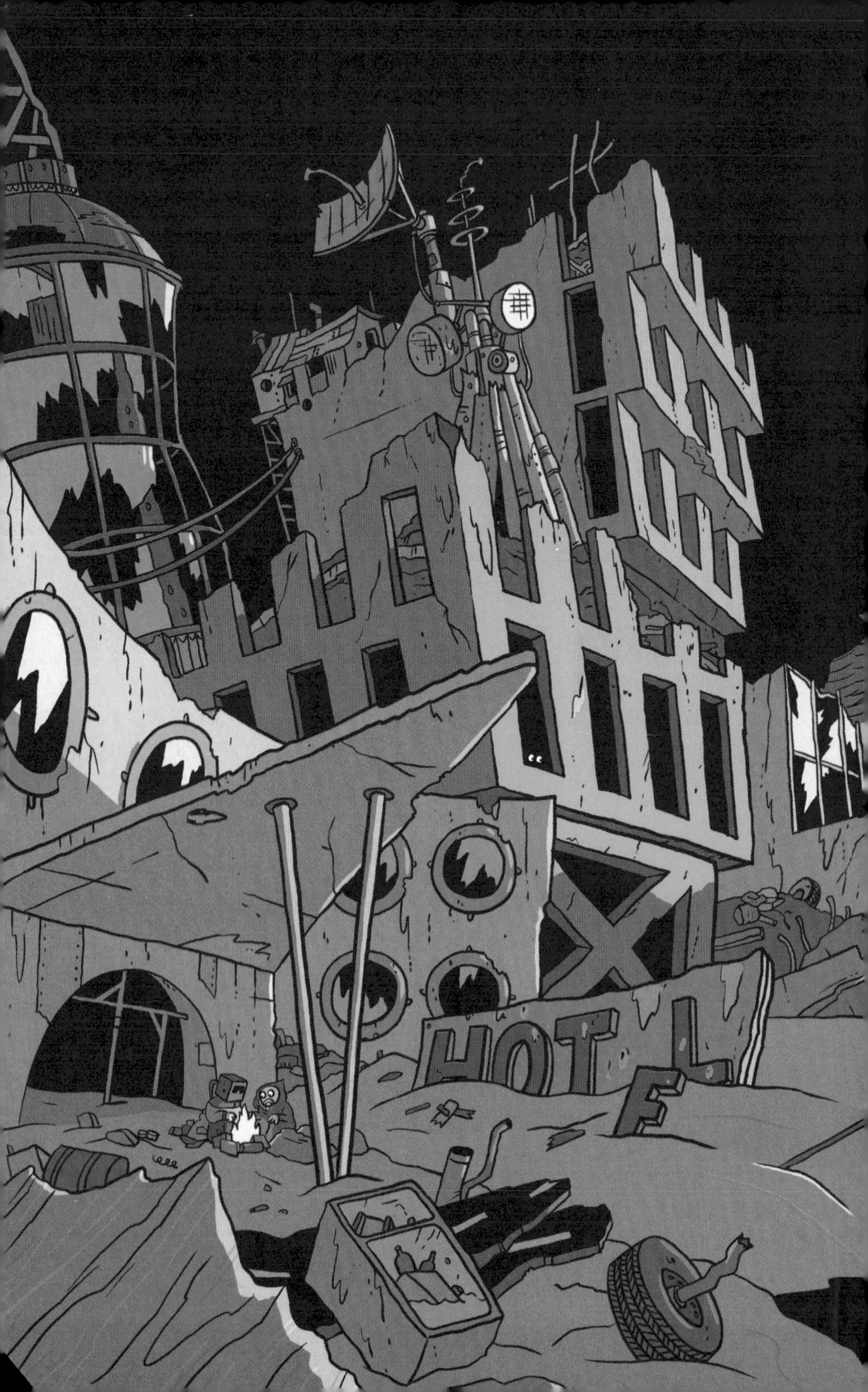
HOT L
E

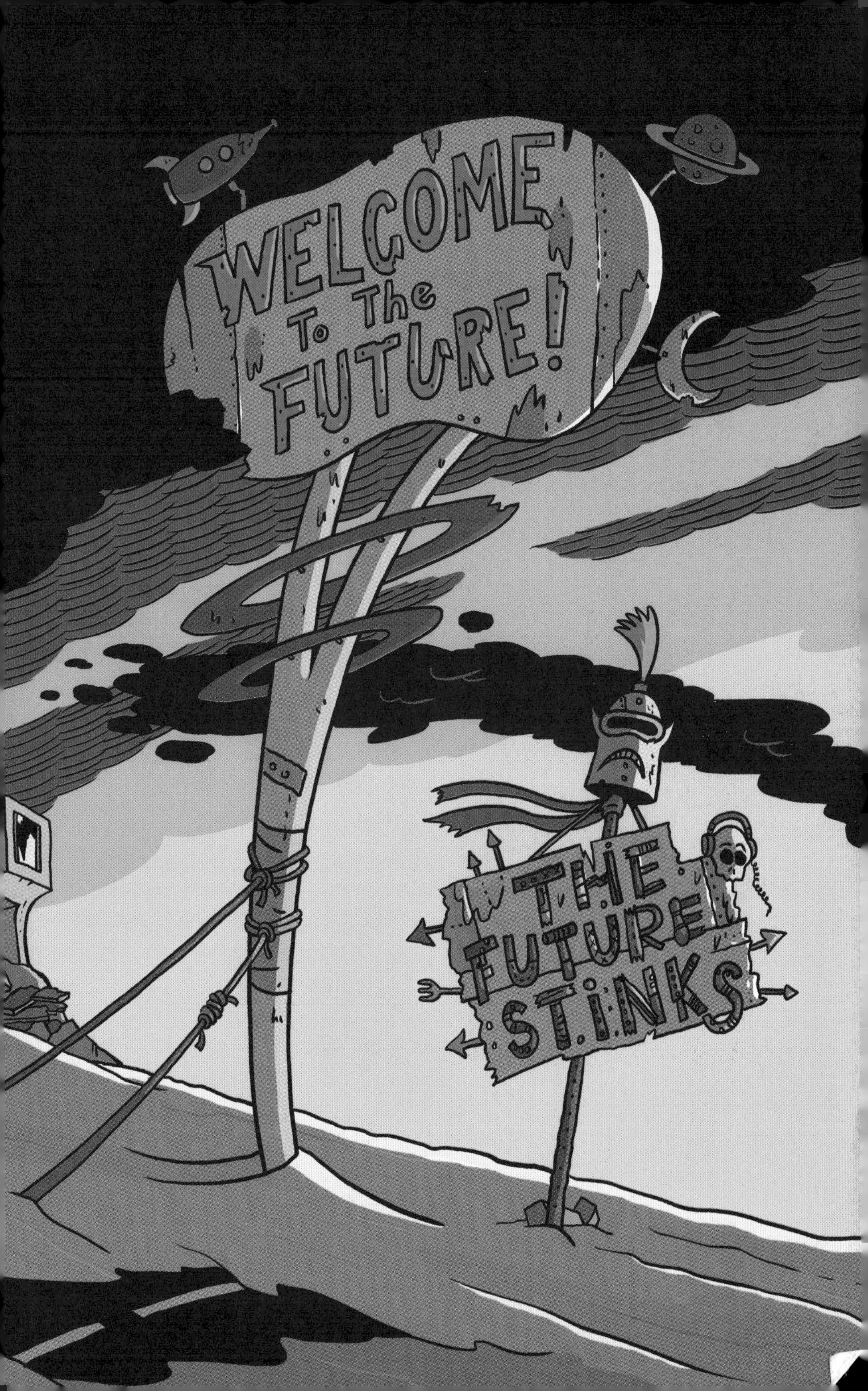
WELCOME
To The
FUTURE!
THE
FUTURE
STINKS

CHAPTER 1

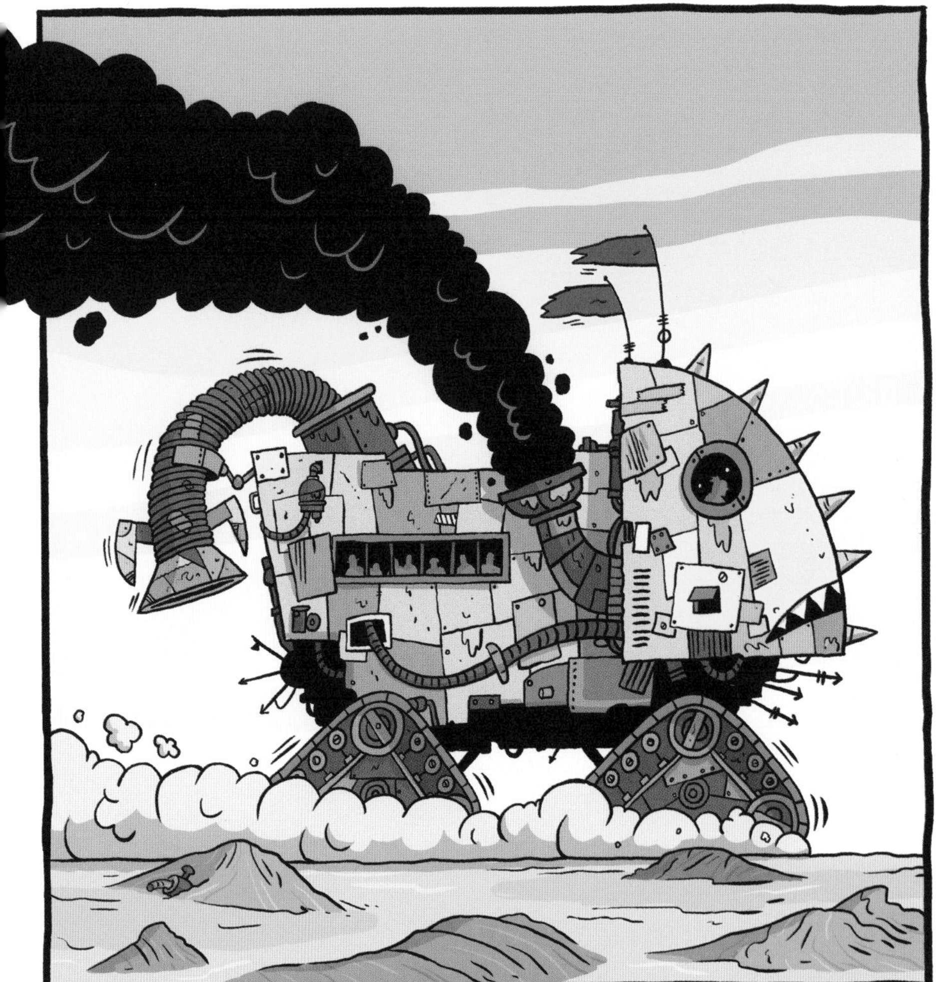

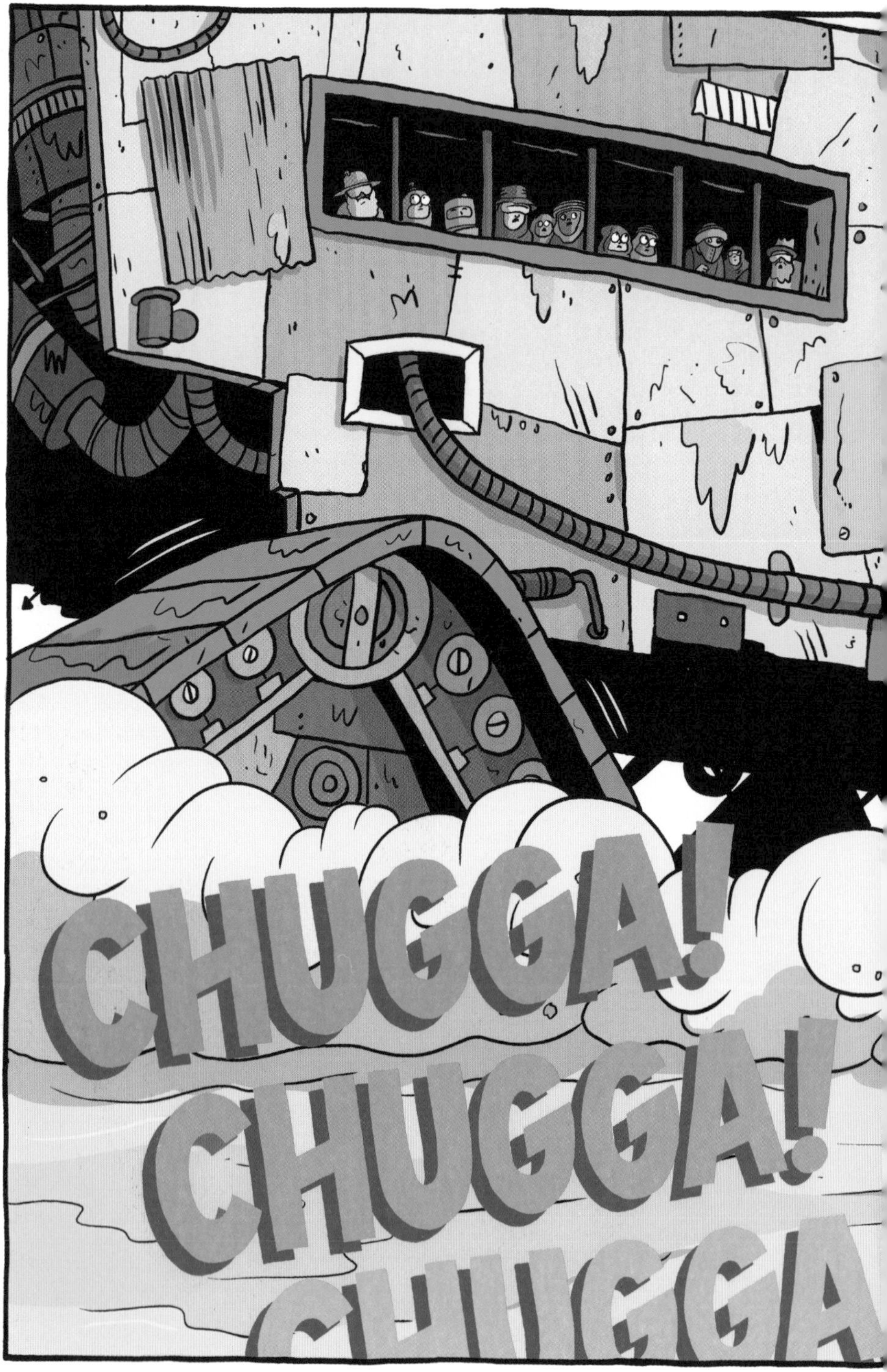
CHUGGA!
CHUGGA!
CHUGGA

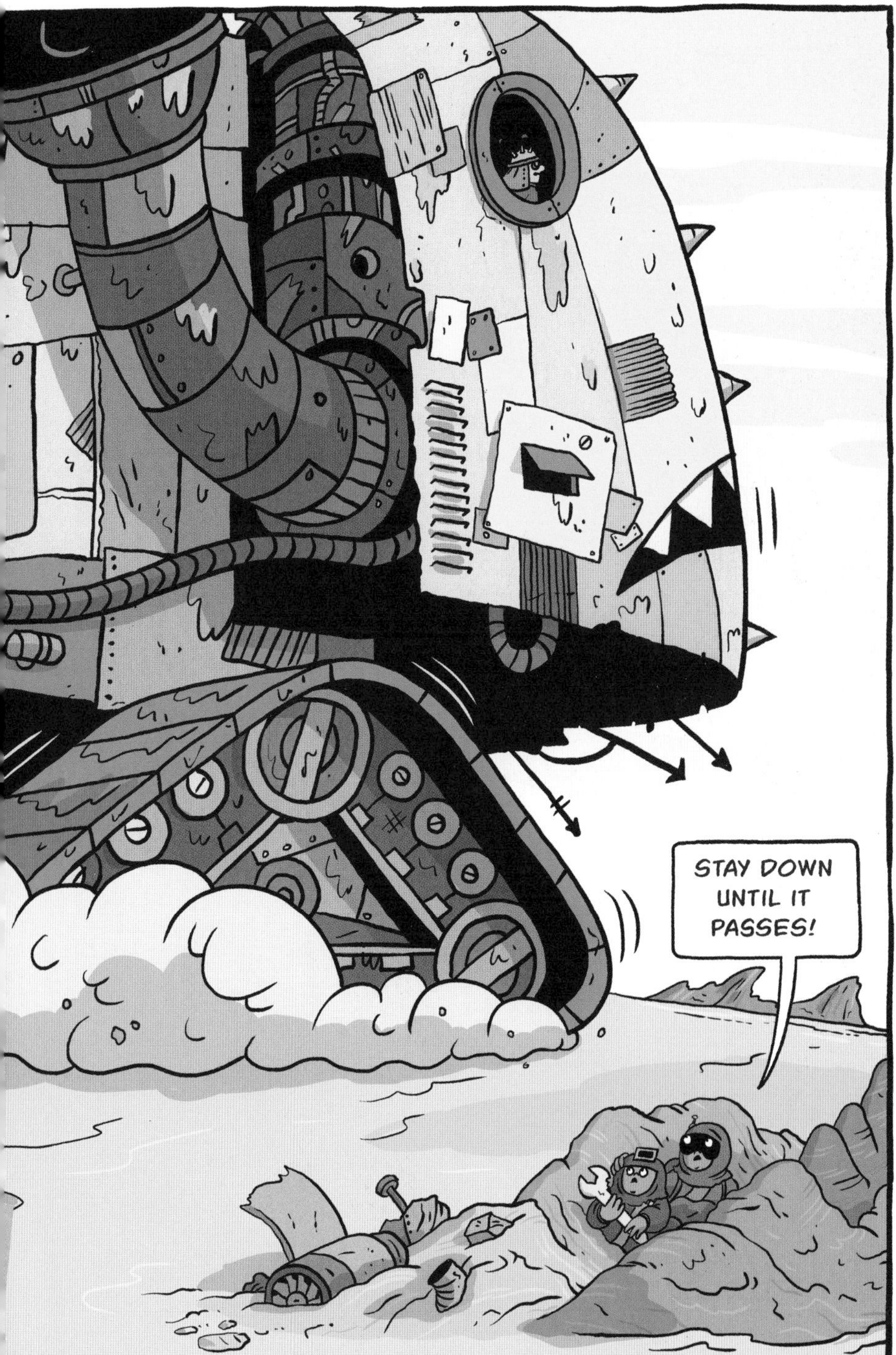
STAY DOWN UNTIL IT PASSES!

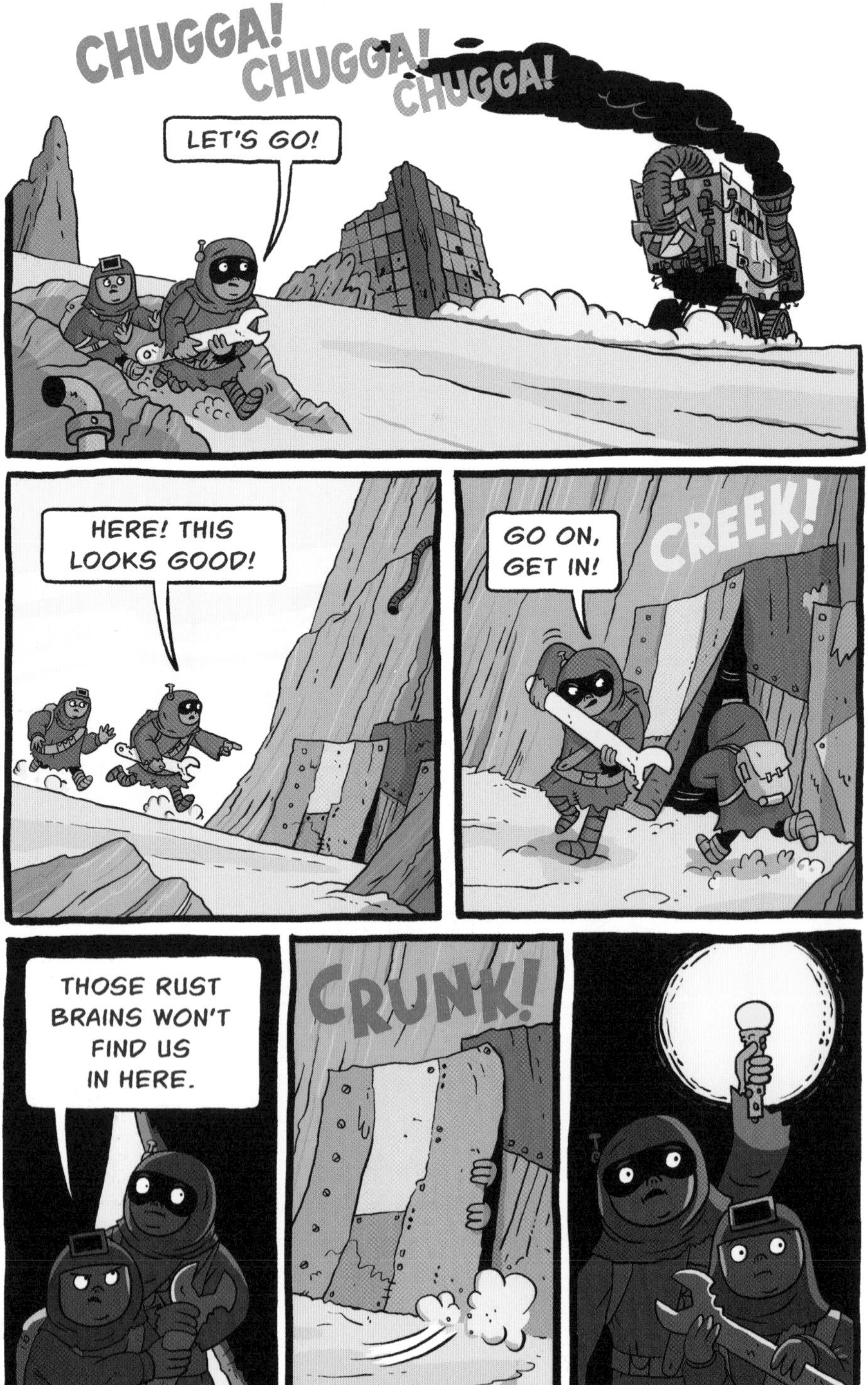
CHUGGA! CHUGGA! CHUGGA!
LET'S GO!
HERE! THIS LOOKS GOOD!
GO ON, GET IN!
CREEK!
THOSE RUST BRAINS WON'T FIND US IN HERE.
CRUNK!

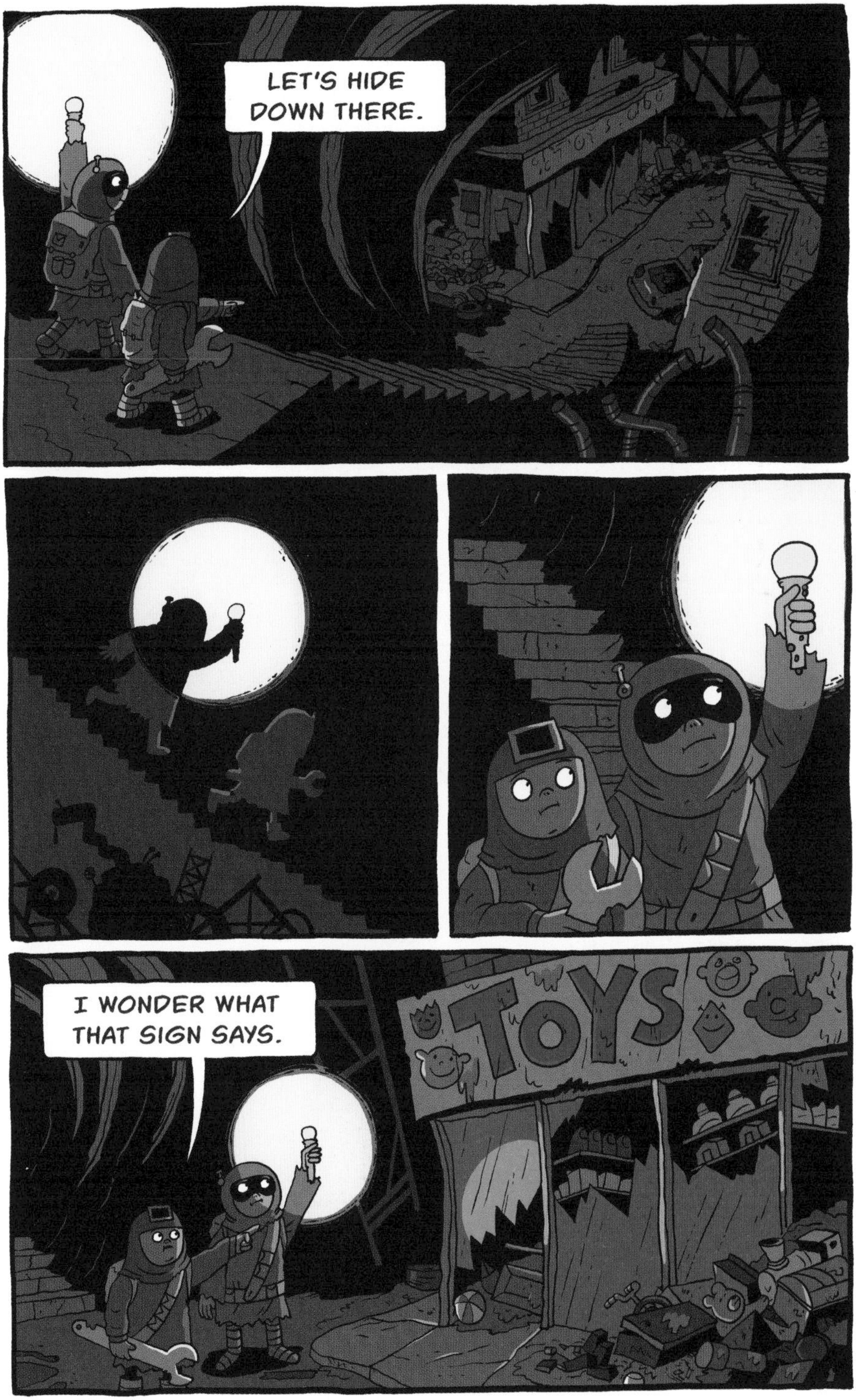
LET'S HIDE DOWN THERE.
I WONDER WHAT THAT SIGN SAYS.
TOYS

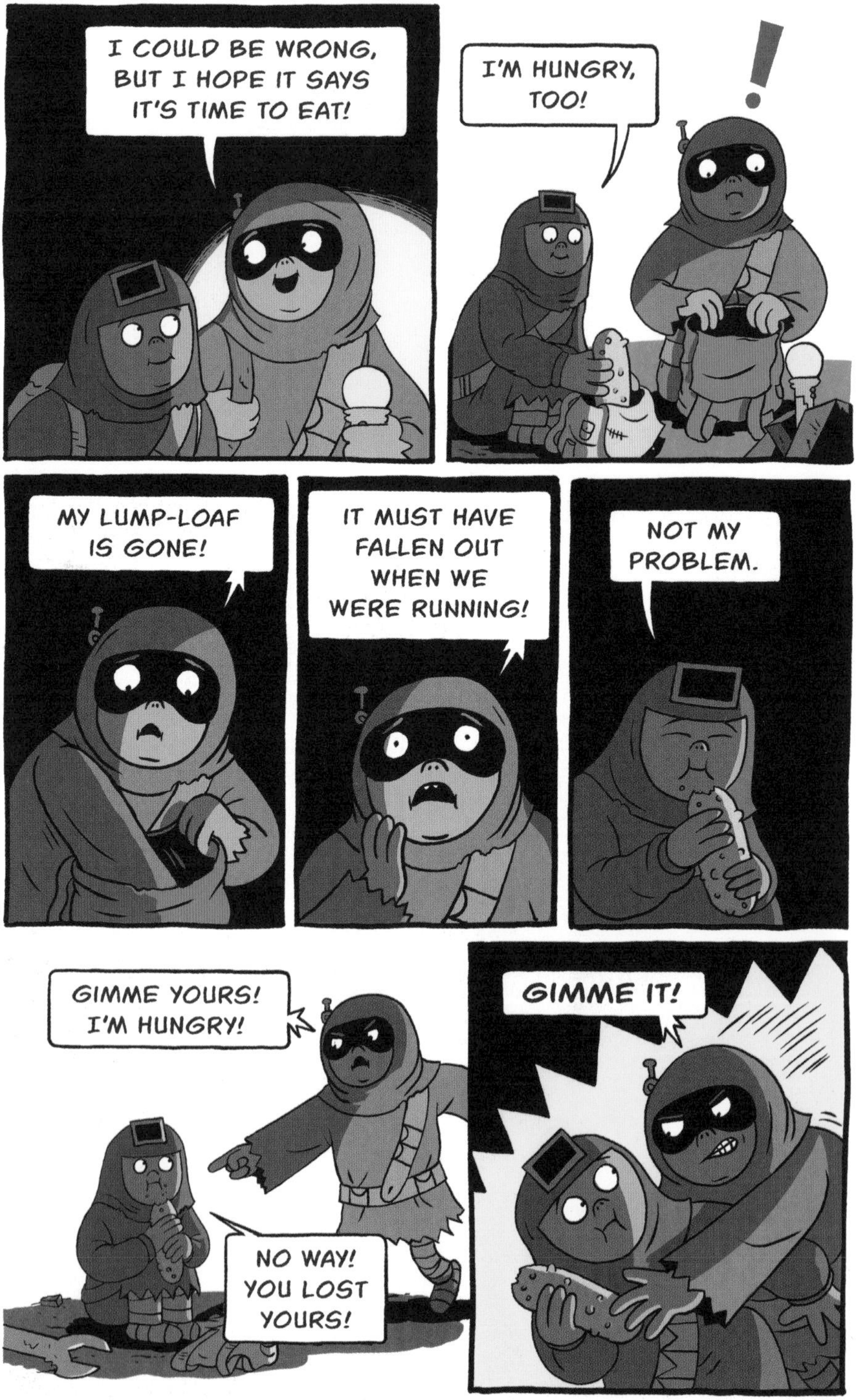

I COULD BE WRONG, BUT I HOPE IT SAYS IT'S TIME TO EAT!
I'M HUNGRY, TOO!
!
MY LUMP-LOAF IS GONE!
IT MUST HAVE FALLEN OUT WHEN WE WERE RUNNING!
NOT MY PROBLEM.
GIMME YOURS! I'M HUNGRY!
NO WAY! YOU LOST YOURS!
GIMME IT!

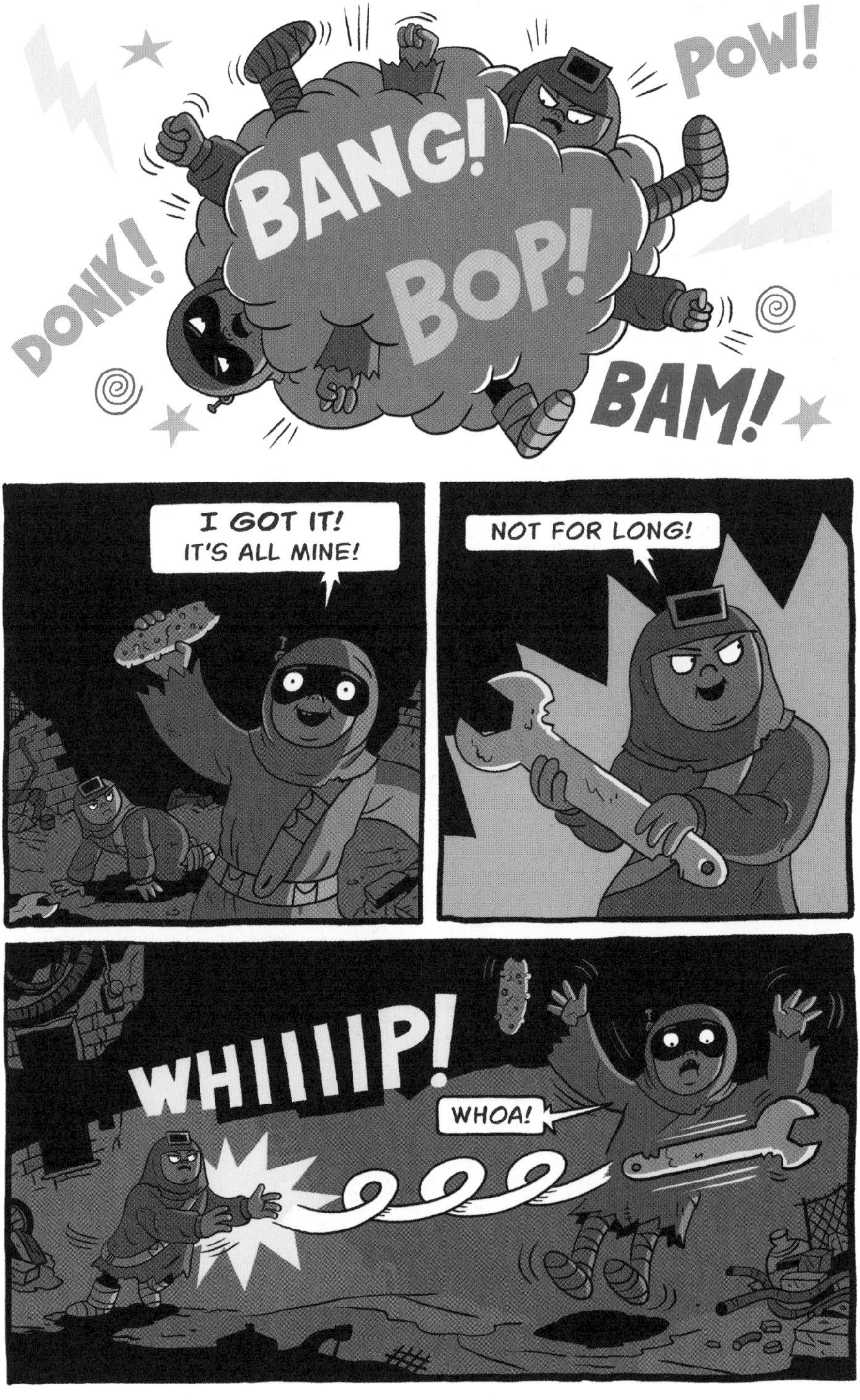
BANG!
BOP!
DONK!
POW!
BAM!
I GOT IT!
IT'S ALL MINE!
NOT FOR LONG!
WHIIIIP!
WHOA!

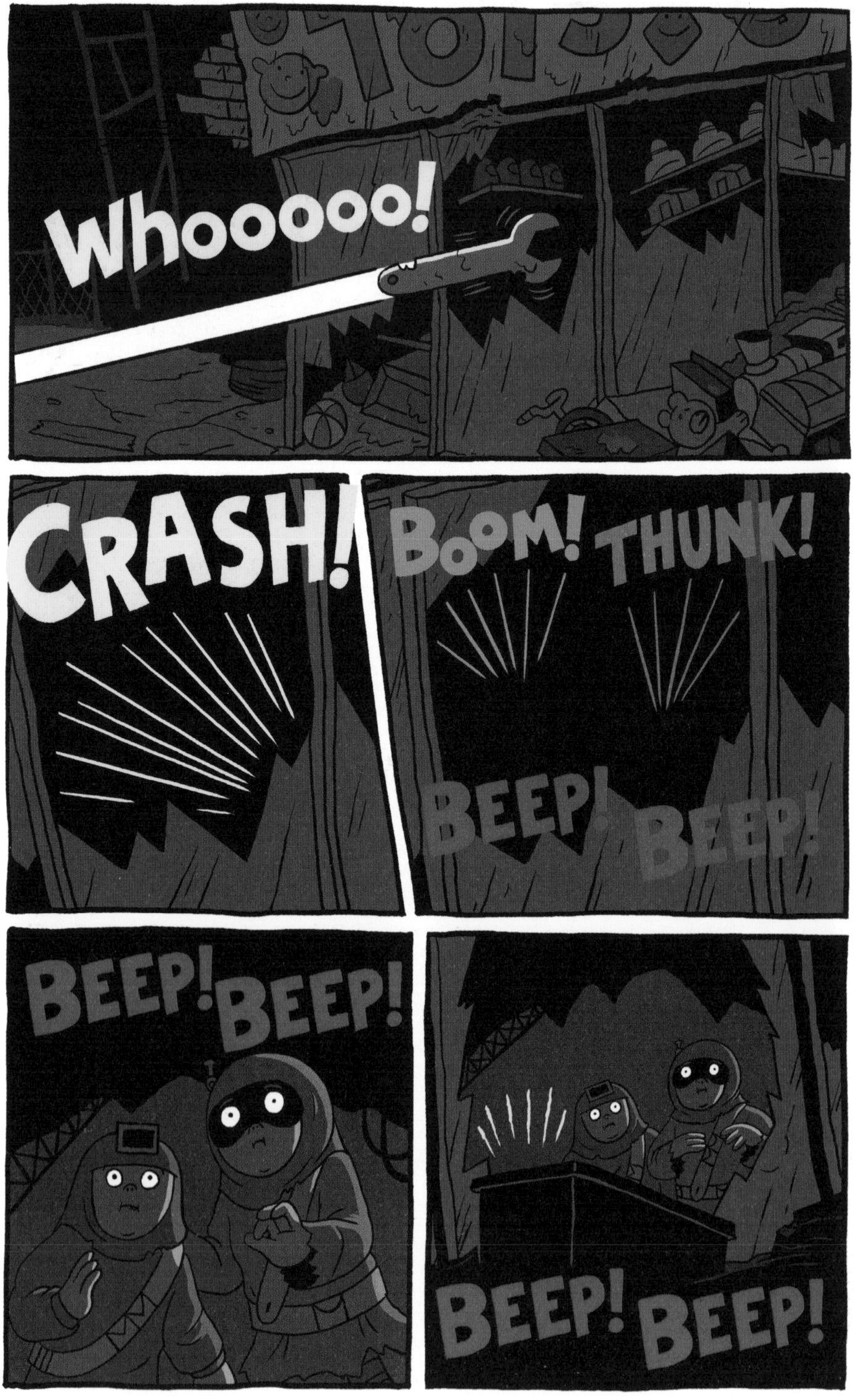
Whooooo!
CRASH!
BOOM! THUNK!
BEEP! BEEP!
BEEP! BEEP!
BEEP! BEEP!

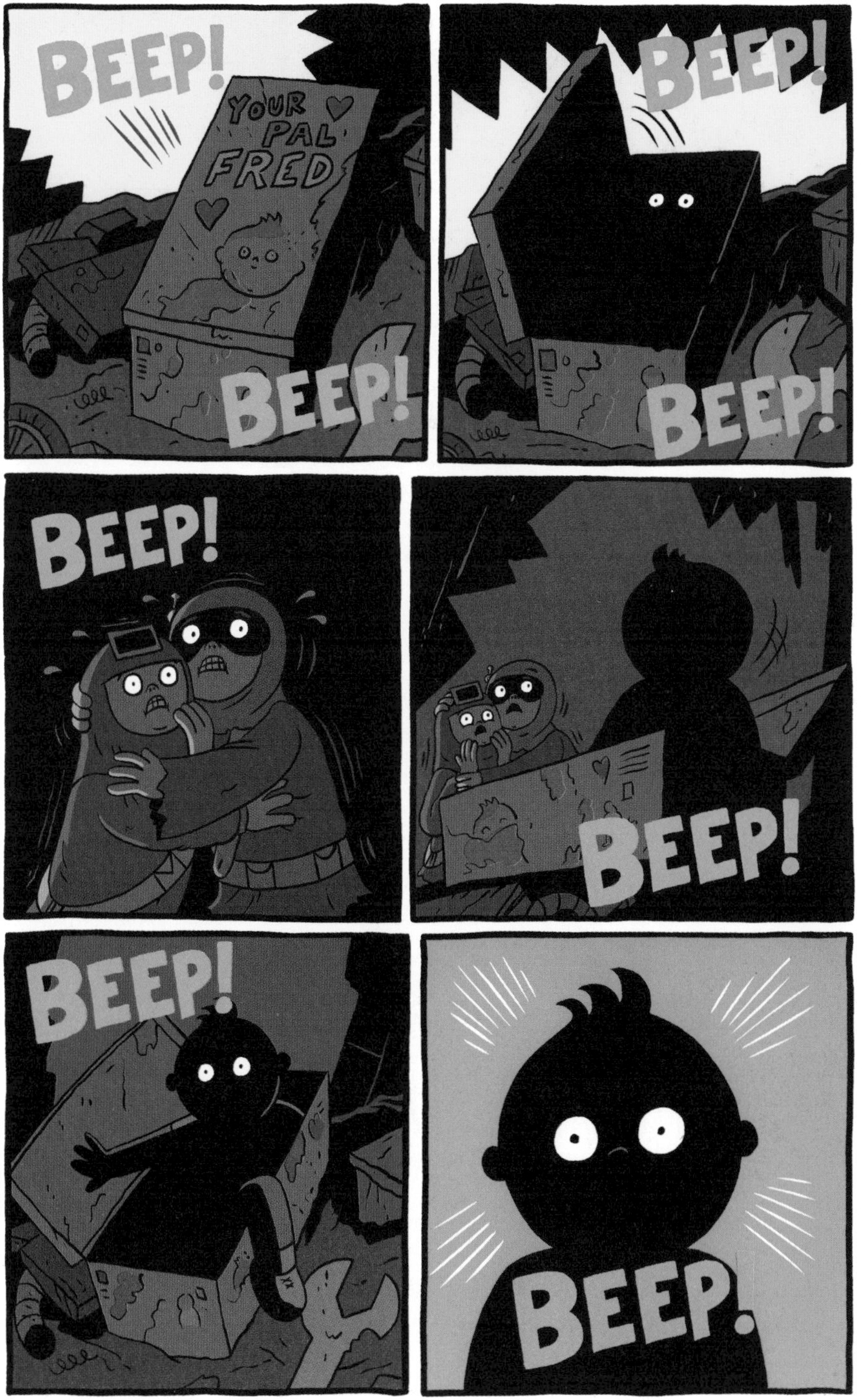
BEEP!
YOUR PAL FRED
BEEP!
BEEP!
BEEP!
BEEP!
BEEP!
BEEP!
BEEP.

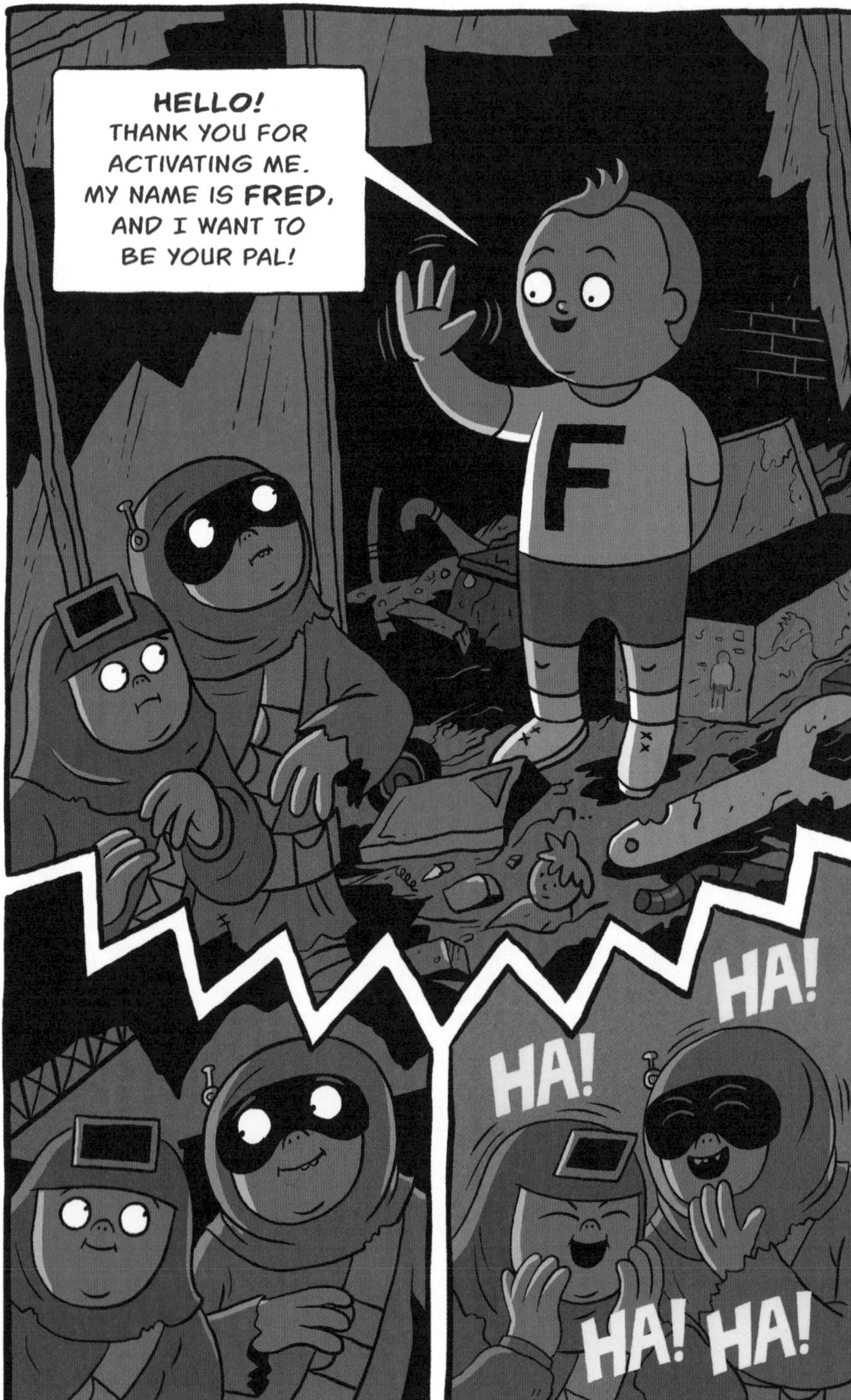
HELLO!
THANK YOU FOR ACTIVATING ME. MY NAME IS FRED, AND I WANT TO BE YOUR PAL!
HA!
HA!
HA! HA!

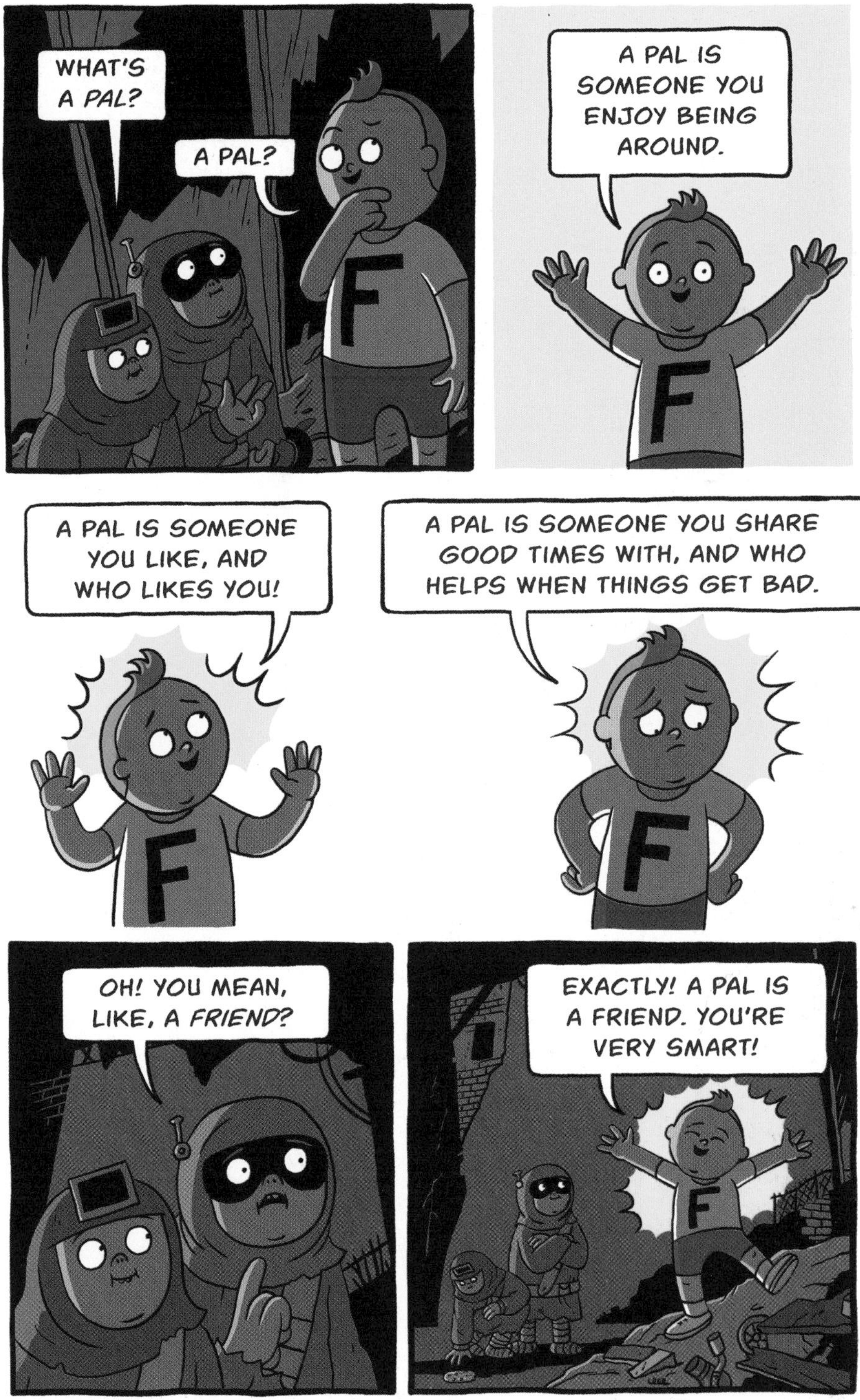
WHAT'S A PAL?
A PAL?
A PAL IS SOMEONE YOU ENJOY BEING AROUND.
A PAL IS SOMEONE YOU LIKE, AND WHO LIKES YOU!
A PAL IS SOMEONE YOU SHARE GOOD TIMES WITH, AND WHO HELPS WHEN THINGS GET BAD.
OH! YOU MEAN, LIKE, A *FRIEND?*
EXACTLY! A PAL IS A FRIEND. YOU'RE VERY SMART!

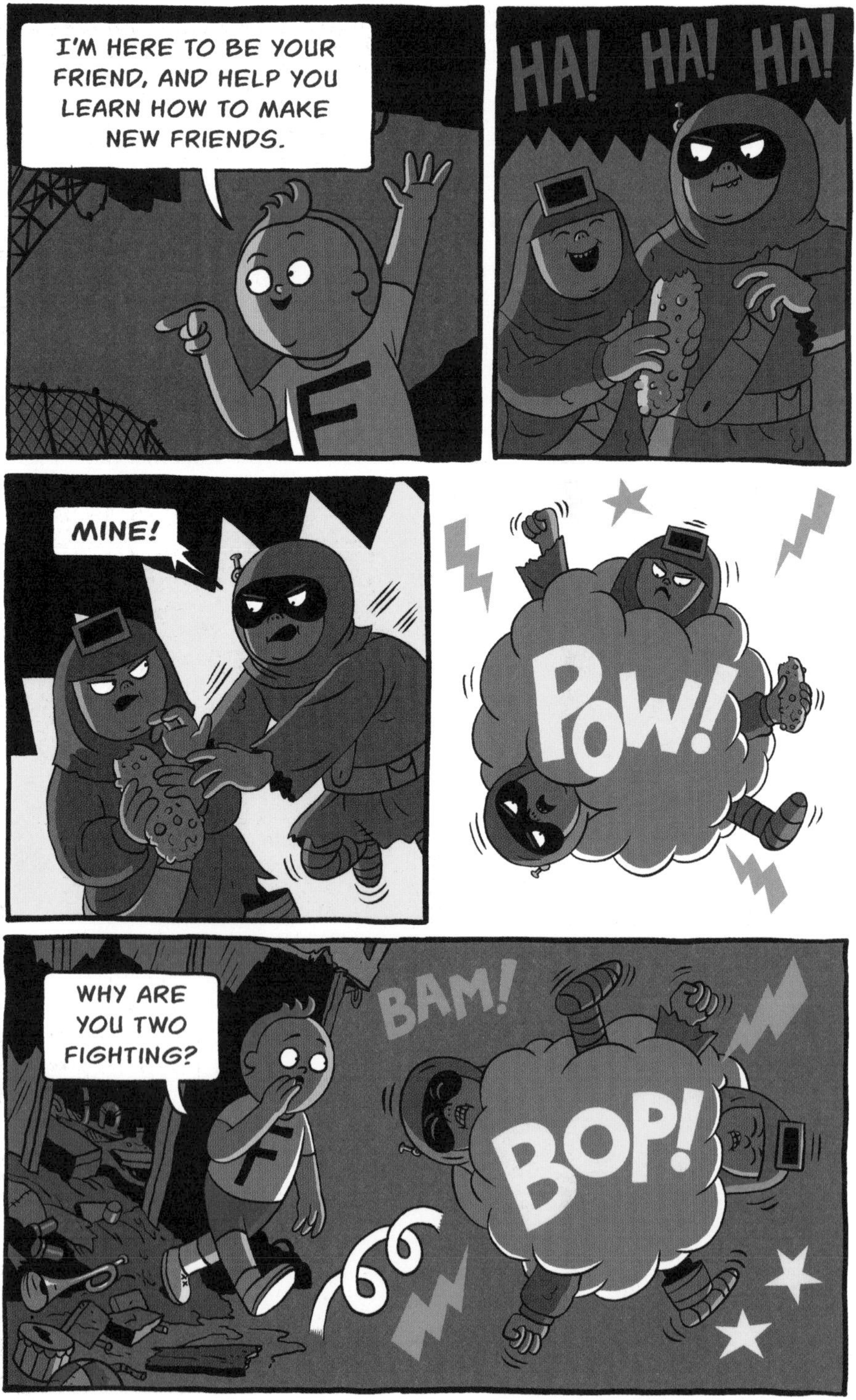
I'M HERE TO BE YOUR FRIEND, AND HELP YOU LEARN HOW TO MAKE NEW FRIENDS.
HA! HA! HA!
MINE!
POW!
WHY ARE YOU TWO FIGHTING?
BAM!
BOP!

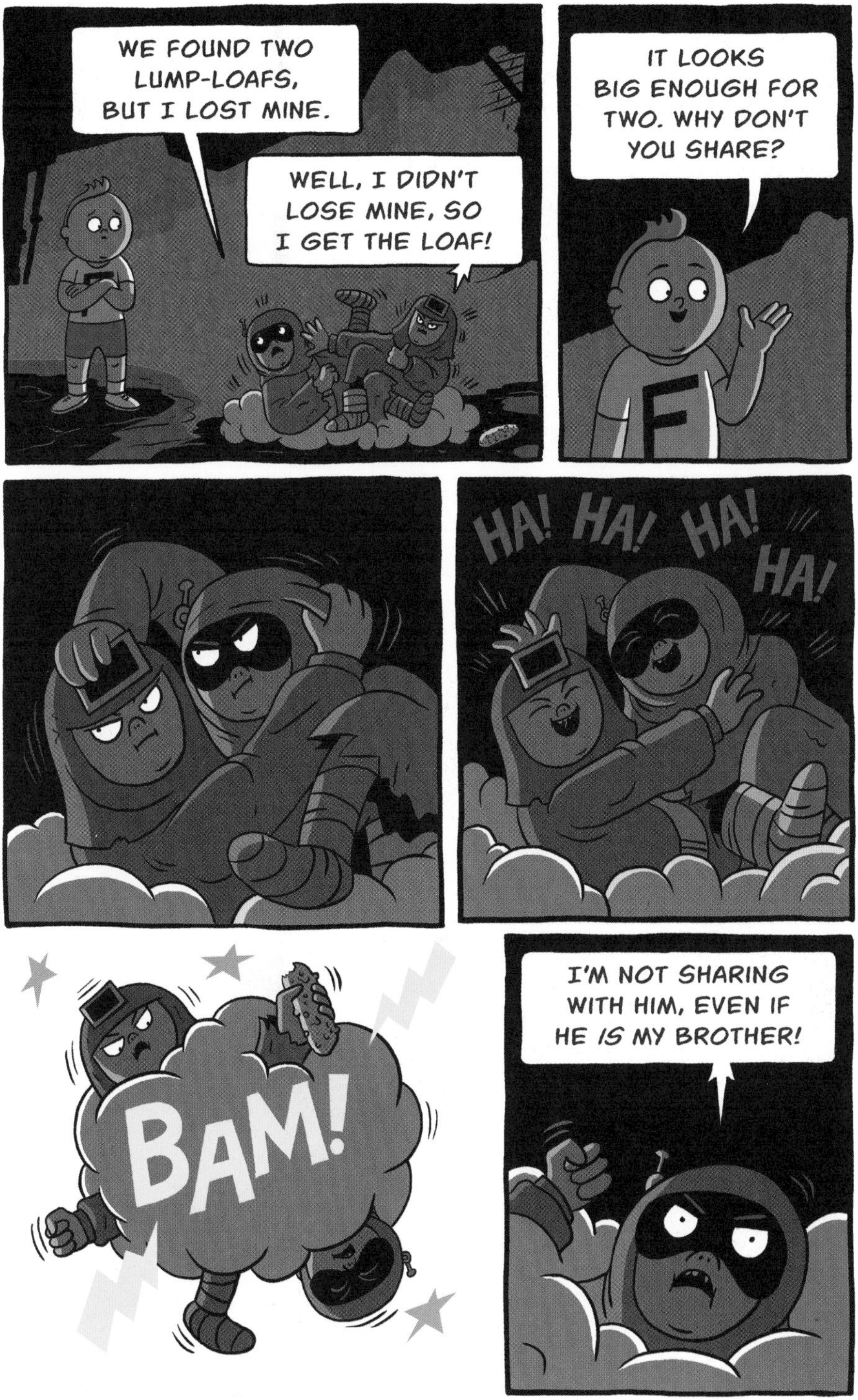
WE FOUND TWO LUMP-LOAFS, BUT I LOST MINE.
WELL, I DIDN'T LOSE MINE, SO I GET THE LOAF!
IT LOOKS BIG ENOUGH FOR TWO. WHY DON'T YOU SHARE?
HA! HA! HA! HA!
BAM!
I'M NOT SHARING WITH HIM, EVEN IF HE *IS* MY BROTHER!

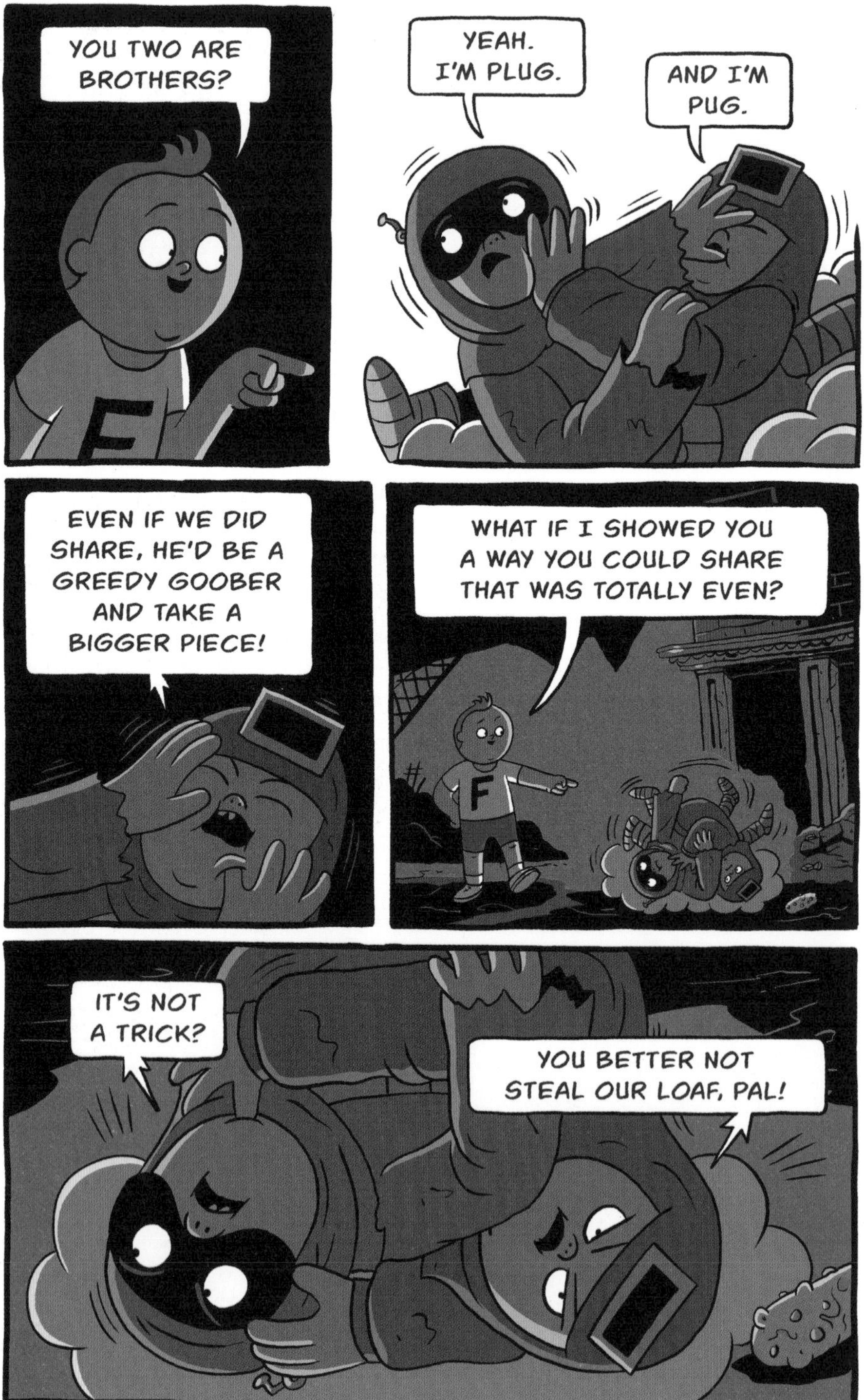
YOU TWO ARE BROTHERS?
YEAH. I'M PLUG.
AND I'M PUG.
EVEN IF WE DID SHARE, HE'D BE A GREEDY GOOBER AND TAKE A BIGGER PIECE!
WHAT IF I SHOWED YOU A WAY YOU COULD SHARE THAT WAS TOTALLY EVEN?
IT'S NOT A TRICK?
YOU BETTER NOT STEAL OUR LOAF, PAL!

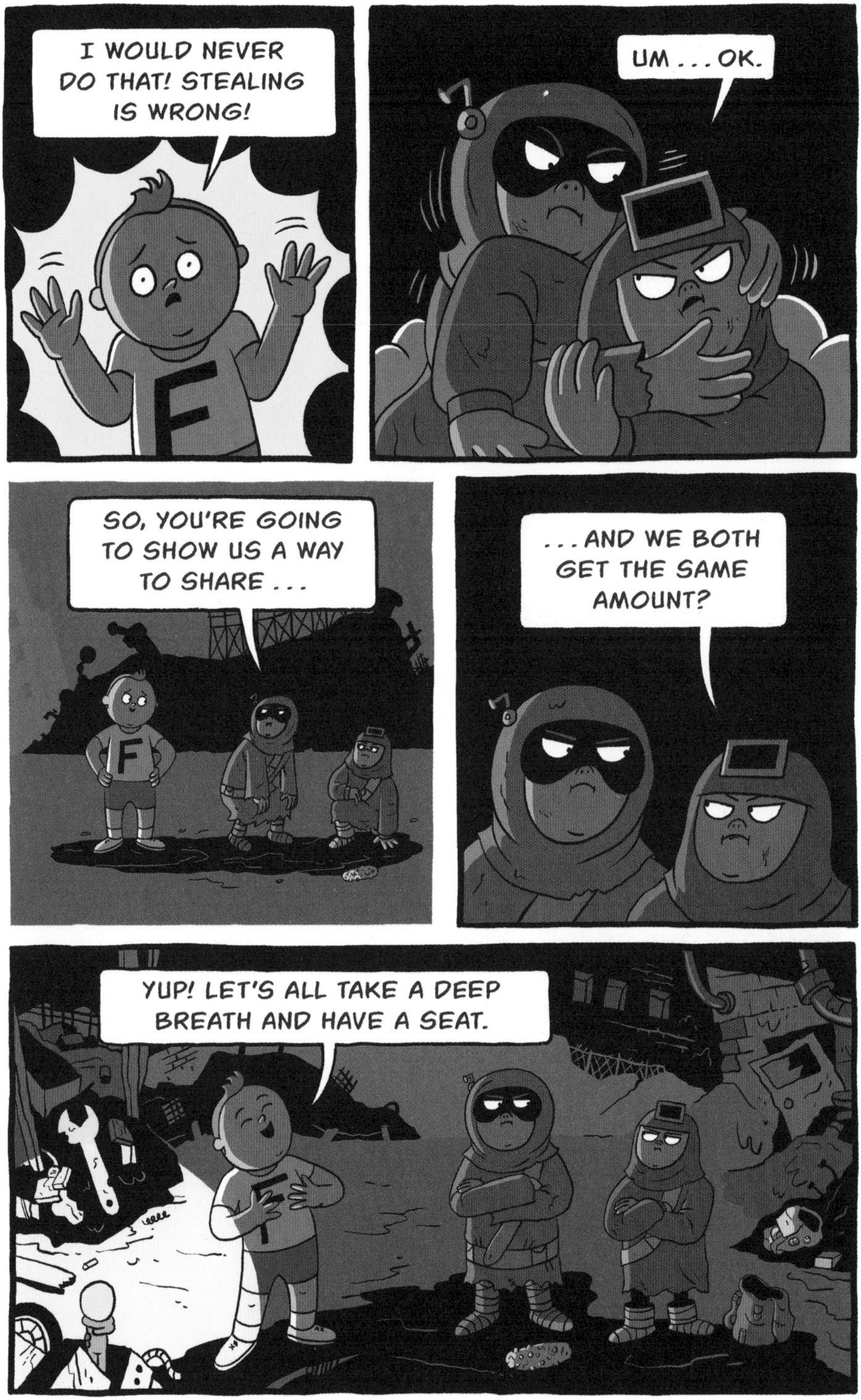
I WOULD NEVER DO THAT! STEALING IS WRONG!
UM . . . OK.
SO, YOU'RE GOING TO SHOW US A WAY TO SHARE . . .
. . . AND WE BOTH GET THE SAME AMOUNT?
YUP! LET'S ALL TAKE A DEEP BREATH AND HAVE A SEAT.

CHAPTER 2

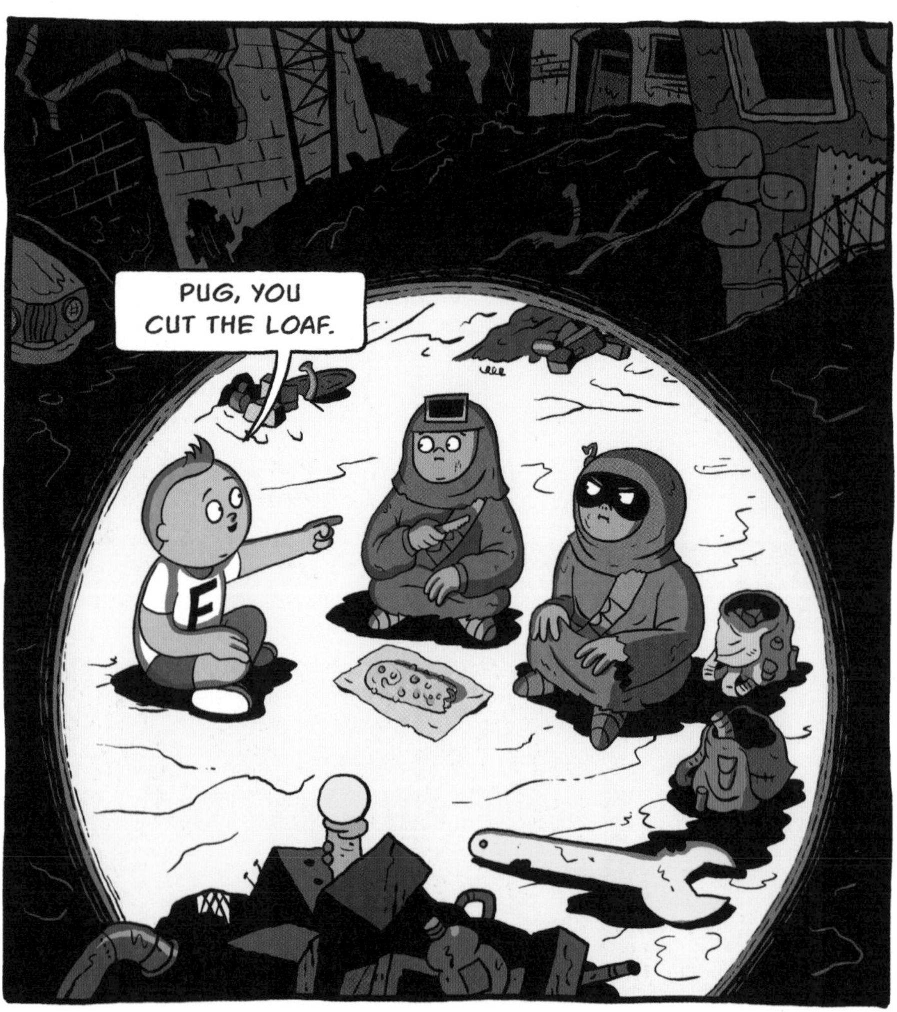
PUG, YOU CUT THE LOAF.

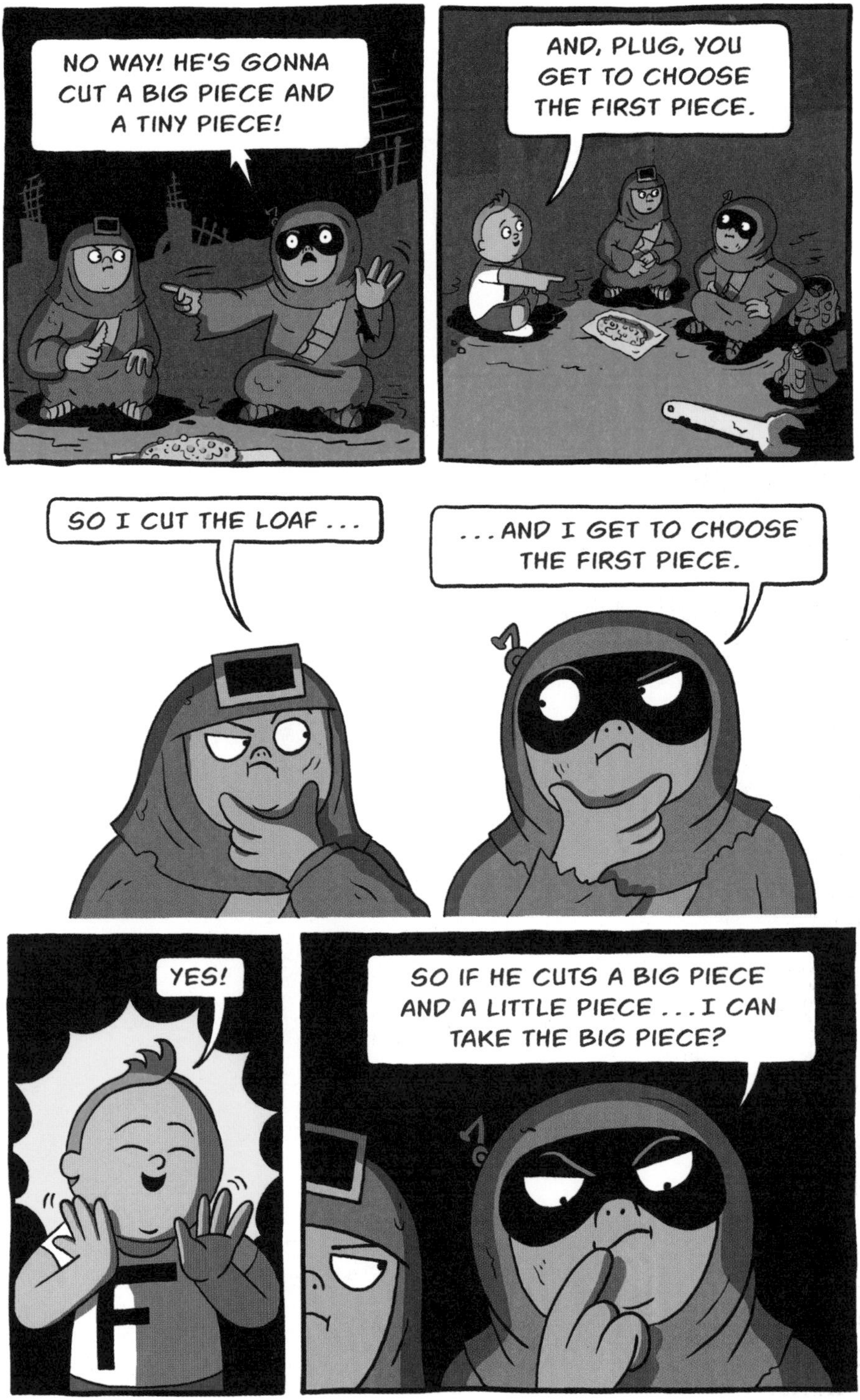
NO WAY! HE'S GONNA CUT A BIG PIECE AND A TINY PIECE!
AND, PLUG, YOU GET TO CHOOSE THE FIRST PIECE.
SO I CUT THE LOAF . . .
. . . AND I GET TO CHOOSE THE FIRST PIECE.
YES!
SO IF HE CUTS A BIG PIECE AND A LITTLE PIECE . . . I CAN TAKE THE BIG PIECE?

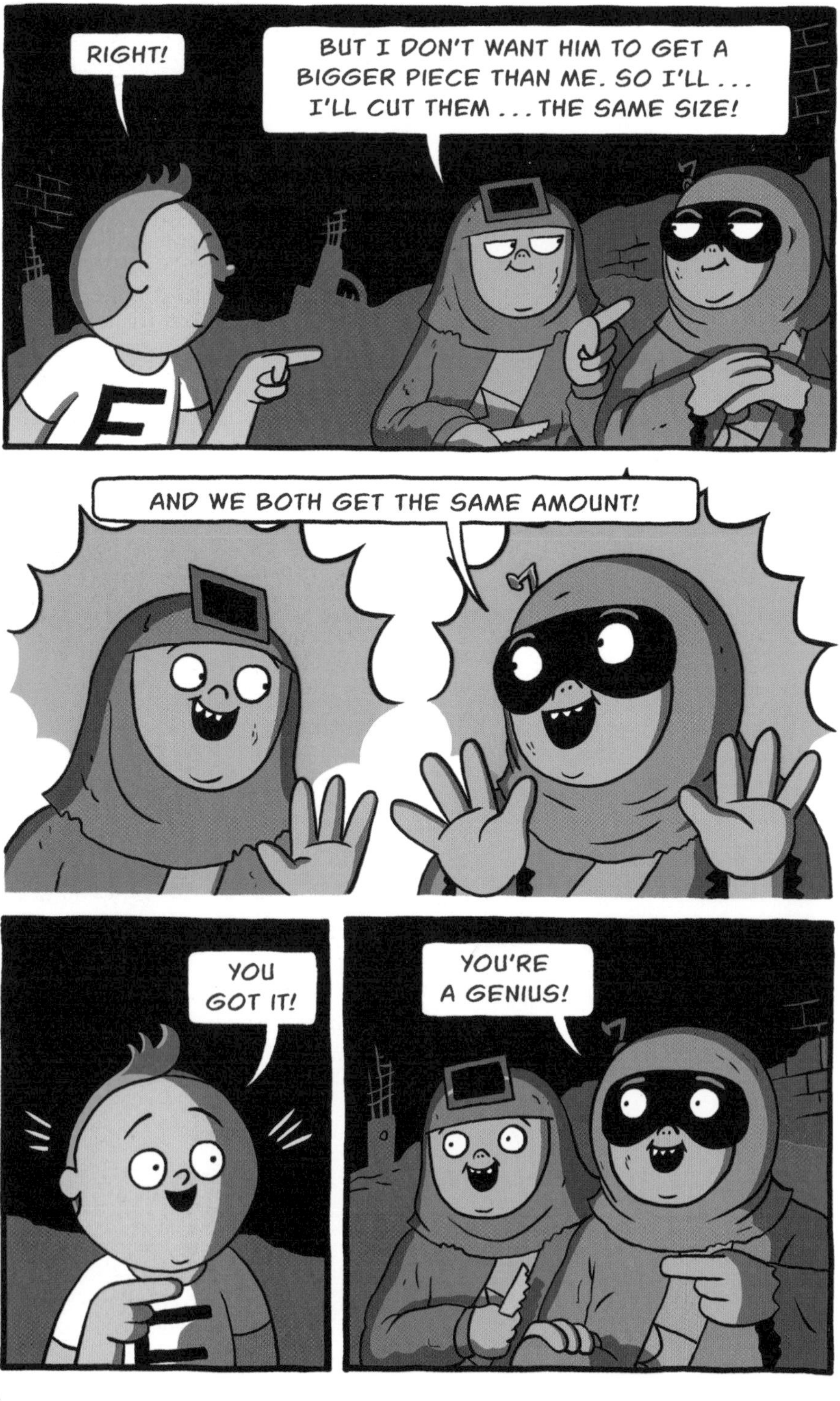
RIGHT!
BUT I DON'T WANT HIM TO GET A BIGGER PIECE THAN ME. SO I'LL . . . I'LL CUT THEM . . . THE SAME SIZE!
AND WE BOTH GET THE SAME AMOUNT!
YOU GOT IT!
YOU'RE A GENIUS!

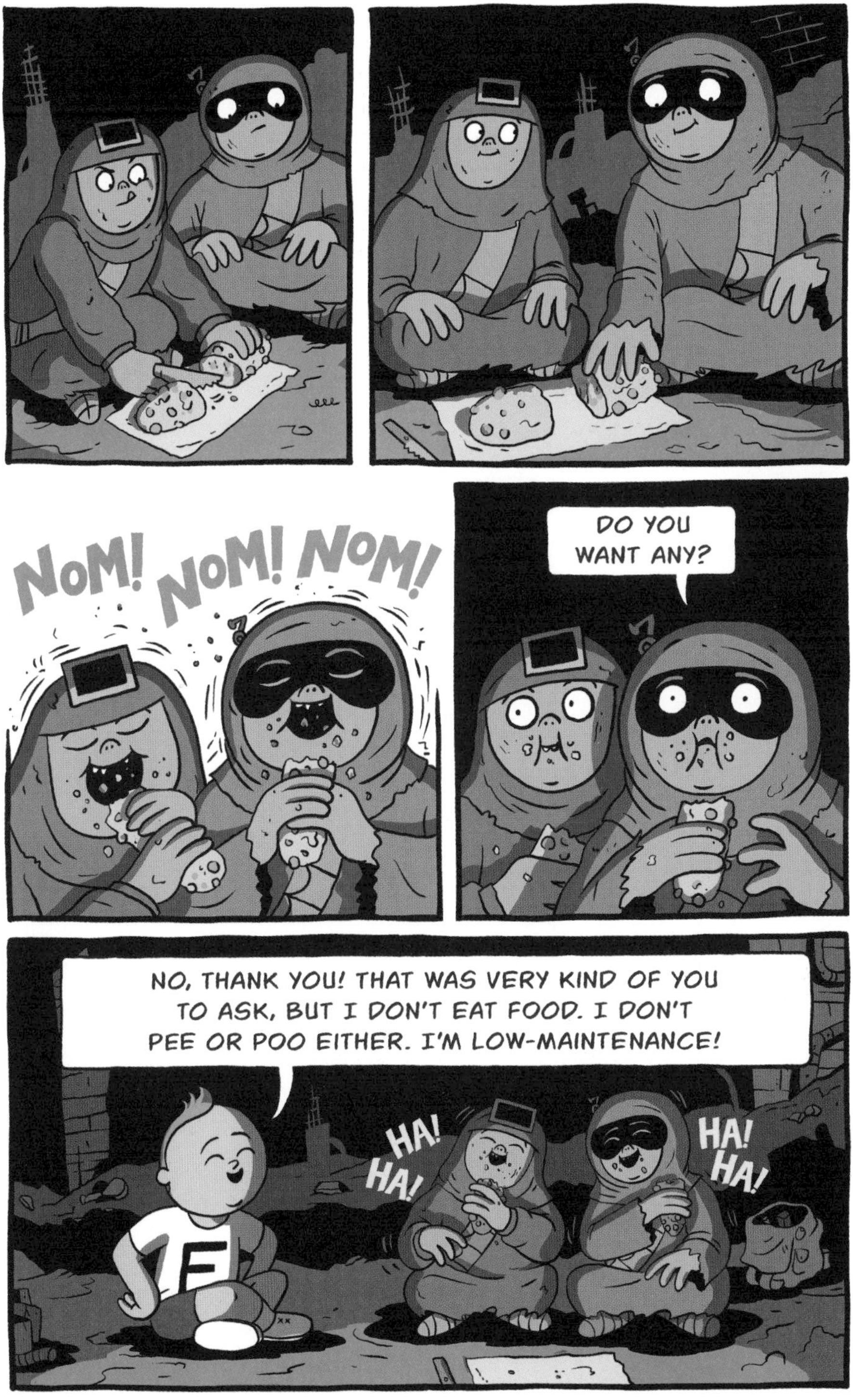
NOM! NOM! NOM!
DO YOU WANT ANY?
NO, THANK YOU! THAT WAS VERY KIND OF YOU TO ASK, BUT I DON'T EAT FOOD. I DON'T PEE OR POO EITHER. I'M LOW-MAINTENANCE!
HA! HA!
HA! HA!

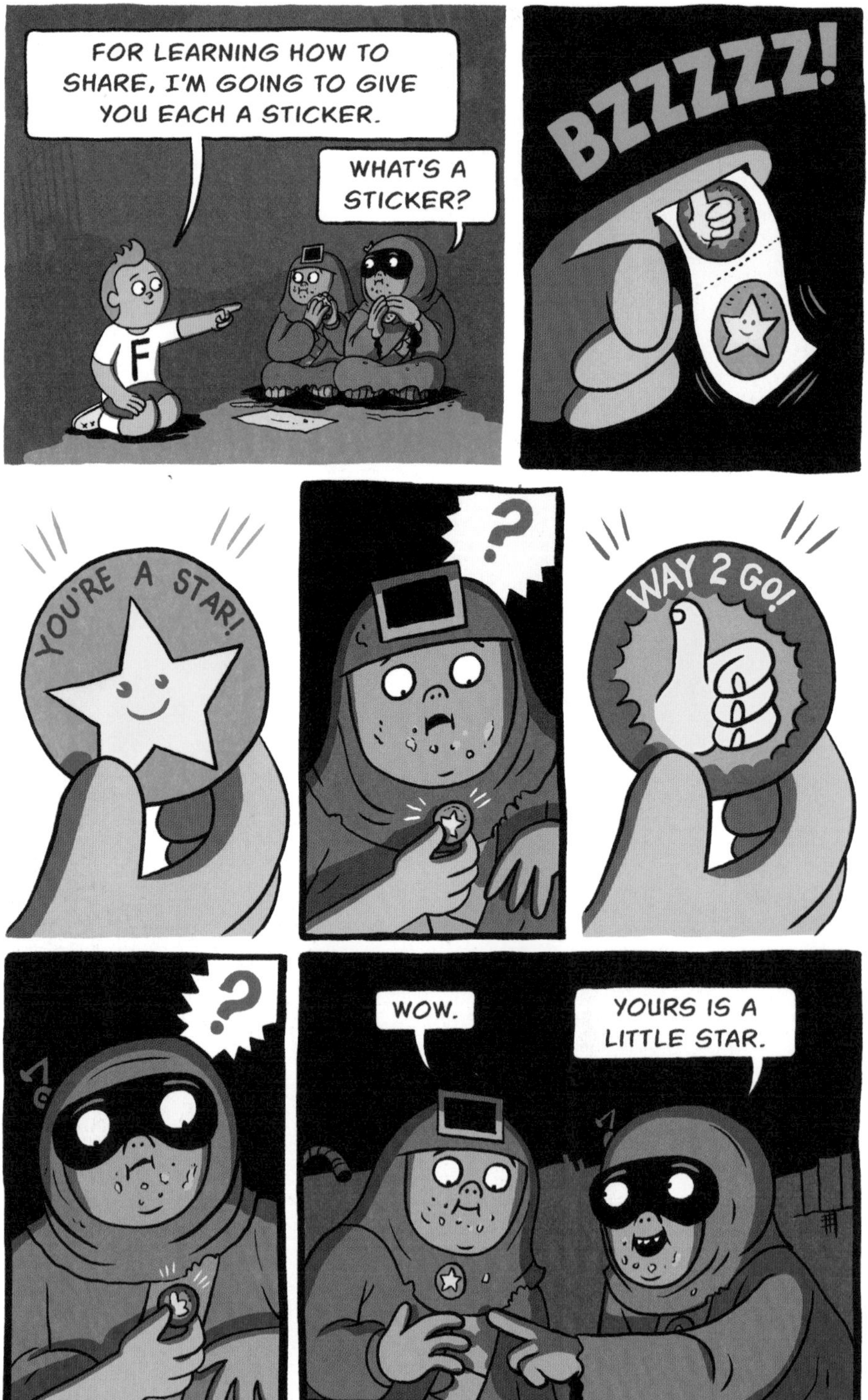
FOR LEARNING HOW TO SHARE, I'M GOING TO GIVE YOU EACH A STICKER.
WHAT'S A STICKER?
BZZZZZ!
YOU'RE A STAR!
?
WAY 2 GO!
?
WOW.
YOURS IS A LITTLE STAR.

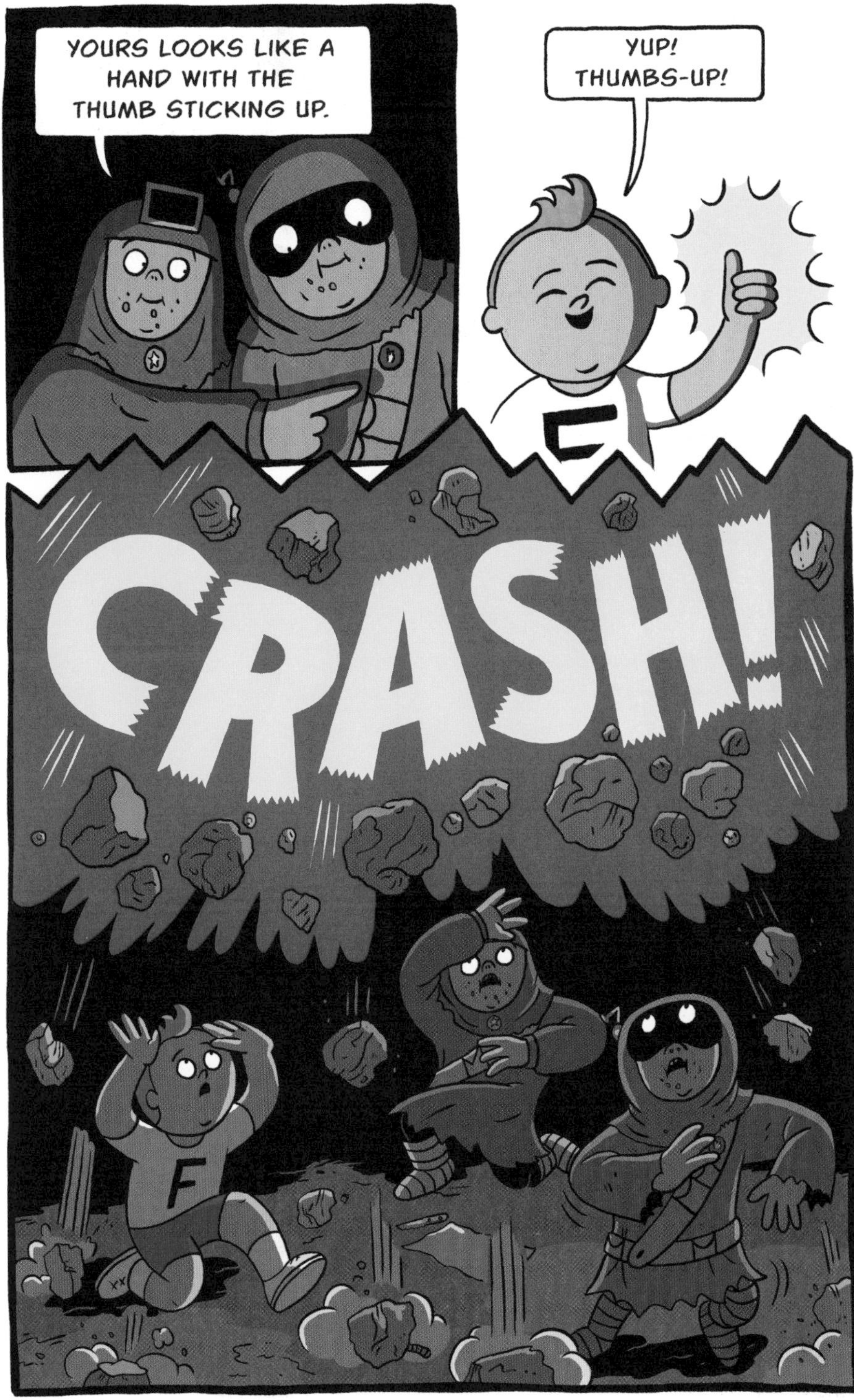
YOURS LOOKS LIKE A HAND WITH THE THUMB STICKING UP.
YUP! THUMBS-UP!
CRASH!

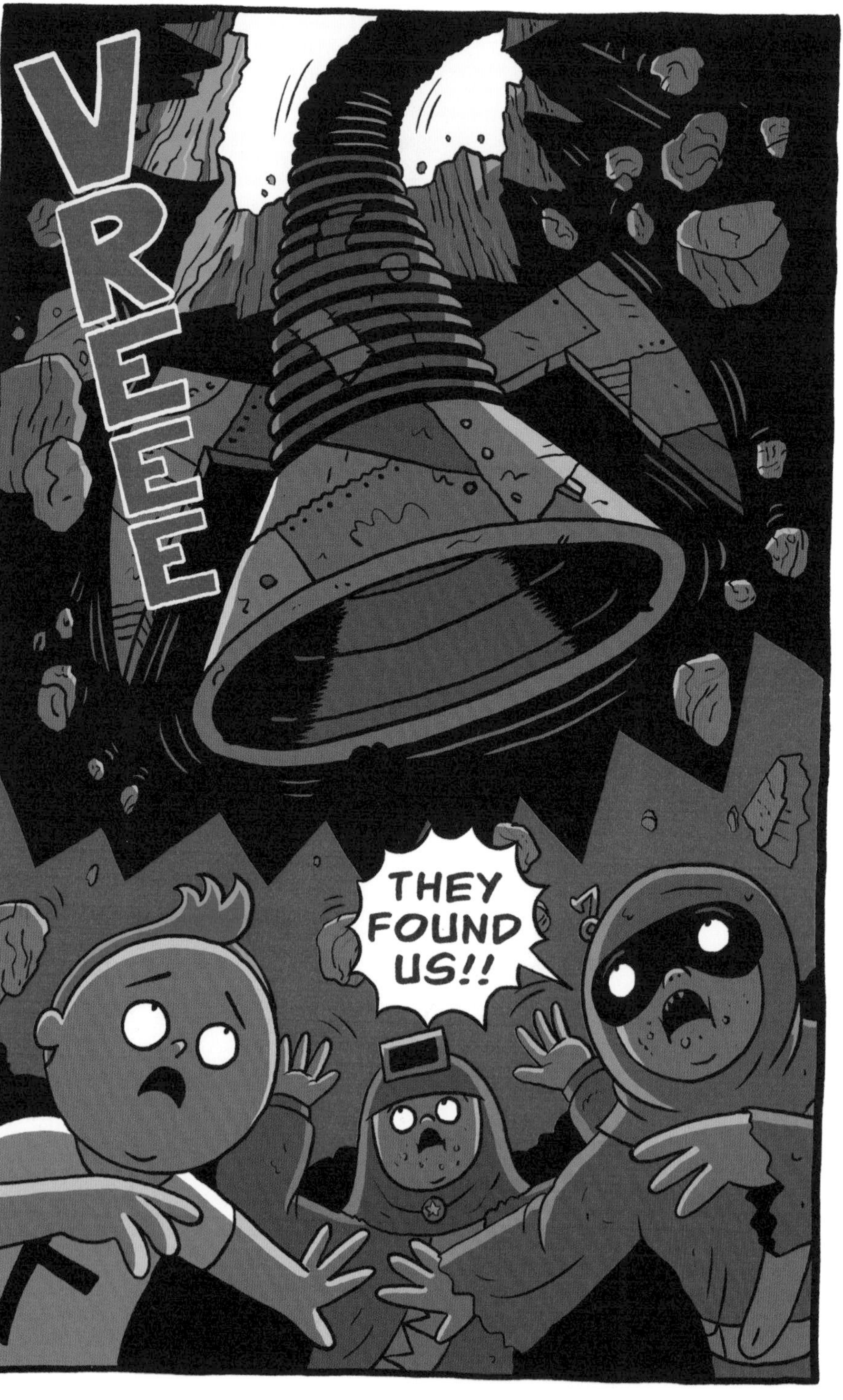
VREEE
THEY FOUND US!!

CHAPTER 3

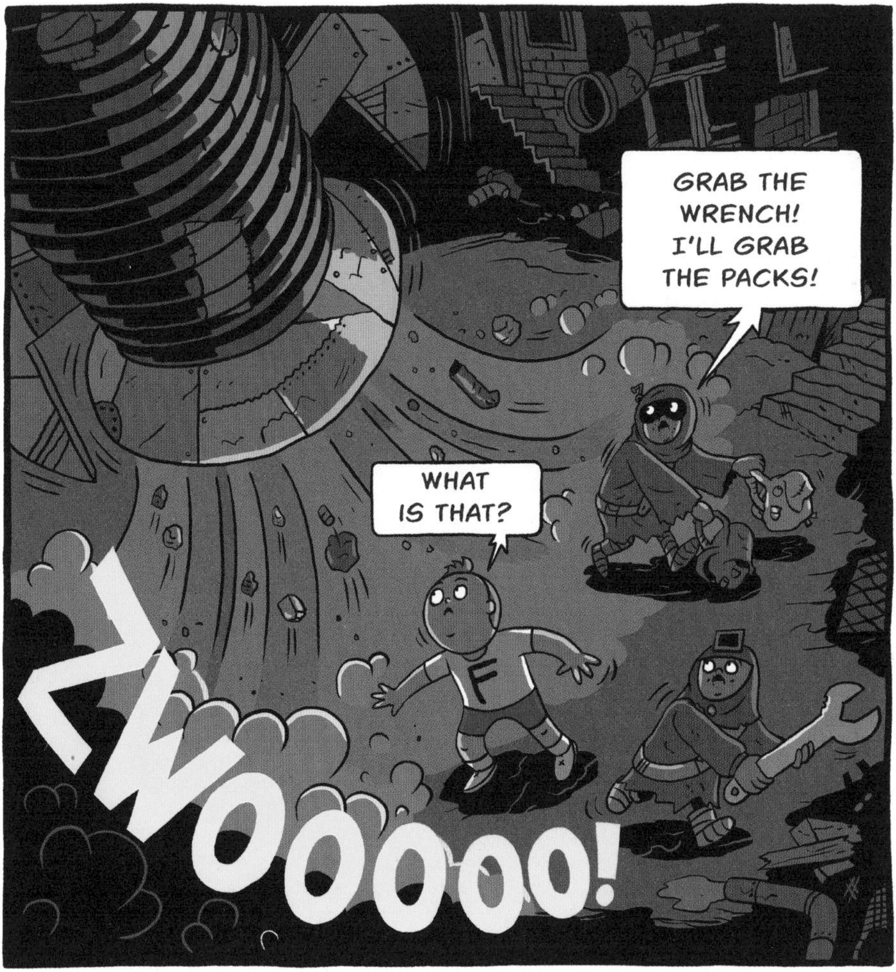
GRAB THE WRENCH! I'LL GRAB THE PACKS!
WHAT IS THAT?
ZWOOOOOO!

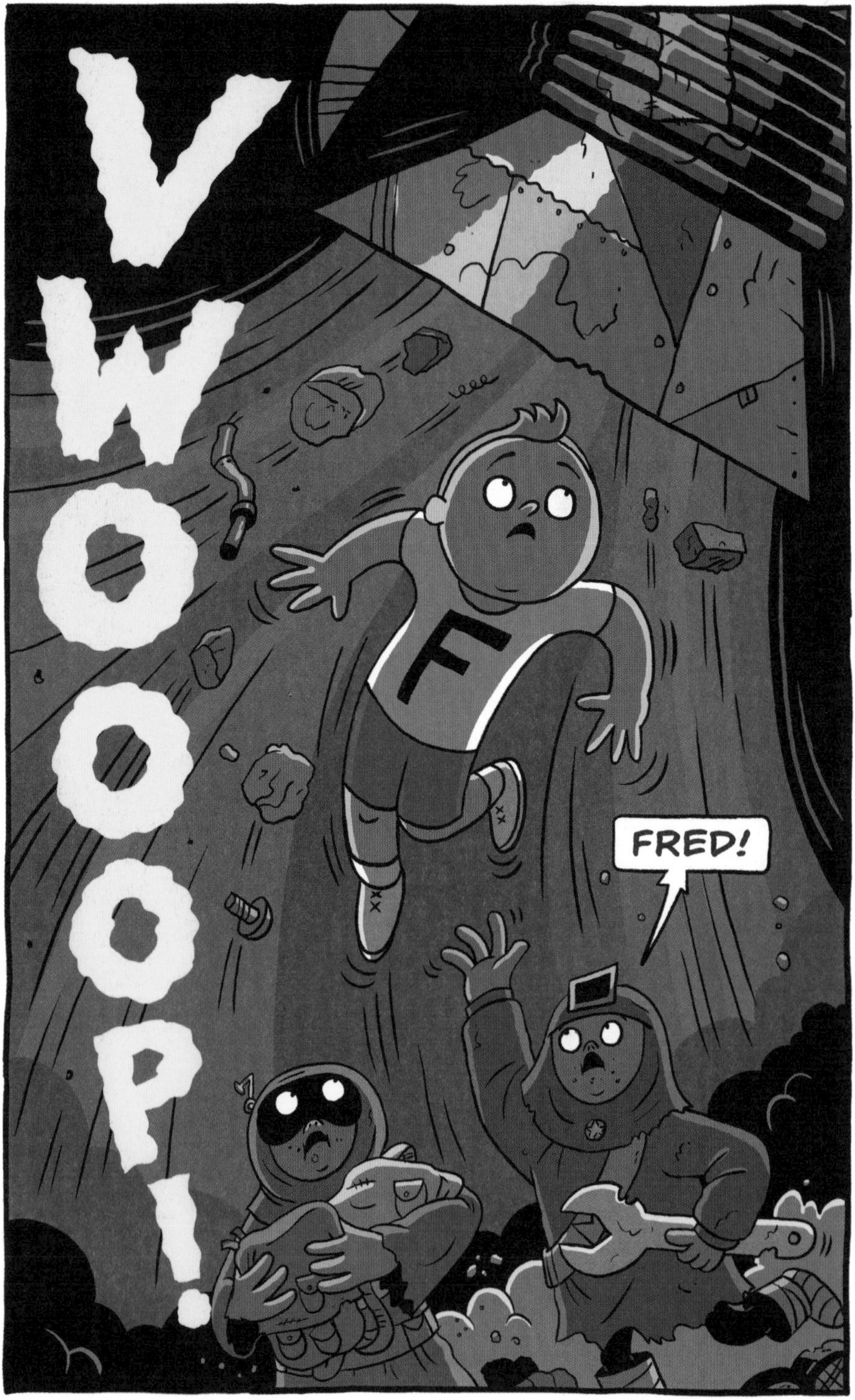
VWOOOOP!
FRED!

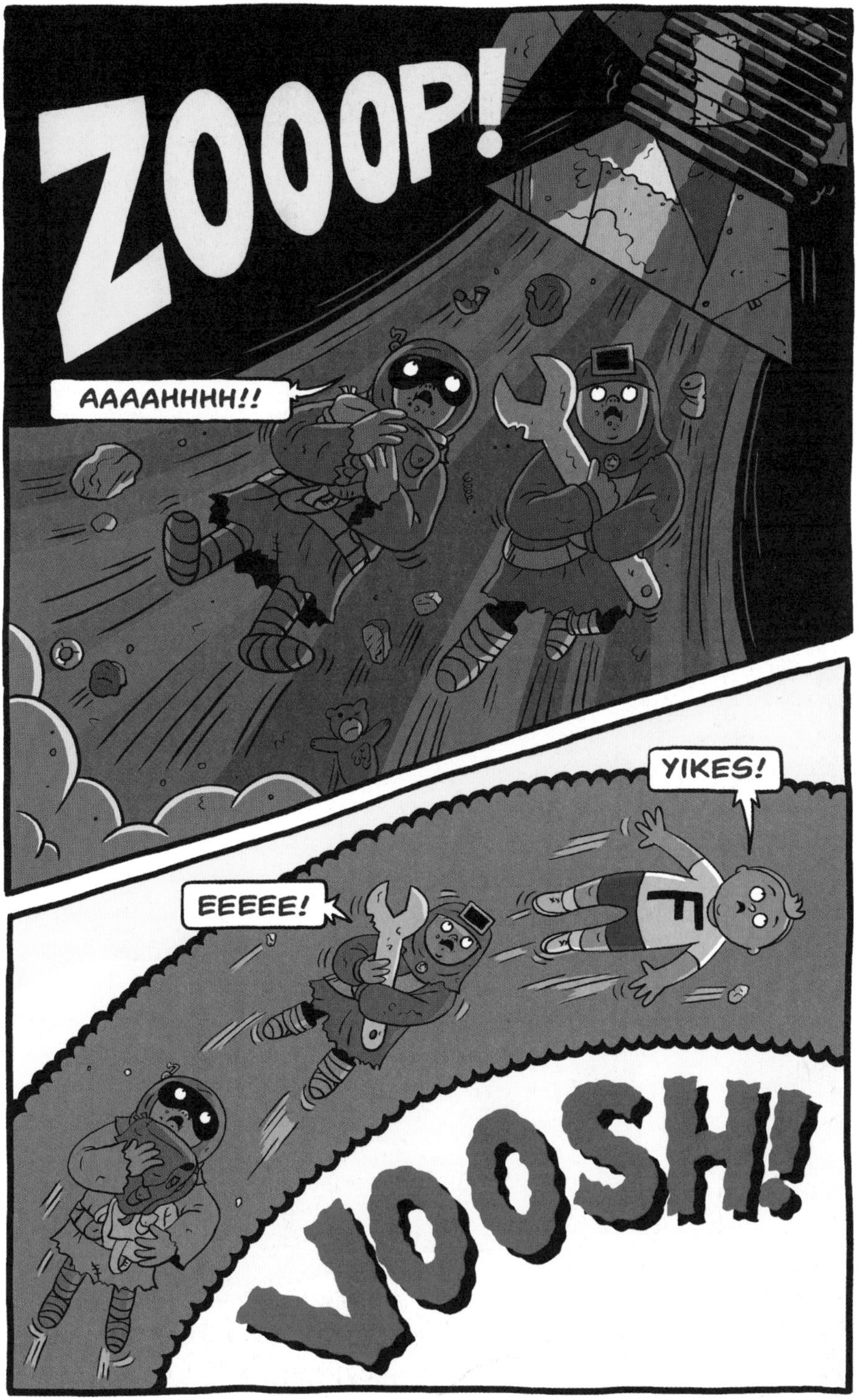
ZOOOP!
AAAAHHHH!!
YIKES!
EEEEE!
VOOSH!

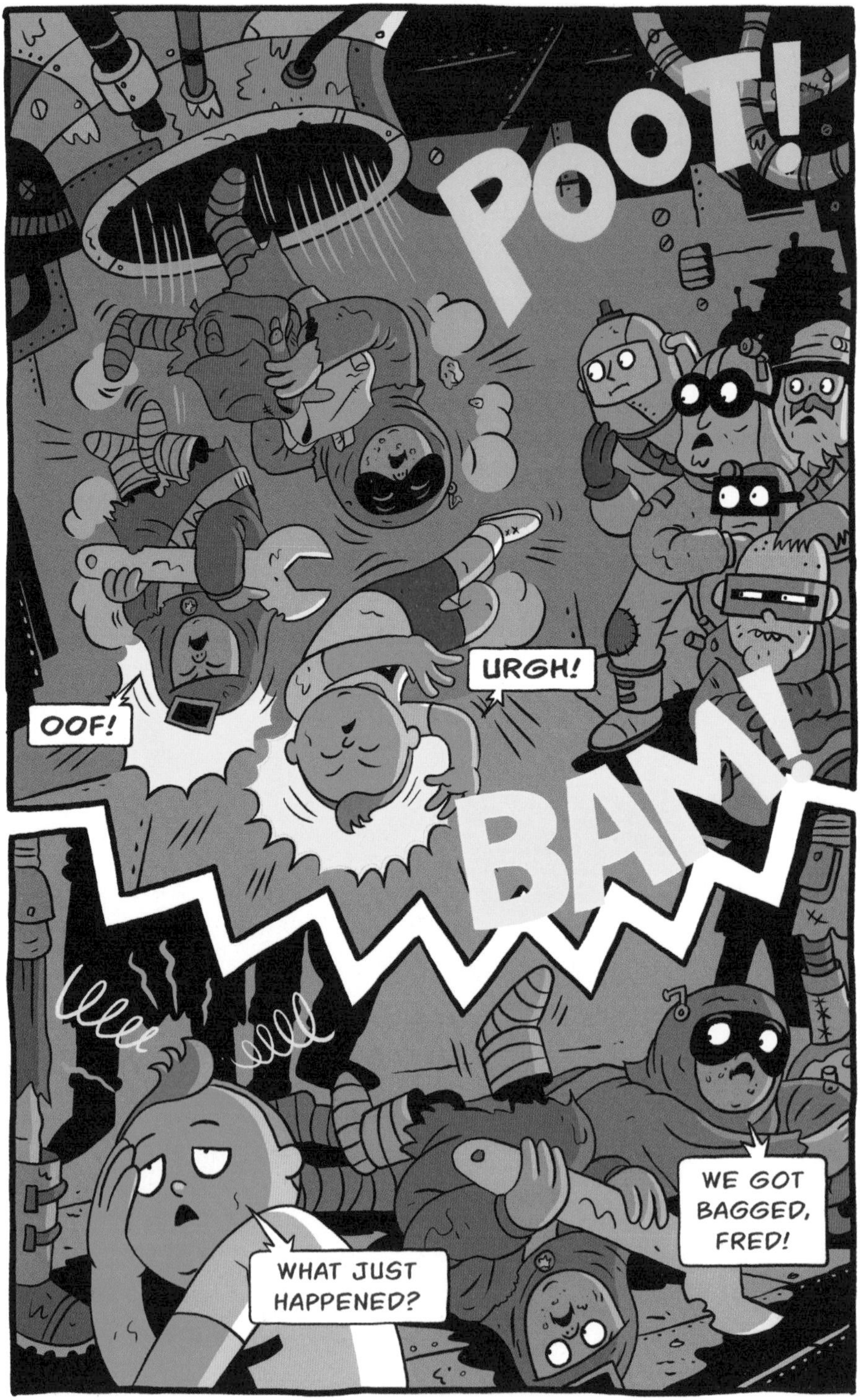
POOT!
OOF!
URGH!
BAM!
WHAT JUST HAPPENED?
WE GOT BAGGED, FRED!

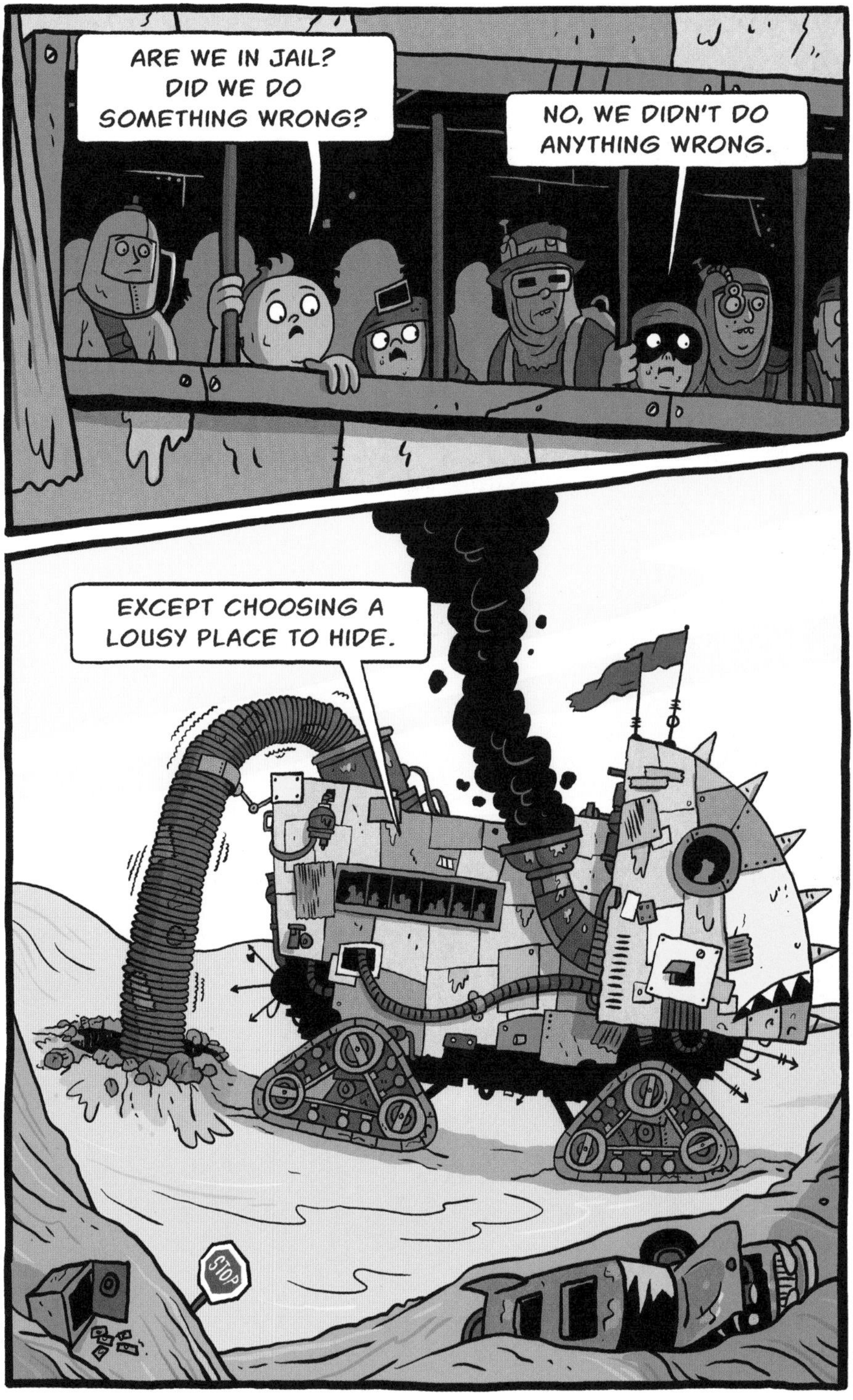
ARE WE IN JAIL? DID WE DO SOMETHING WRONG?
NO, WE DIDN'T DO ANYTHING WRONG.
EXCEPT CHOOSING A LOUSY PLACE TO HIDE.
STOP

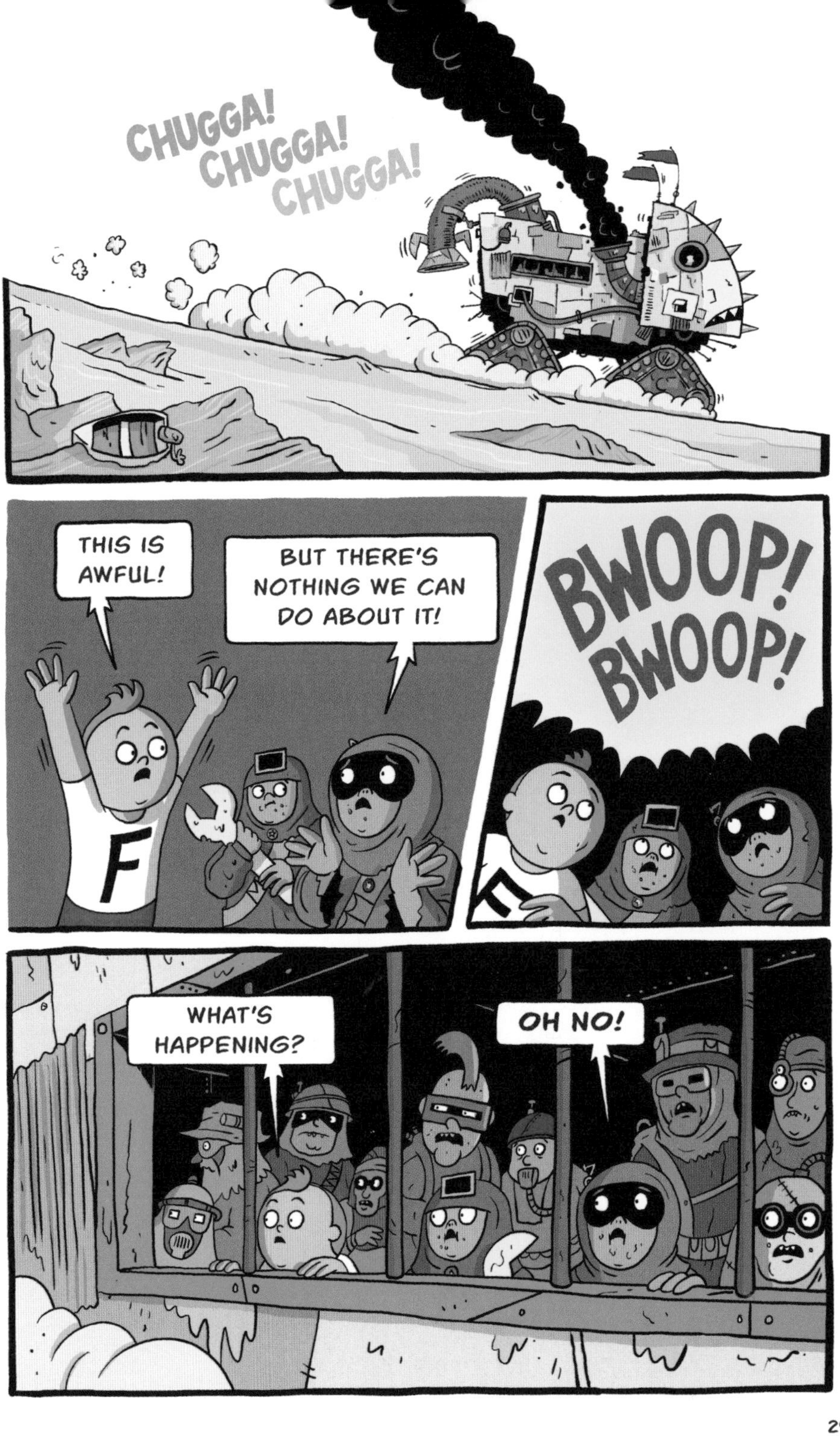
CHUGGA! CHUGGA! CHUGGA!
THIS IS AWFUL!
BUT THERE'S NOTHING WE CAN DO ABOUT IT!
BWOOP! BWOOP!
WHAT'S HAPPENING?
OH NO!

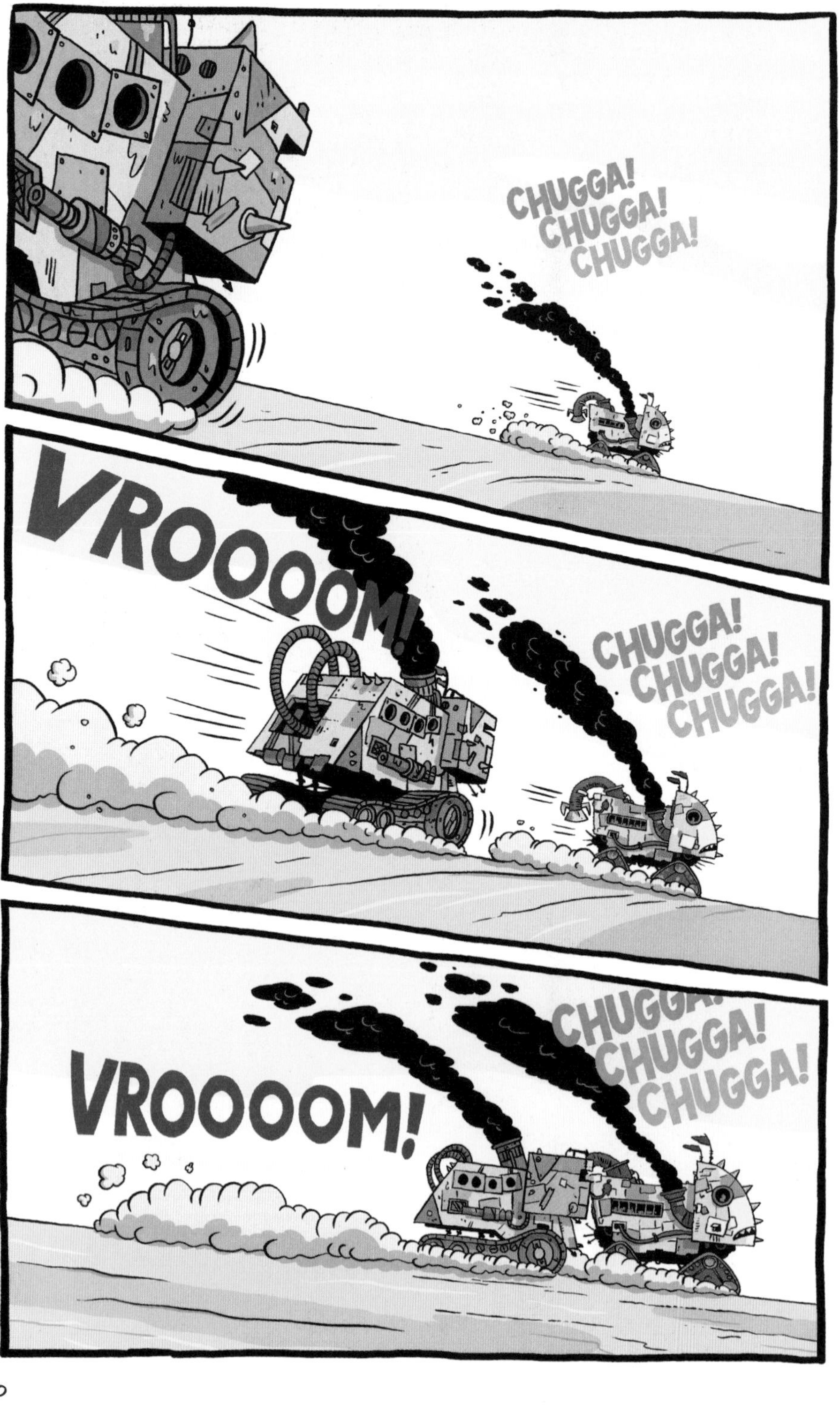
CHUGGA!
CHUGGA!
CHUGGA!
VROOOOM!
CHUGGA!
CHUGGA!
CHUGGA!
VROOOOM!
CHUGGA!
CHUGGA!

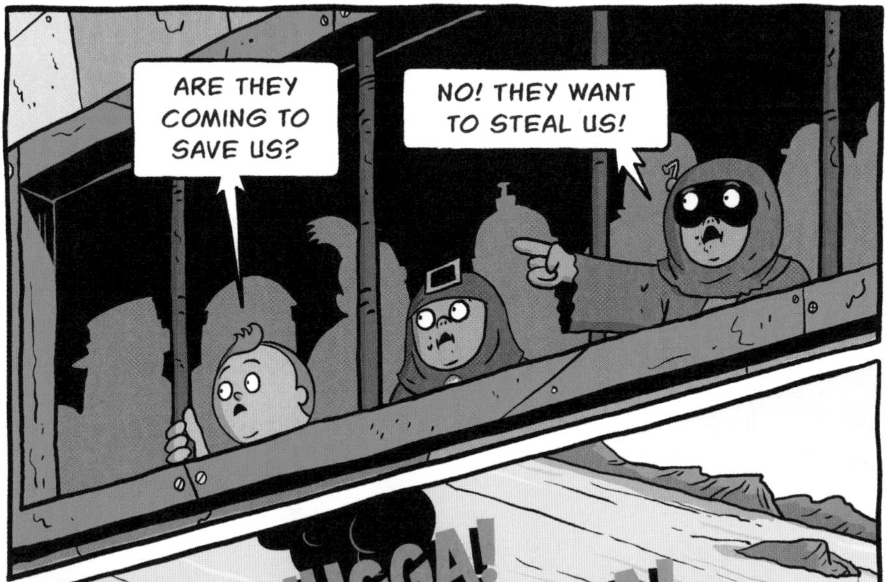
ARE THEY COMING TO SAVE US?
NO! THEY WANT TO STEAL US!

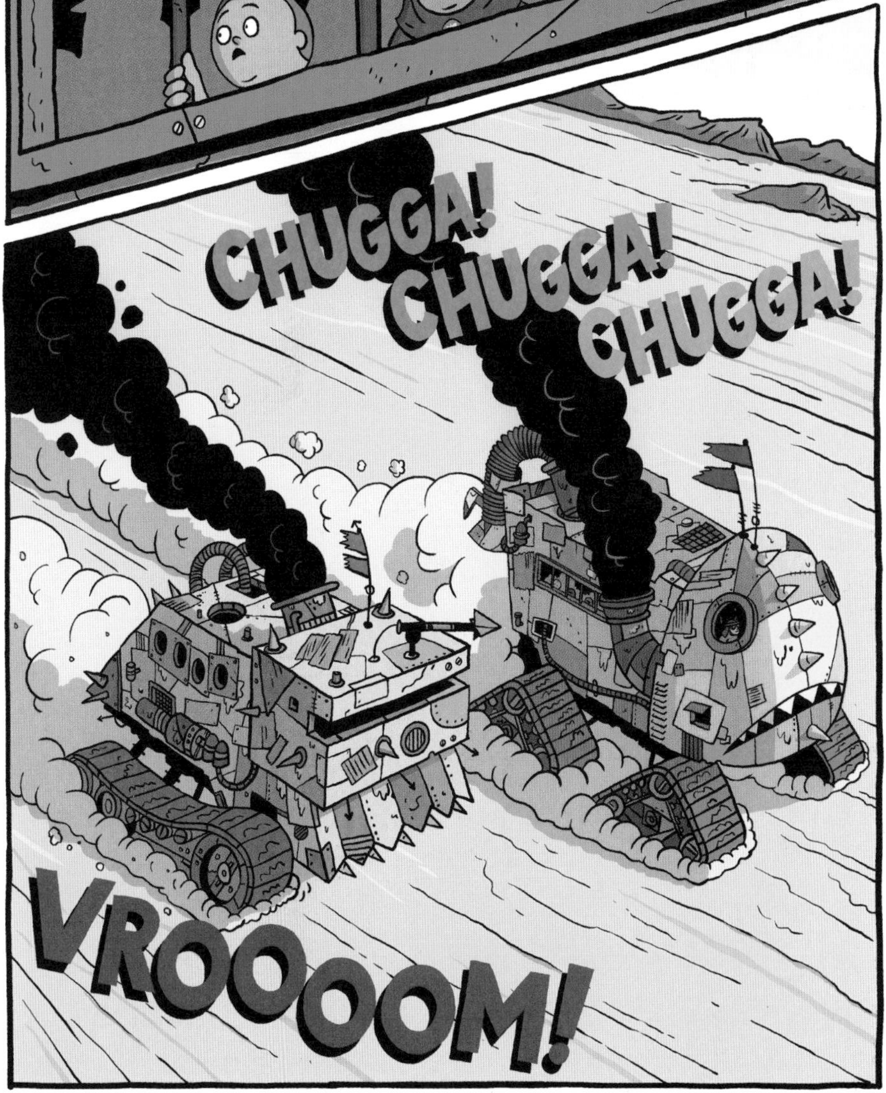
CHUGGA! CHUGGA! CHUGGA!
VROOOOOM!

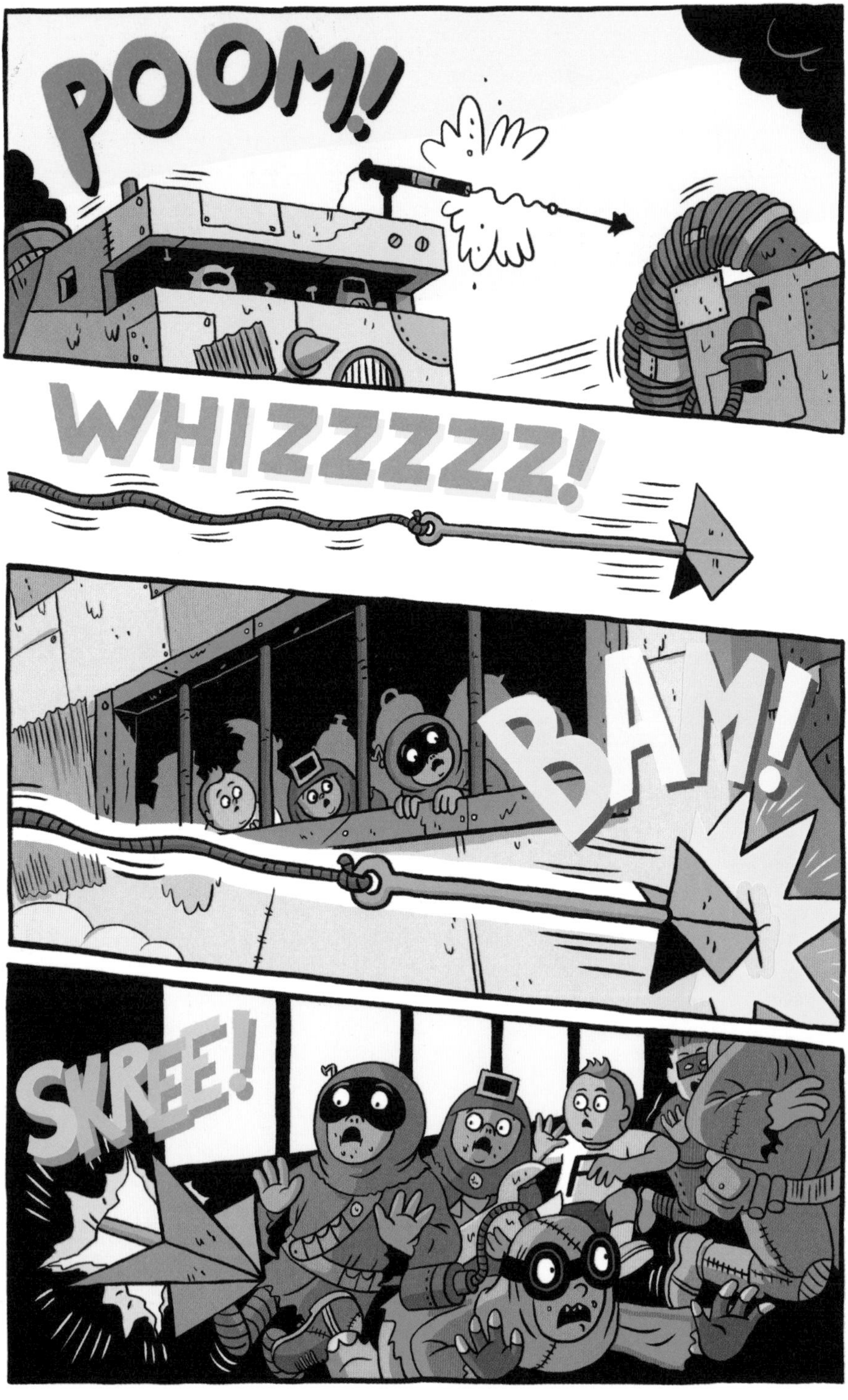
POOM!
WHIZZZZZ!
BAM!
SKREE!

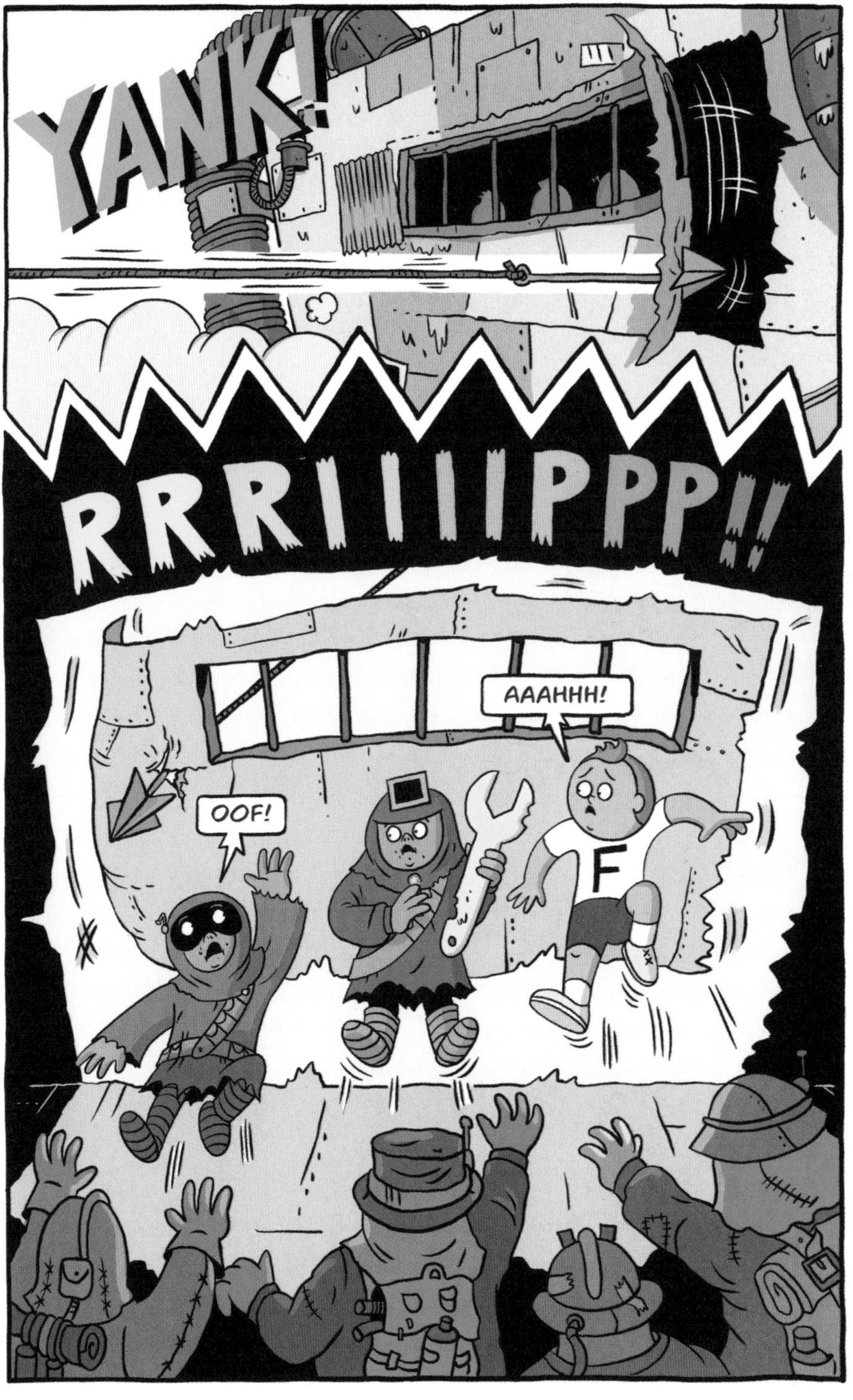
YANK!
RRRIIIIPPPP!!
OOF!
AAAHHH!
F

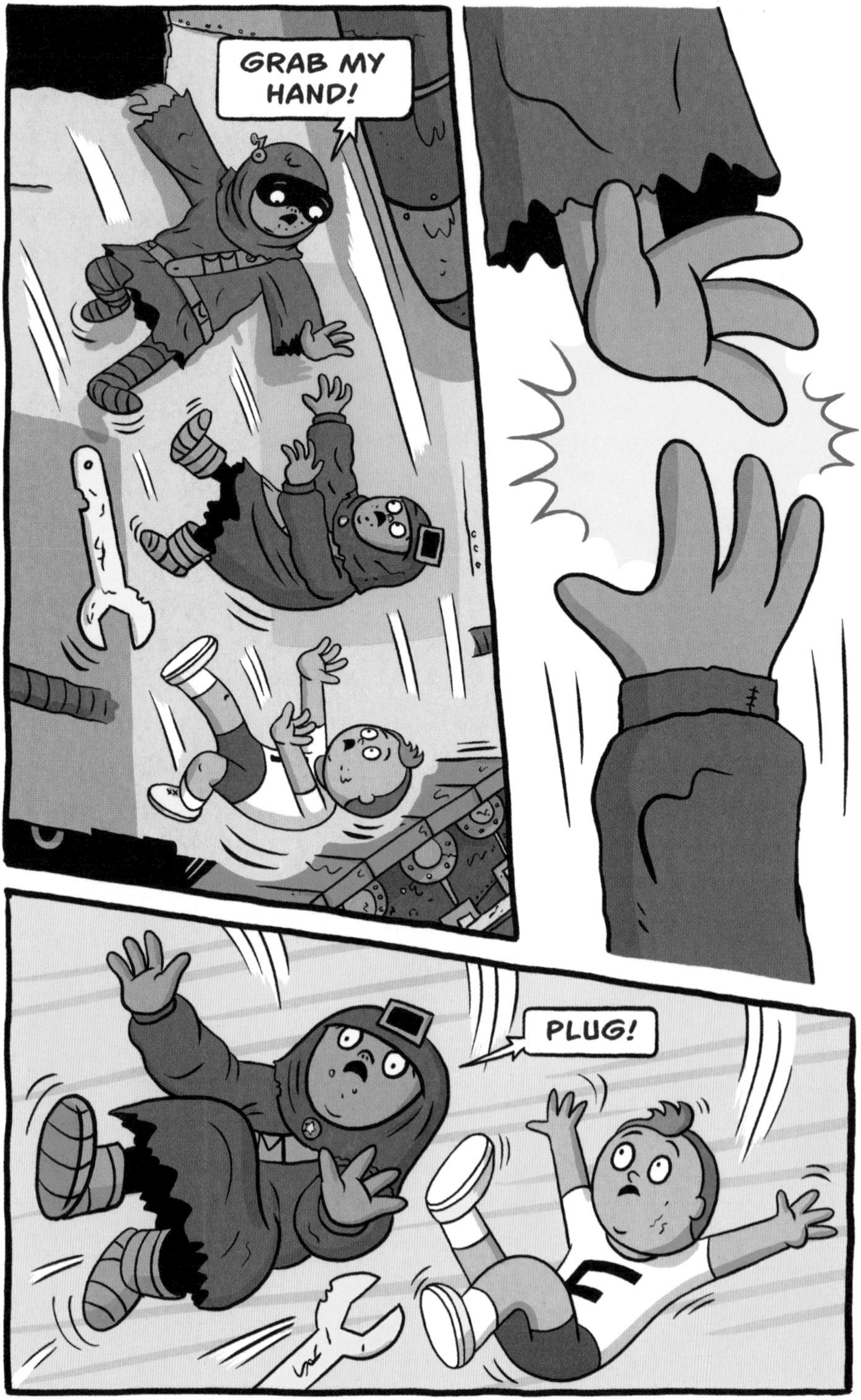
GRAB MY HAND!
PLUG!

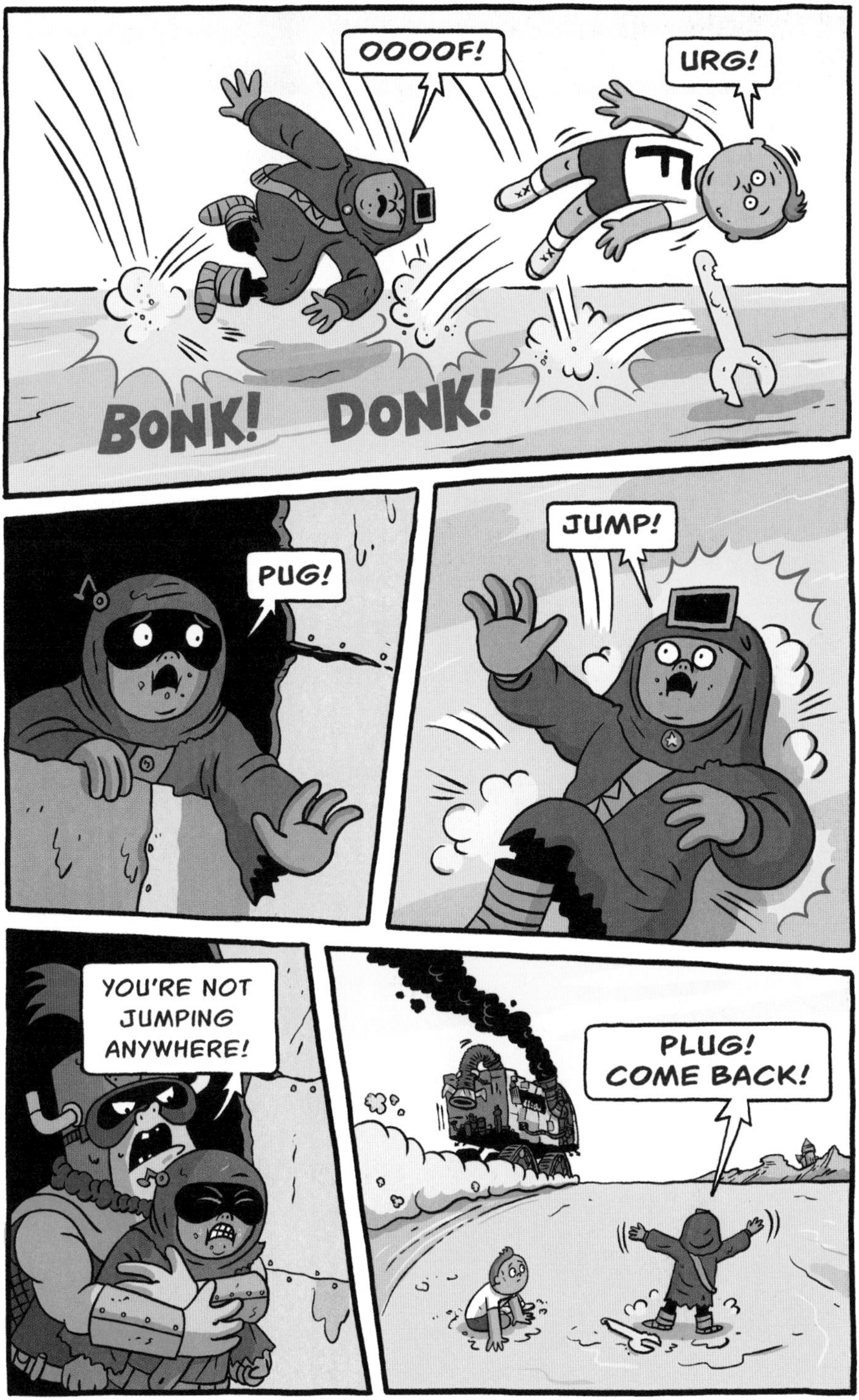
OOOOF!
URG!
BONK!
DONK!
PUG!
JUMP!
YOU'RE NOT JUMPING ANYWHERE!
PLUG! COME BACK!

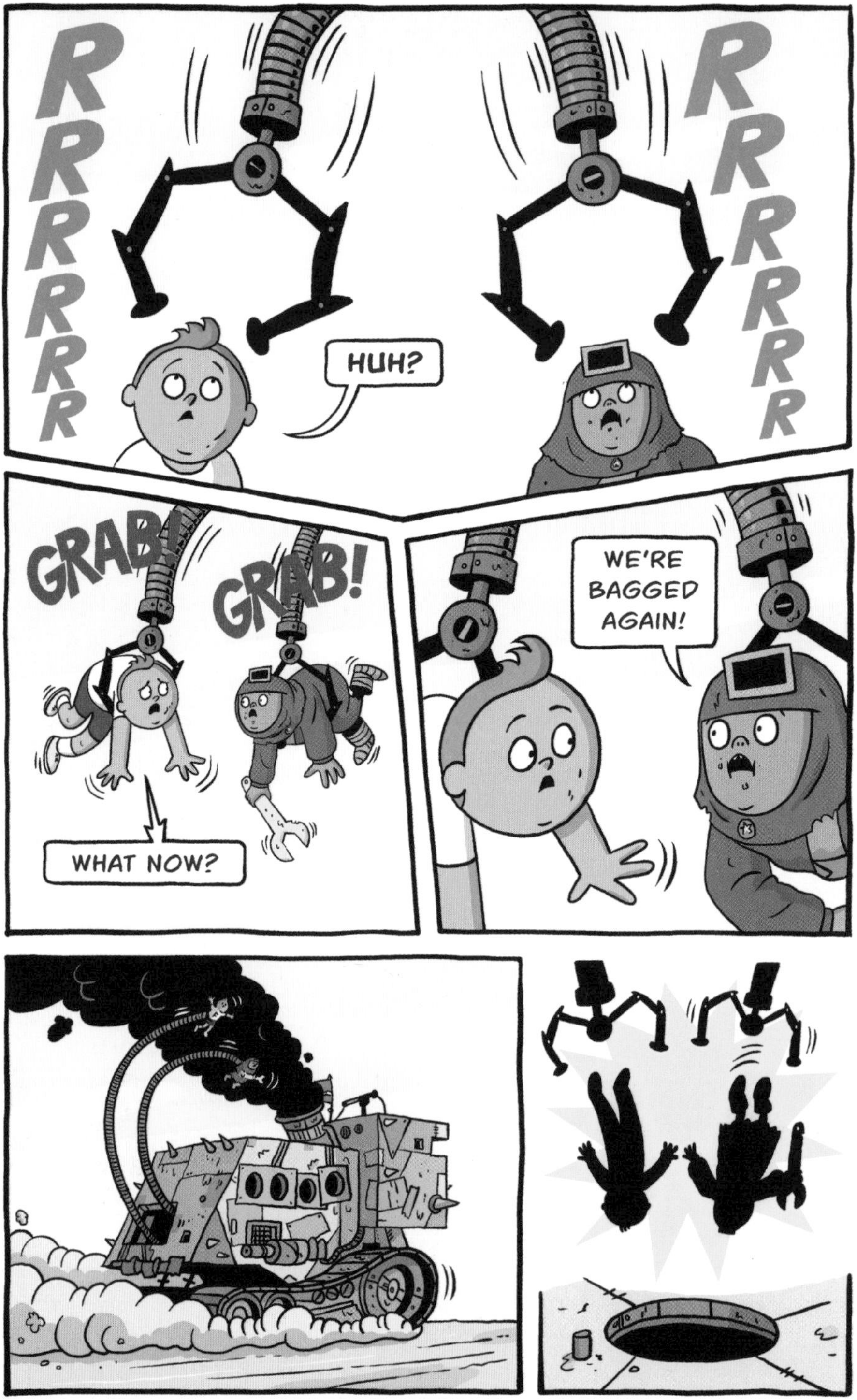
RRRRRRR
RRRRRRR
HUH?
GRAB!
GRAB!
WHAT NOW?
WE'RE BAGGED AGAIN!

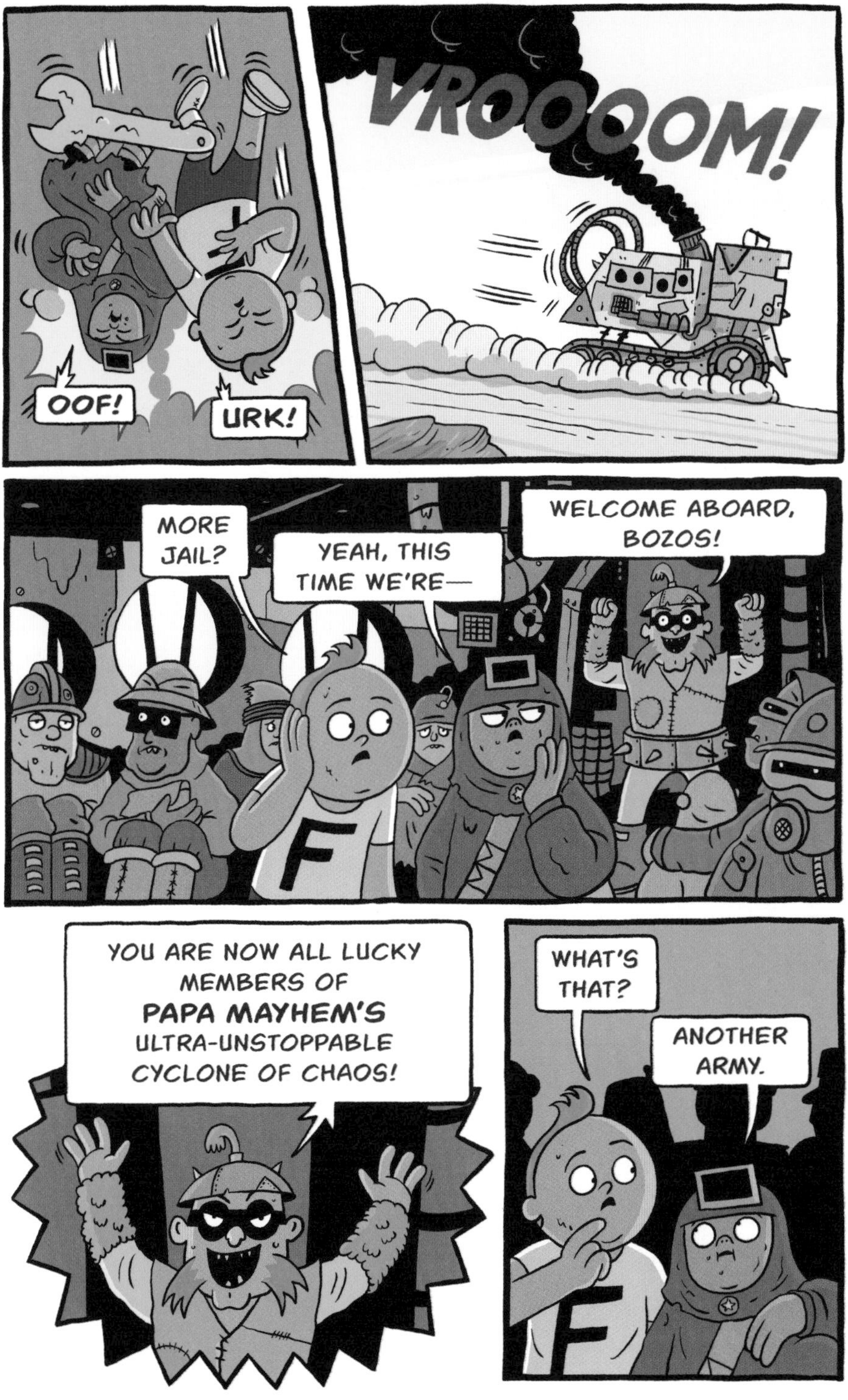
OOF!
URK!
VROOOOM!
MORE JAIL?
YEAH, THIS TIME WE'RE—
WELCOME ABOARD, BOZOS!
YOU ARE NOW ALL LUCKY MEMBERS OF PAPA MAYHEM'S ULTRA-UNSTOPPABLE CYCLONE OF CHAOS!
WHAT'S THAT?
ANOTHER ARMY.

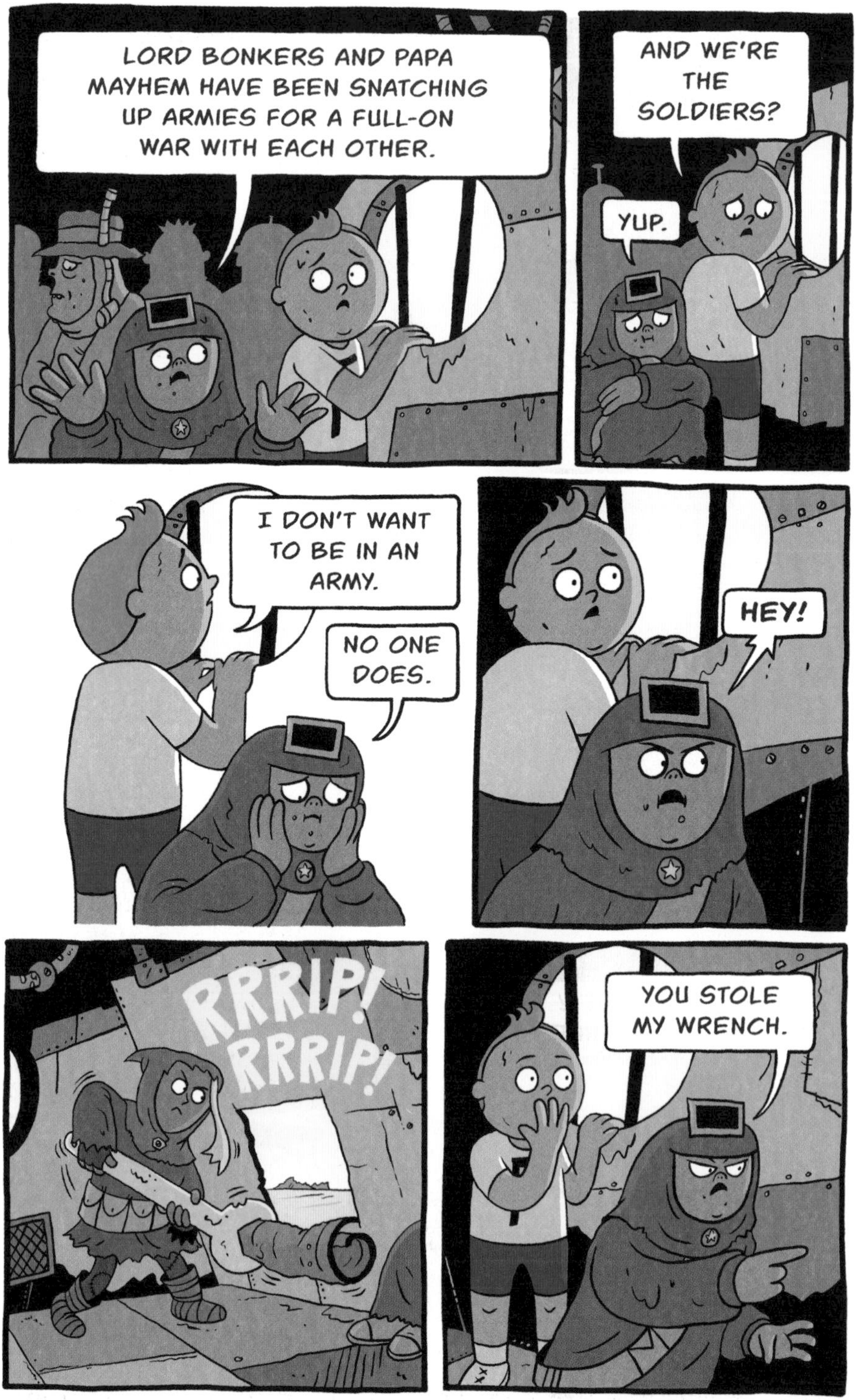
LORD BONKERS AND PAPA MAYHEM HAVE BEEN SNATCHING UP ARMIES FOR A FULL-ON WAR WITH EACH OTHER.
AND WE'RE THE SOLDIERS?
YUP.
I DON'T WANT TO BE IN AN ARMY.
NO ONE DOES.
HEY!
RRRIP! RRRIP!
YOU STOLE MY WRENCH.

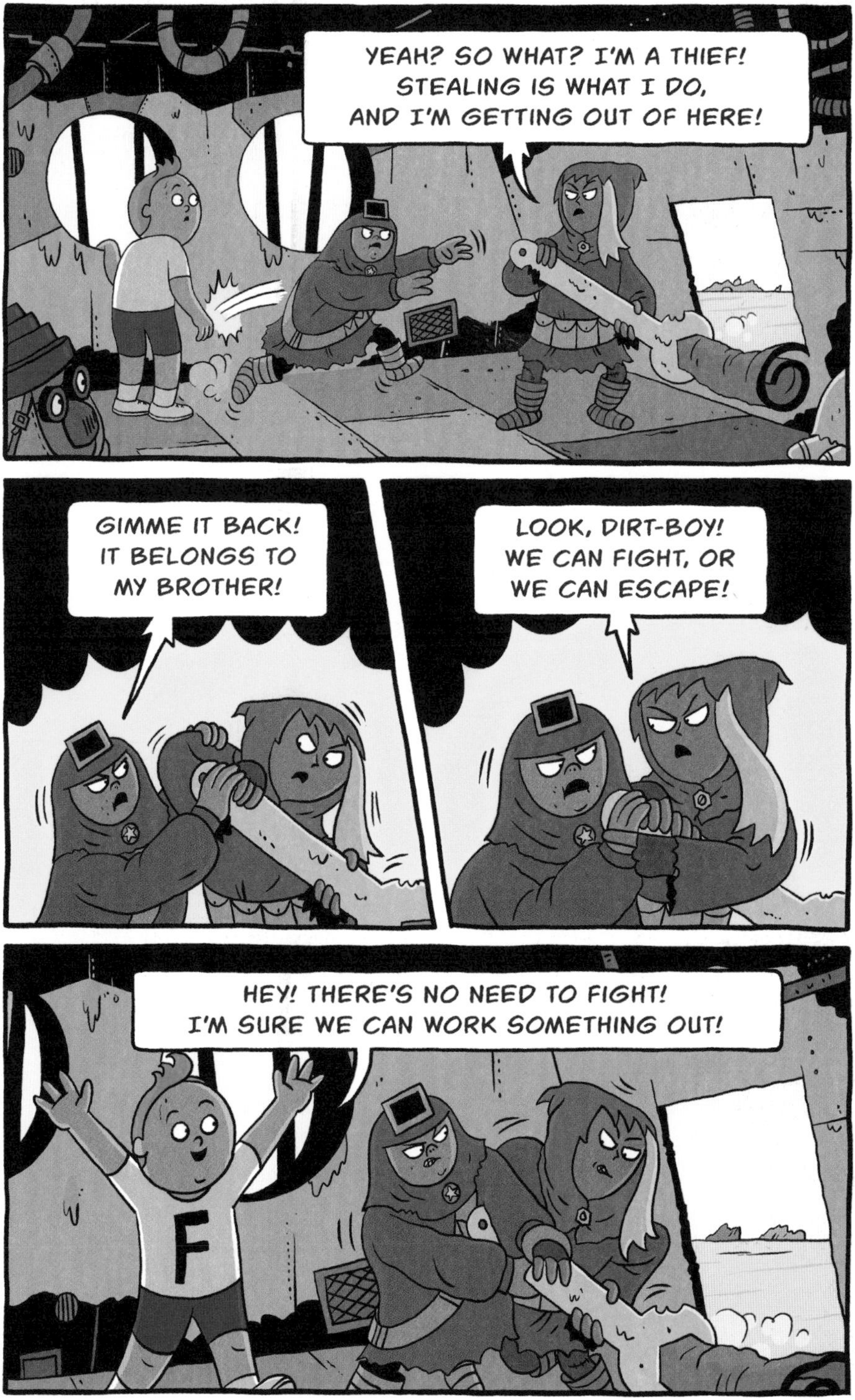
YEAH? SO WHAT? I'M A THIEF! STEALING IS WHAT I DO, AND I'M GETTING OUT OF HERE!
GIMME IT BACK! IT BELONGS TO MY BROTHER!
LOOK, DIRT-BOY! WE CAN FIGHT, OR WE CAN ESCAPE!
HEY! THERE'S NO NEED TO FIGHT! I'M SURE WE CAN WORK SOMETHING OUT!

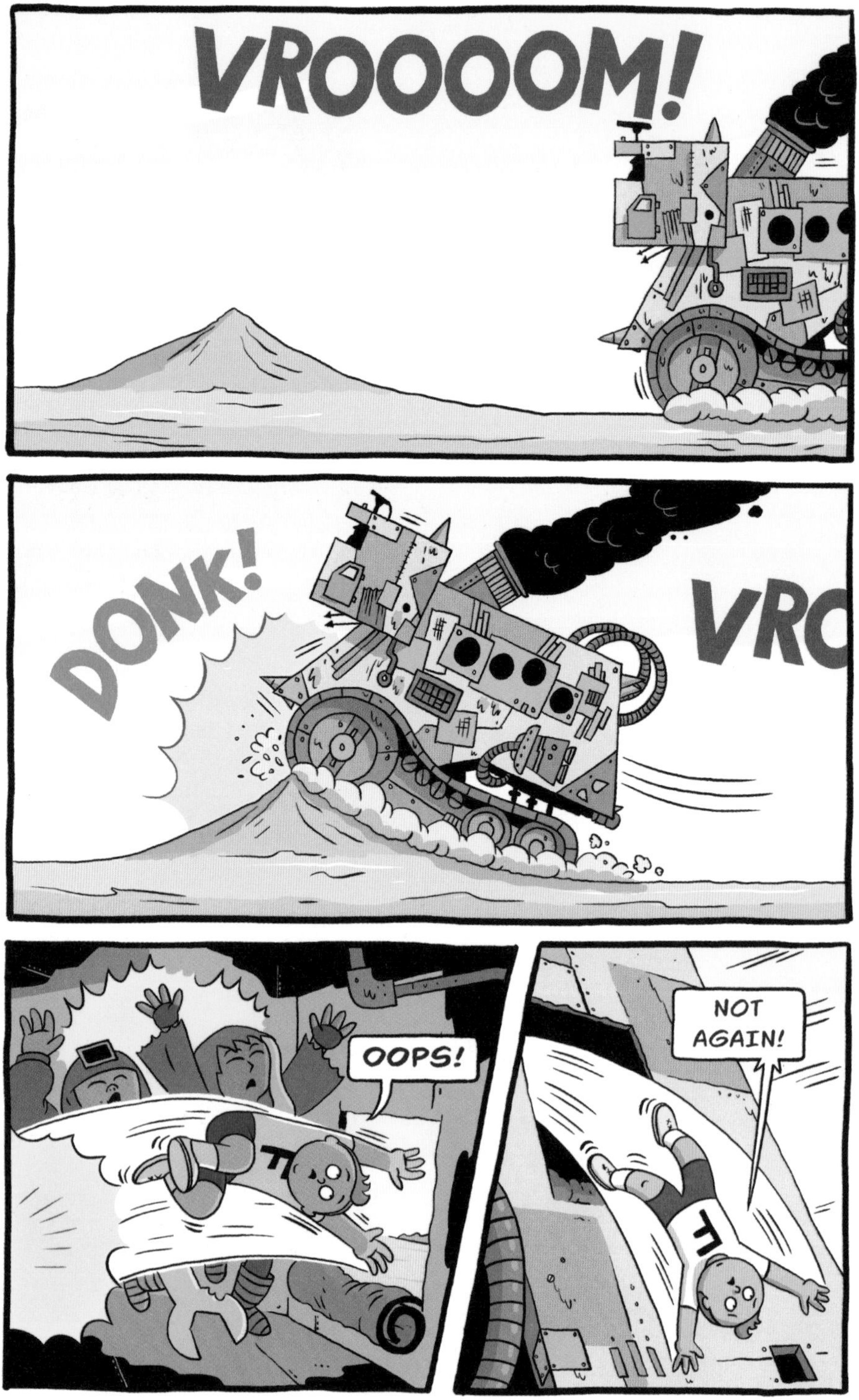
VROOOOM!
DONK!
VRO
OOPS!
NOT AGAIN!

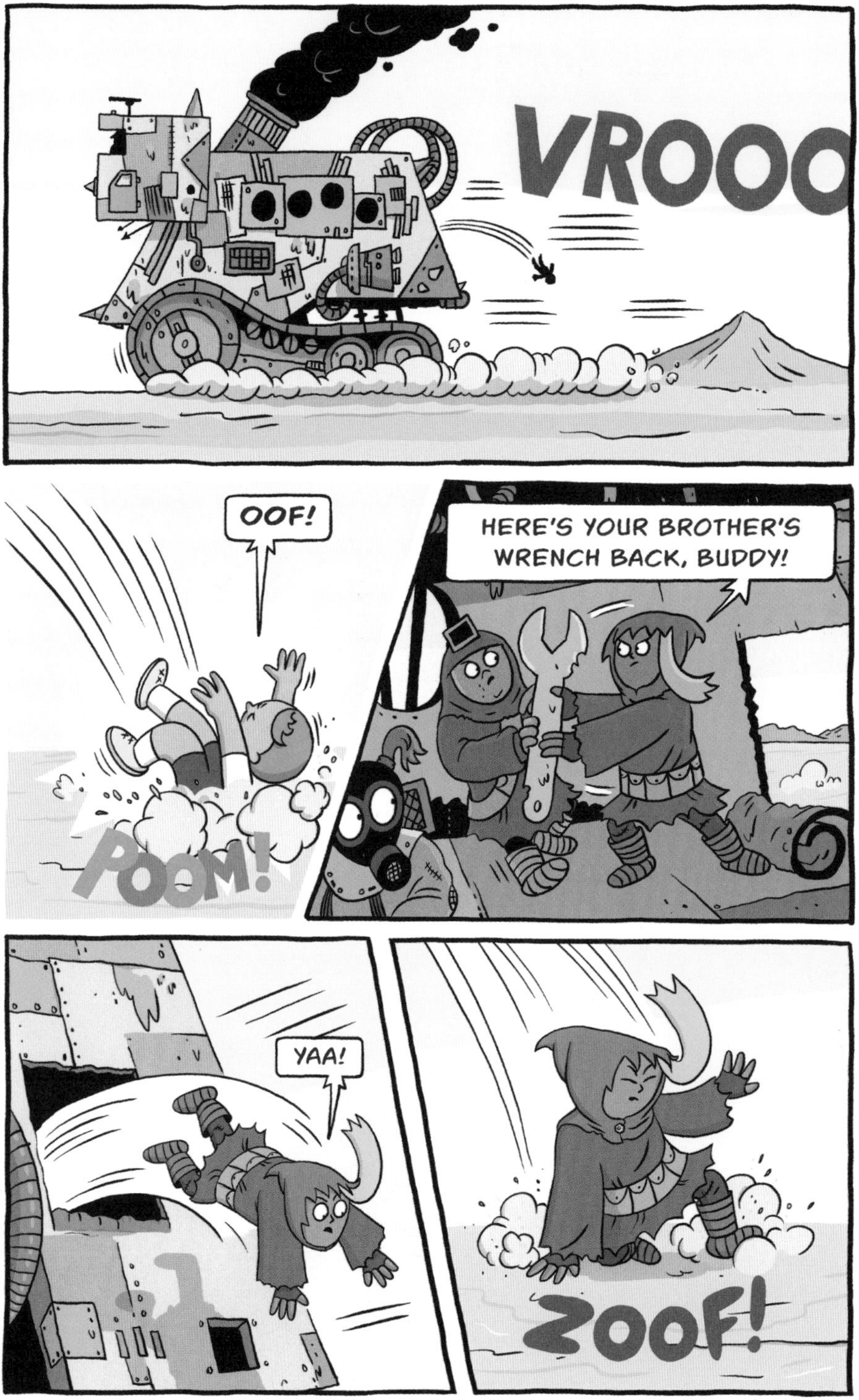

VROOO
OOF!
POOM!
HERE'S YOUR BROTHER'S WRENCH BACK, BUDDY!
YAA!
ZOOF!

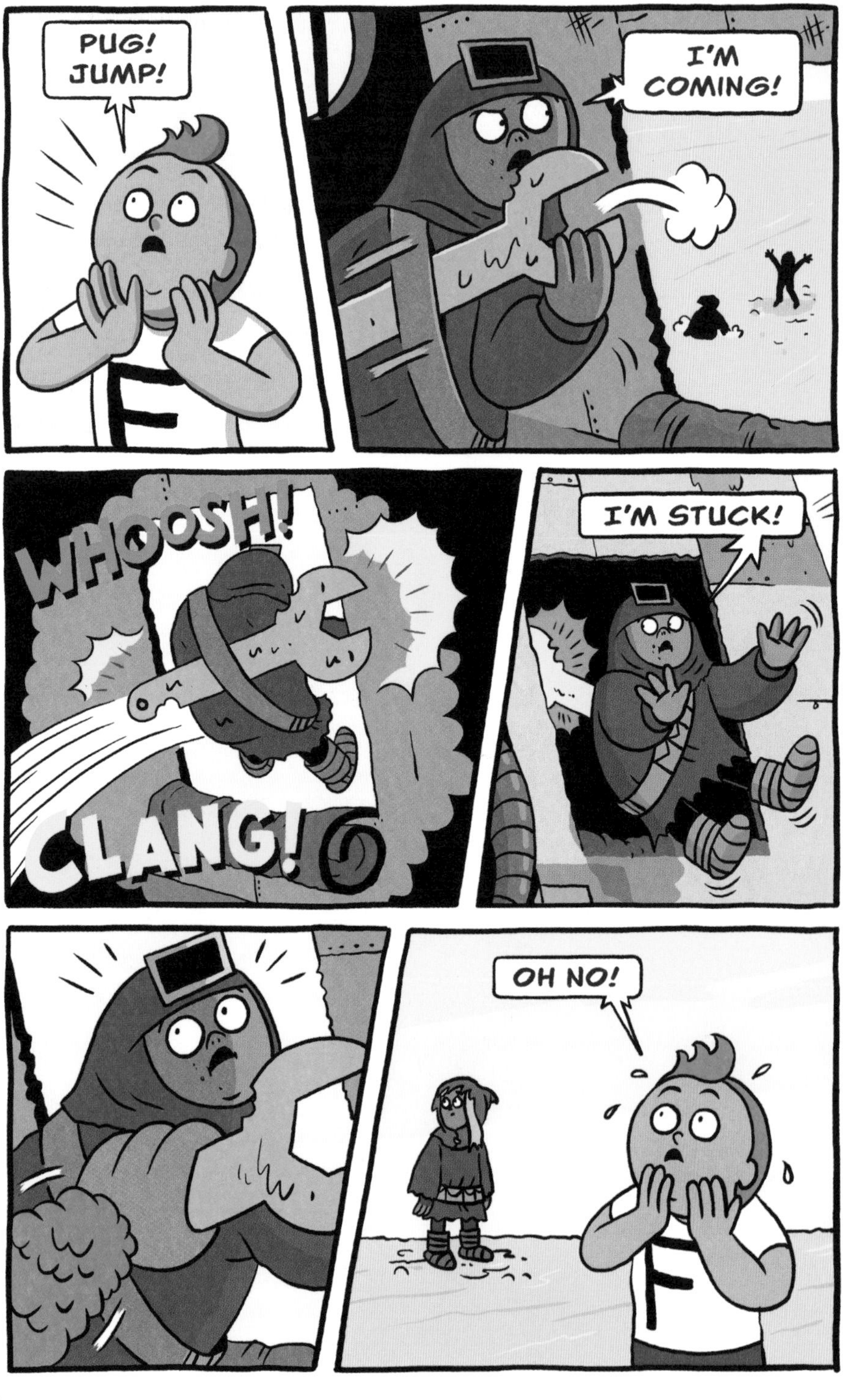
PUG! JUMP!
I'M COMING!
WHOOSH!
CLANG!
I'M STUCK!
OH NO!

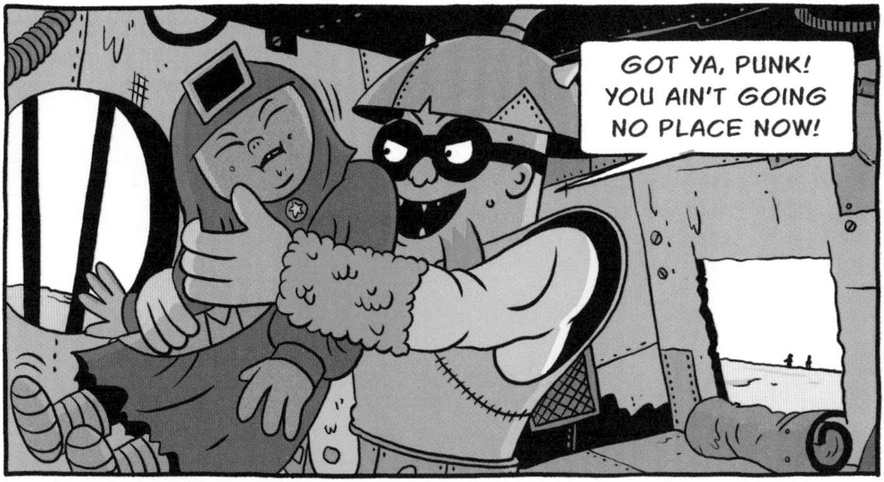
GOT YA, PUNK!
YOU AIN'T GOING
NO PLACE NOW!

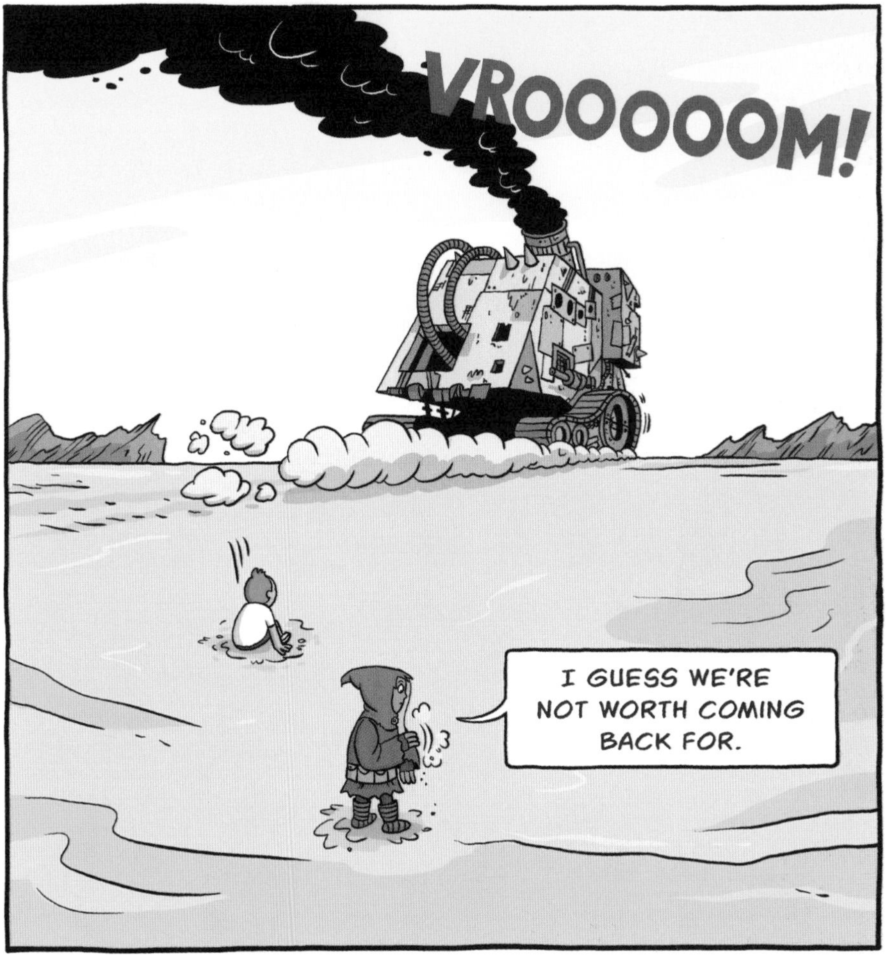
VROOOOOM!
I GUESS WE'RE
NOT WORTH COMING
BACK FOR.

CHAPTER 4

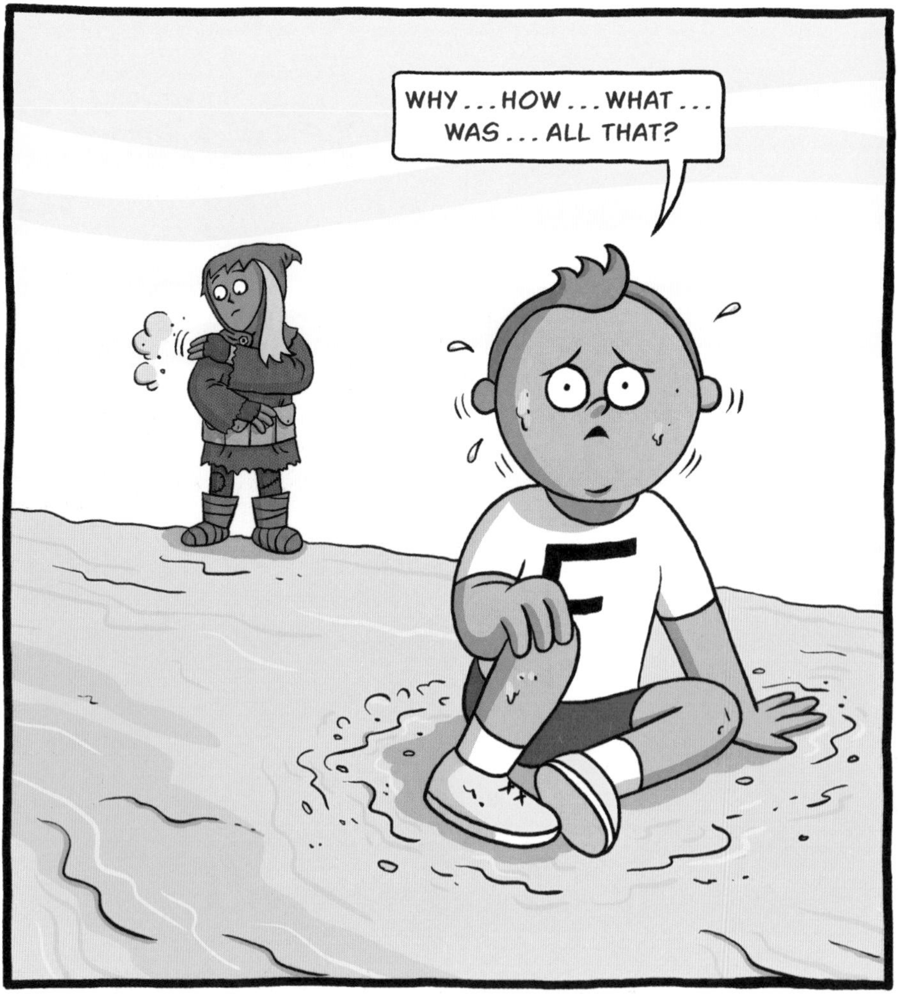
WHY . . . HOW . . . WHAT . . .
WAS . . . ALL THAT?

45

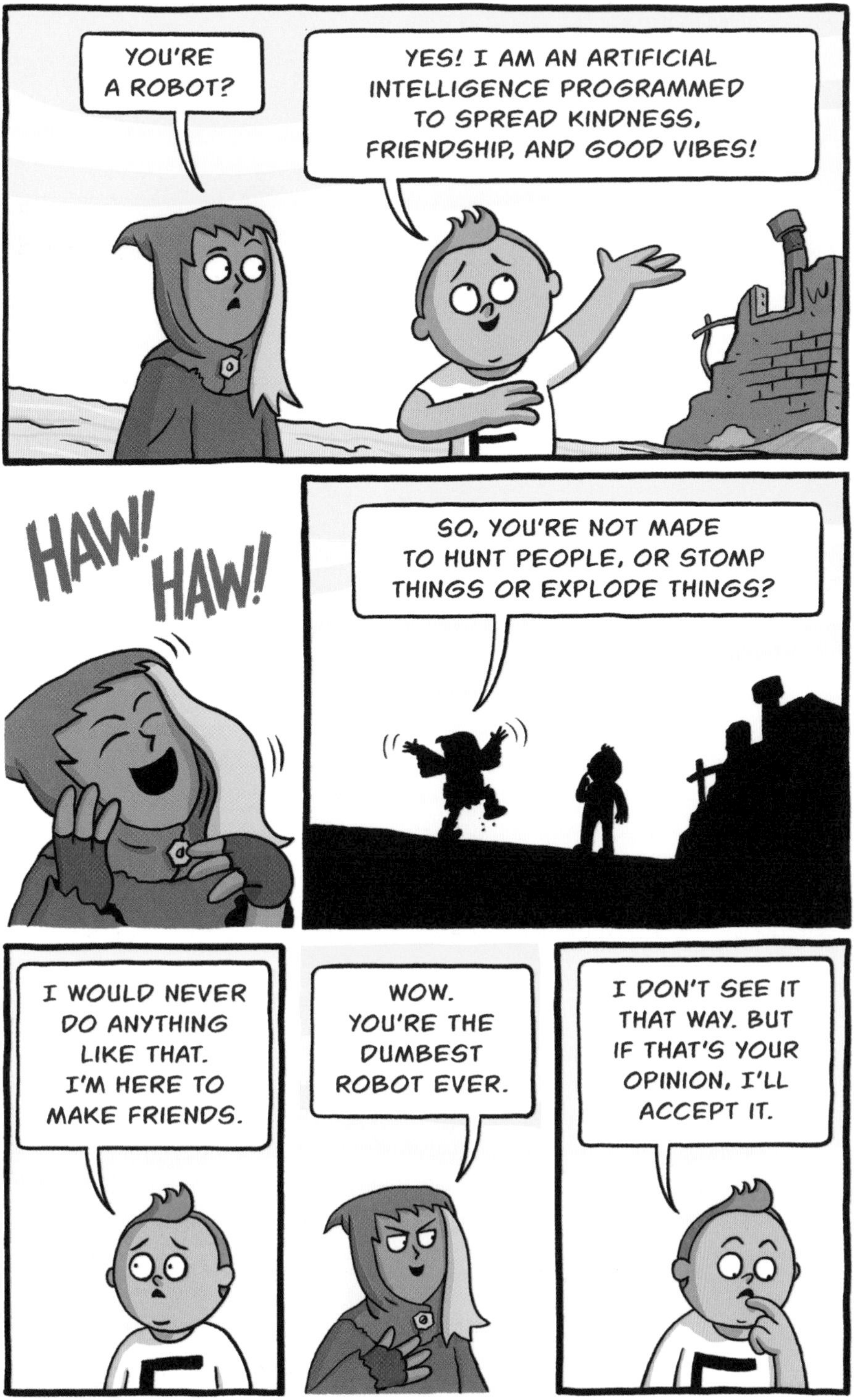
YOU'RE A ROBOT?
YES! I AM AN ARTIFICIAL INTELLIGENCE PROGRAMMED TO SPREAD KINDNESS, FRIENDSHIP, AND GOOD VIBES!
HAW! HAW!
SO, YOU'RE NOT MADE TO HUNT PEOPLE, OR STOMP THINGS OR EXPLODE THINGS?
I WOULD NEVER DO ANYTHING LIKE THAT. I'M HERE TO MAKE FRIENDS.
WOW. YOU'RE THE DUMBEST ROBOT EVER.
I DON'T SEE IT THAT WAY. BUT IF THAT'S YOUR OPINION, I'LL ACCEPT IT.

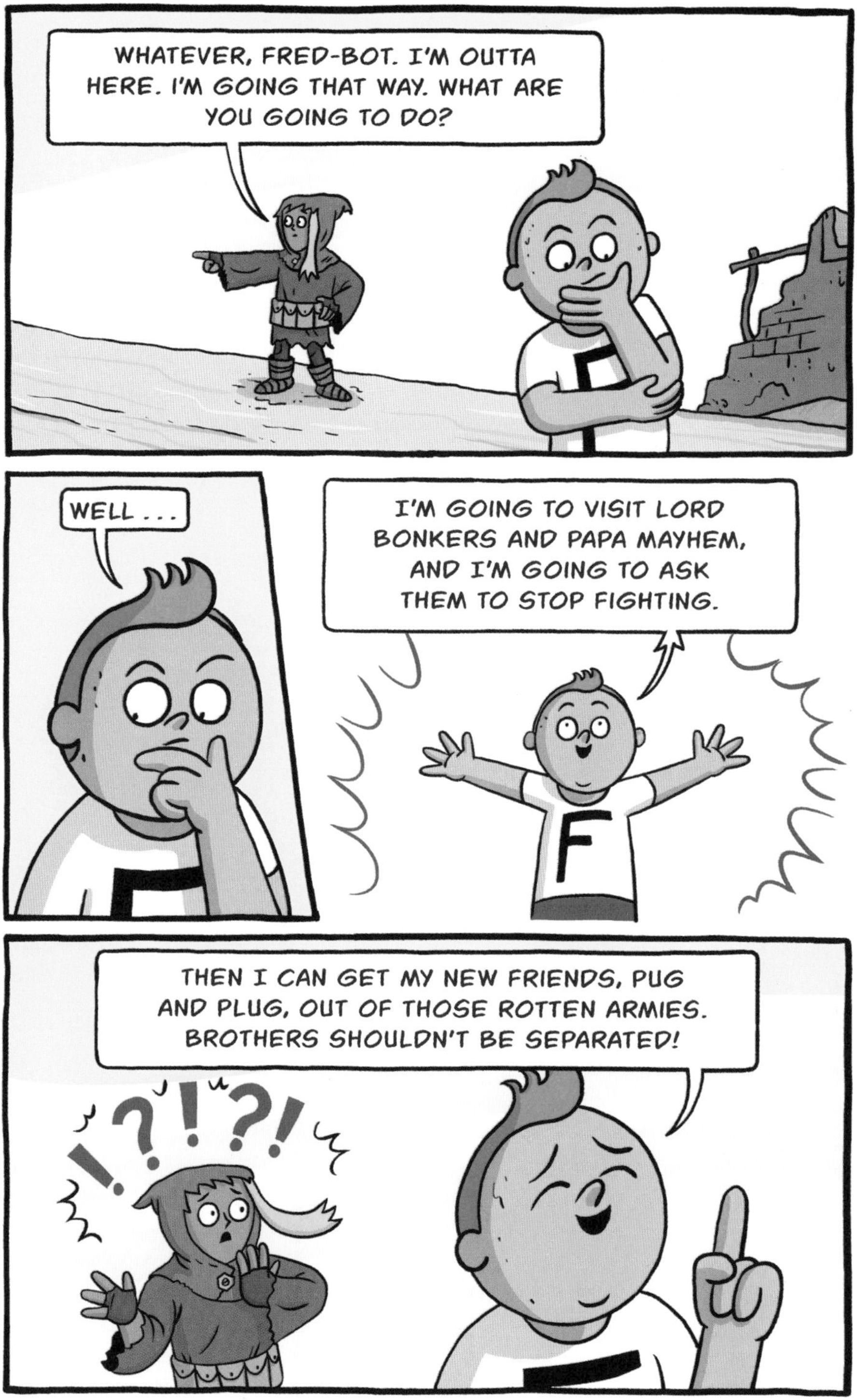
WHATEVER, FRED-BOT. I'M OUTTA HERE. I'M GOING THAT WAY. WHAT ARE YOU GOING TO DO?
WELL . . .
I'M GOING TO VISIT LORD BONKERS AND PAPA MAYHEM, AND I'M GOING TO ASK THEM TO STOP FIGHTING.
THEN I CAN GET MY NEW FRIENDS, PUG AND PLUG, OUT OF THOSE ROTTEN ARMIES. BROTHERS SHOULDN'T BE SEPARATED!
!?!?!

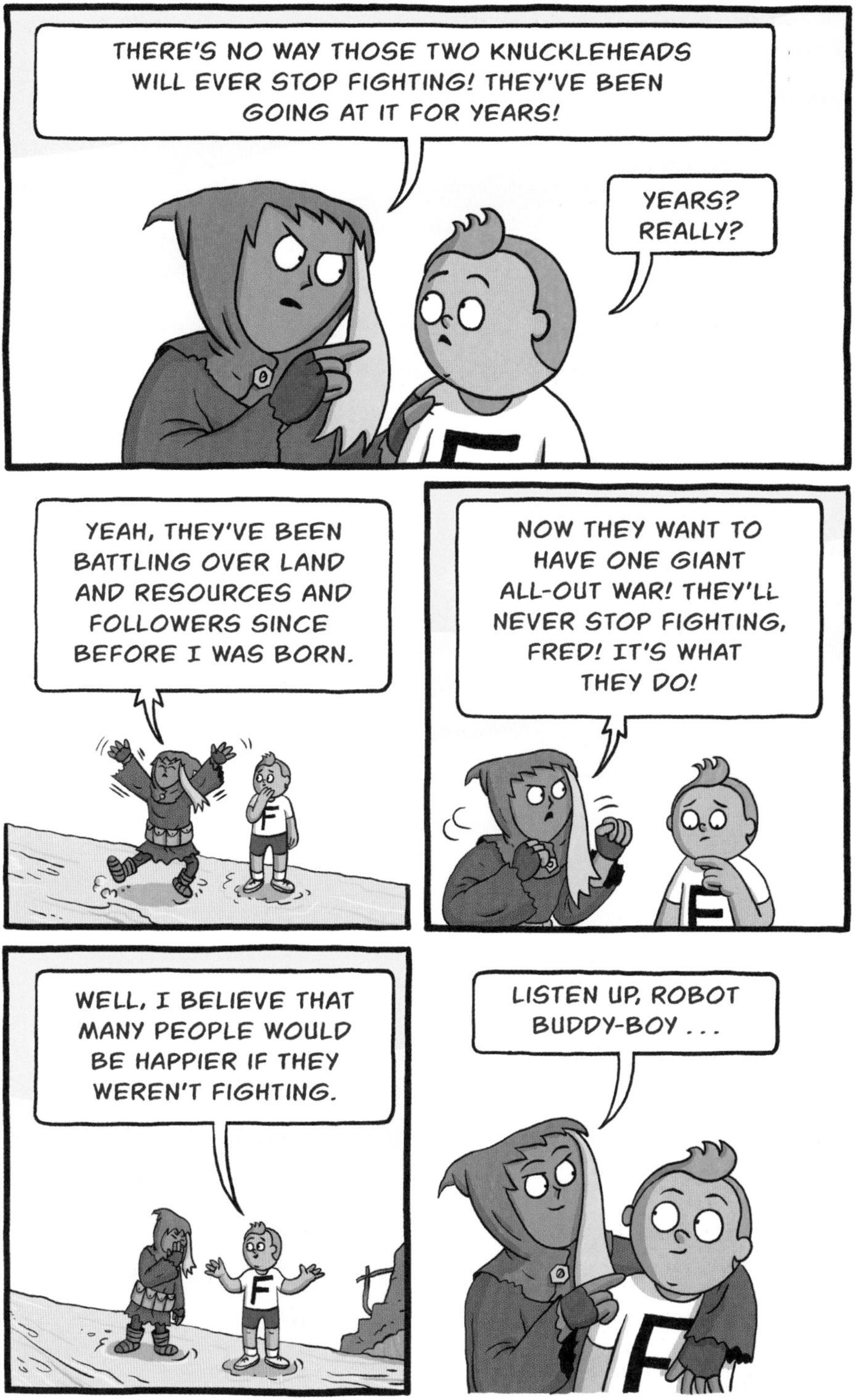
THERE'S NO WAY THOSE TWO KNUCKLEHEADS WILL EVER STOP FIGHTING! THEY'VE BEEN GOING AT IT FOR YEARS!
YEARS? REALLY?
YEAH, THEY'VE BEEN BATTLING OVER LAND AND RESOURCES AND FOLLOWERS SINCE BEFORE I WAS BORN.
NOW THEY WANT TO HAVE ONE GIANT ALL-OUT WAR! THEY'LL NEVER STOP FIGHTING, FRED! IT'S WHAT THEY DO!
WELL, I BELIEVE THAT MANY PEOPLE WOULD BE HAPPIER IF THEY WEREN'T FIGHTING.
LISTEN UP, ROBOT BUDDY-BOY . . .

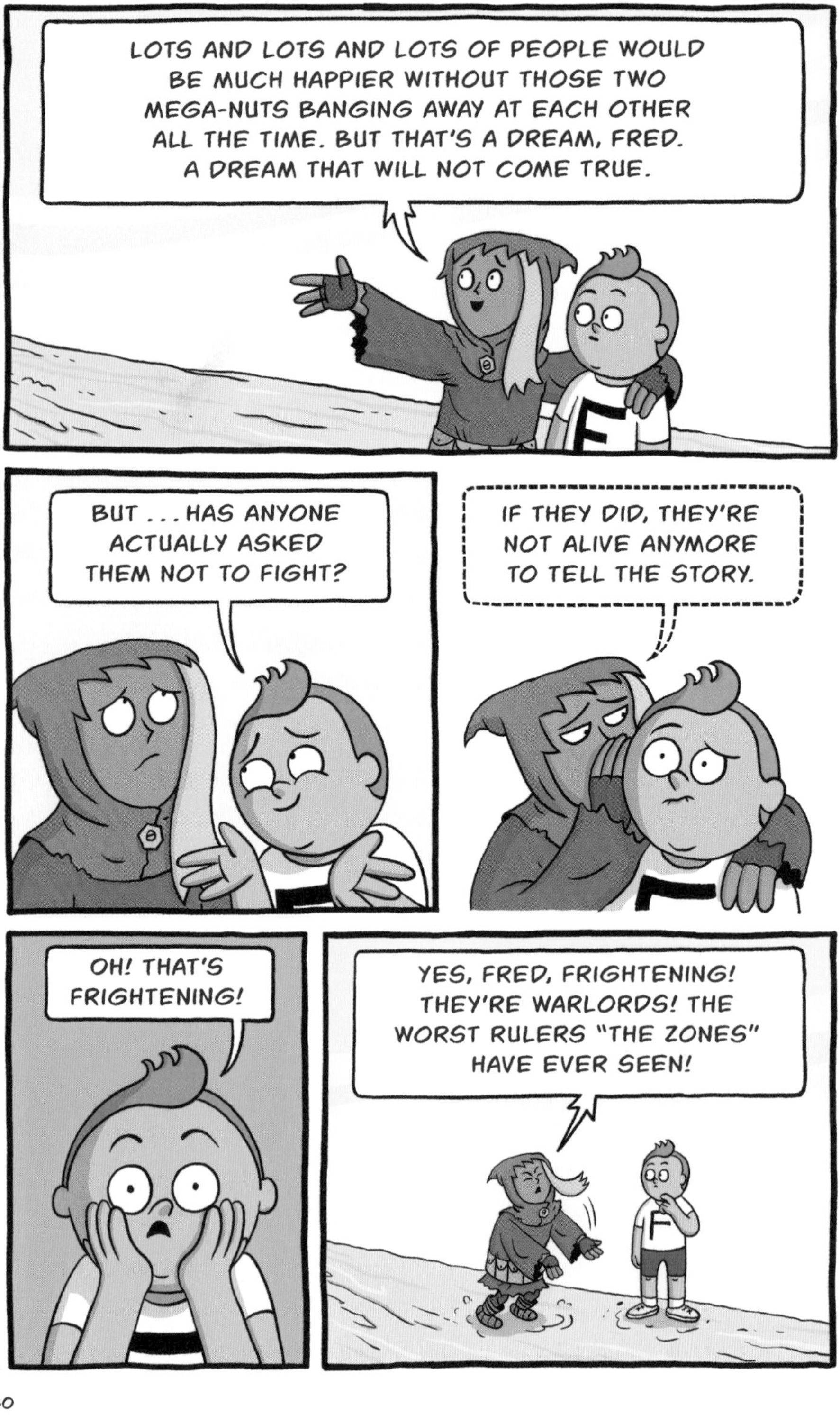
LOTS AND LOTS AND LOTS OF PEOPLE WOULD BE MUCH HAPPIER WITHOUT THOSE TWO MEGA-NUTS BANGING AWAY AT EACH OTHER ALL THE TIME. BUT THAT'S A DREAM, FRED. A DREAM THAT WILL NOT COME TRUE.
BUT . . . HAS ANYONE ACTUALLY ASKED THEM NOT TO FIGHT?
IF THEY DID, THEY'RE NOT ALIVE ANYMORE TO TELL THE STORY.
OH! THAT'S FRIGHTENING!
YES, FRED, FRIGHTENING! THEY'RE WARLORDS! THE WORST RULERS "THE ZONES" HAVE EVER SEEN!

FRED, THIS IS A ROUGH WORLD, AND I THINK YOU MIGHT BE TOO INNOCENT FOR IT. MAYBE YOU SHOULD JUST DIG A HOLE AND HIDE IN IT FOR AS LONG AS YOU CAN.

I COULD NEVER HIDE IN A HOLE WHEN THERE ARE SO MANY UNHAPPY PEOPLE AROUND.

WHATEVER, FRED.

ONE MORE QUESTION?

WHO LIVES CLOSER? LORD BONKERS OR PAPA MAYHEM?

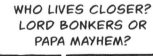

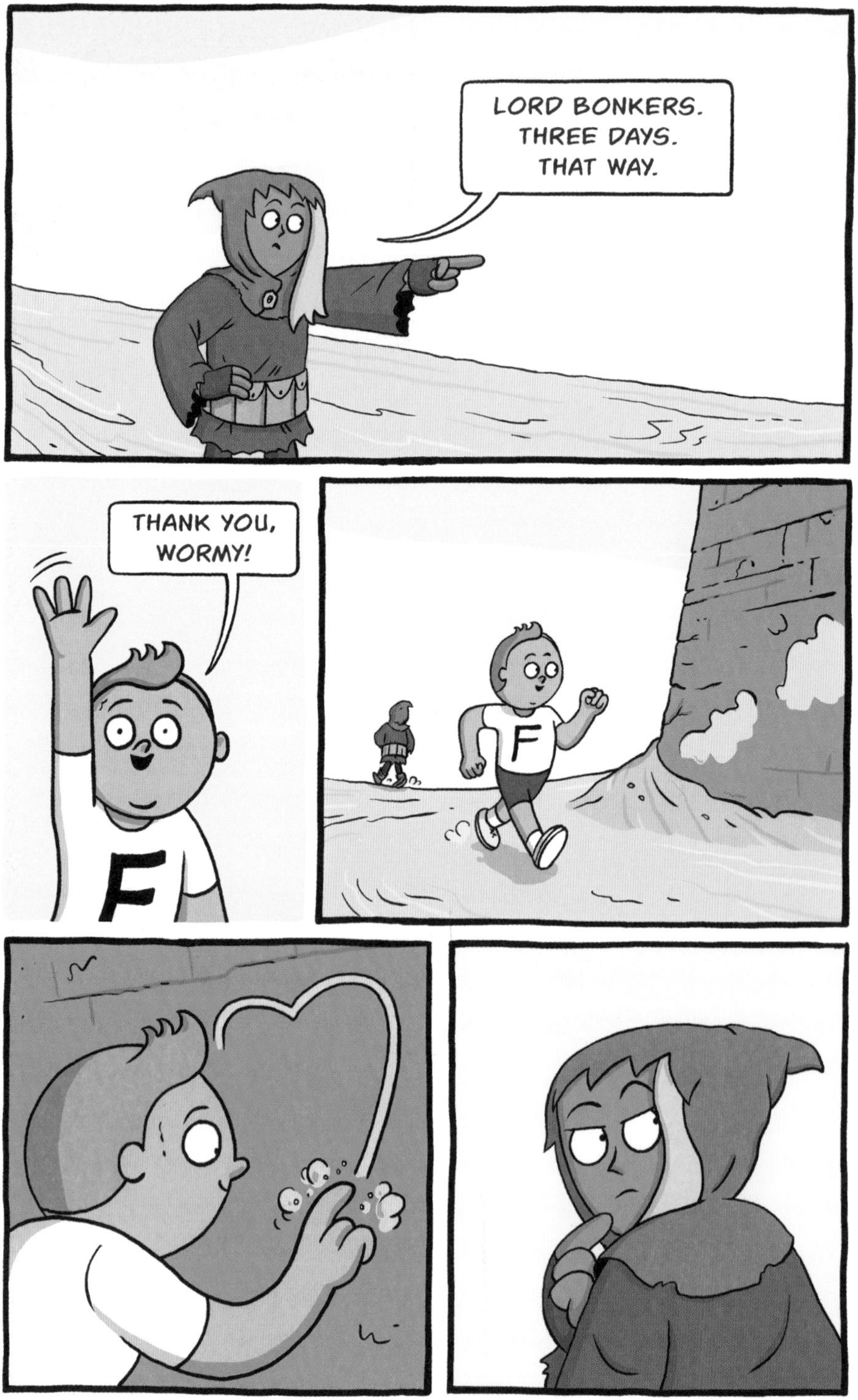
LORD BONKERS. THREE DAYS. THAT WAY.
THANK YOU, WORMY!

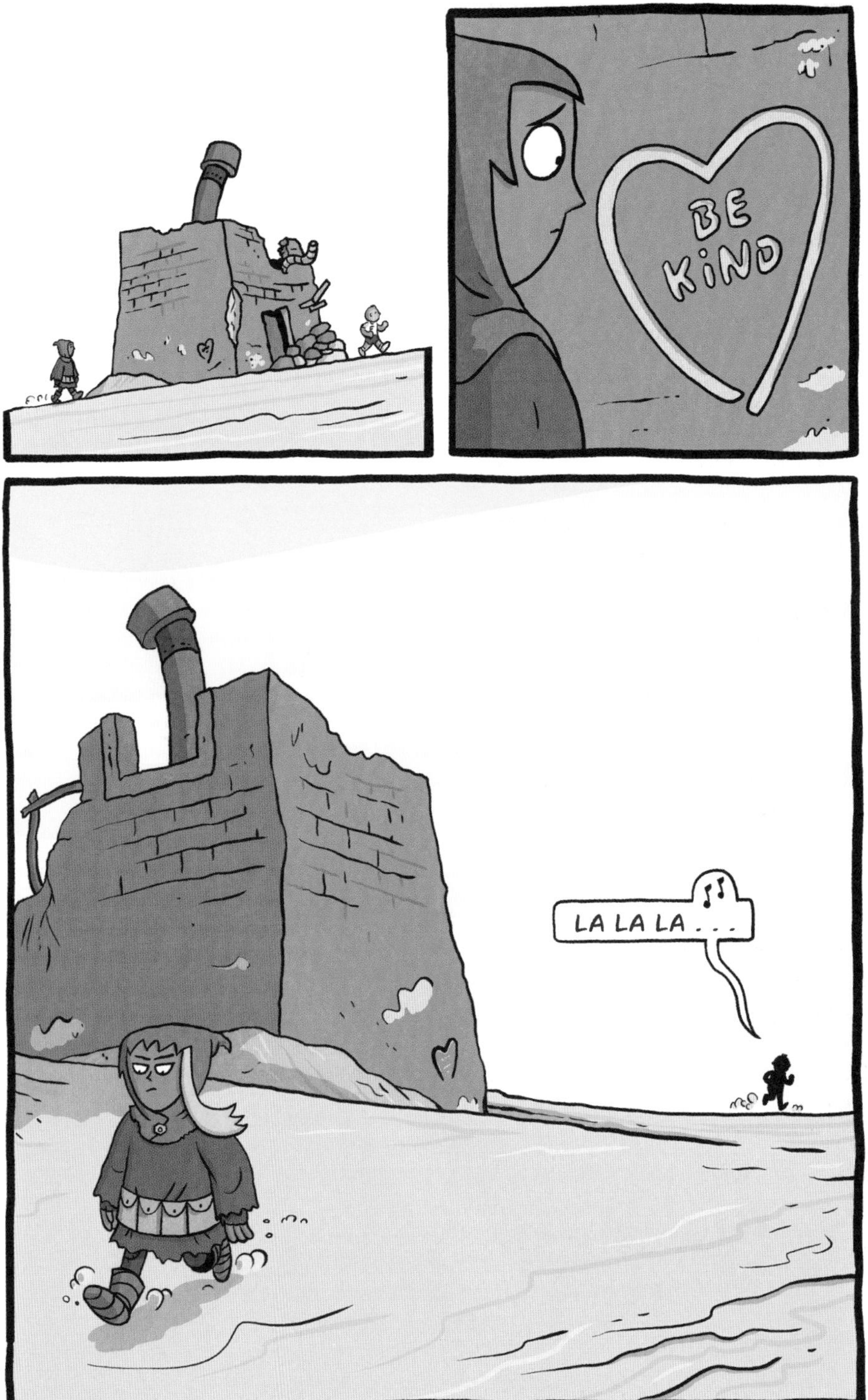
BE KIND
LA LA LA . . .

CHAPTER 5

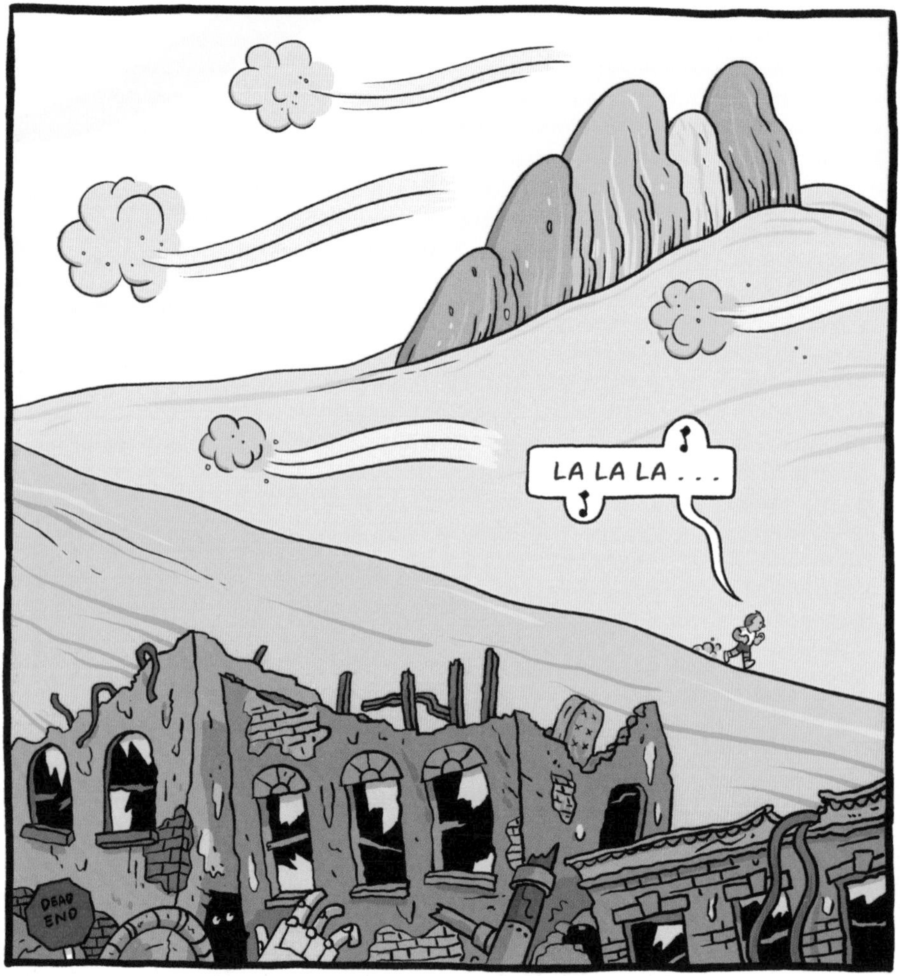
LA LA LA . . .
DEAD END

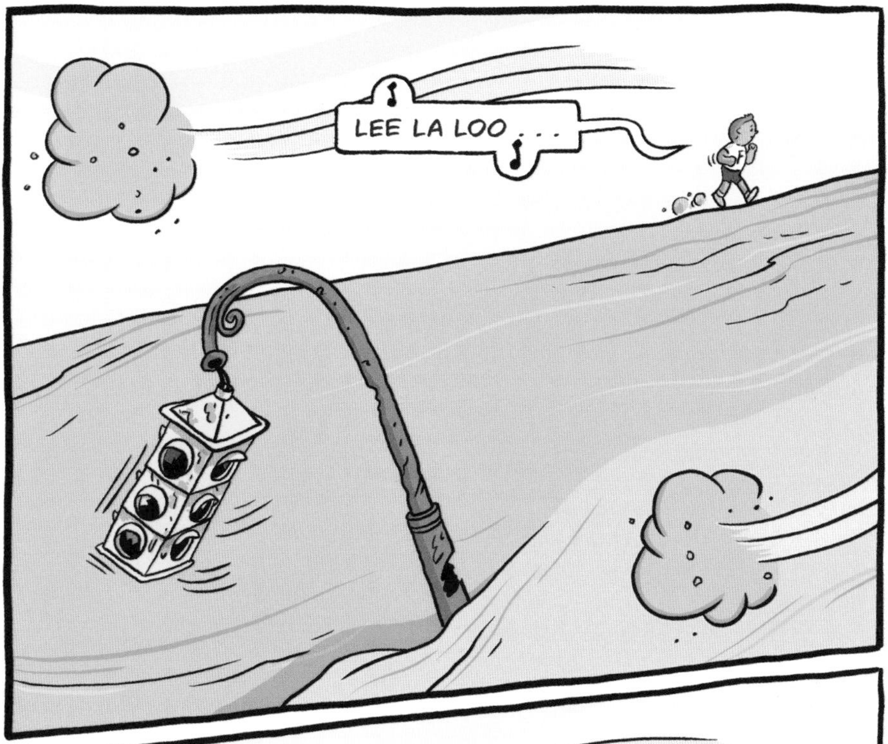
LEE LA LOO . . .

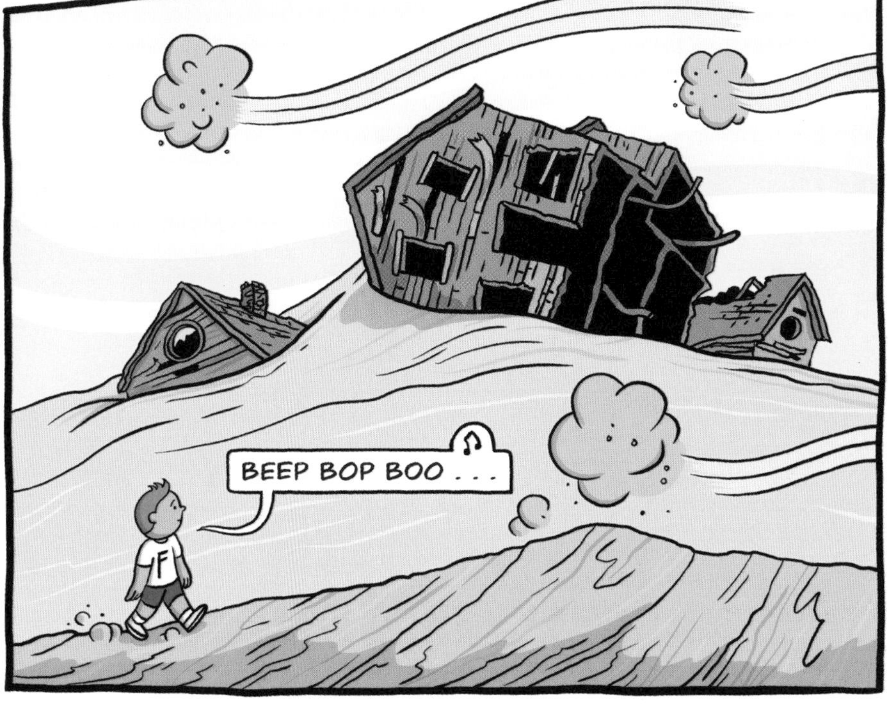
BEEP BOP BOO . . .

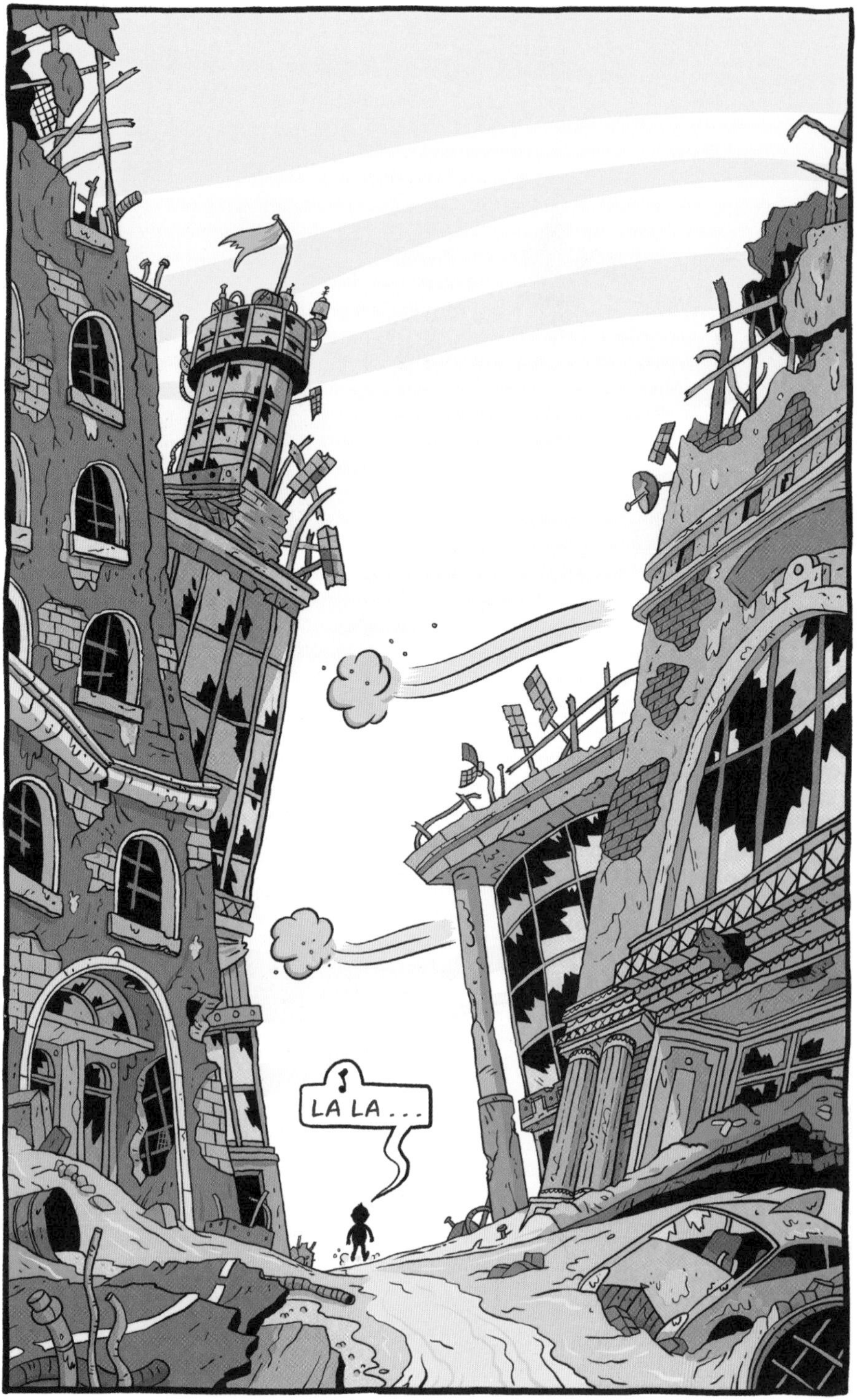
♪ LA LA . . .

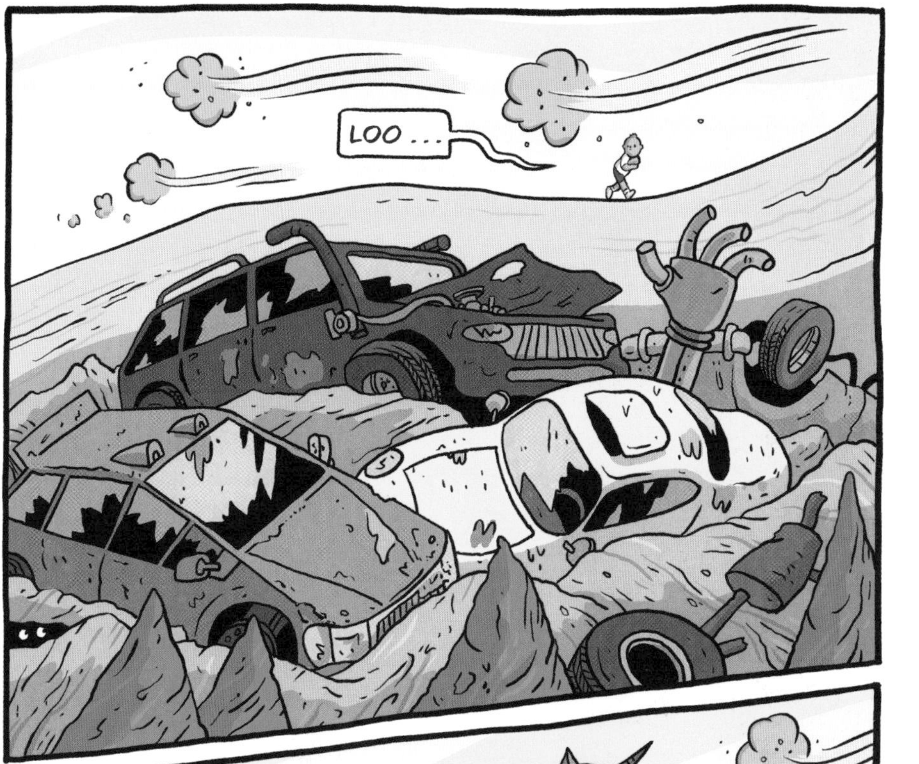
LOO . . .

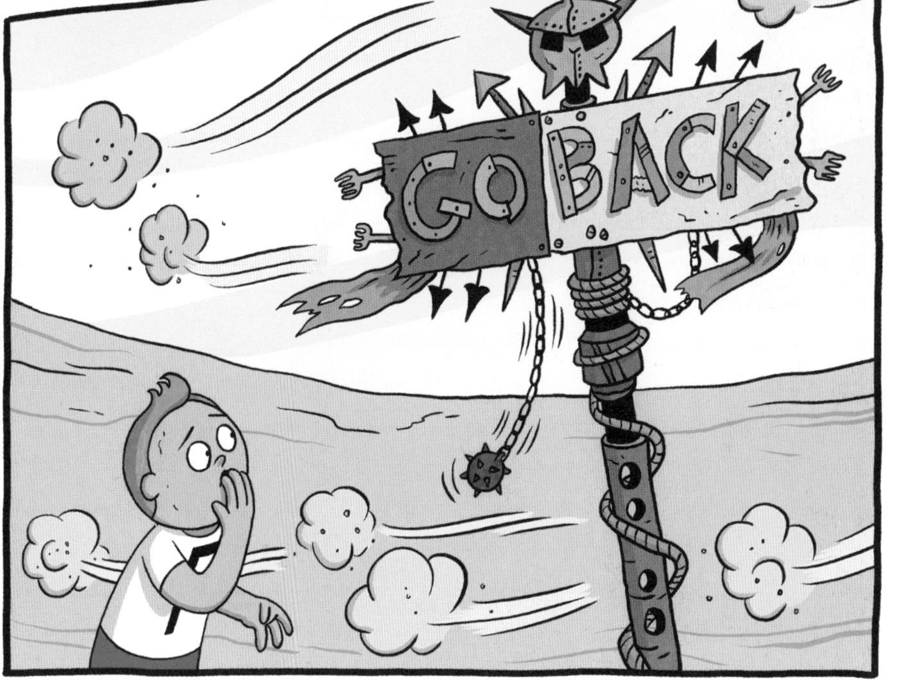
GO BACK

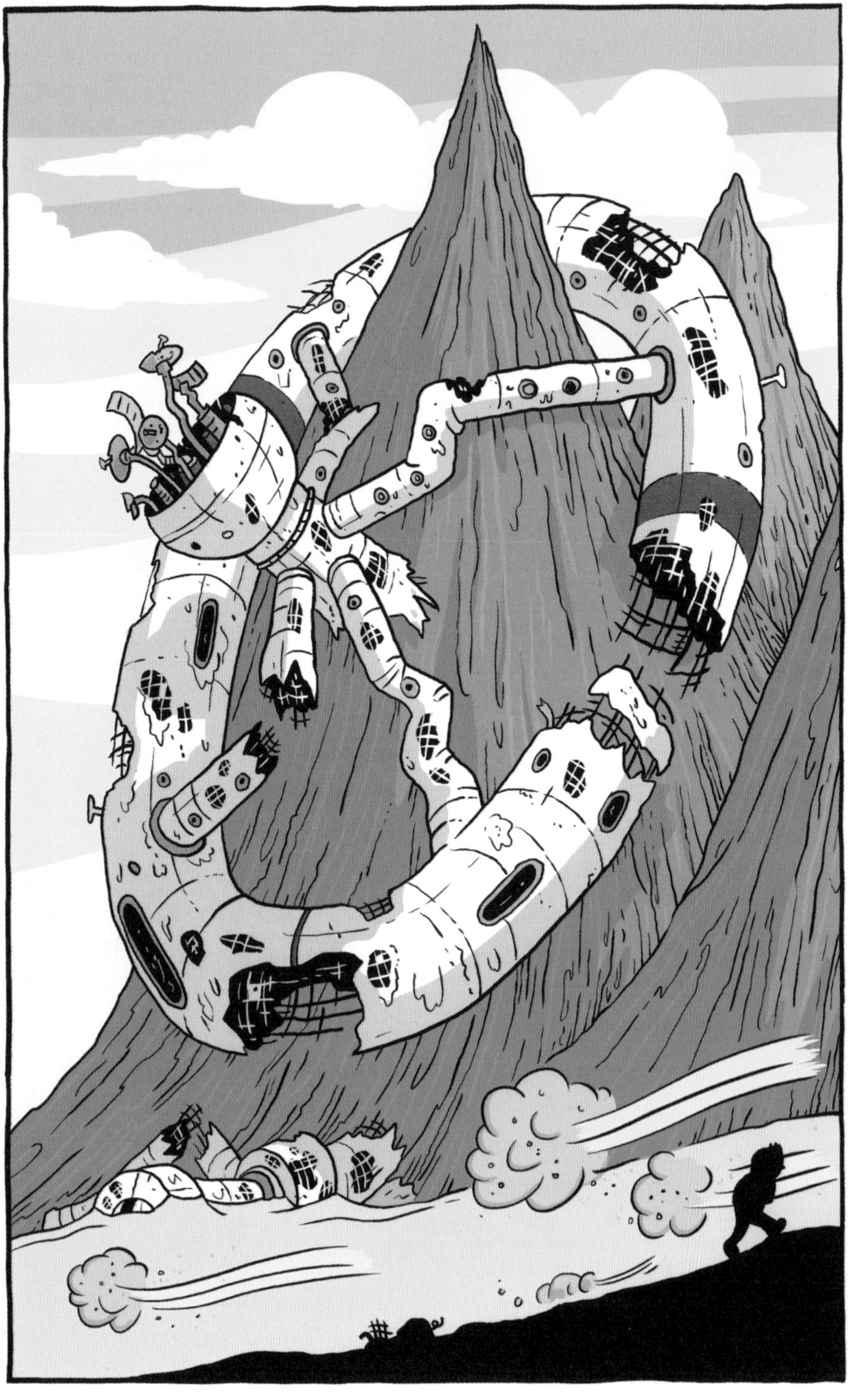

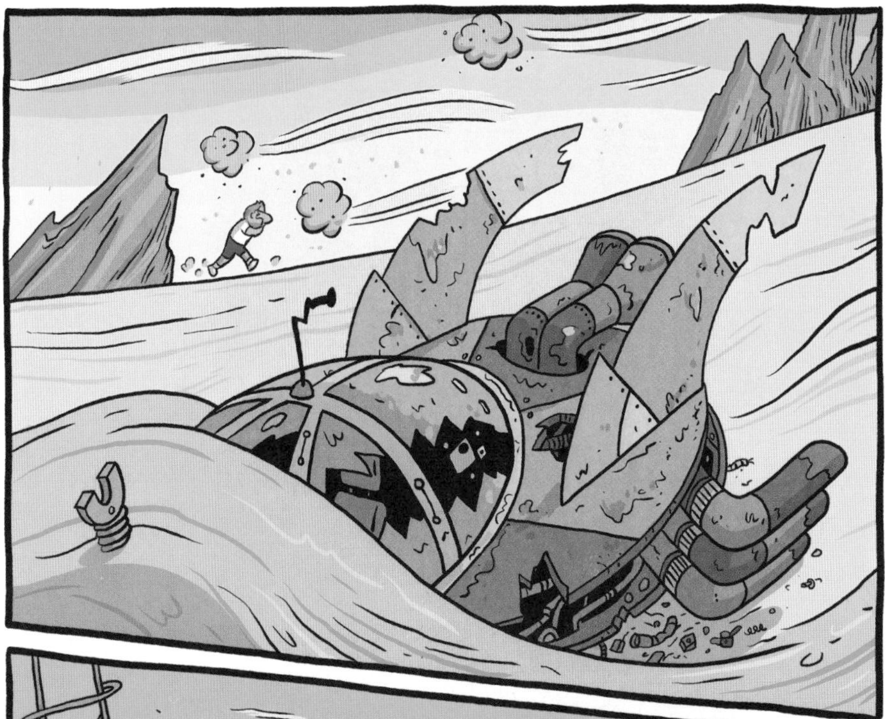

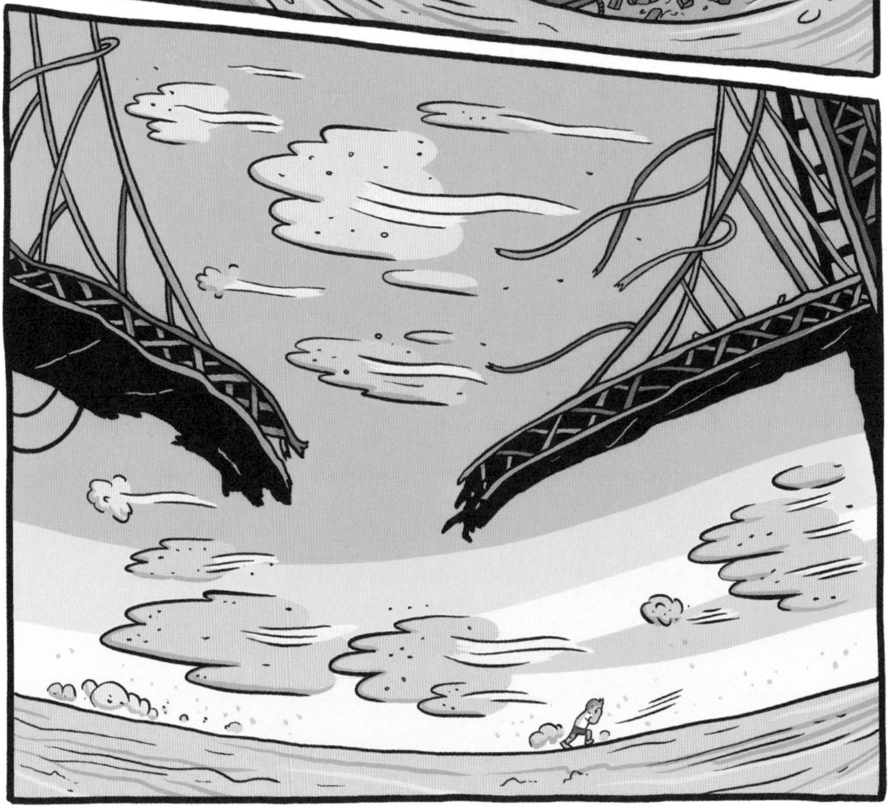

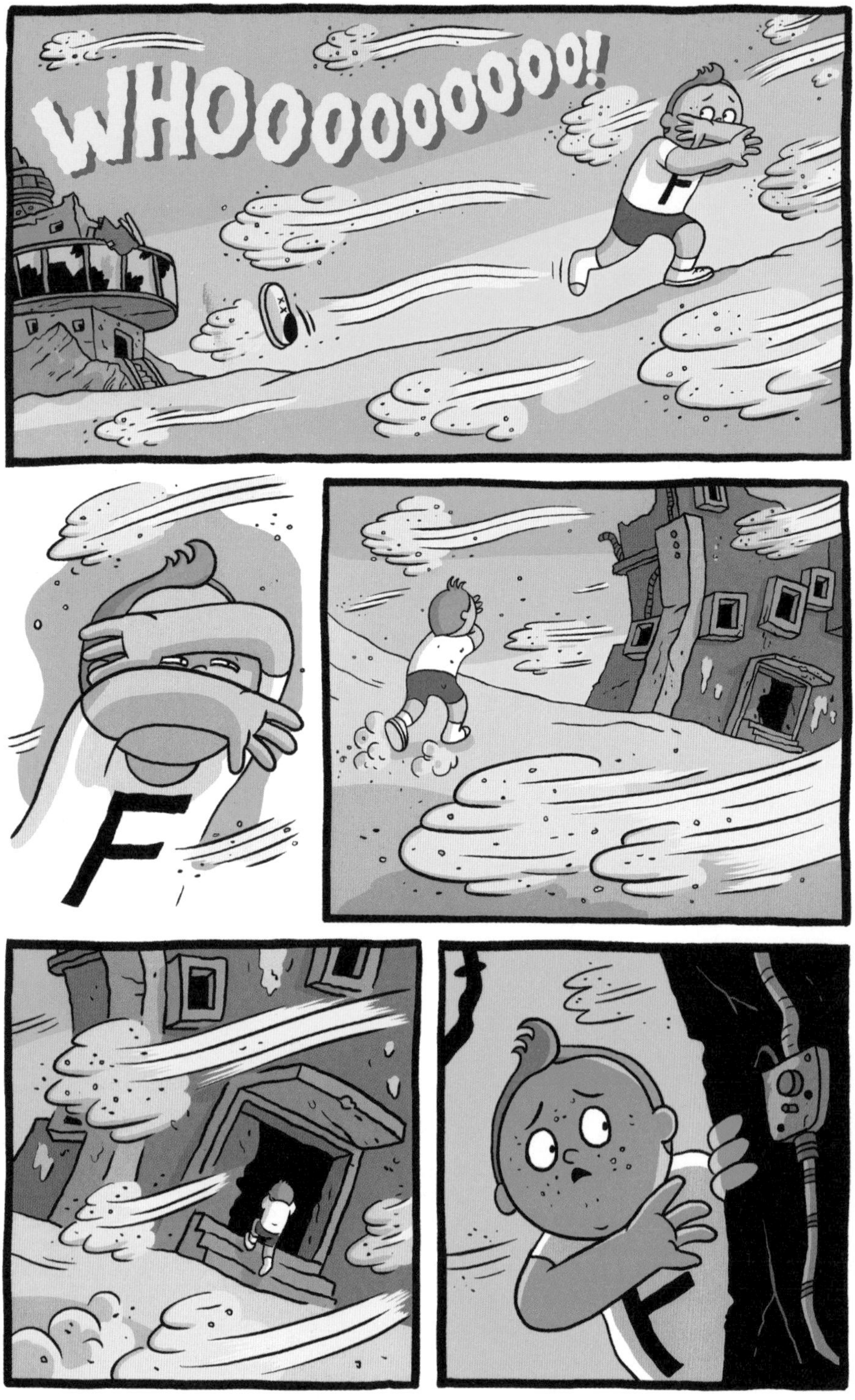
WHOOOOOOOOO!

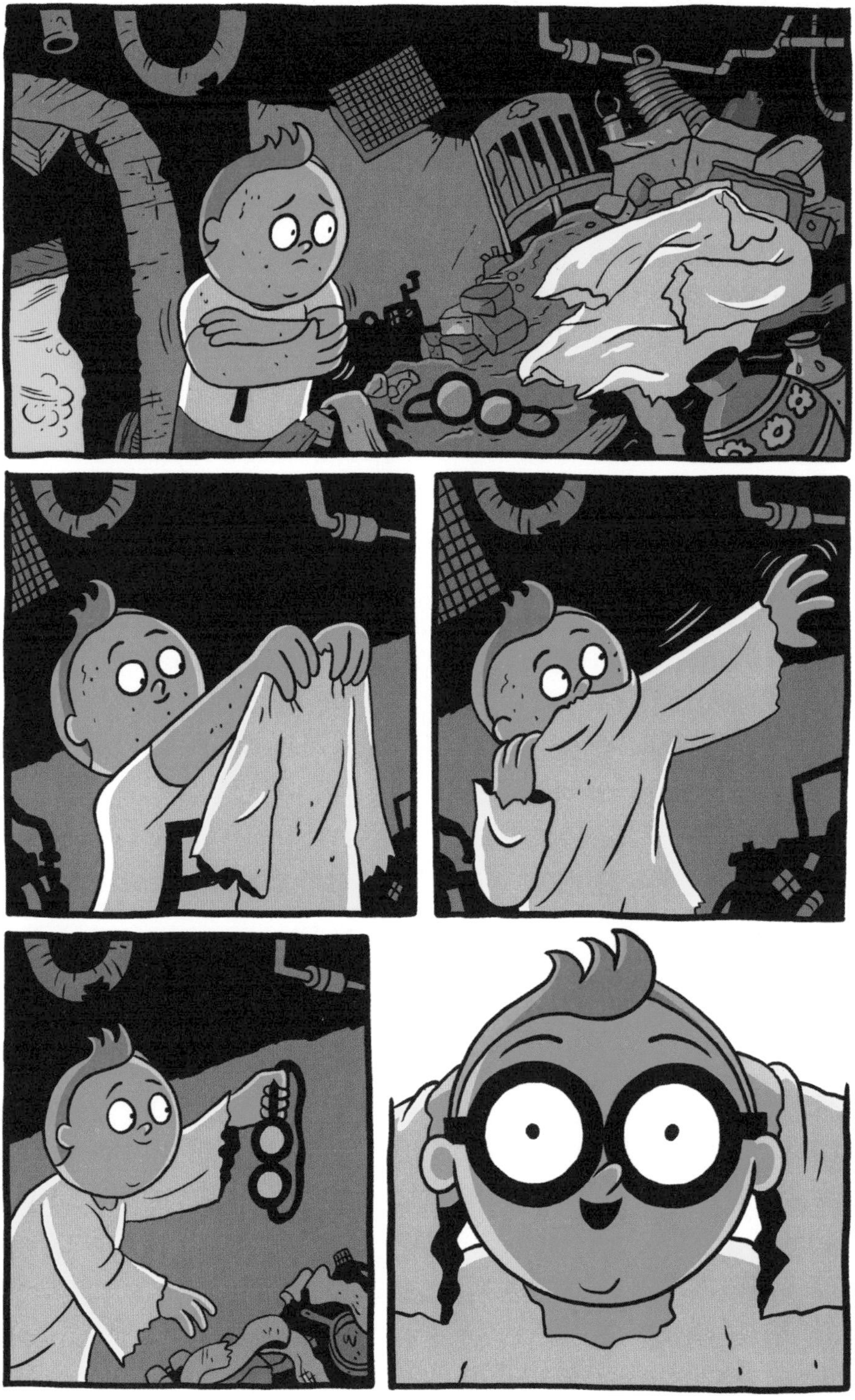

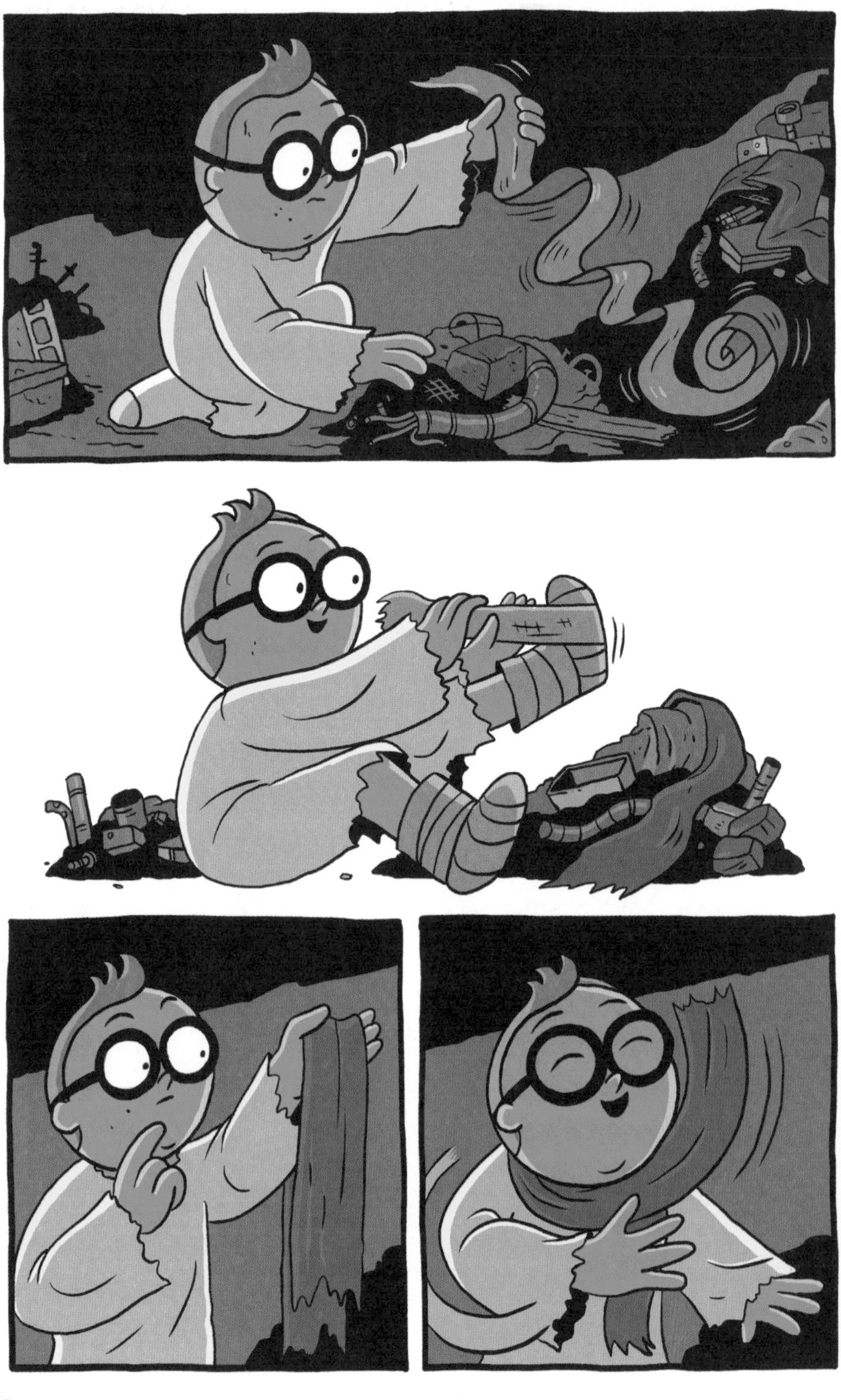

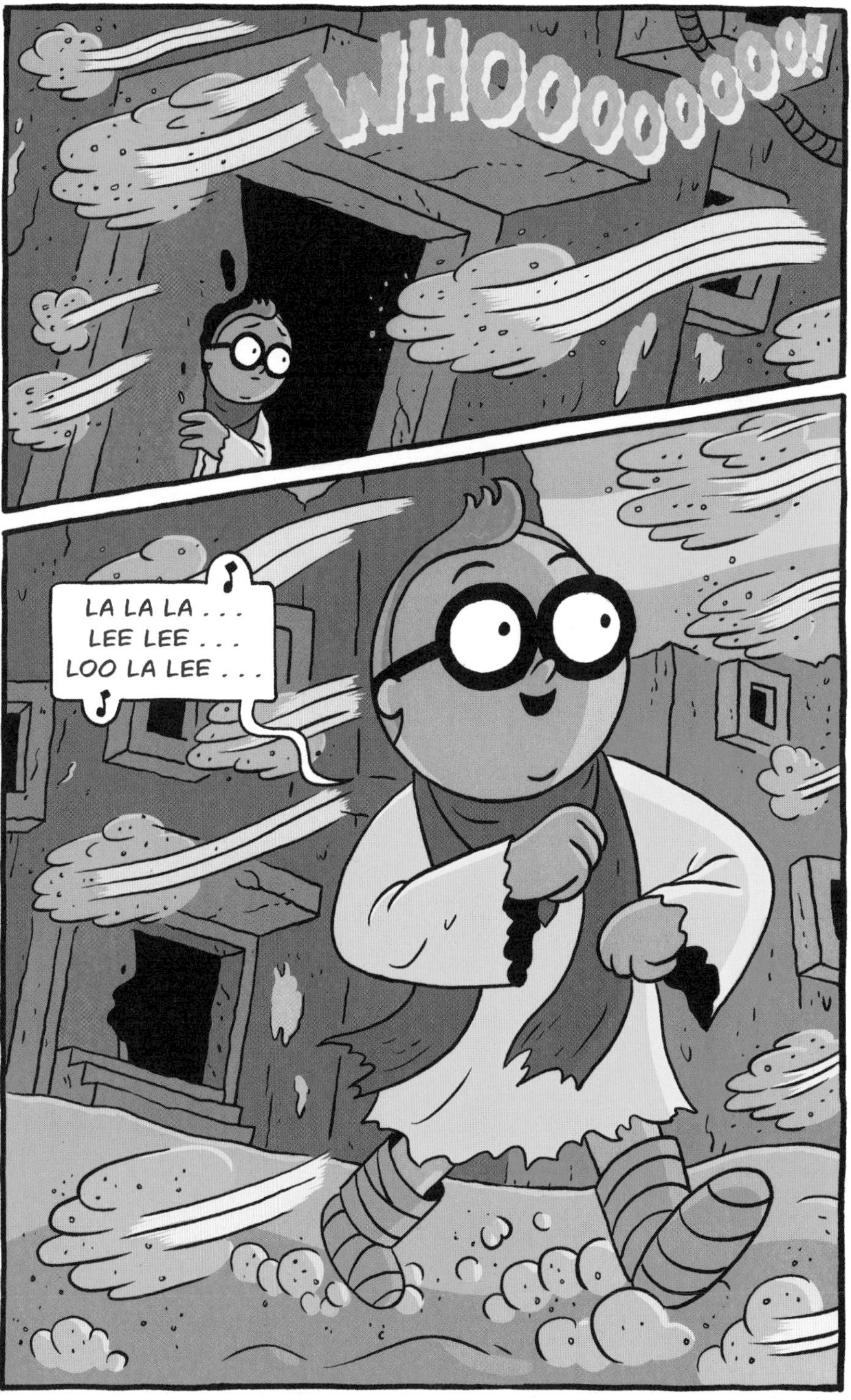
WHOOOOOOOO!
LA LA LA . . .
LEE LEE . . .
LOO LA LEE . . .

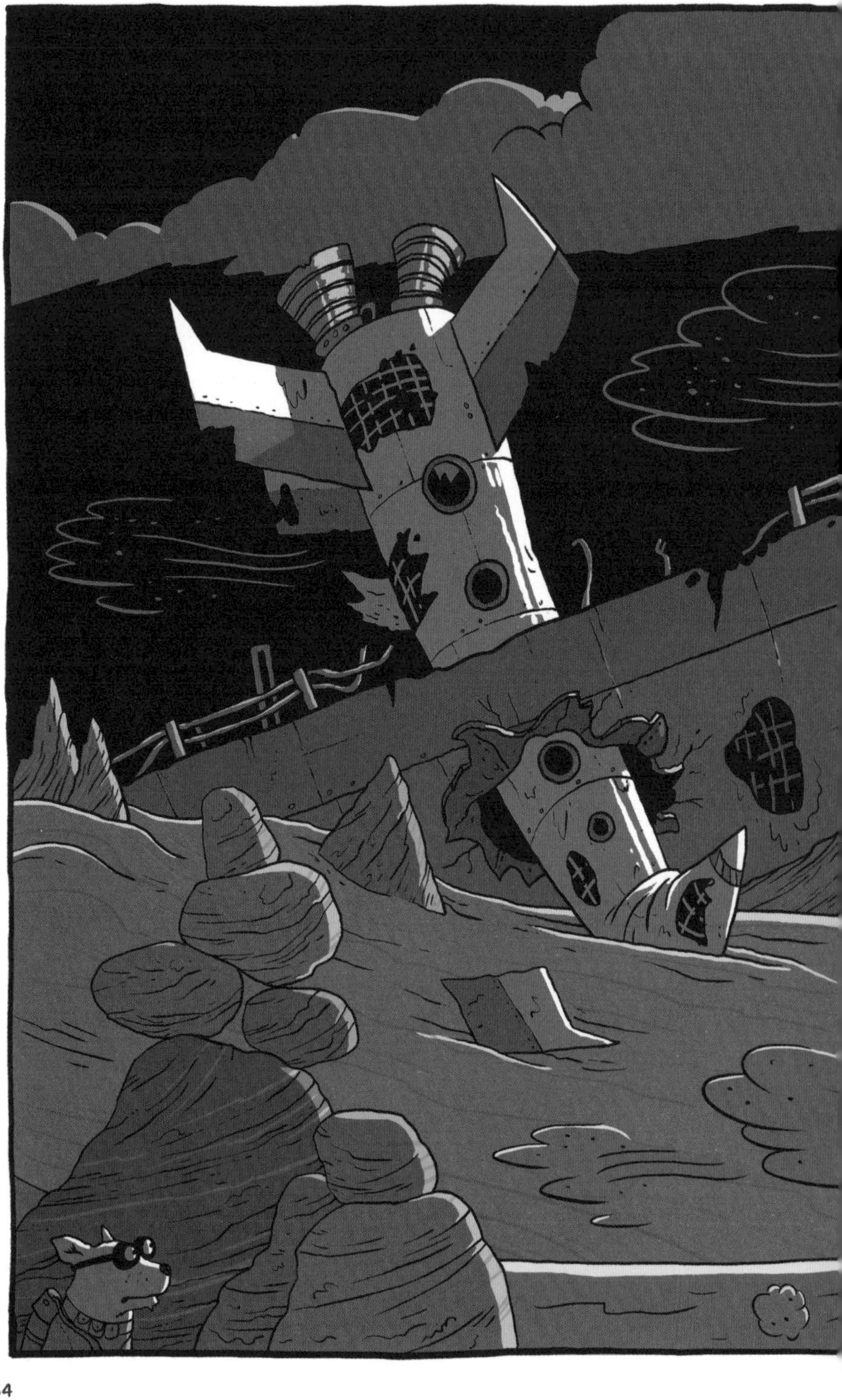

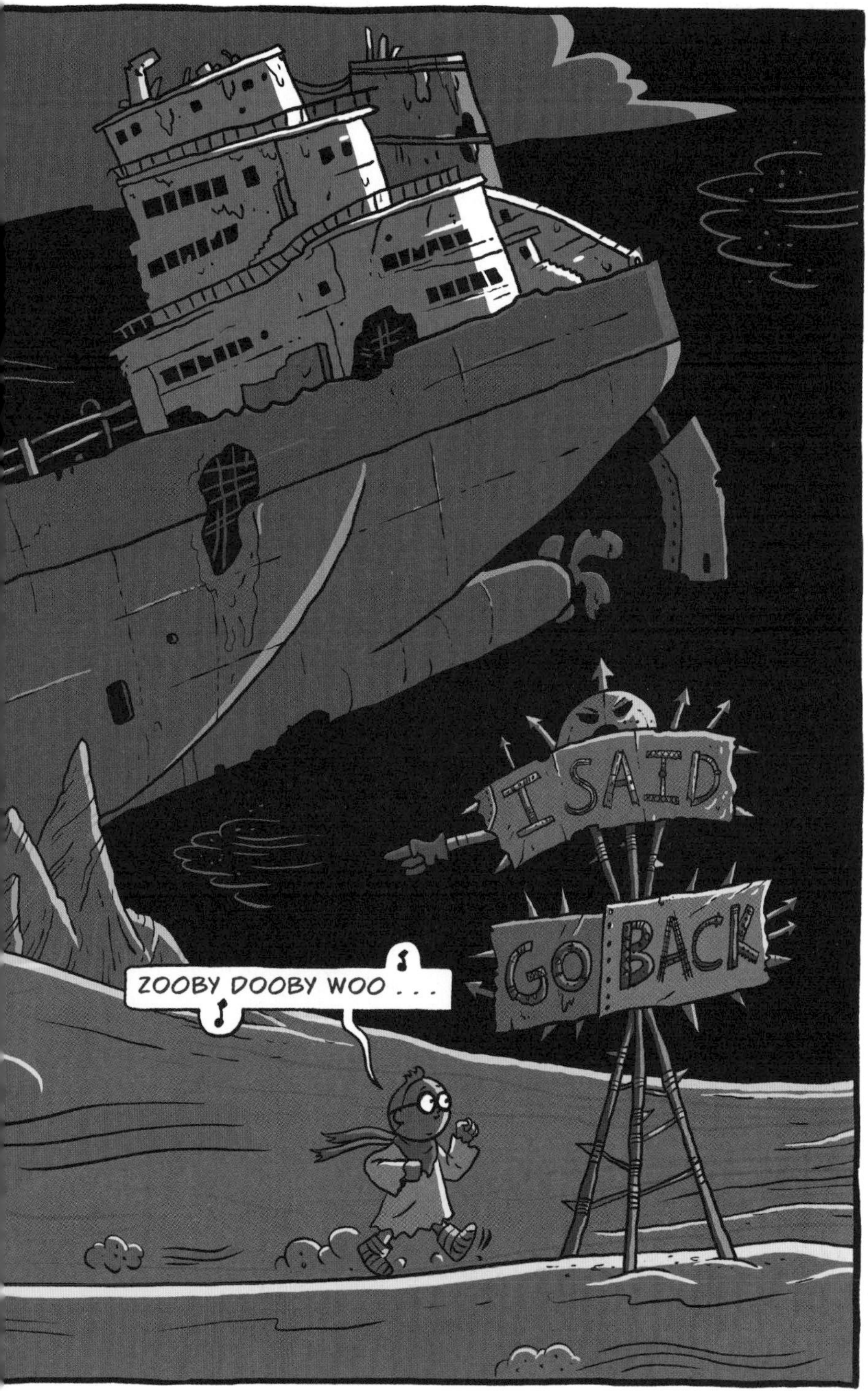
I SAID
GO BACK
ZOOBY DOOBY WOO . . .

CHAPTER 6

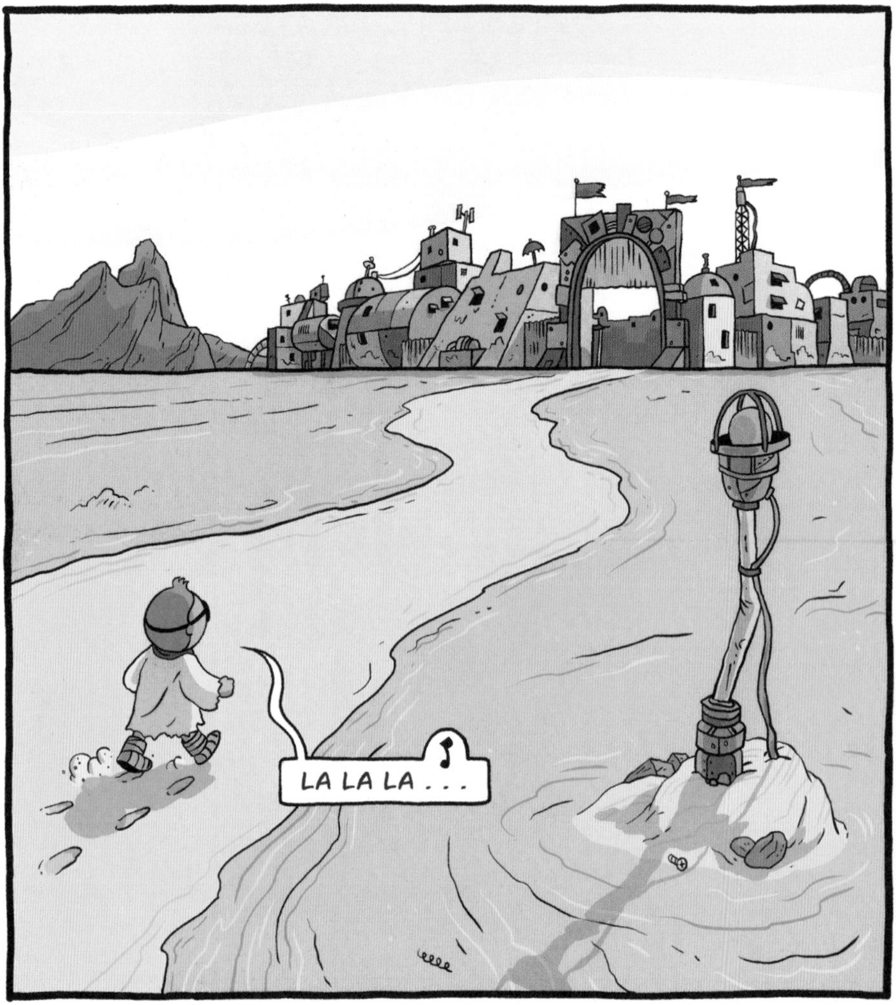
LA LA LA . . .

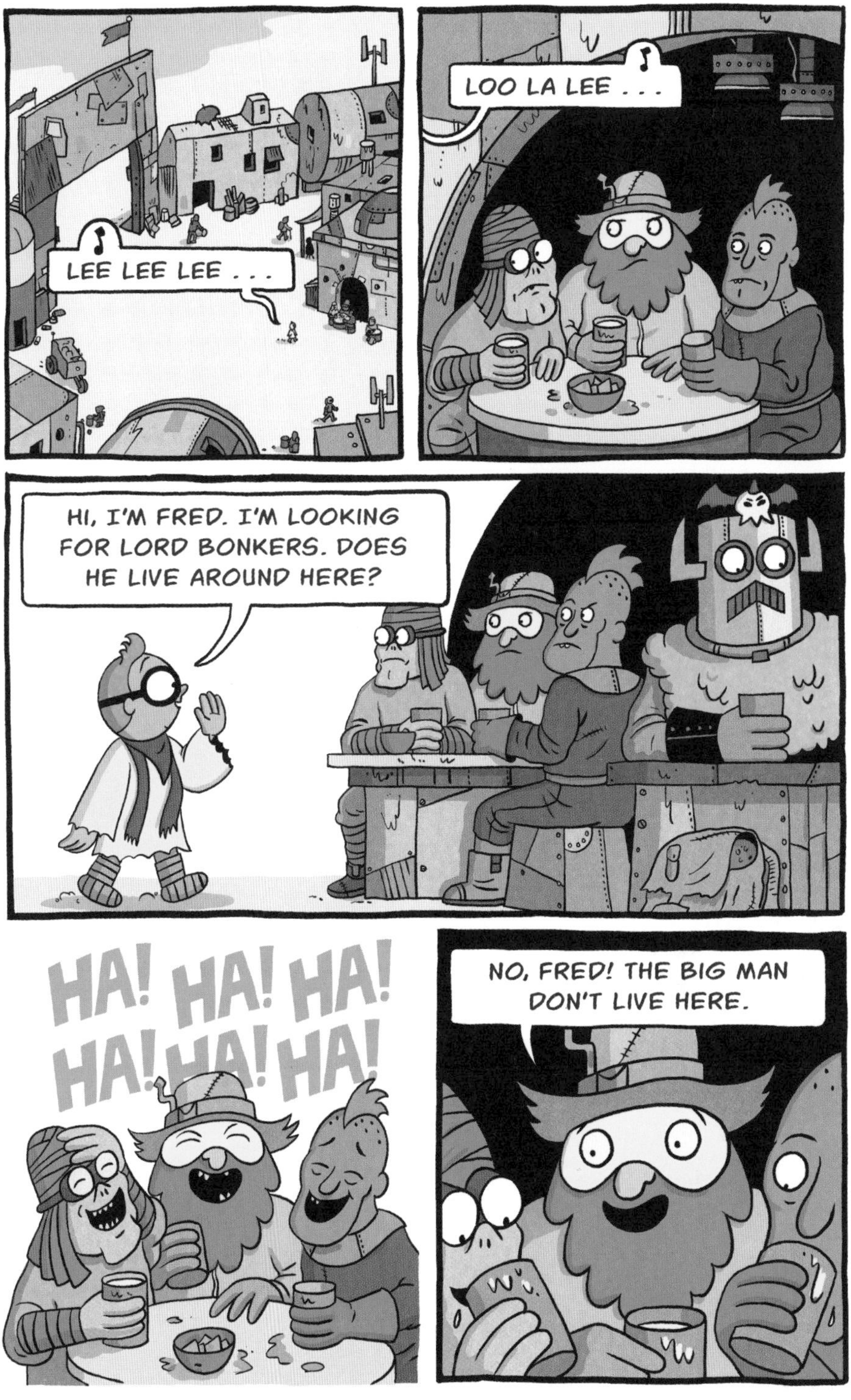
LEE LEE LEE . . .
LOO LA LEE . . .
HI, I'M FRED. I'M LOOKING FOR LORD BONKERS. DOES HE LIVE AROUND HERE?
HA! HA! HA! HA! HA! HA!
NO, FRED! THE BIG MAN DON'T LIVE HERE.

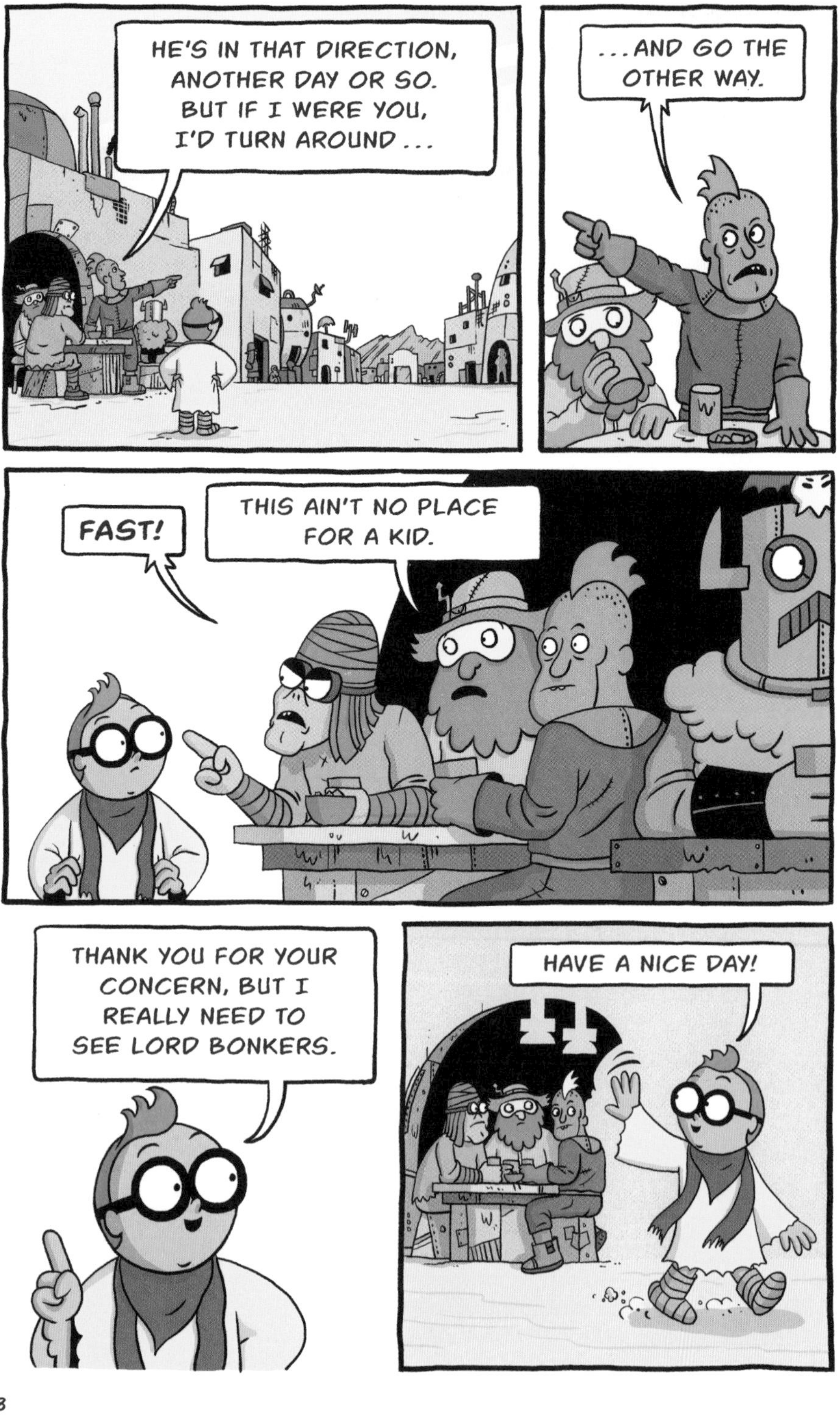
HE'S IN THAT DIRECTION, ANOTHER DAY OR SO. BUT IF I WERE YOU, I'D TURN AROUND . . .
. . . AND GO THE OTHER WAY.
FAST!
THIS AIN'T NO PLACE FOR A KID.
THANK YOU FOR YOUR CONCERN, BUT I REALLY NEED TO SEE LORD BONKERS.
HAVE A NICE DAY!

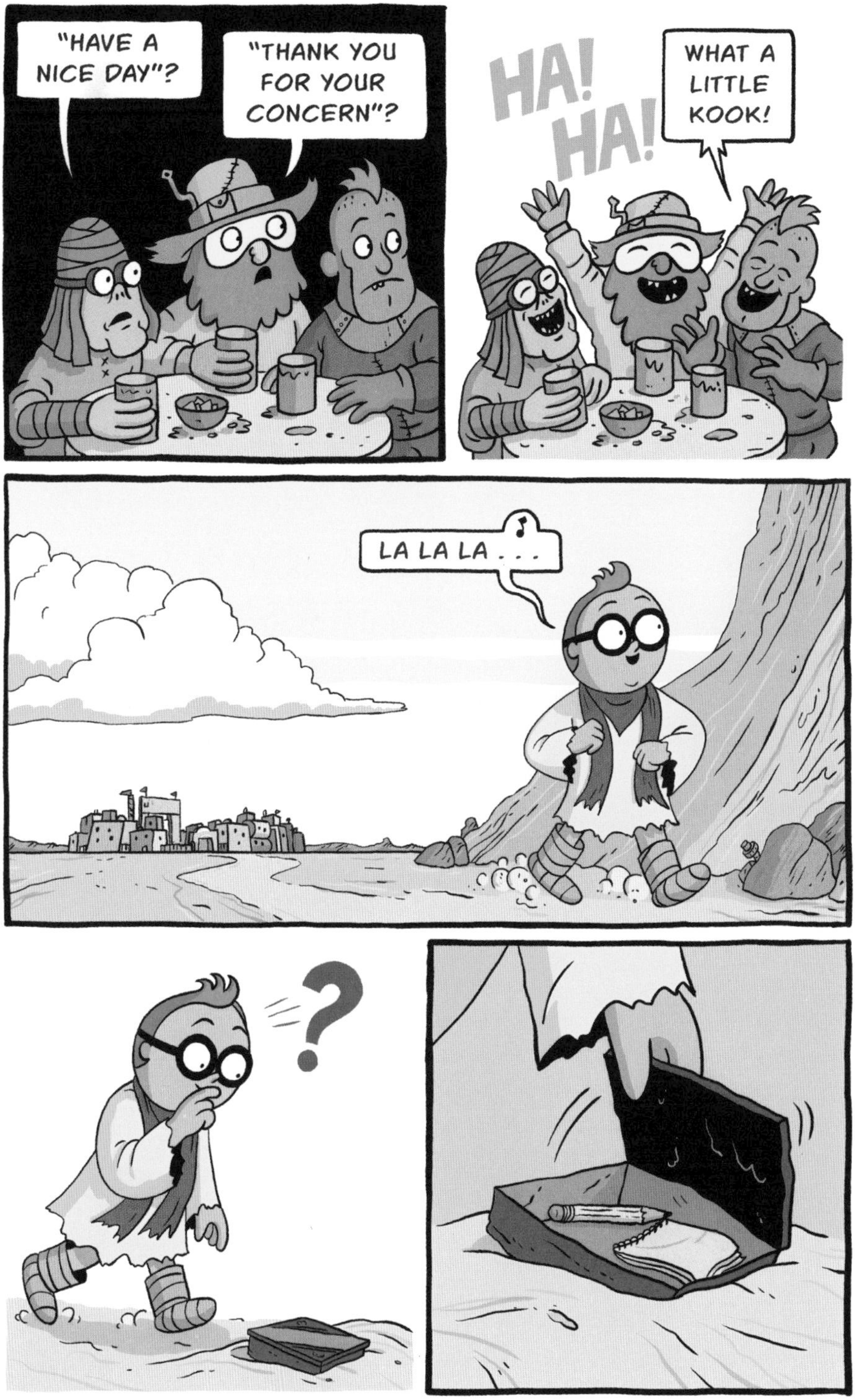
"HAVE A NICE DAY"?
"THANK YOU FOR YOUR CONCERN"?
HA! HA!
WHAT A LITTLE KOOK!
LA LA LA . . .
?

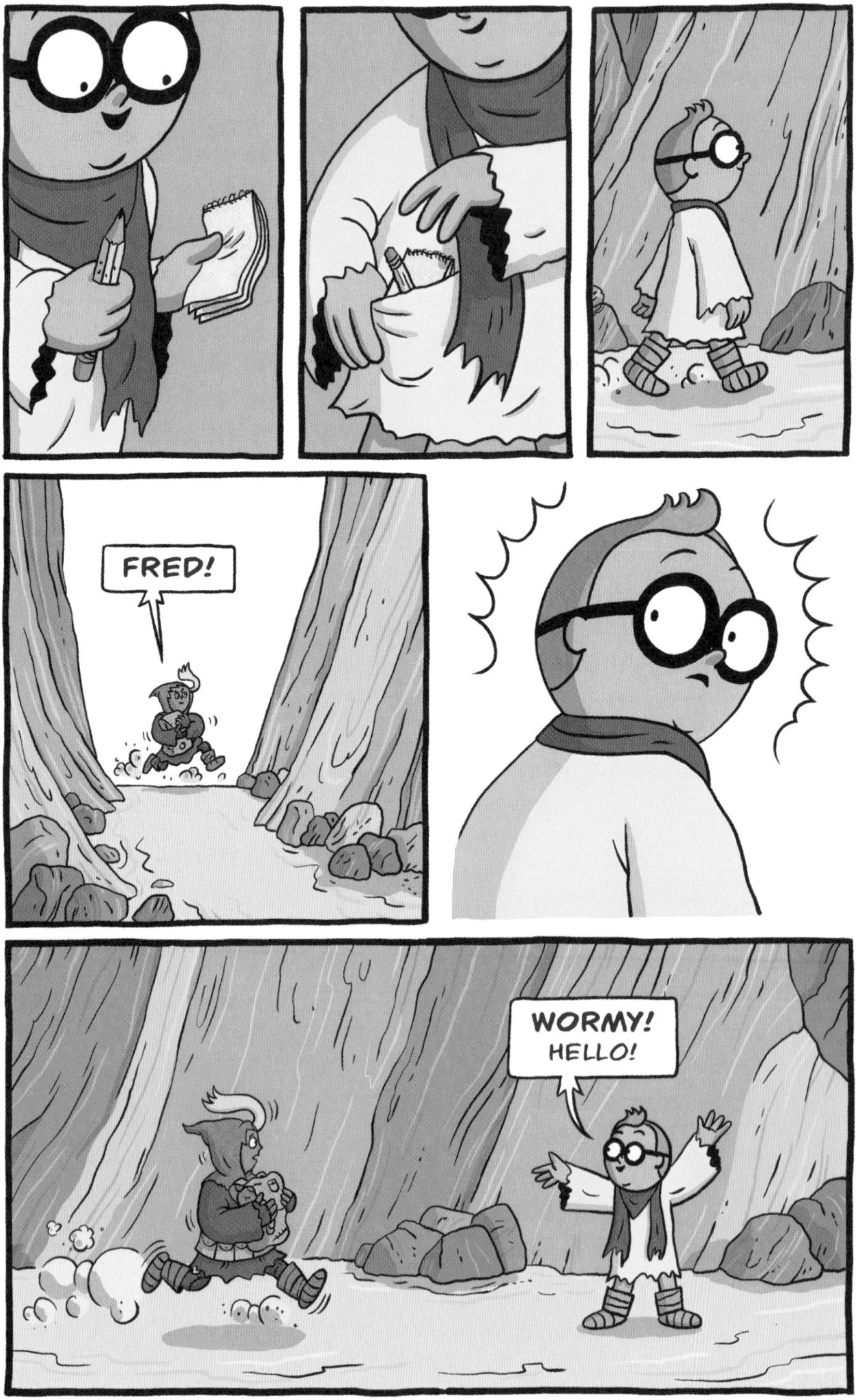
FRED!
WORMY!
HELLO!

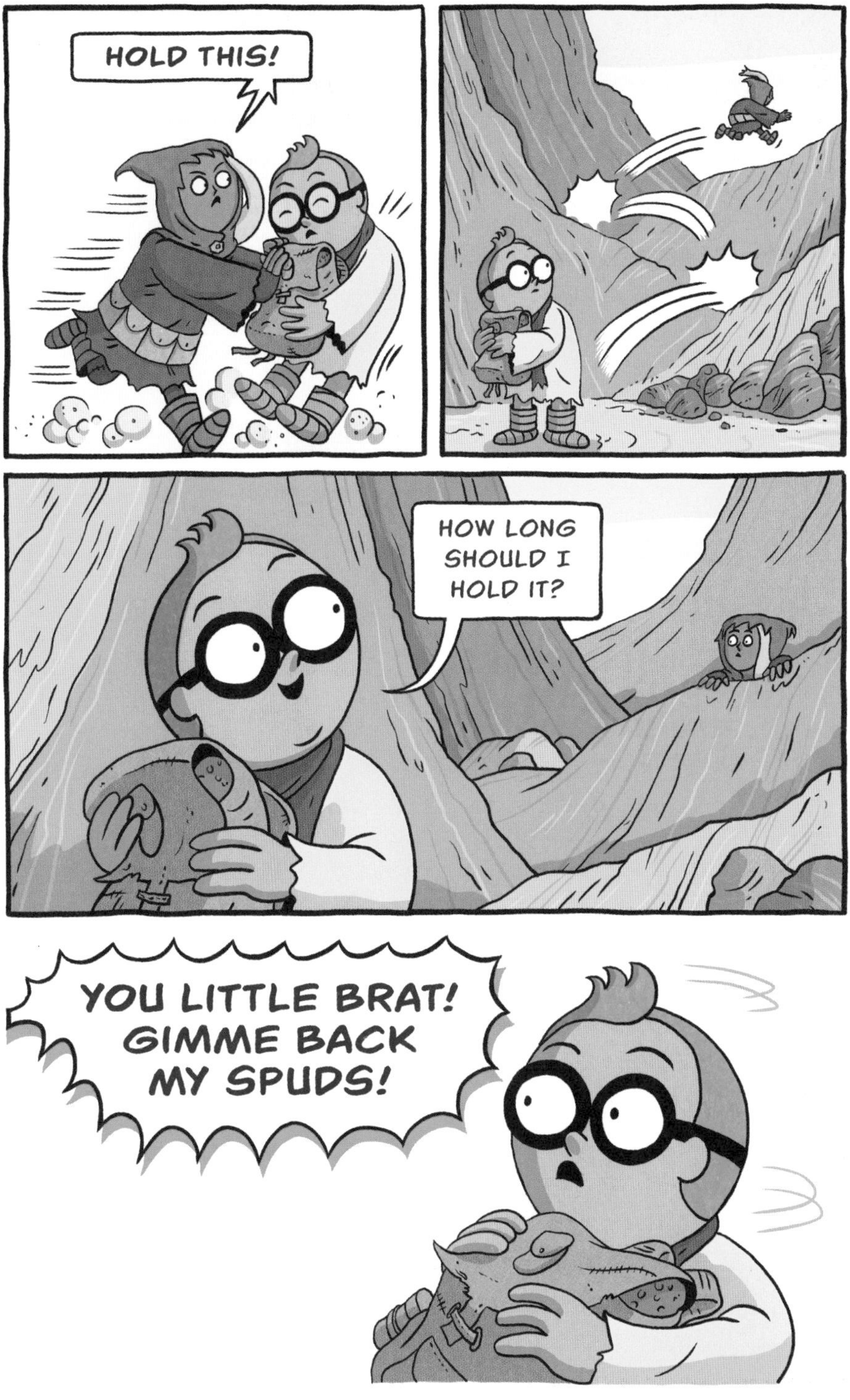
HOLD THIS!
HOW LONG SHOULD I HOLD IT?
YOU LITTLE BRAT! GIMME BACK MY SPUDS!

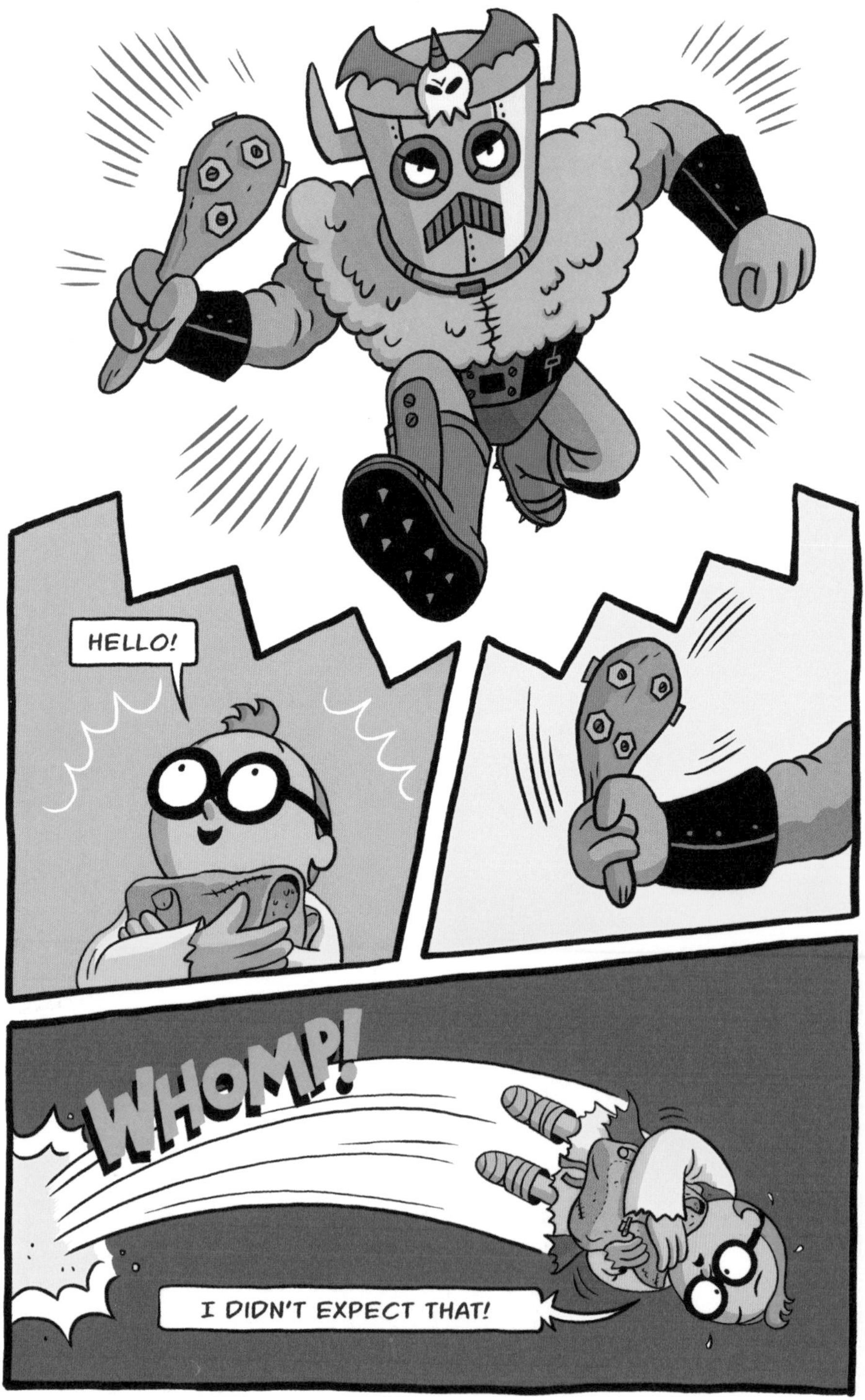
HELLO!
WHOMP!
I DIDN'T EXPECT THAT!

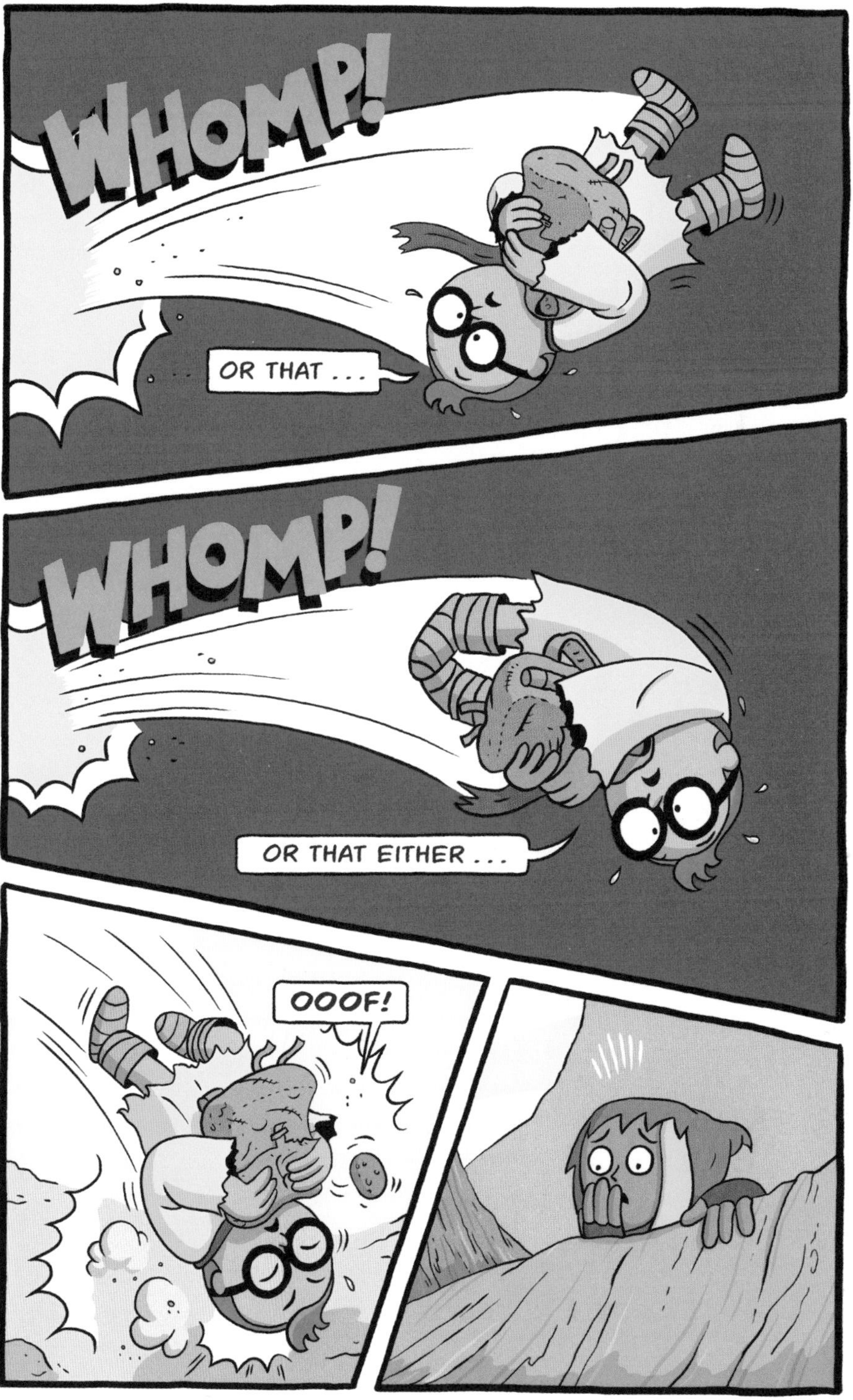
WHOMP!
OR THAT . . .
WHOMP!
OR THAT EITHER . . .
OOOF!

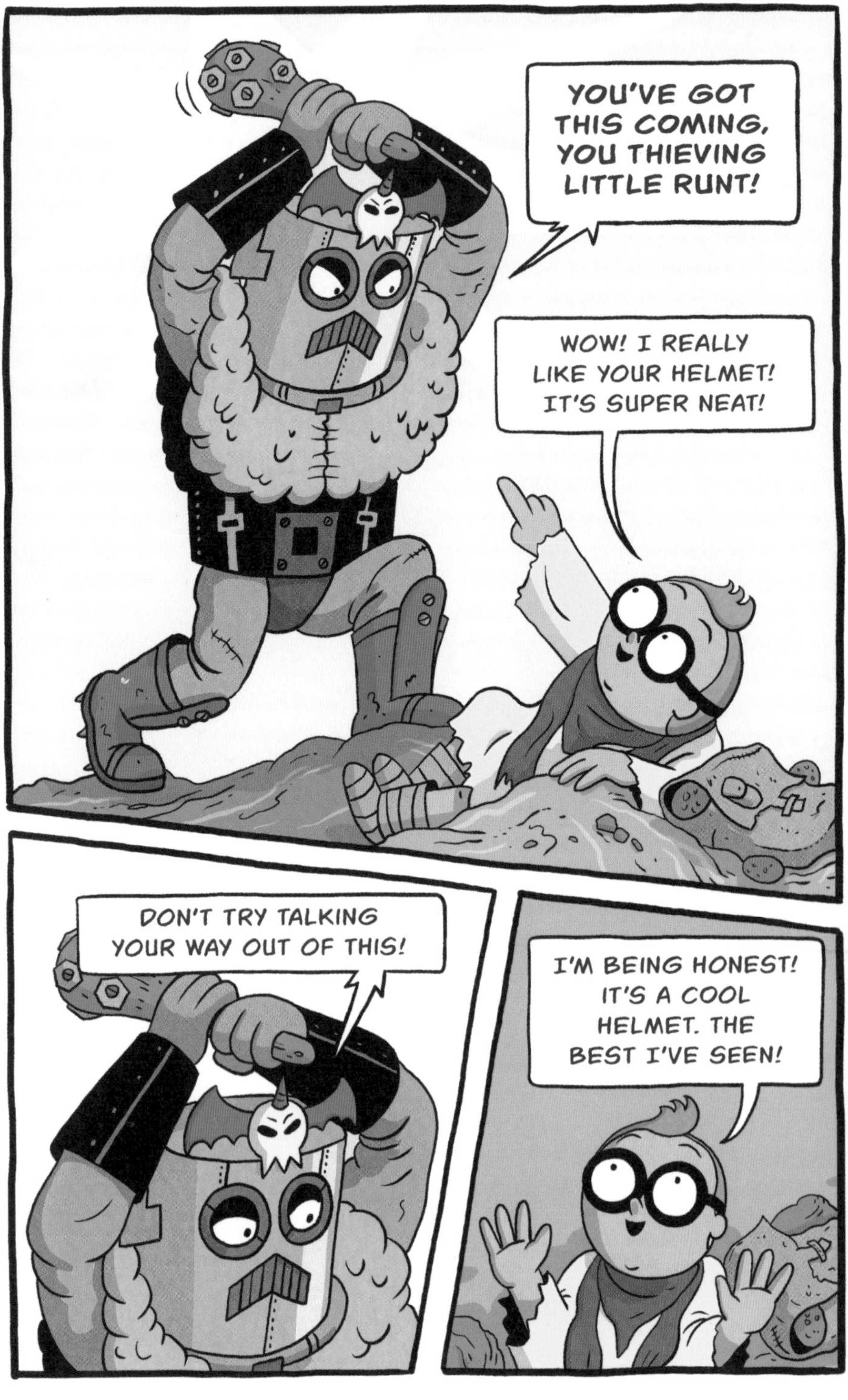
YOU'VE GOT THIS COMING, YOU THIEVING LITTLE RUNT!
WOW! I REALLY LIKE YOUR HELMET! IT'S SUPER NEAT!
DON'T TRY TALKING YOUR WAY OUT OF THIS!
I'M BEING HONEST! IT'S A COOL HELMET. THE BEST I'VE SEEN!

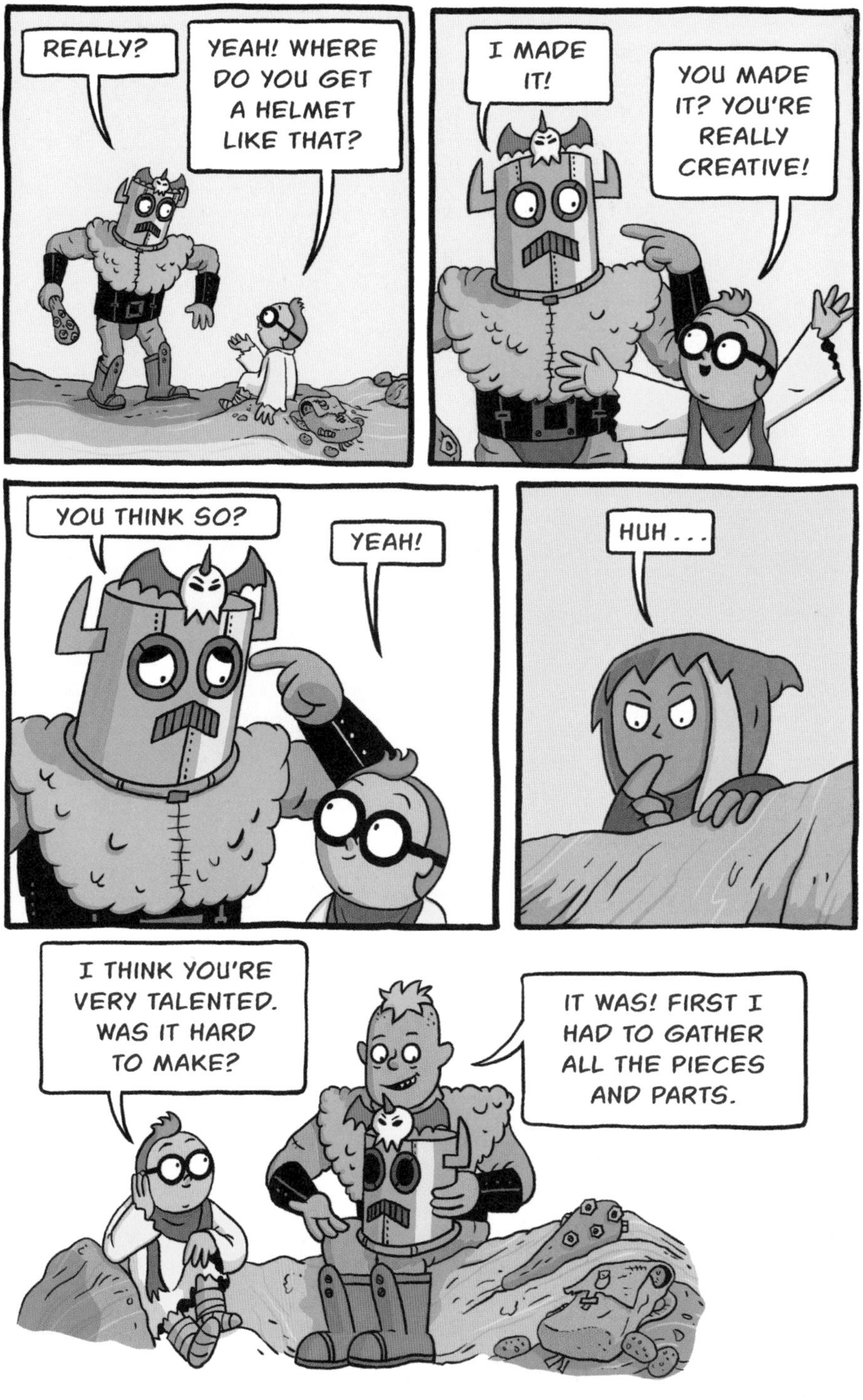
REALLY?
YEAH! WHERE DO YOU GET A HELMET LIKE THAT?
I MADE IT!
YOU MADE IT? YOU'RE REALLY CREATIVE!
YOU THINK SO?
YEAH!
HUH . . .
I THINK YOU'RE VERY TALENTED. WAS IT HARD TO MAKE?
IT WAS! FIRST I HAD TO GATHER ALL THE PIECES AND PARTS.

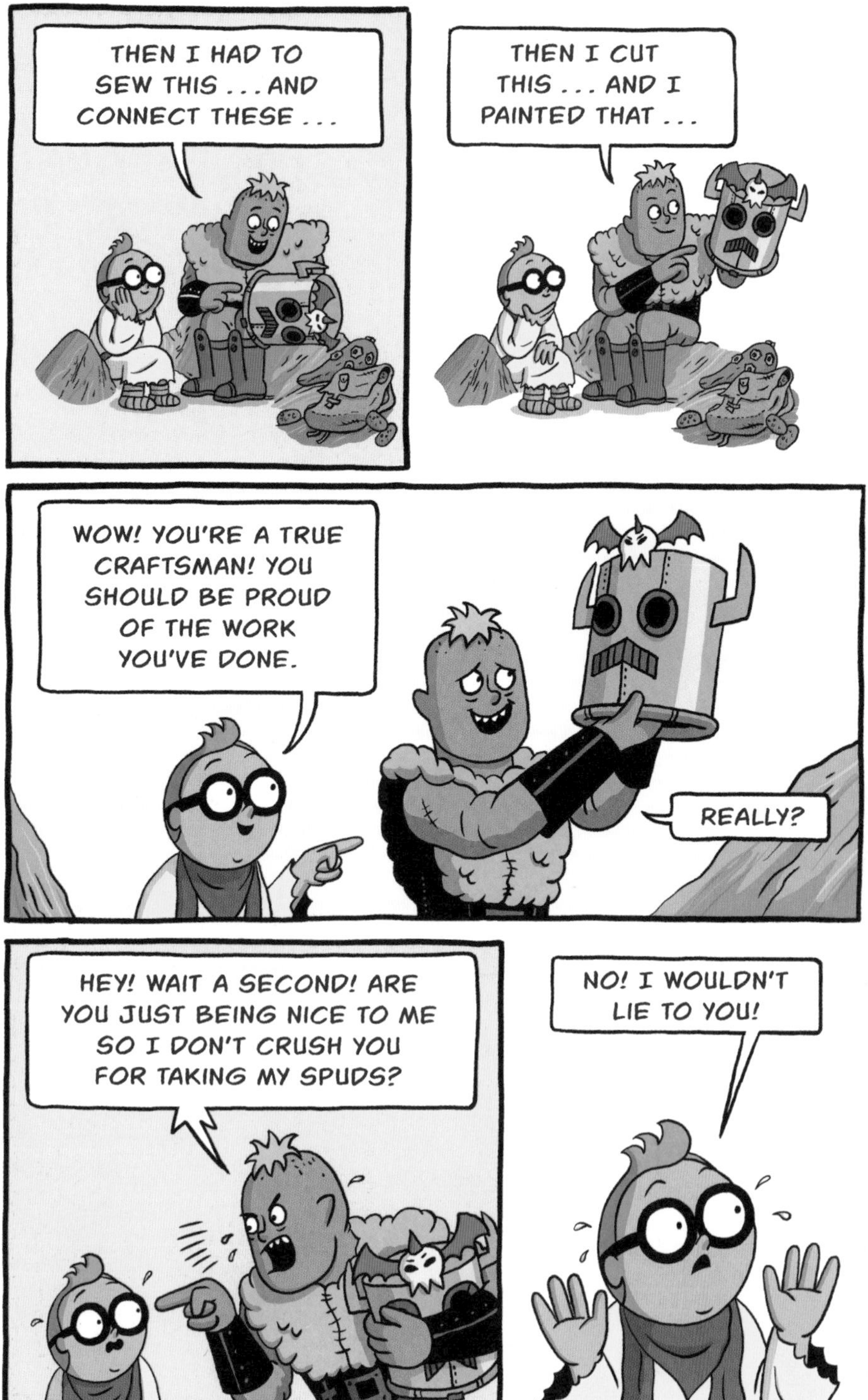
THEN I HAD TO SEW THIS . . . AND CONNECT THESE . . .
THEN I CUT THIS . . . AND I PAINTED THAT . . .
WOW! YOU'RE A TRUE CRAFTSMAN! YOU SHOULD BE PROUD OF THE WORK YOU'VE DONE.
REALLY?
HEY! WAIT A SECOND! ARE YOU JUST BEING NICE TO ME SO I DON'T CRUSH YOU FOR TAKING MY SPUDS?
NO! I WOULDN'T LIE TO YOU!

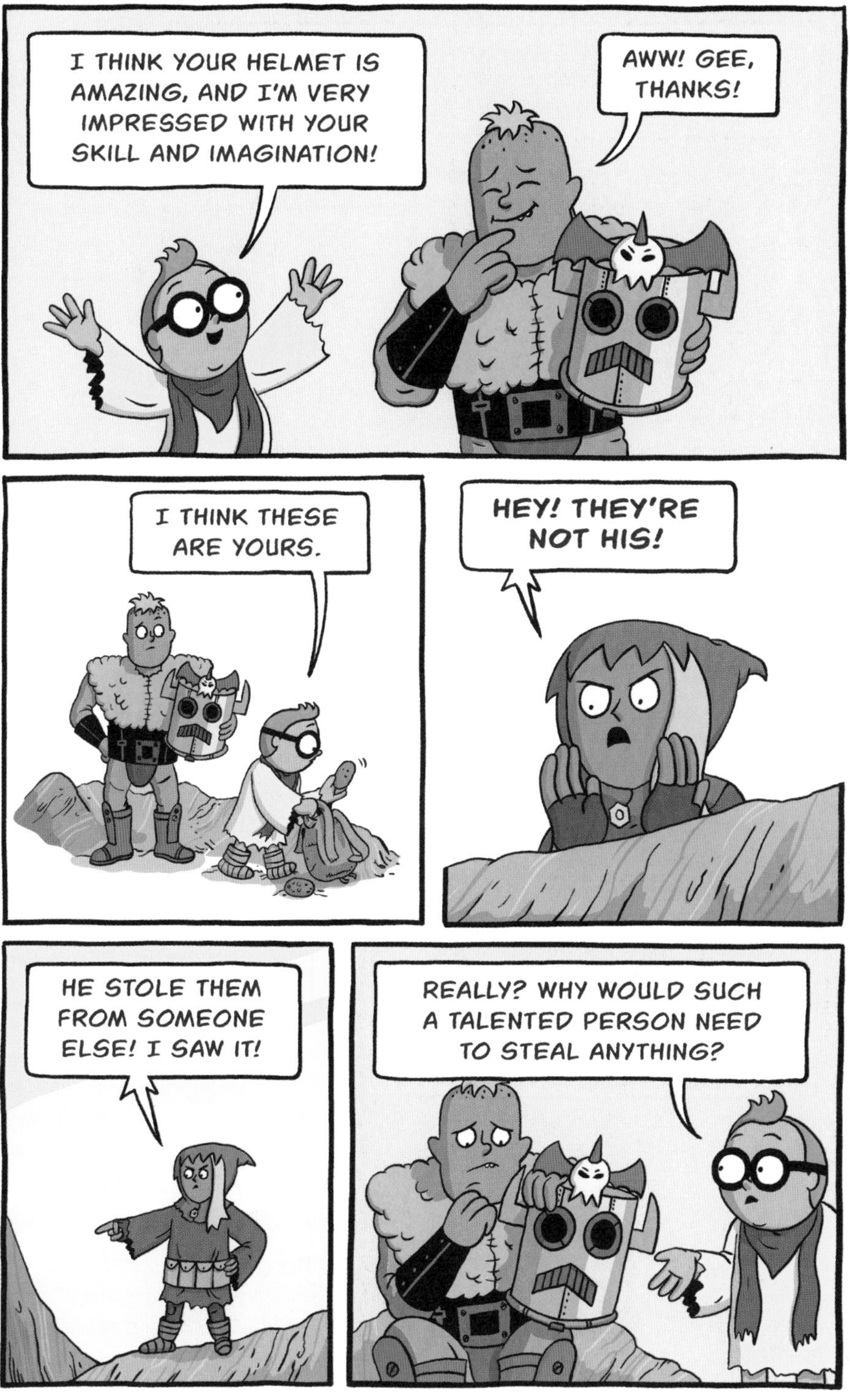
I THINK YOUR HELMET IS AMAZING, AND I'M VERY IMPRESSED WITH YOUR SKILL AND IMAGINATION!
AWW! GEE, THANKS!
I THINK THESE ARE YOURS.
HEY! THEY'RE NOT HIS!
HE STOLE THEM FROM SOMEONE ELSE! I SAW IT!
REALLY? WHY WOULD SUCH A TALENTED PERSON NEED TO STEAL ANYTHING?

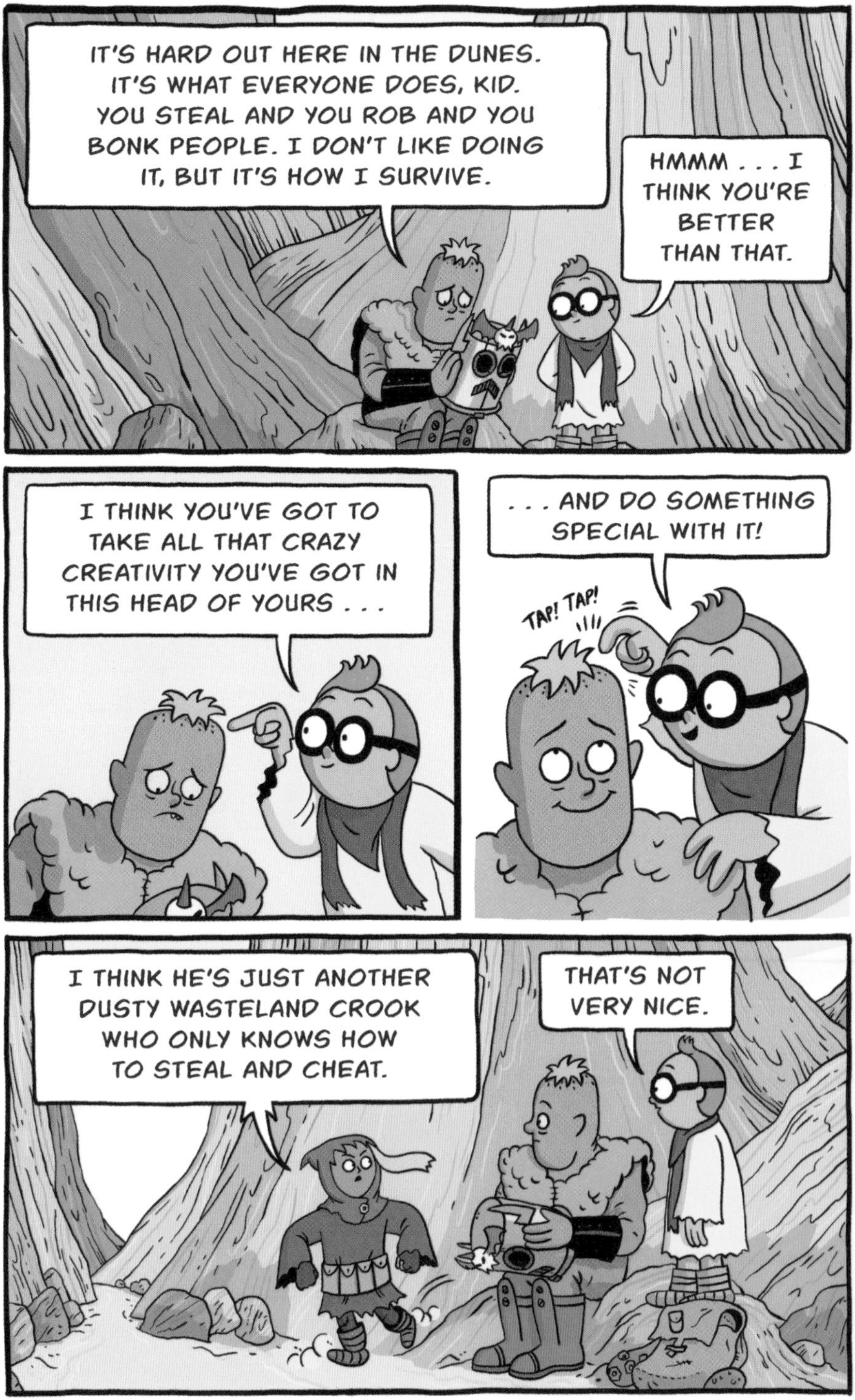
IT'S HARD OUT HERE IN THE DUNES. IT'S WHAT EVERYONE DOES, KID. YOU STEAL AND YOU ROB AND YOU BONK PEOPLE. I DON'T LIKE DOING IT, BUT IT'S HOW I SURVIVE.
HMMM . . . I THINK YOU'RE BETTER THAN THAT.
I THINK YOU'VE GOT TO TAKE ALL THAT CRAZY CREATIVITY YOU'VE GOT IN THIS HEAD OF YOURS . . .
. . . AND DO SOMETHING SPECIAL WITH IT!
TAP! TAP!
I THINK HE'S JUST ANOTHER DUSTY WASTELAND CROOK WHO ONLY KNOWS HOW TO STEAL AND CHEAT.
THAT'S NOT VERY NICE.

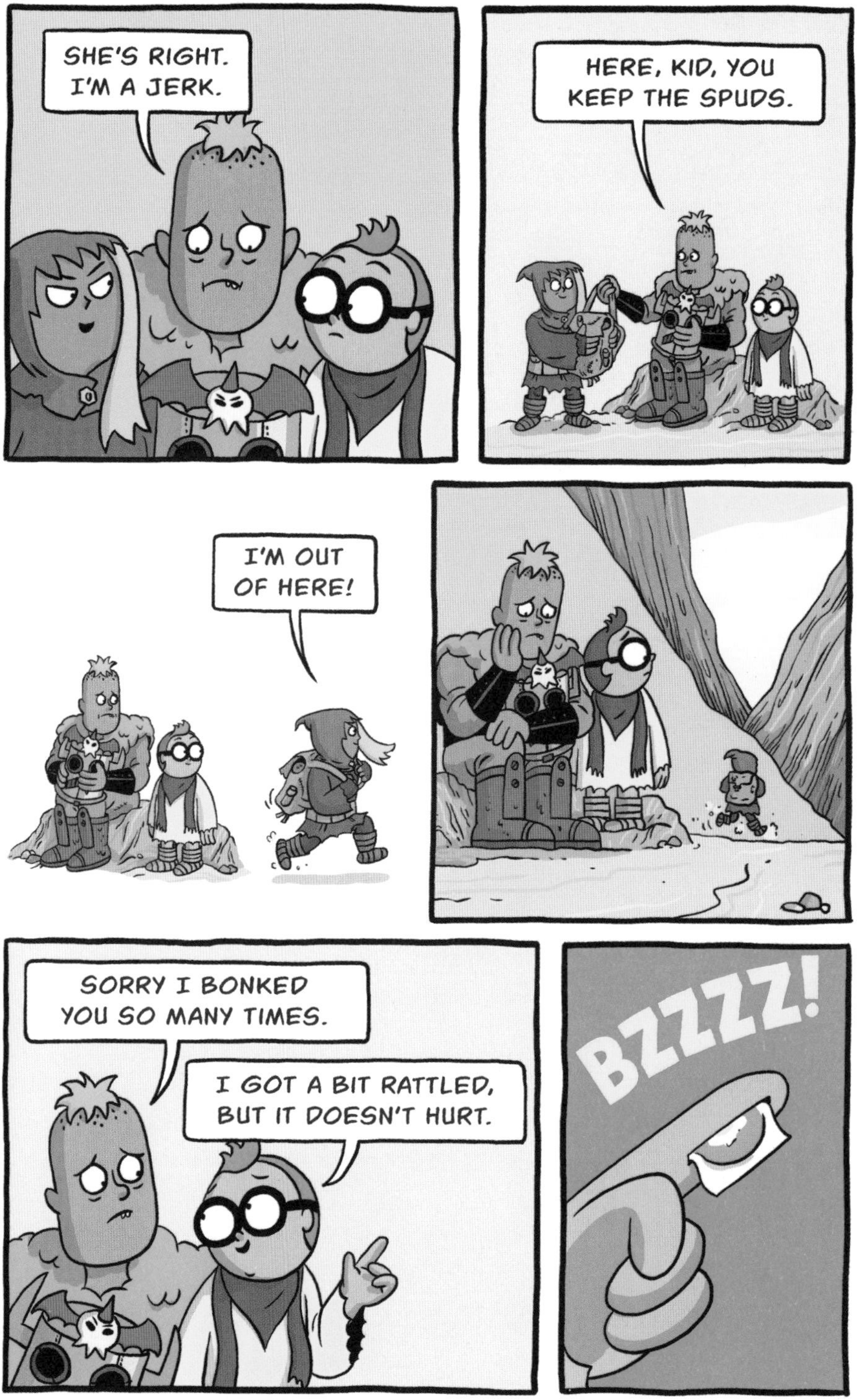
SHE'S RIGHT. I'M A JERK.
HERE, KID, YOU KEEP THE SPUDS.
I'M OUT OF HERE!
SORRY I BONKED YOU SO MANY TIMES.
I GOT A BIT RATTLED, BUT IT DOESN'T HURT.
BZZZZ!

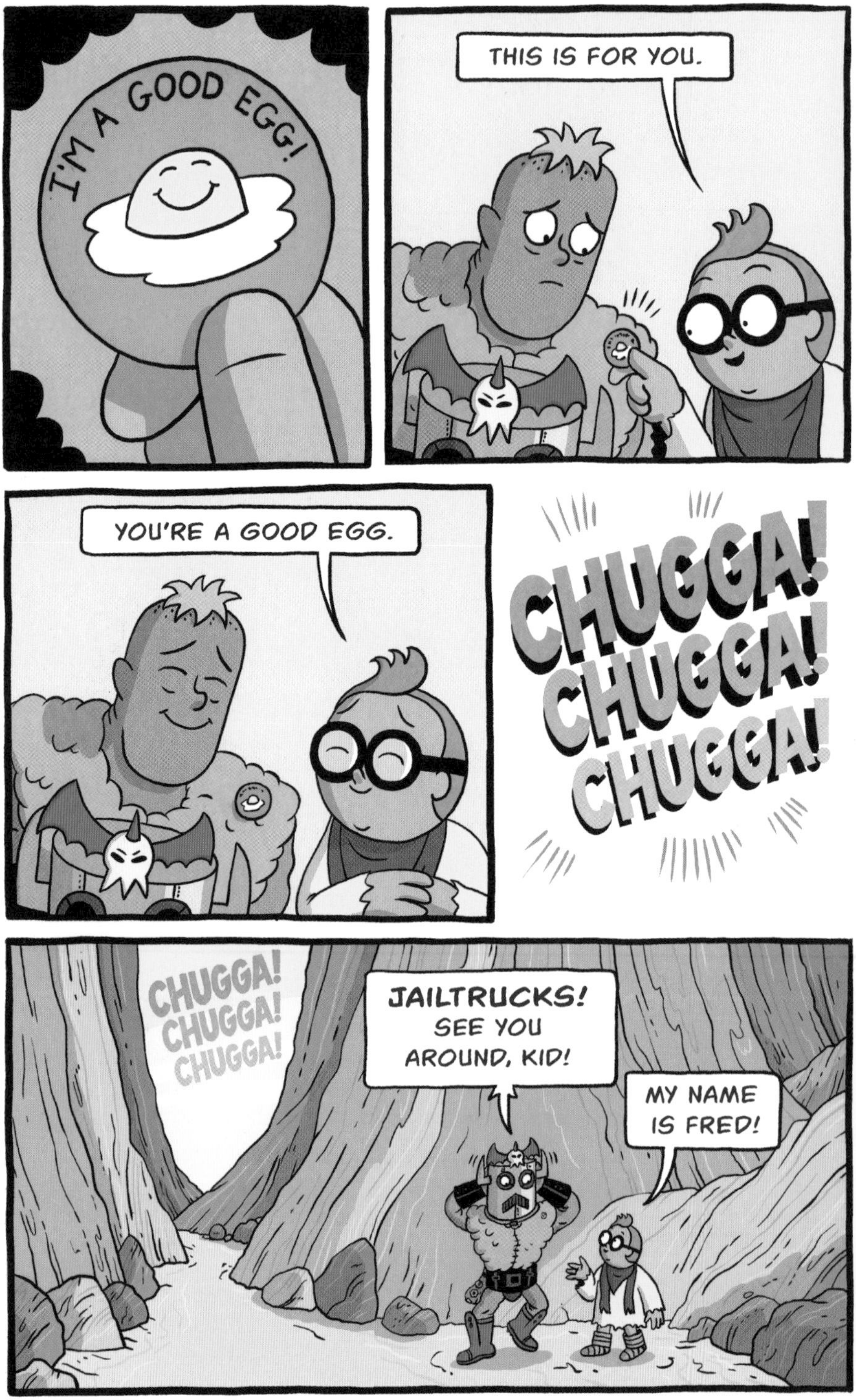
I'M A GOOD EGG!
THIS IS FOR YOU.
YOU'RE A GOOD EGG.
CHUGGA! CHUGGA! CHUGGA!
CHUGGA! CHUGGA! CHUGGA!
JAILTRUCKS! SEE YOU AROUND, KID!
MY NAME IS FRED!

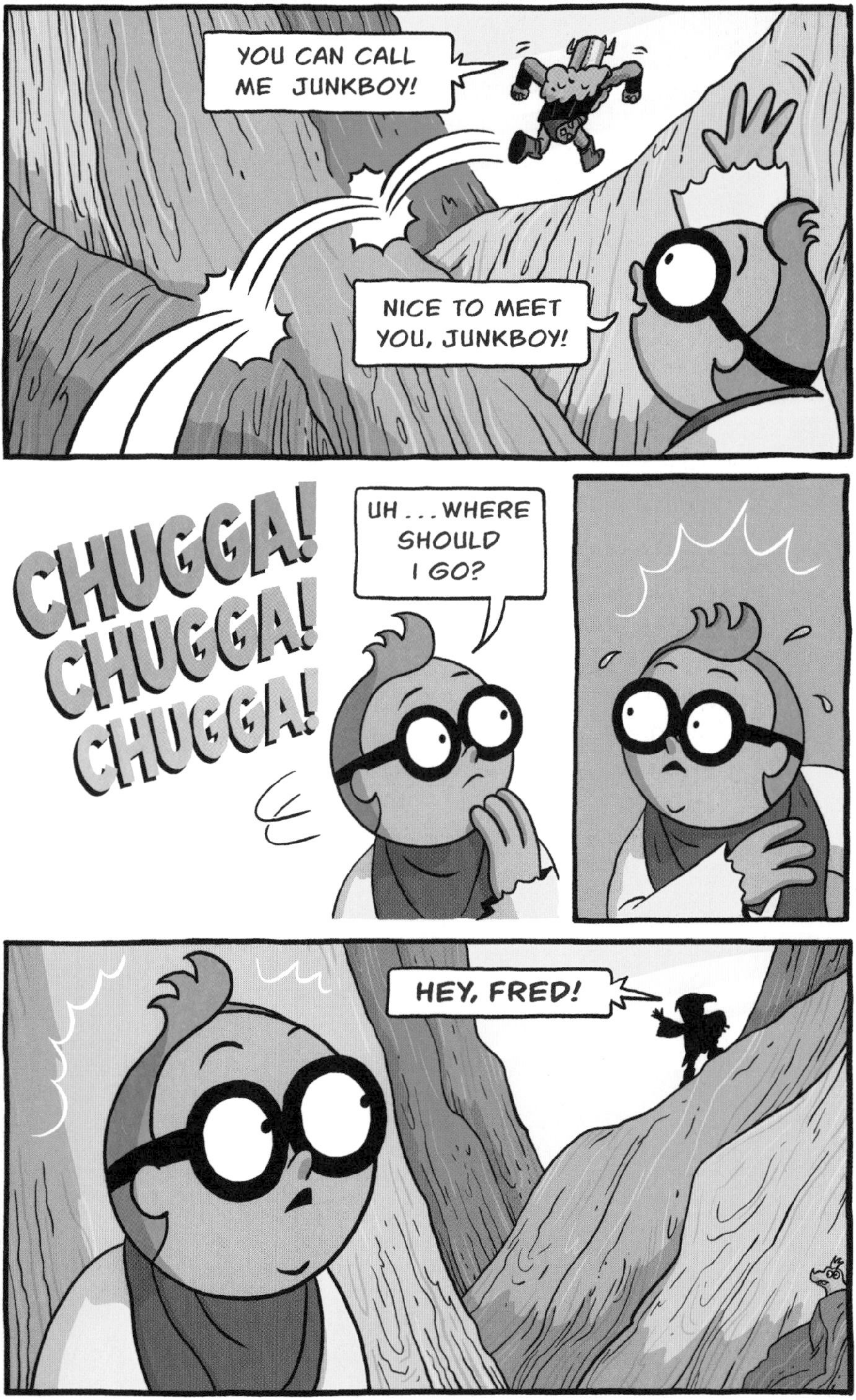
YOU CAN CALL ME JUNKBOY!
NICE TO MEET YOU, JUNKBOY!
CHUGGA! CHUGGA! CHUGGA!
UH . . . WHERE SHOULD I GO?
HEY, FRED!

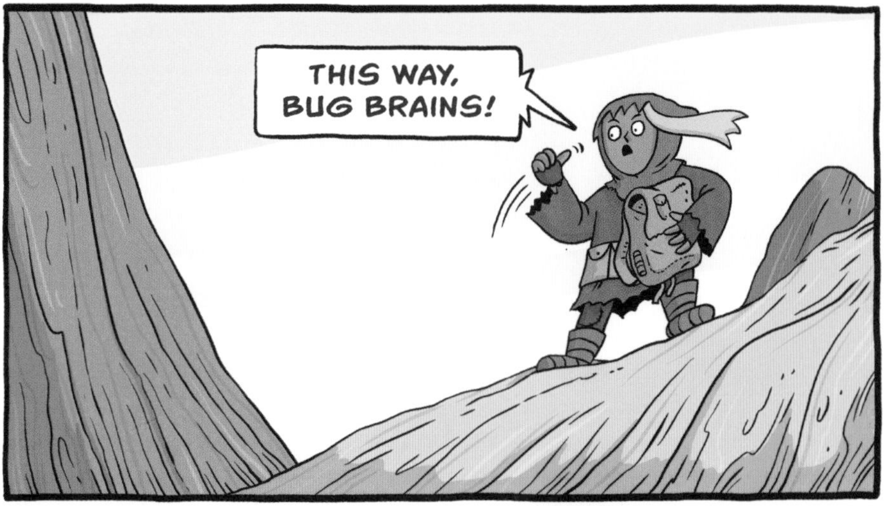
THIS WAY,
BUG BRAINS!

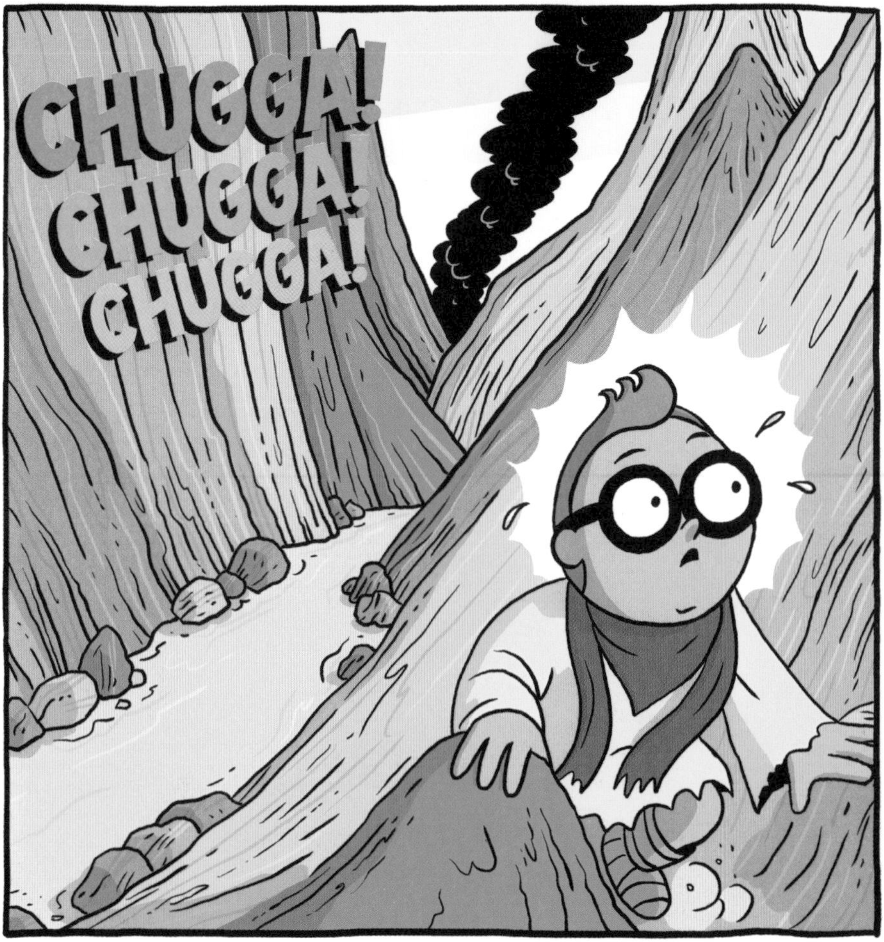
CHUGGA!
CHUGGA!
CHUGGA!

CHAPTER 7

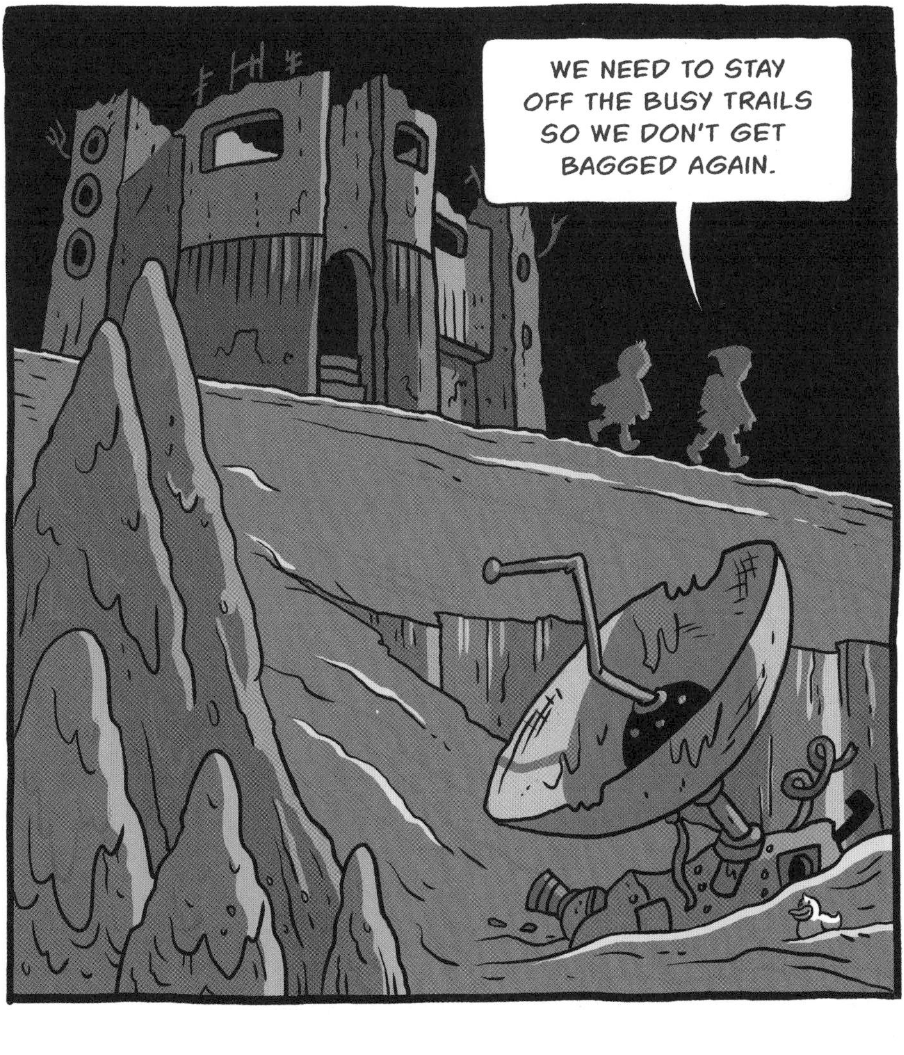
WE NEED TO STAY OFF THE BUSY TRAILS SO WE DON'T GET BAGGED AGAIN.

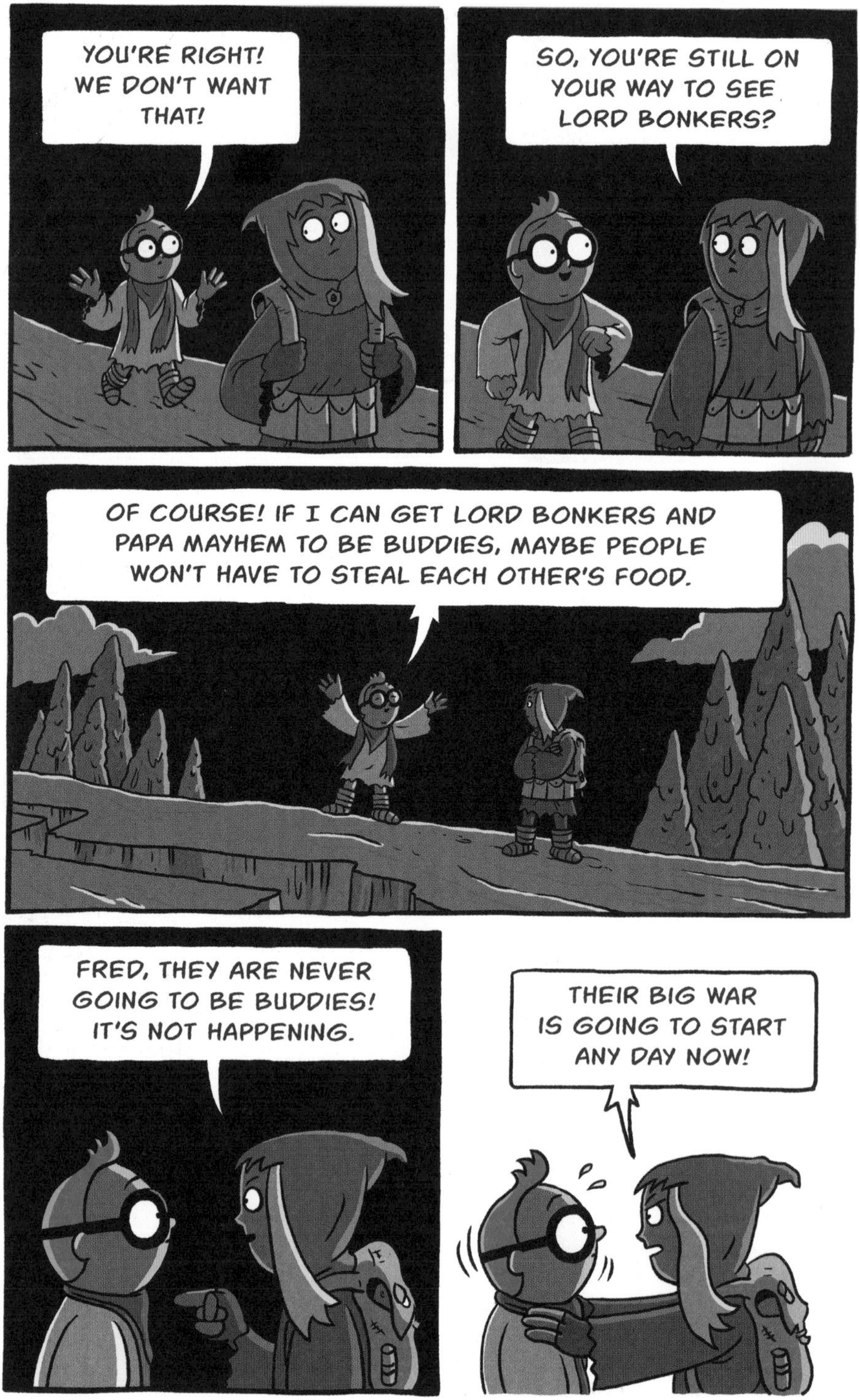
YOU'RE RIGHT! WE DON'T WANT THAT!
SO, YOU'RE STILL ON YOUR WAY TO SEE LORD BONKERS?
OF COURSE! IF I CAN GET LORD BONKERS AND PAPA MAYHEM TO BE BUDDIES, MAYBE PEOPLE WON'T HAVE TO STEAL EACH OTHER'S FOOD.
FRED, THEY ARE NEVER GOING TO BE BUDDIES! IT'S NOT HAPPENING.
THEIR BIG WAR IS GOING TO START ANY DAY NOW!

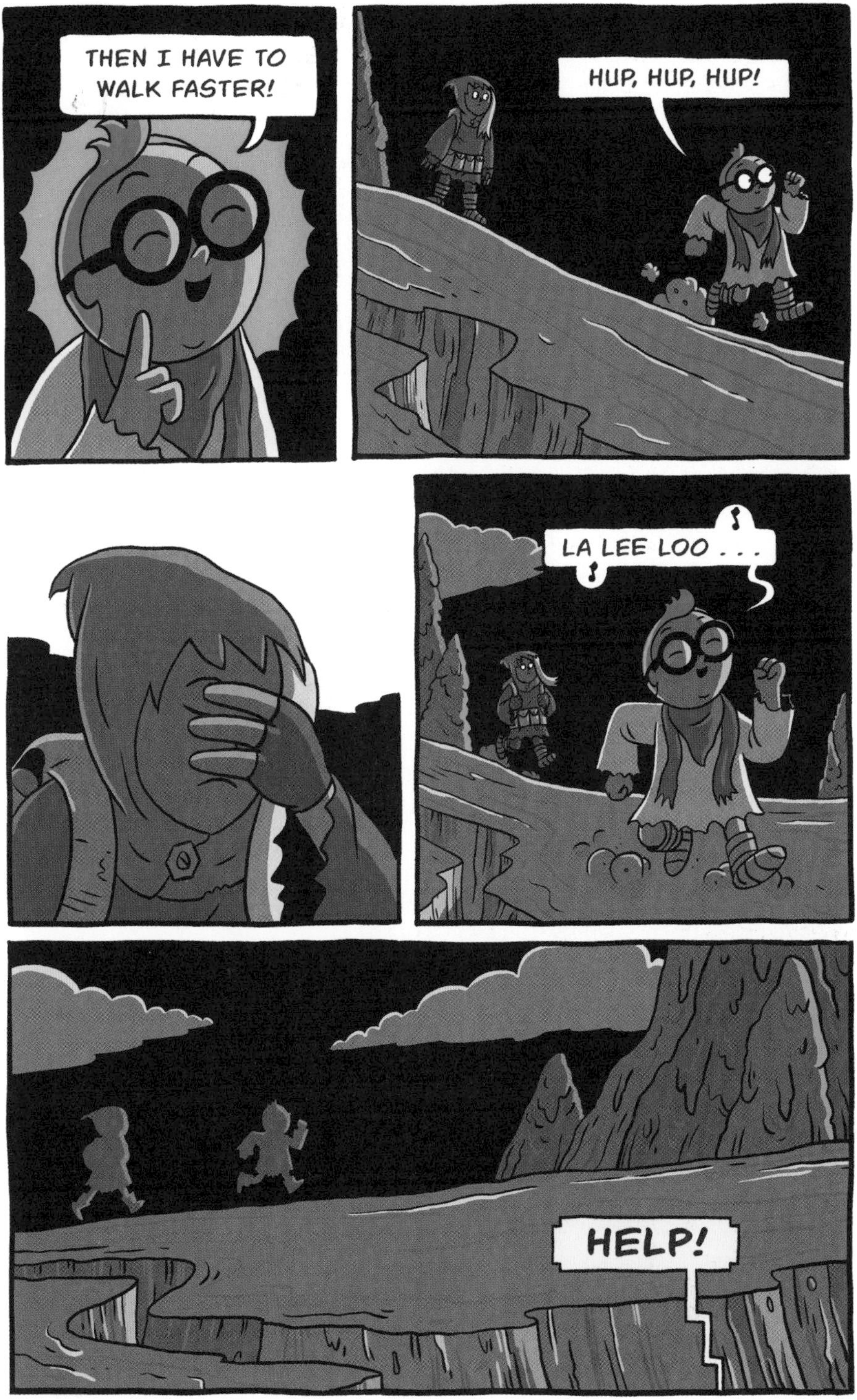
THEN I HAVE TO WALK FASTER!
HUP, HUP, HUP!
LA LEE LOO . . .
HELP!

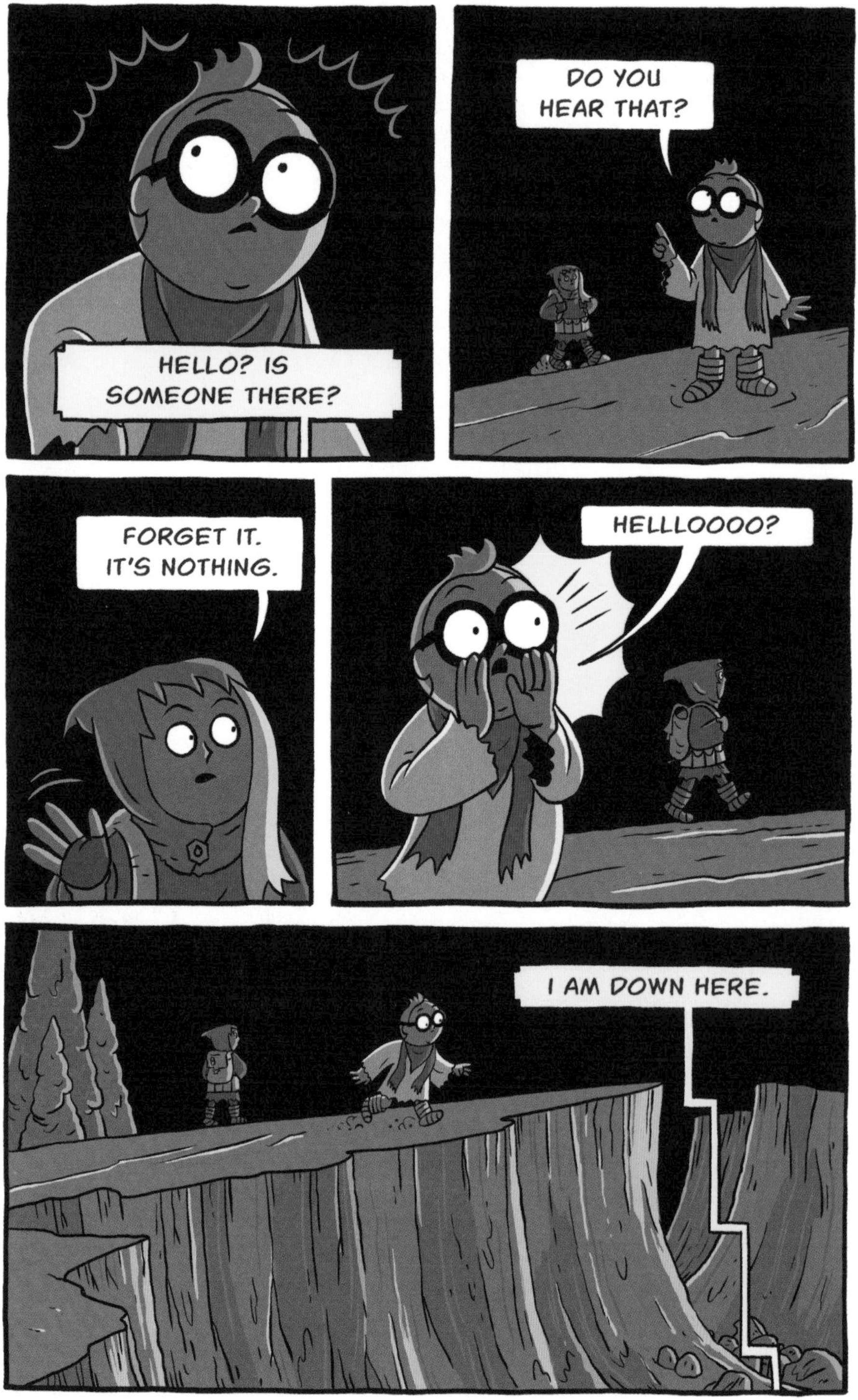
HELLO? IS SOMEONE THERE?
DO YOU HEAR THAT?
FORGET IT. IT'S NOTHING.
HELLLOOOO?
I AM DOWN HERE.

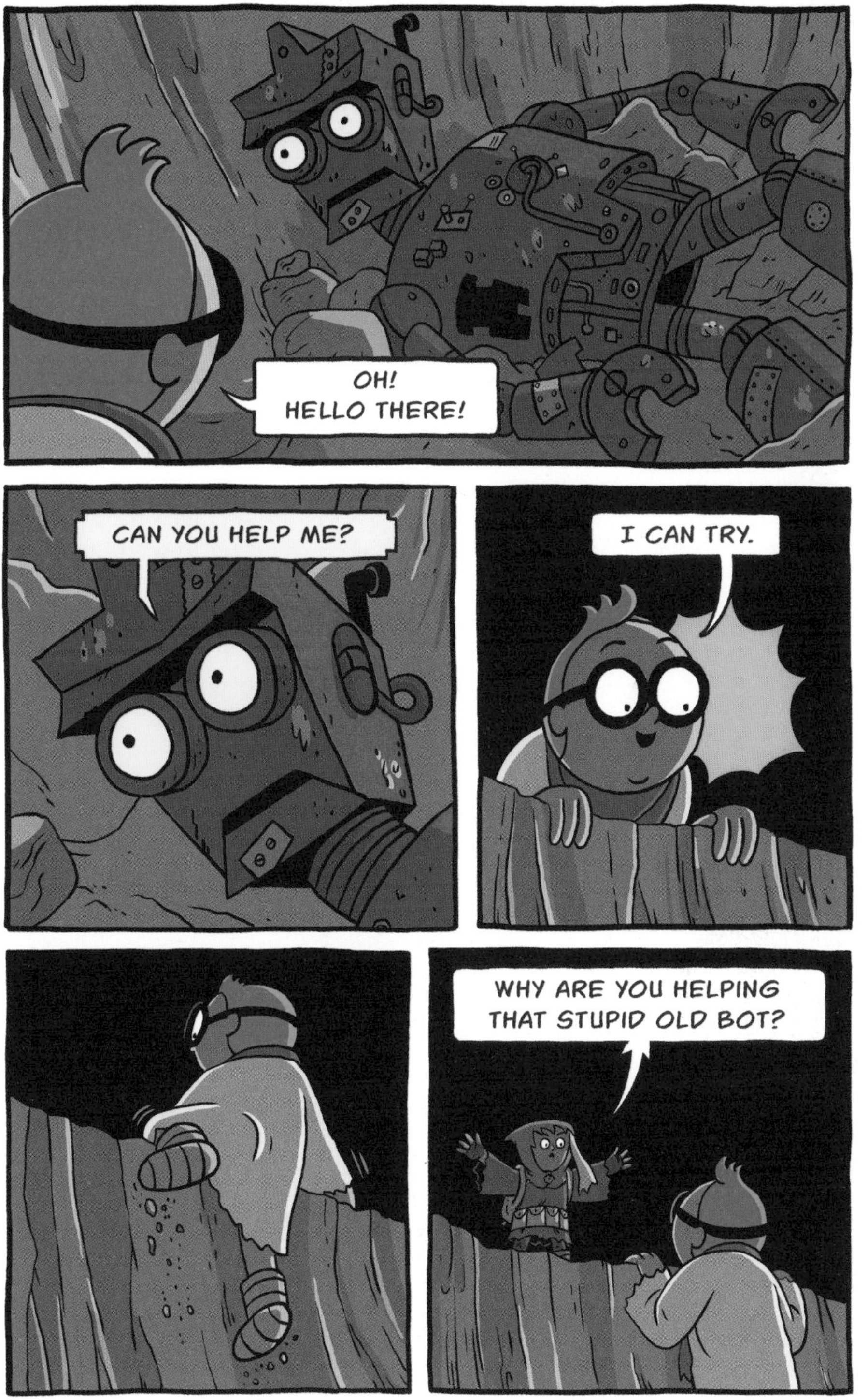
OH!
HELLO THERE!
CAN YOU HELP ME?
I CAN TRY.
WHY ARE YOU HELPING THAT STUPID OLD BOT?

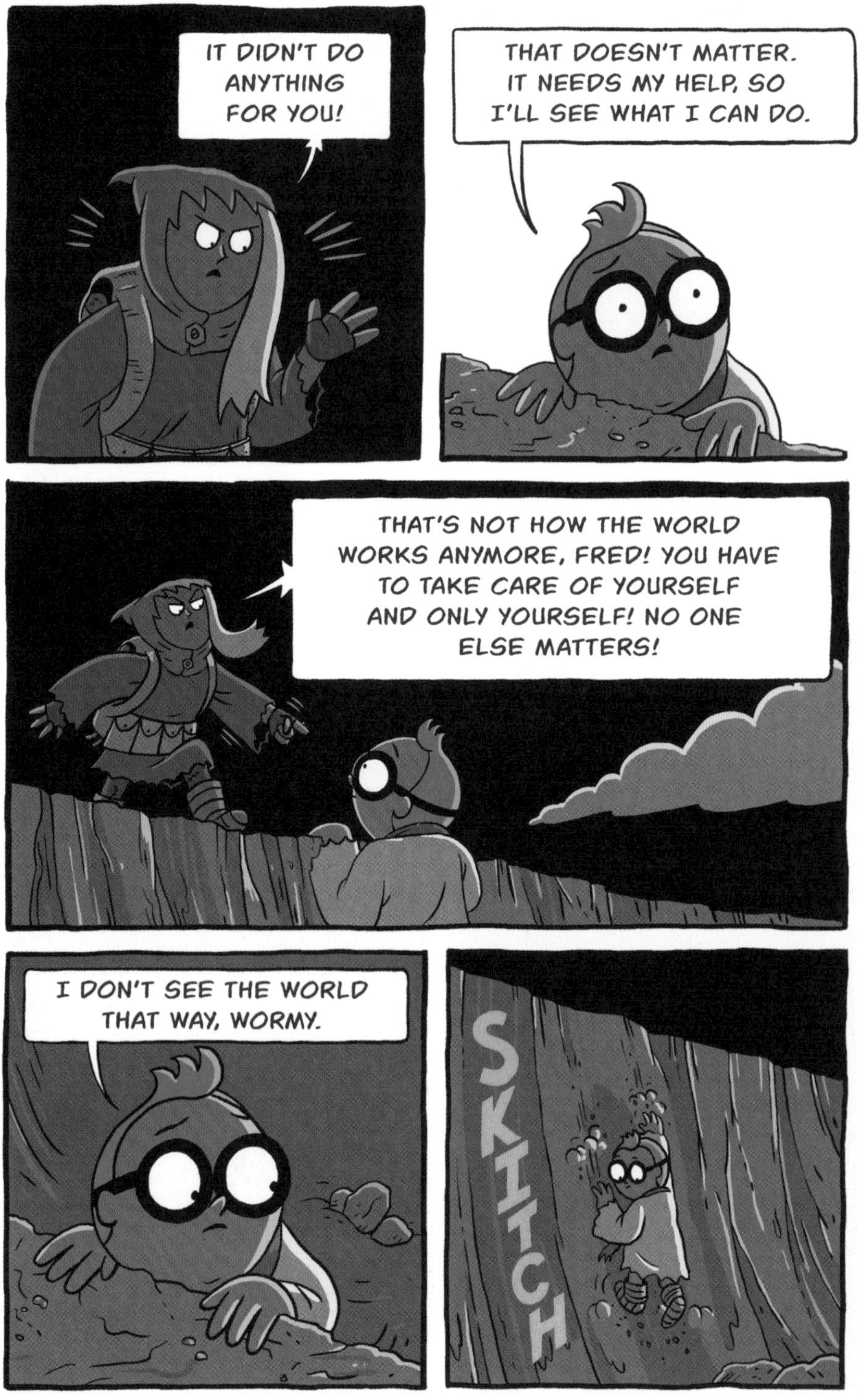
IT DIDN'T DO ANYTHING FOR YOU!
THAT DOESN'T MATTER. IT NEEDS MY HELP, SO I'LL SEE WHAT I CAN DO.
THAT'S NOT HOW THE WORLD WORKS ANYMORE, FRED! YOU HAVE TO TAKE CARE OF YOURSELF AND ONLY YOURSELF! NO ONE ELSE MATTERS!
I DON'T SEE THE WORLD THAT WAY, WORMY.
SKITCH

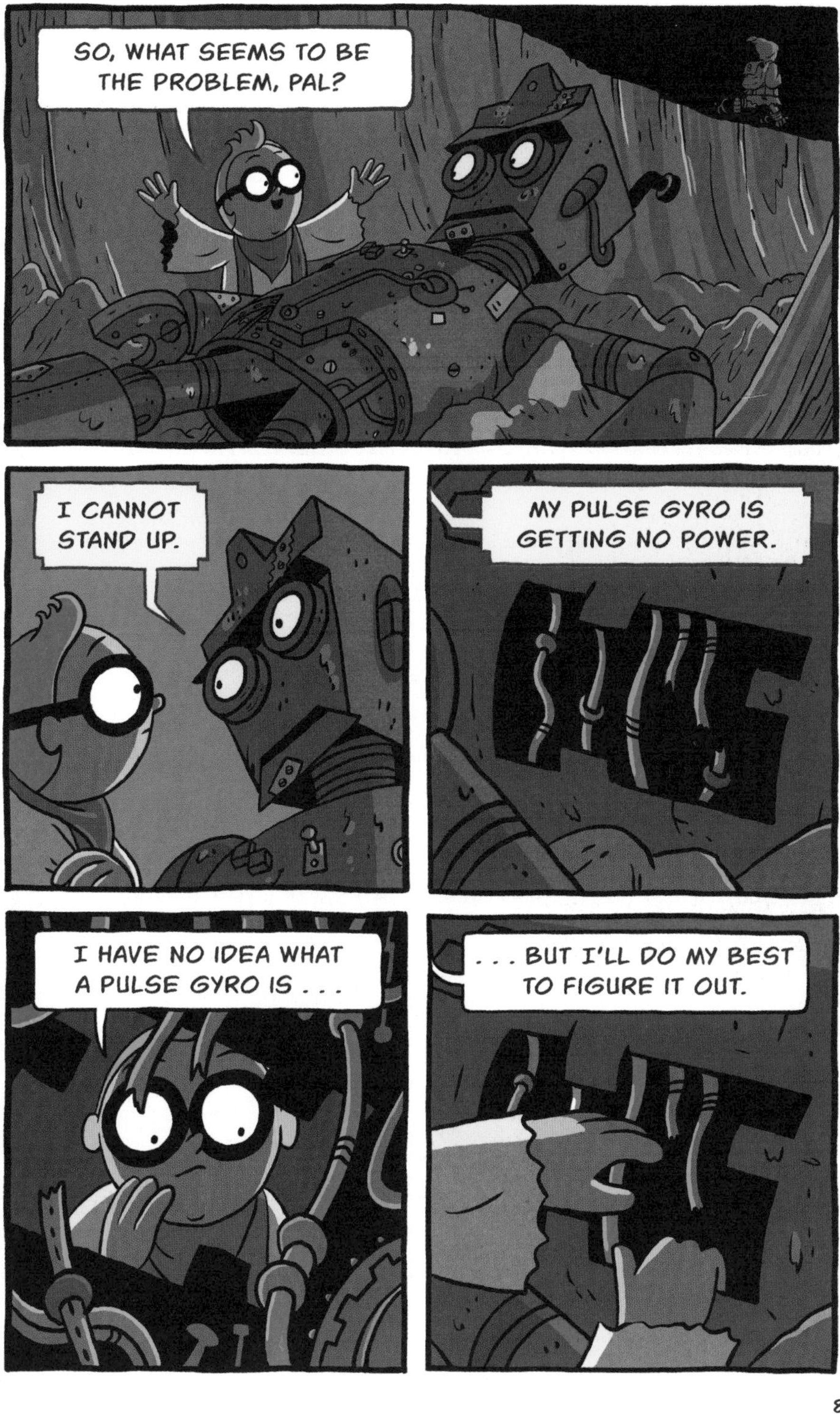
SO, WHAT SEEMS TO BE THE PROBLEM, PAL?
I CANNOT STAND UP.
MY PULSE GYRO IS GETTING NO POWER.
I HAVE NO IDEA WHAT A PULSE GYRO IS . . .
. . . BUT I'LL DO MY BEST TO FIGURE IT OUT.

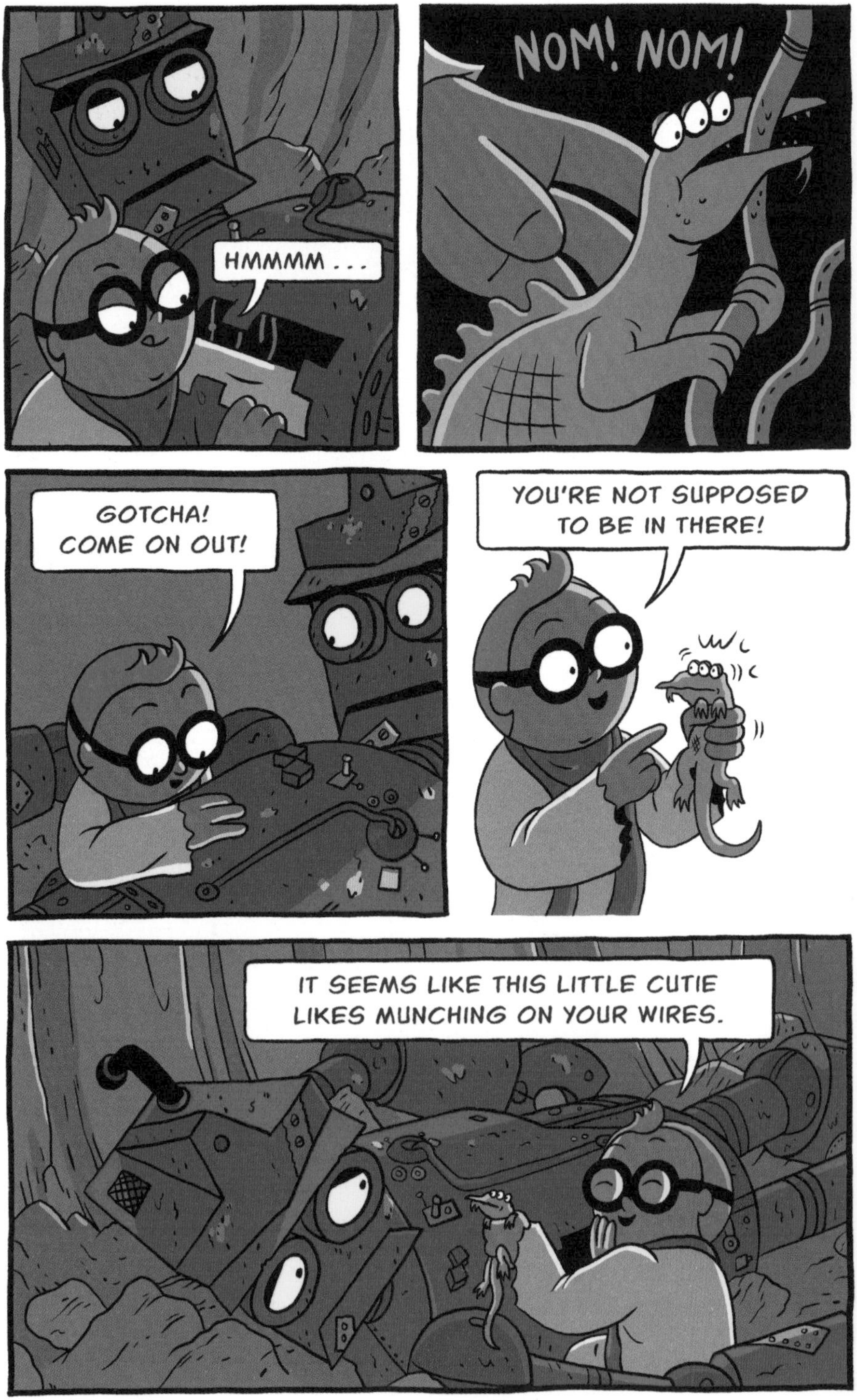
HMMMM . . .
NOM! NOM!
GOTCHA!
COME ON OUT!
YOU'RE NOT SUPPOSED
TO BE IN THERE!
IT SEEMS LIKE THIS LITTLE CUTIE
LIKES MUNCHING ON YOUR WIRES.

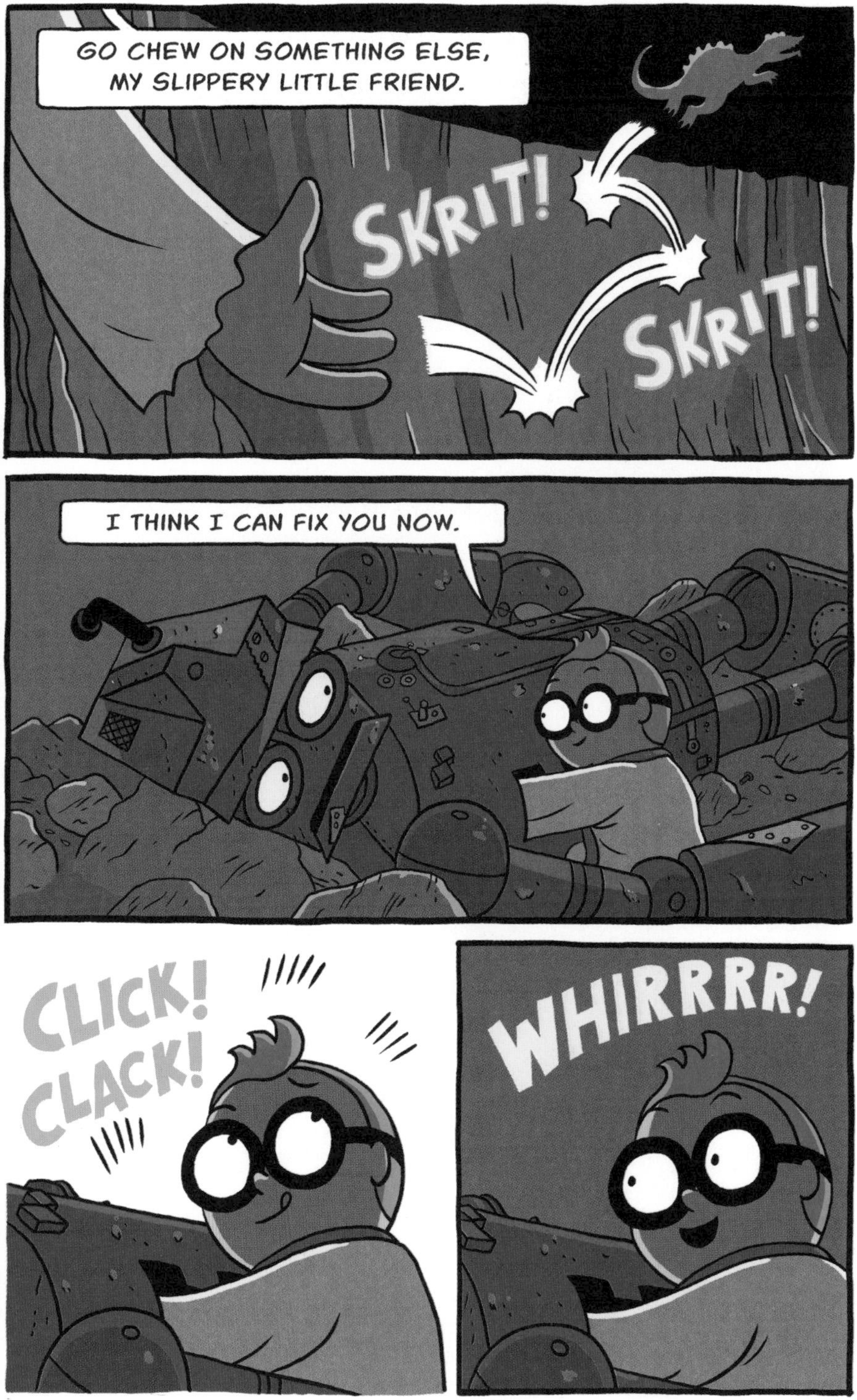
GO CHEW ON SOMETHING ELSE, MY SLIPPERY LITTLE FRIEND.
SKRIT!
SKRIT!
I THINK I CAN FIX YOU NOW.
CLICK! CLACK!
WHIRRRR!

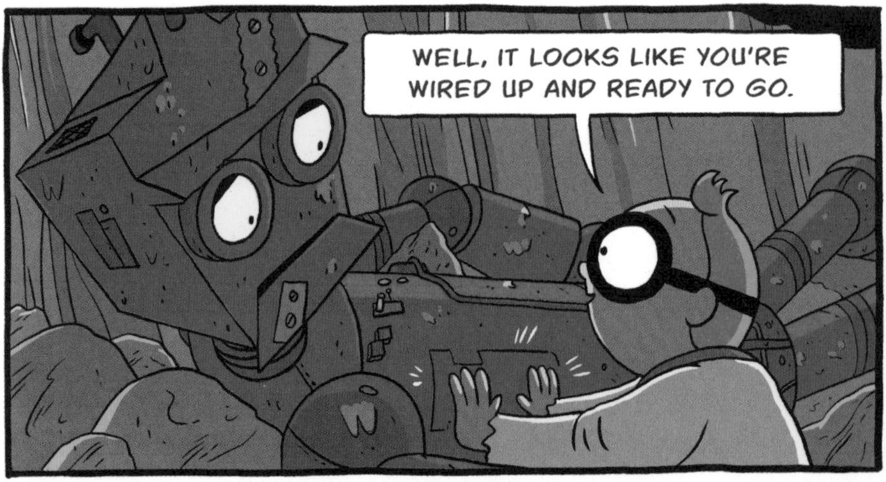
WELL, IT LOOKS LIKE YOU'RE WIRED UP AND READY TO GO.

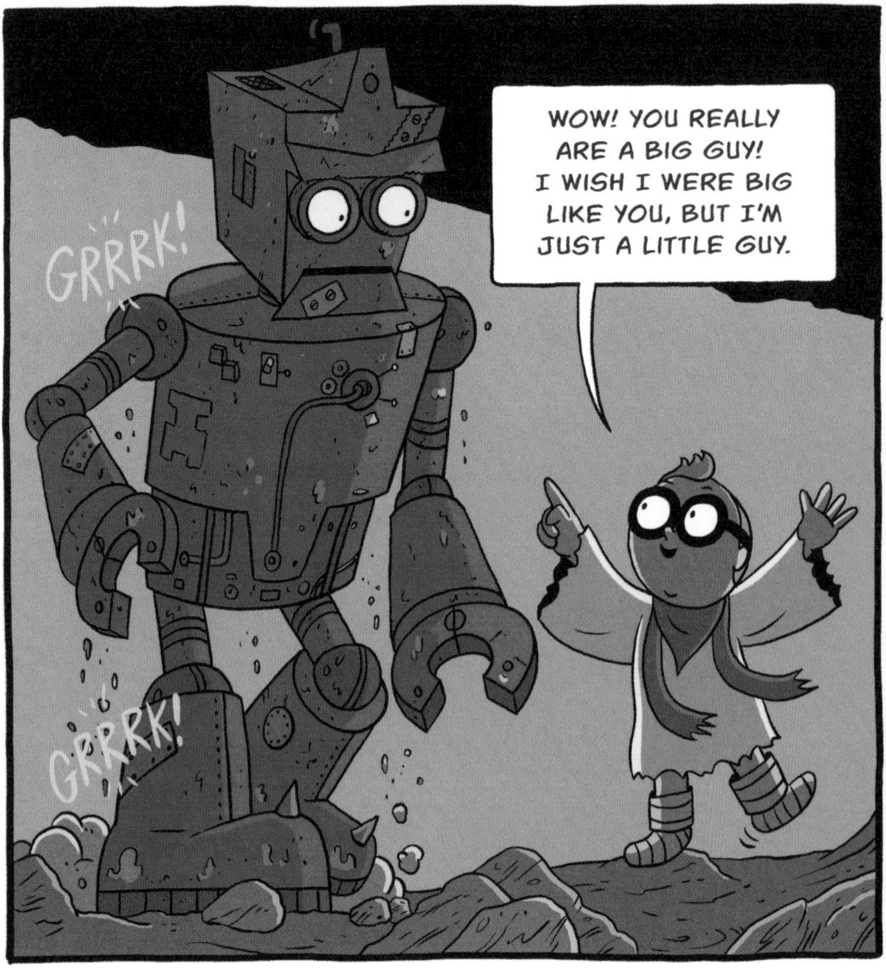
GRRRK!
WOW! YOU REALLY ARE A BIG GUY! I WISH I WERE BIG LIKE YOU, BUT I'M JUST A LITTLE GUY.
GRRRK!

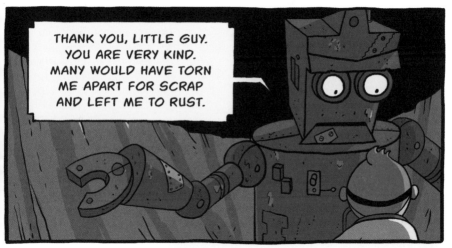

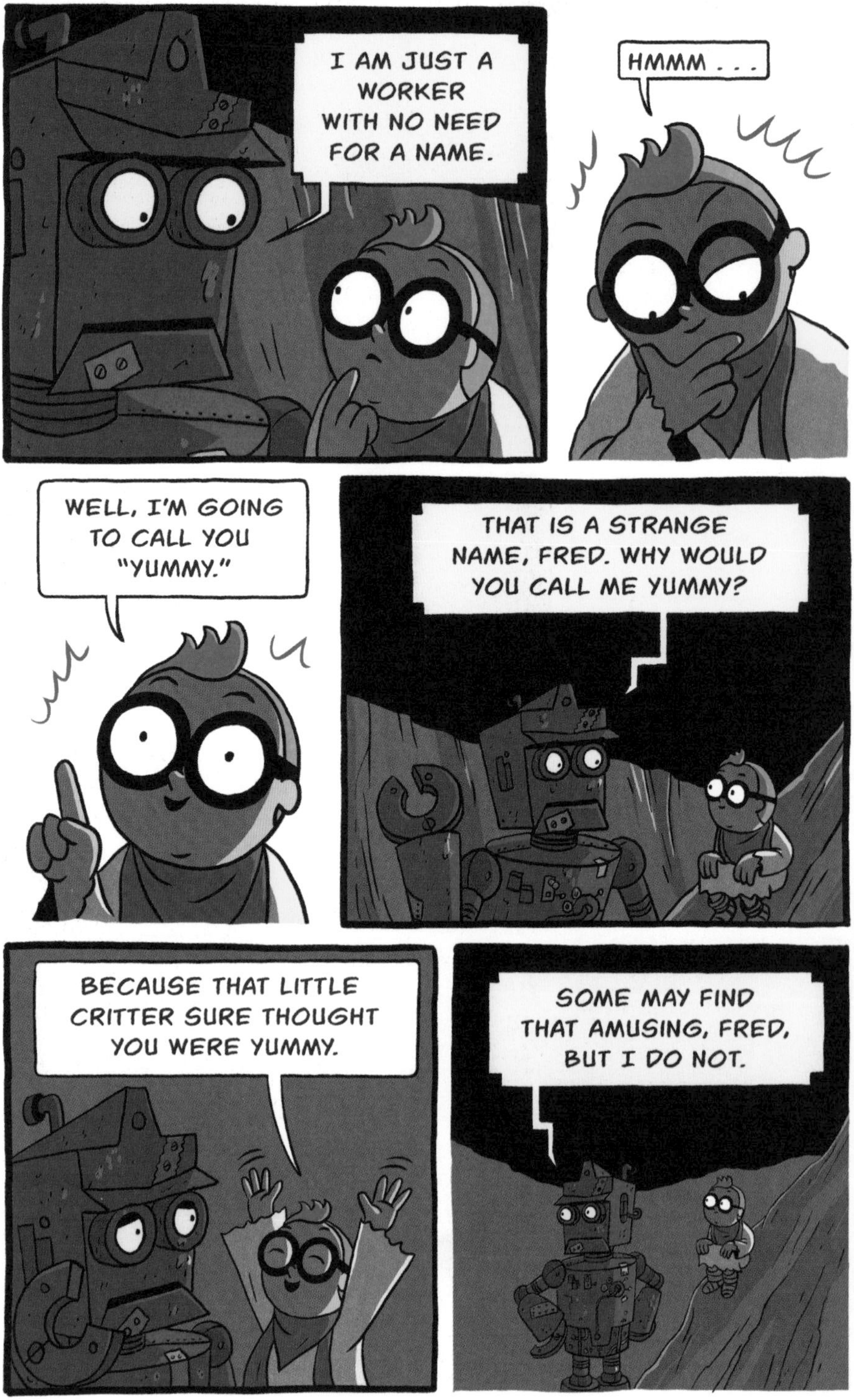
I AM JUST A WORKER WITH NO NEED FOR A NAME.
HMMM . . .
WELL, I'M GOING TO CALL YOU "YUMMY."
THAT IS A STRANGE NAME, FRED. WHY WOULD YOU CALL ME YUMMY?
BECAUSE THAT LITTLE CRITTER SURE THOUGHT YOU WERE YUMMY.
SOME MAY FIND THAT AMUSING, FRED, BUT I DO NOT.

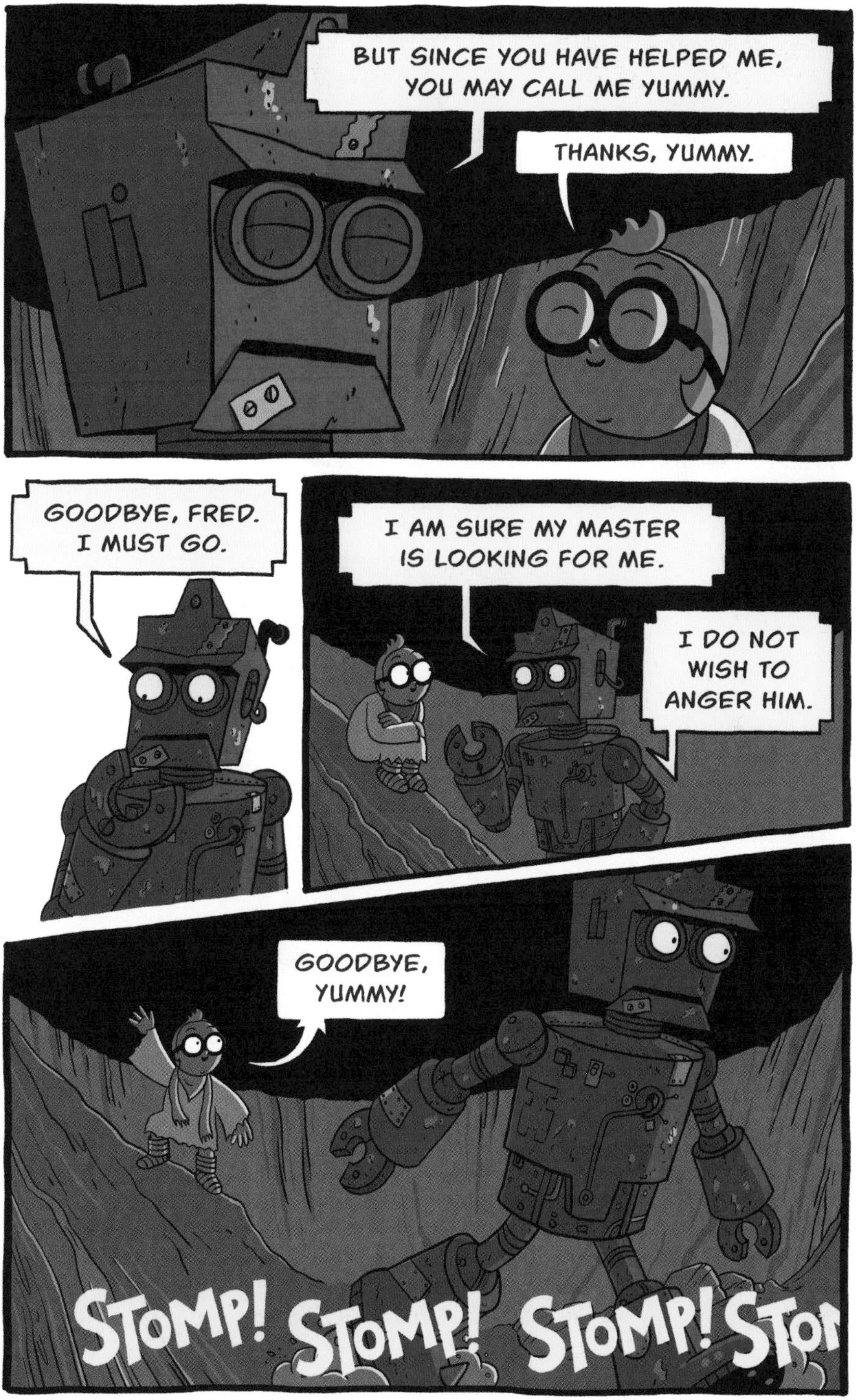
BUT SINCE YOU HAVE HELPED ME, YOU MAY CALL ME YUMMY.
THANKS, YUMMY.
GOODBYE, FRED. I MUST GO.
I AM SURE MY MASTER IS LOOKING FOR ME.
I DO NOT WISH TO ANGER HIM.
GOODBYE, YUMMY!
STOMP! STOMP! STOMP!

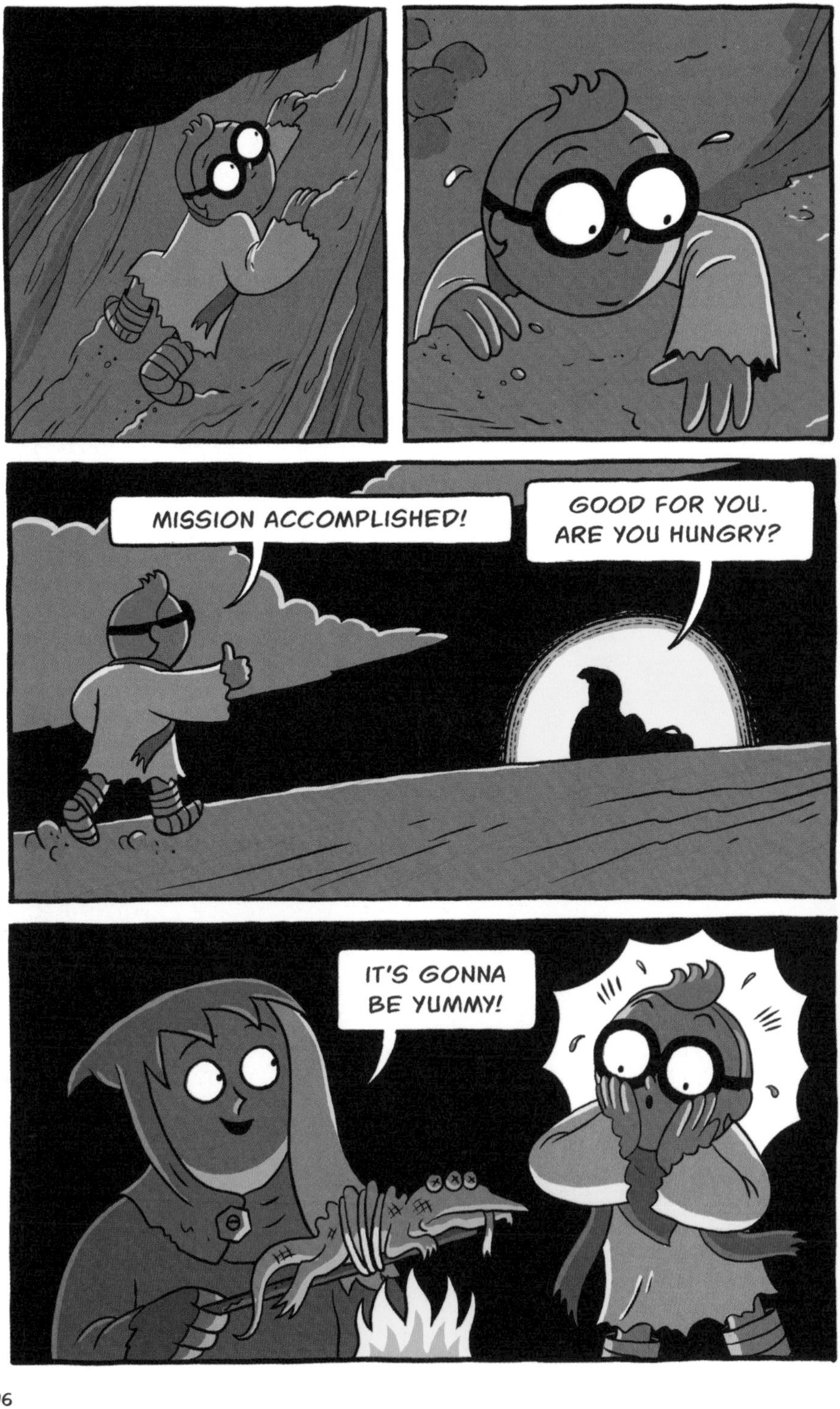
MISSION ACCOMPLISHED!
GOOD FOR YOU. ARE YOU HUNGRY?
IT'S GONNA BE YUMMY!

CHAPTER 8

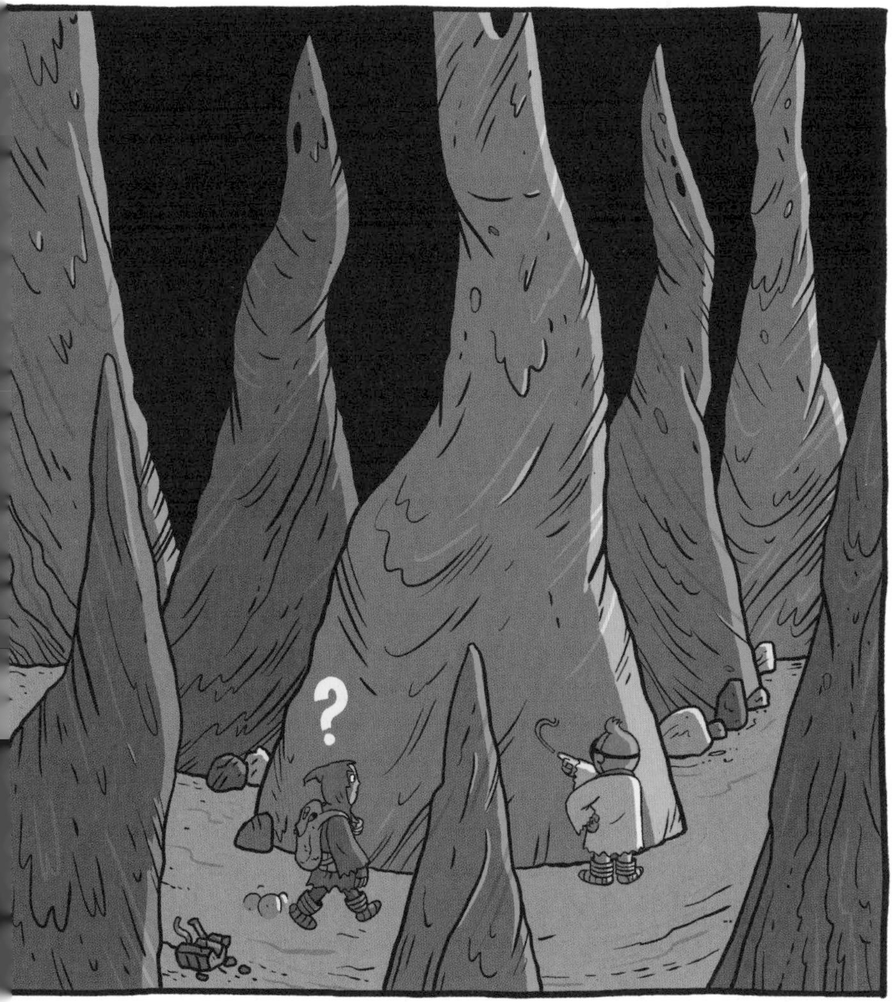
?

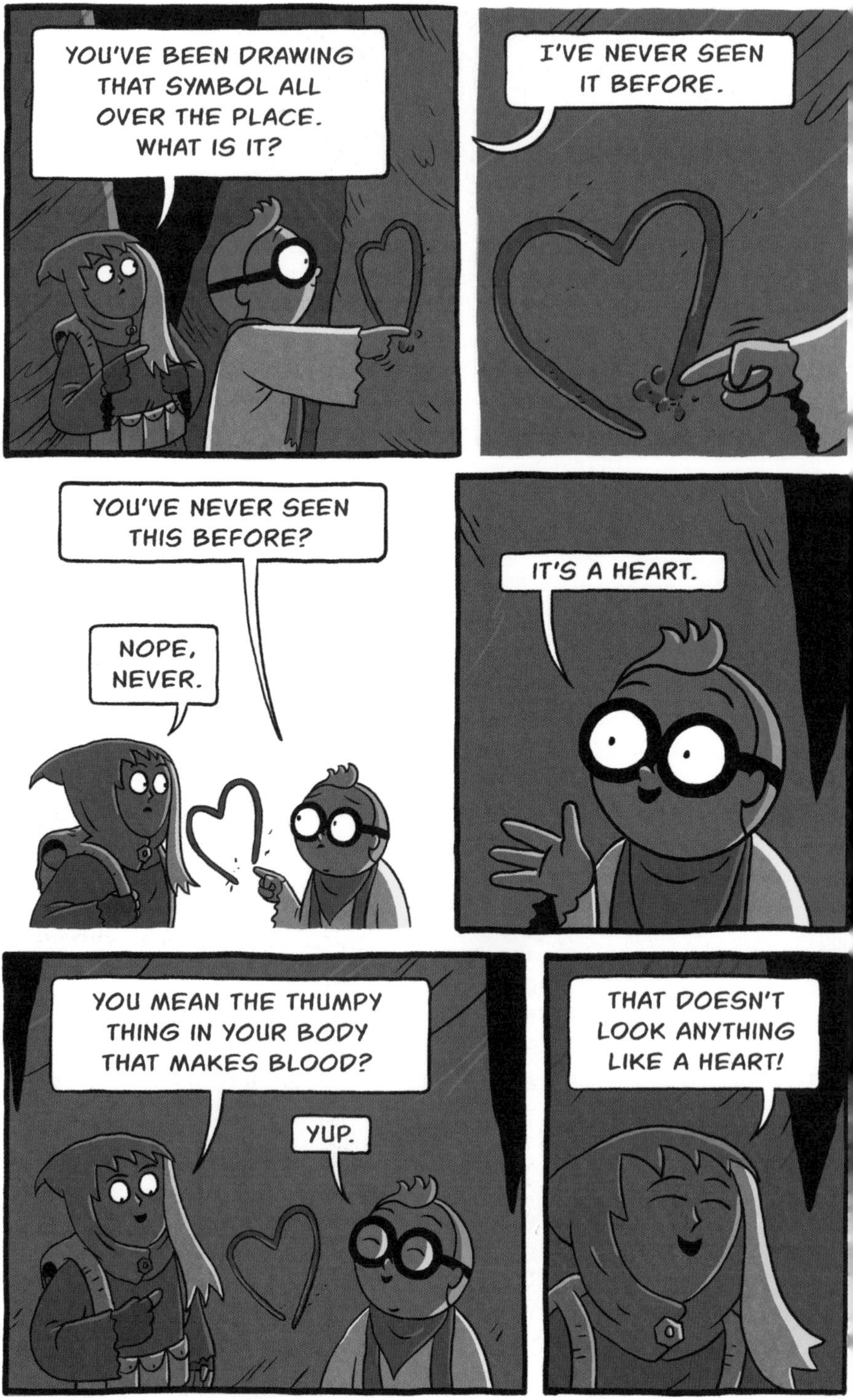

YOU'VE BEEN DRAWING THAT SYMBOL ALL OVER THE PLACE. WHAT IS IT?
I'VE NEVER SEEN IT BEFORE.
YOU'VE NEVER SEEN THIS BEFORE?
NOPE, NEVER.
IT'S A HEART.
YOU MEAN THE THUMPY THING IN YOUR BODY THAT MAKES BLOOD?
YUP.
THAT DOESN'T LOOK ANYTHING LIKE A HEART!

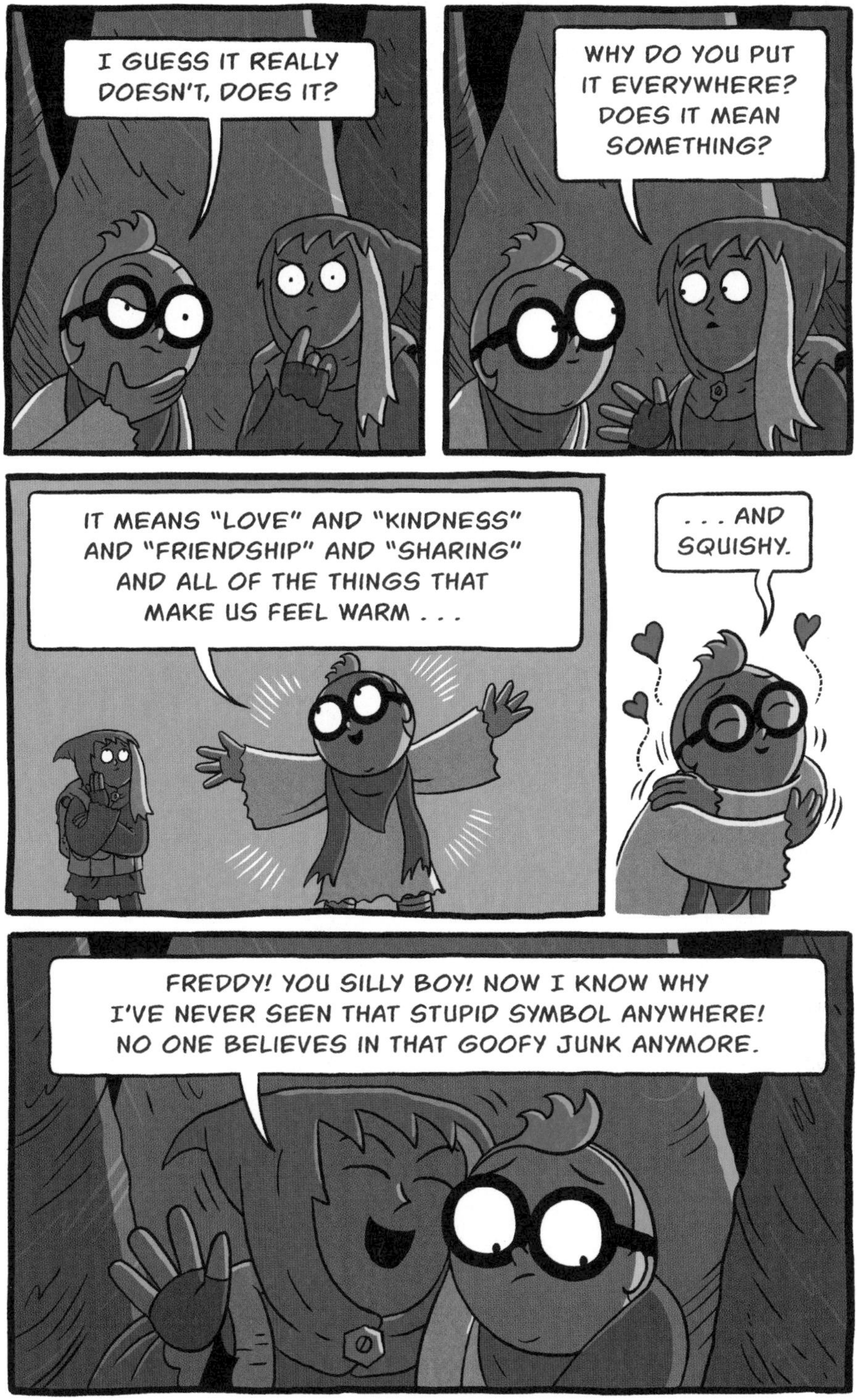
I GUESS IT REALLY DOESN'T, DOES IT?
WHY DO YOU PUT IT EVERYWHERE? DOES IT MEAN SOMETHING?
IT MEANS "LOVE" AND "KINDNESS" AND "FRIENDSHIP" AND "SHARING" AND ALL OF THE THINGS THAT MAKE US FEEL WARM . . .
. . . AND SQUISHY.
FREDDY! YOU SILLY BOY! NOW I KNOW WHY I'VE NEVER SEEN THAT STUPID SYMBOL ANYWHERE! NO ONE BELIEVES IN THAT GOOFY JUNK ANYMORE.

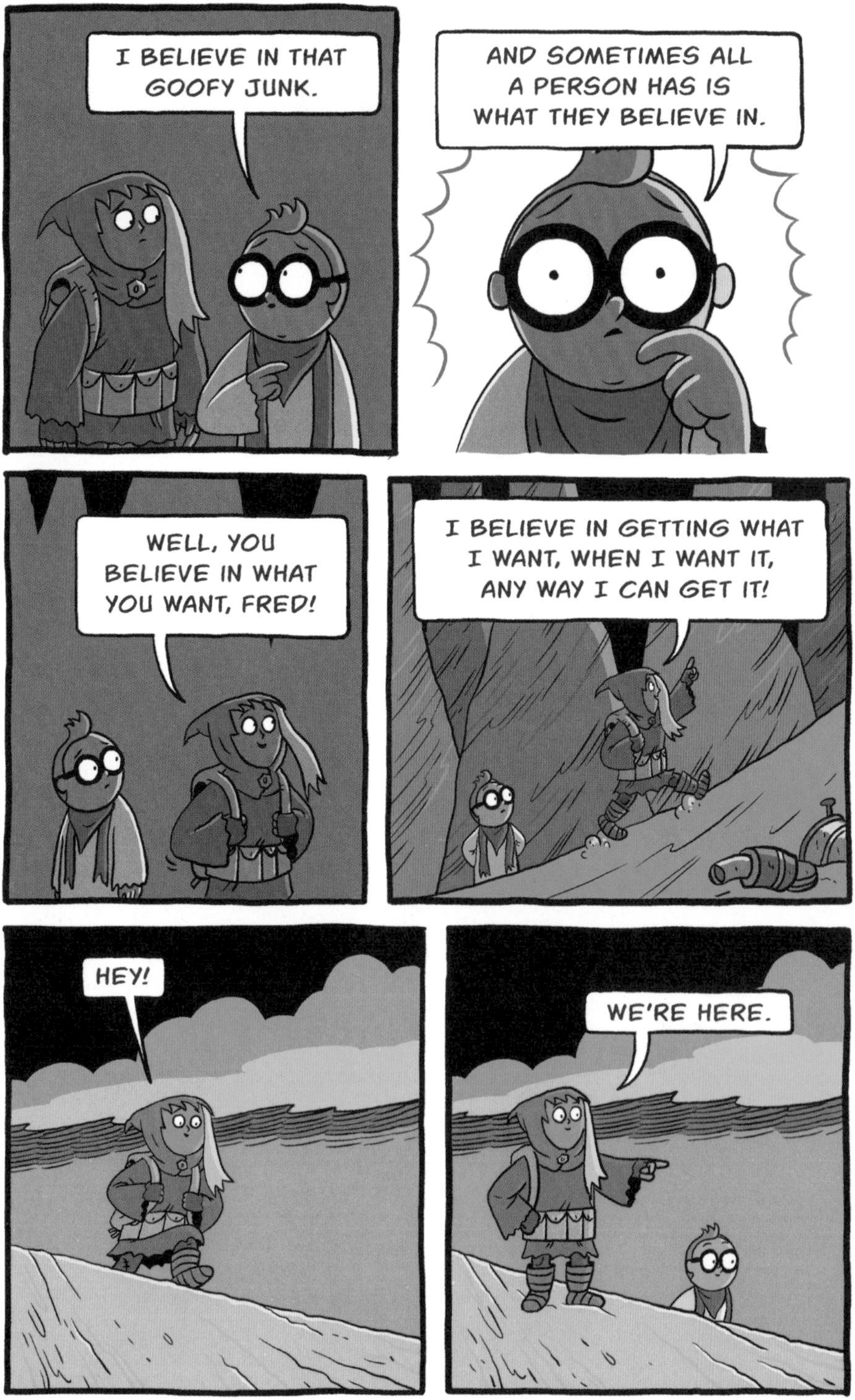
I BELIEVE IN THAT GOOFY JUNK.
AND SOMETIMES ALL A PERSON HAS IS WHAT THEY BELIEVE IN.
WELL, YOU BELIEVE IN WHAT YOU WANT, FRED!
I BELIEVE IN GETTING WHAT I WANT, WHEN I WANT IT, ANY WAY I CAN GET IT!
HEY!
WE'RE HERE.

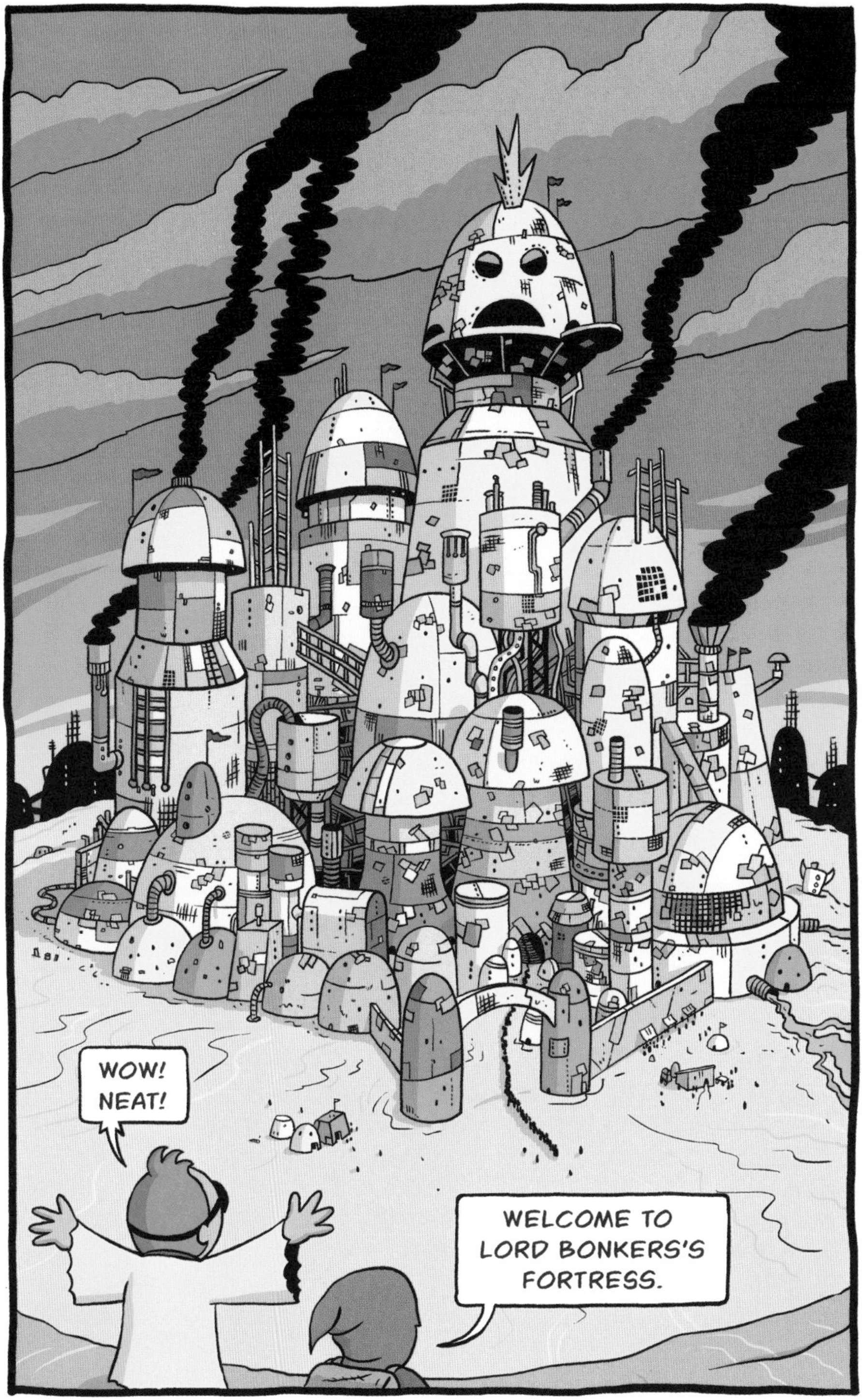
WOW! NEAT!
WELCOME TO LORD BONKERS'S FORTRESS.

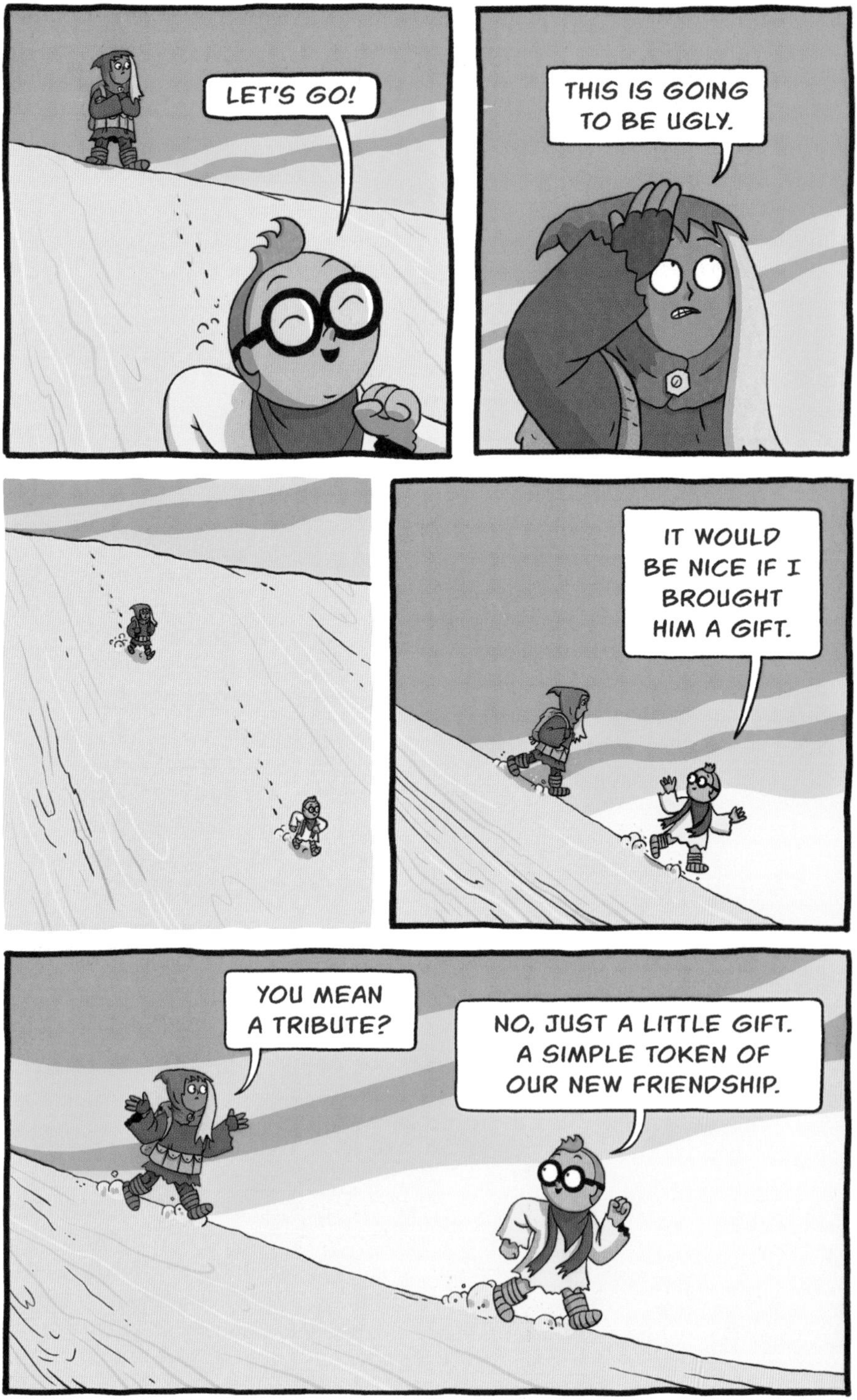
LET'S GO!
THIS IS GOING TO BE UGLY.
IT WOULD BE NICE IF I BROUGHT HIM A GIFT.
YOU MEAN A TRIBUTE?
NO, JUST A LITTLE GIFT. A SIMPLE TOKEN OF OUR NEW FRIENDSHIP.

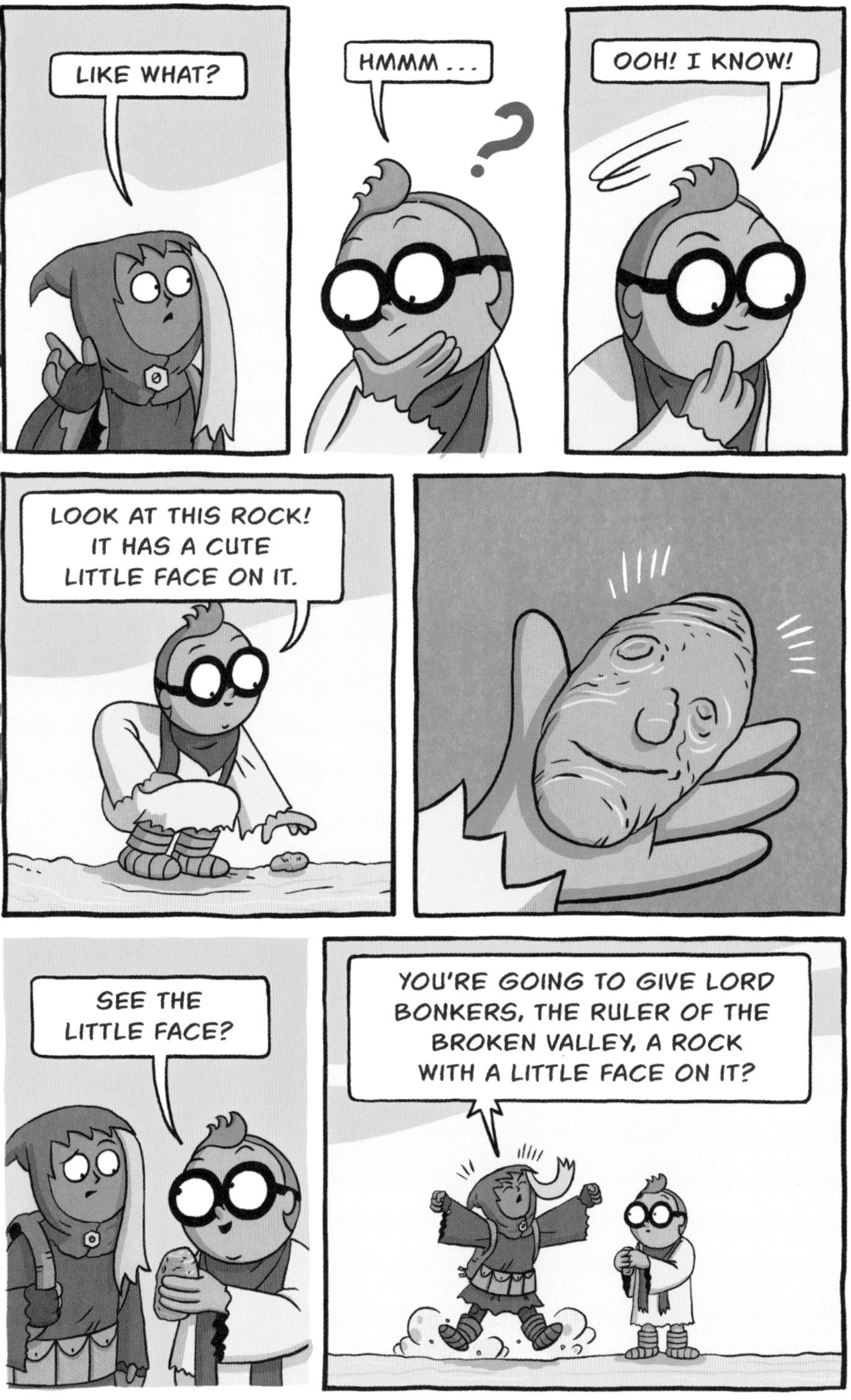
LIKE WHAT?
HMMM . . .
?
OOH! I KNOW!
LOOK AT THIS ROCK! IT HAS A CUTE LITTLE FACE ON IT.
SEE THE LITTLE FACE?
YOU'RE GOING TO GIVE LORD BONKERS, THE RULER OF THE BROKEN VALLEY, A ROCK WITH A LITTLE FACE ON IT?

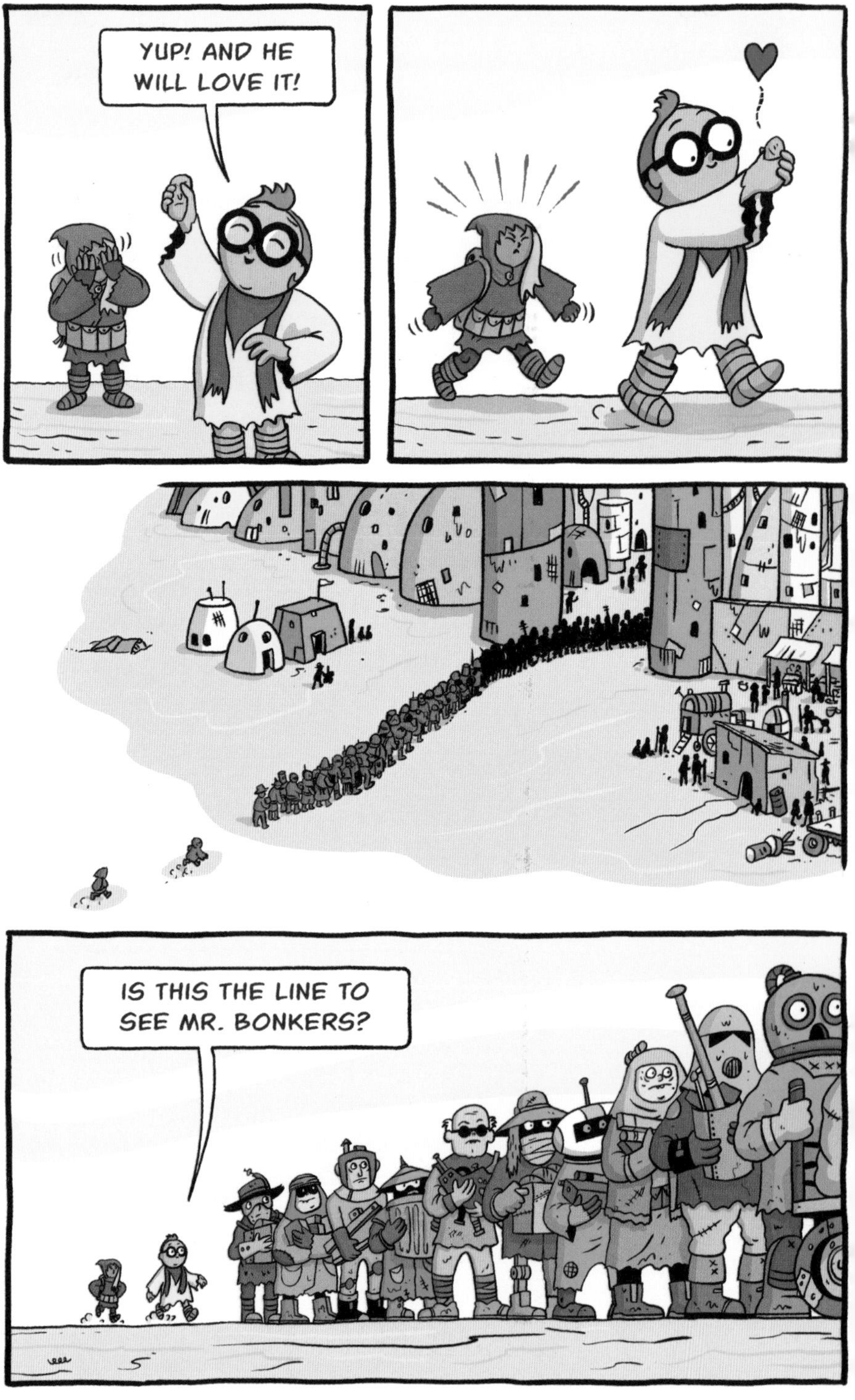
YUP! AND HE WILL LOVE IT!
IS THIS THE LINE TO SEE MR. BONKERS?

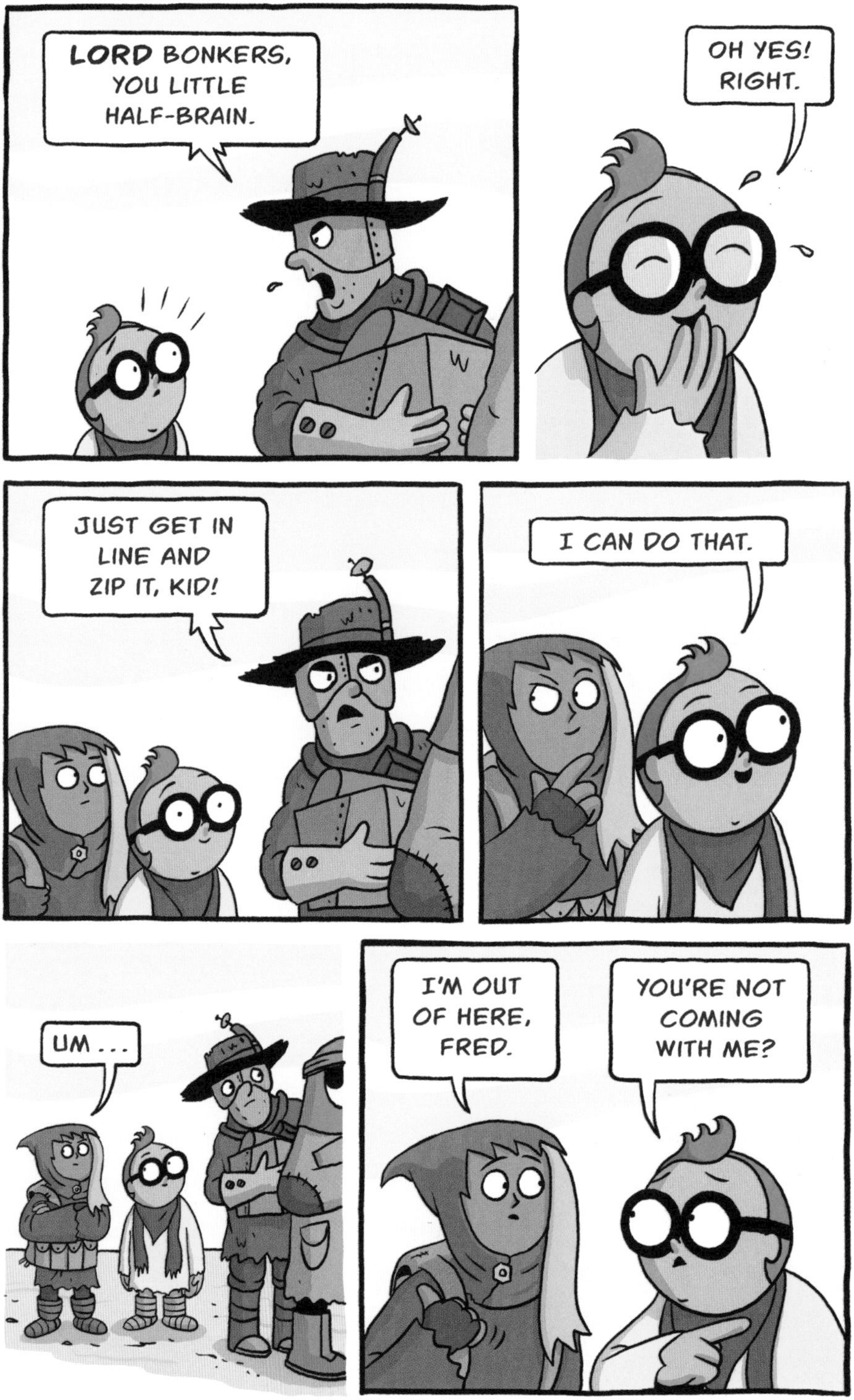
LORD BONKERS, YOU LITTLE HALF-BRAIN.
OH YES! RIGHT.
JUST GET IN LINE AND ZIP IT, KID!
I CAN DO THAT.
UM . . .
I'M OUT OF HERE, FRED.
YOU'RE NOT COMING WITH ME?

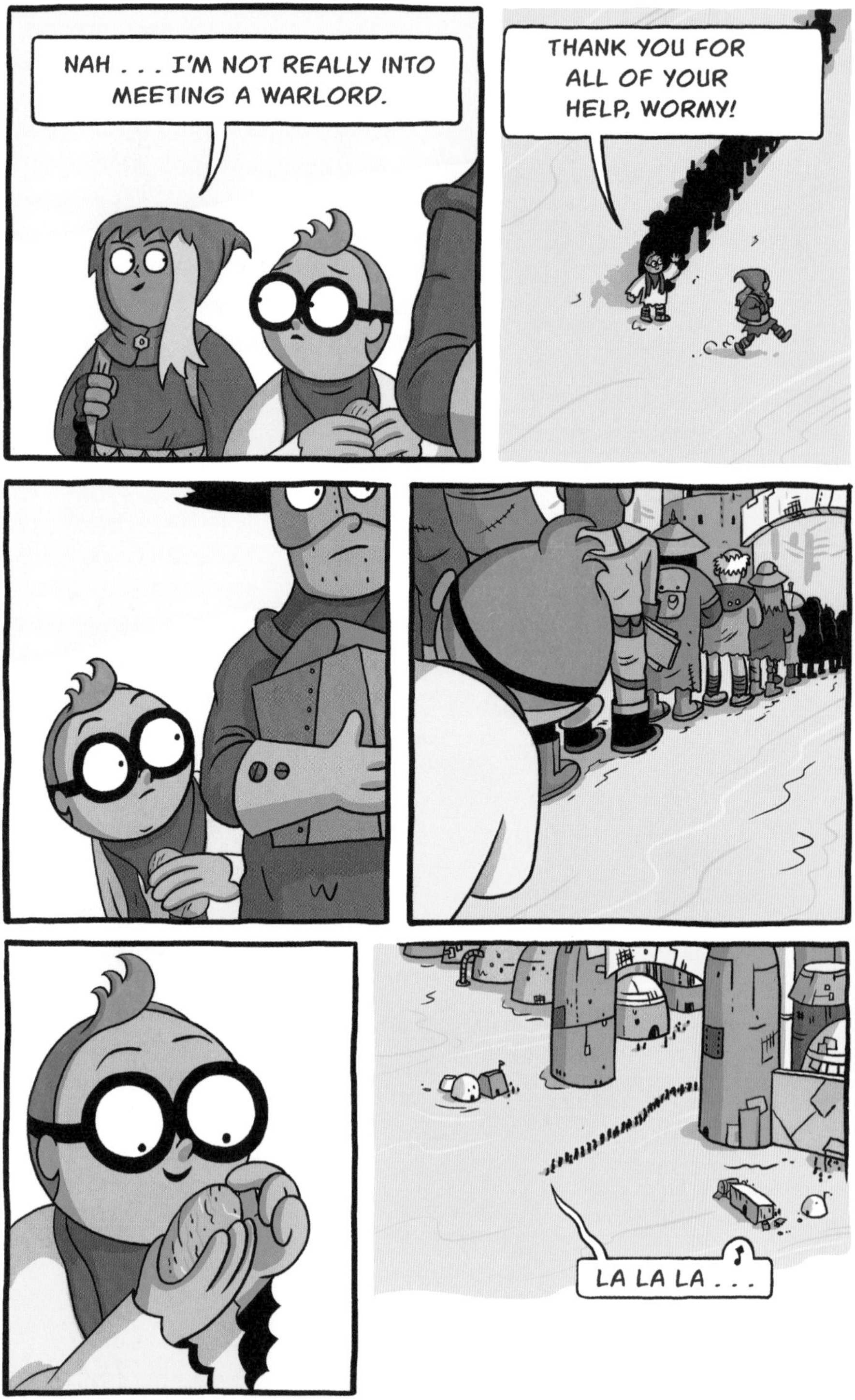

NAH . . . I'M NOT REALLY INTO MEETING A WARLORD.
THANK YOU FOR ALL OF YOUR HELP, WORMY!
LA LA LA . . .

CHAPTER 9

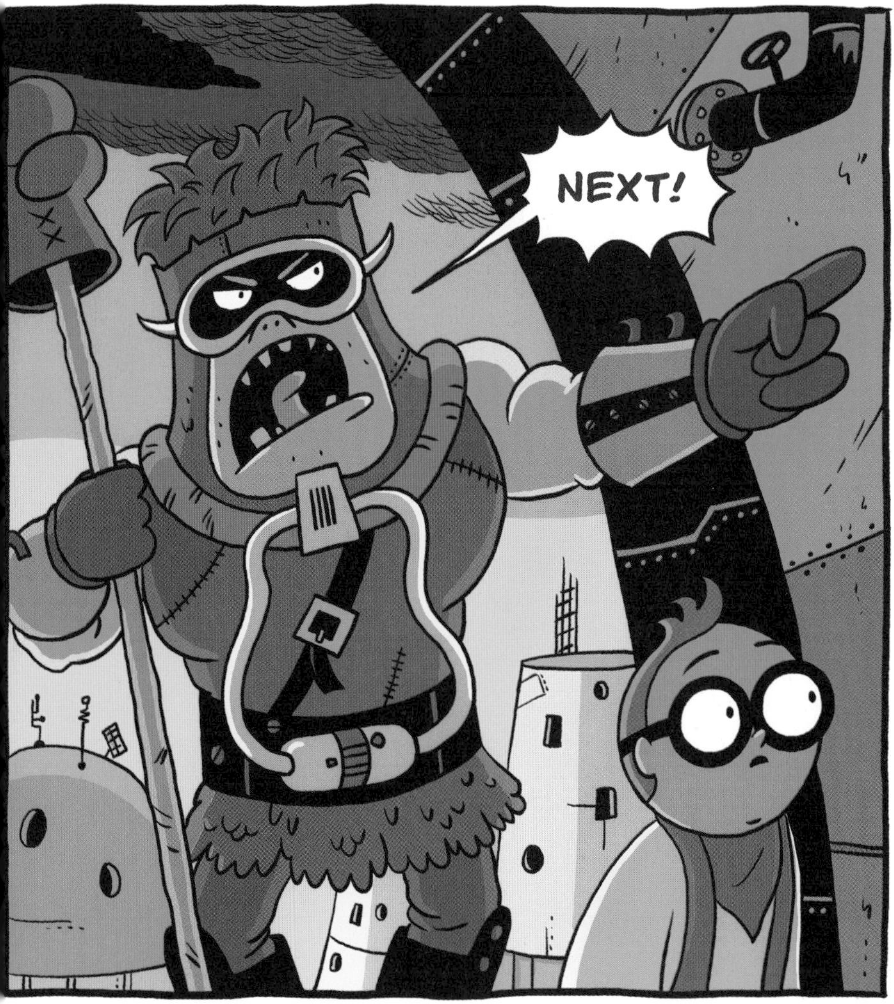
NEXT!

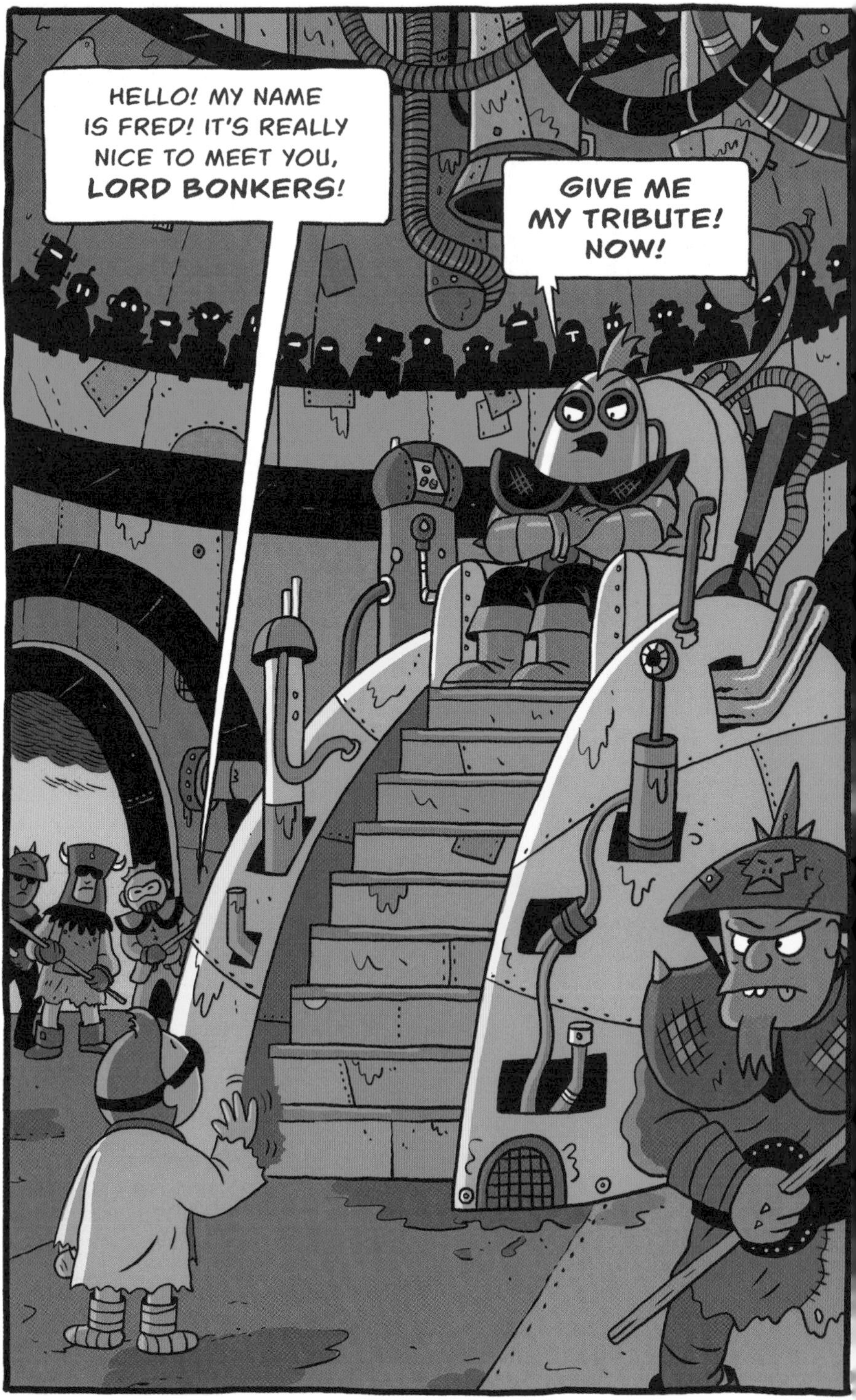
HELLO! MY NAME IS FRED! IT'S REALLY NICE TO MEET YOU, LORD BONKERS!
GIVE ME MY TRIBUTE! NOW!

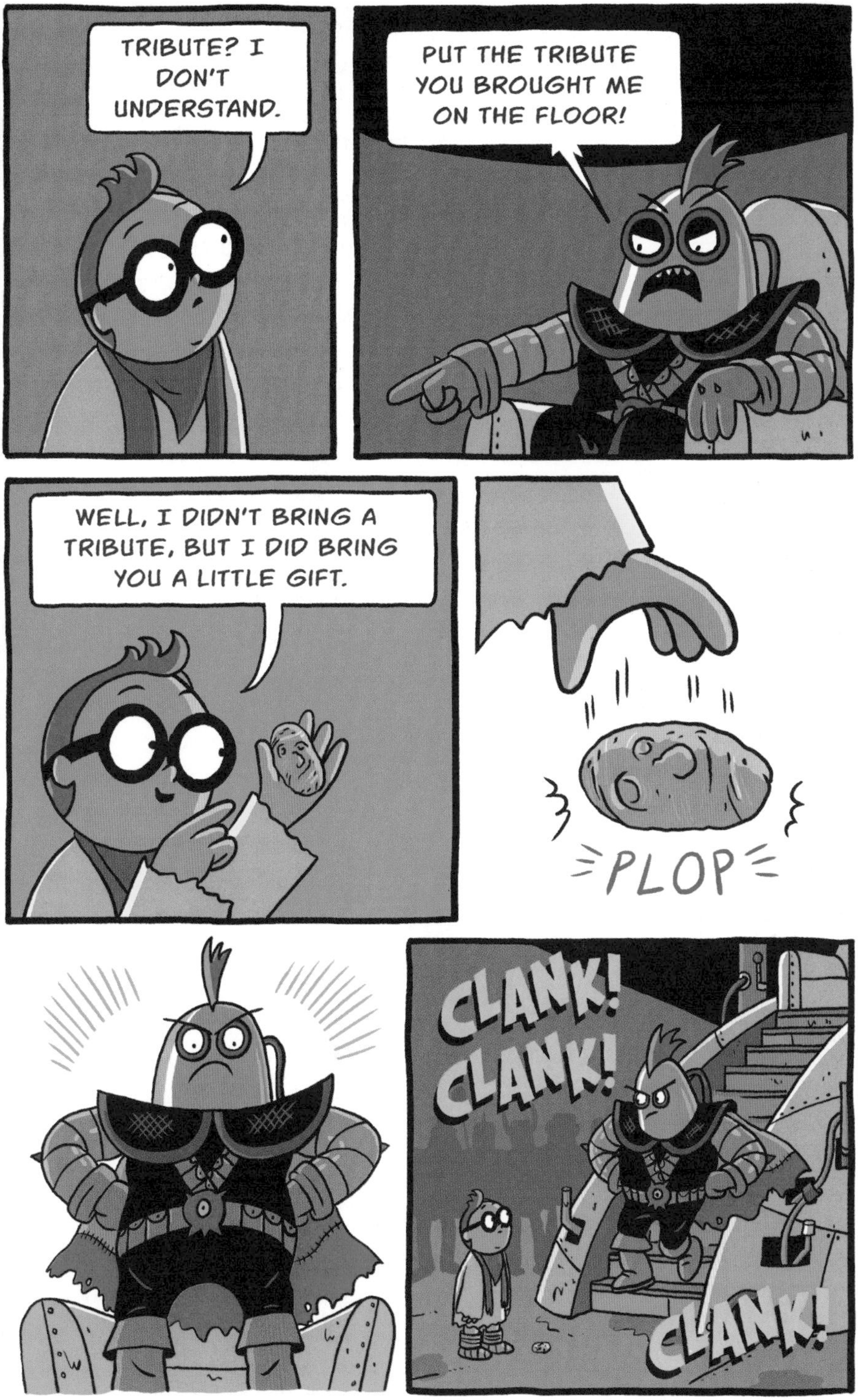
TRIBUTE? I DON'T UNDERSTAND.
PUT THE TRIBUTE YOU BROUGHT ME ON THE FLOOR!
WELL, I DIDN'T BRING A TRIBUTE, BUT I DID BRING YOU A LITTLE GIFT.
PLOP
CLANK! CLANK!
CLANK!

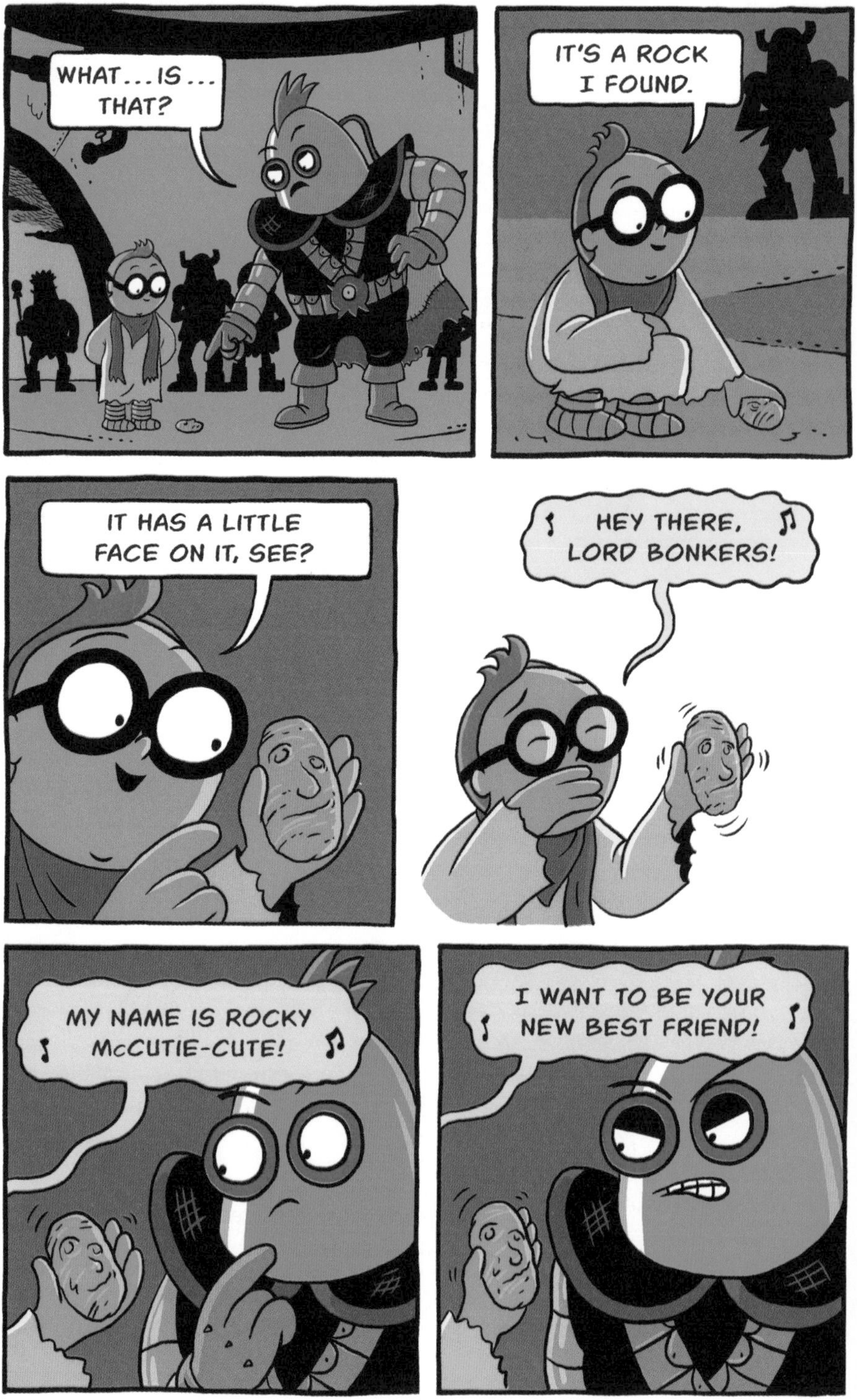
WHAT...IS... THAT?
IT'S A ROCK I FOUND.
IT HAS A LITTLE FACE ON IT, SEE?
HEY THERE, LORD BONKERS!
MY NAME IS ROCKY McCUTIE-CUTE!
I WANT TO BE YOUR NEW BEST FRIEND!

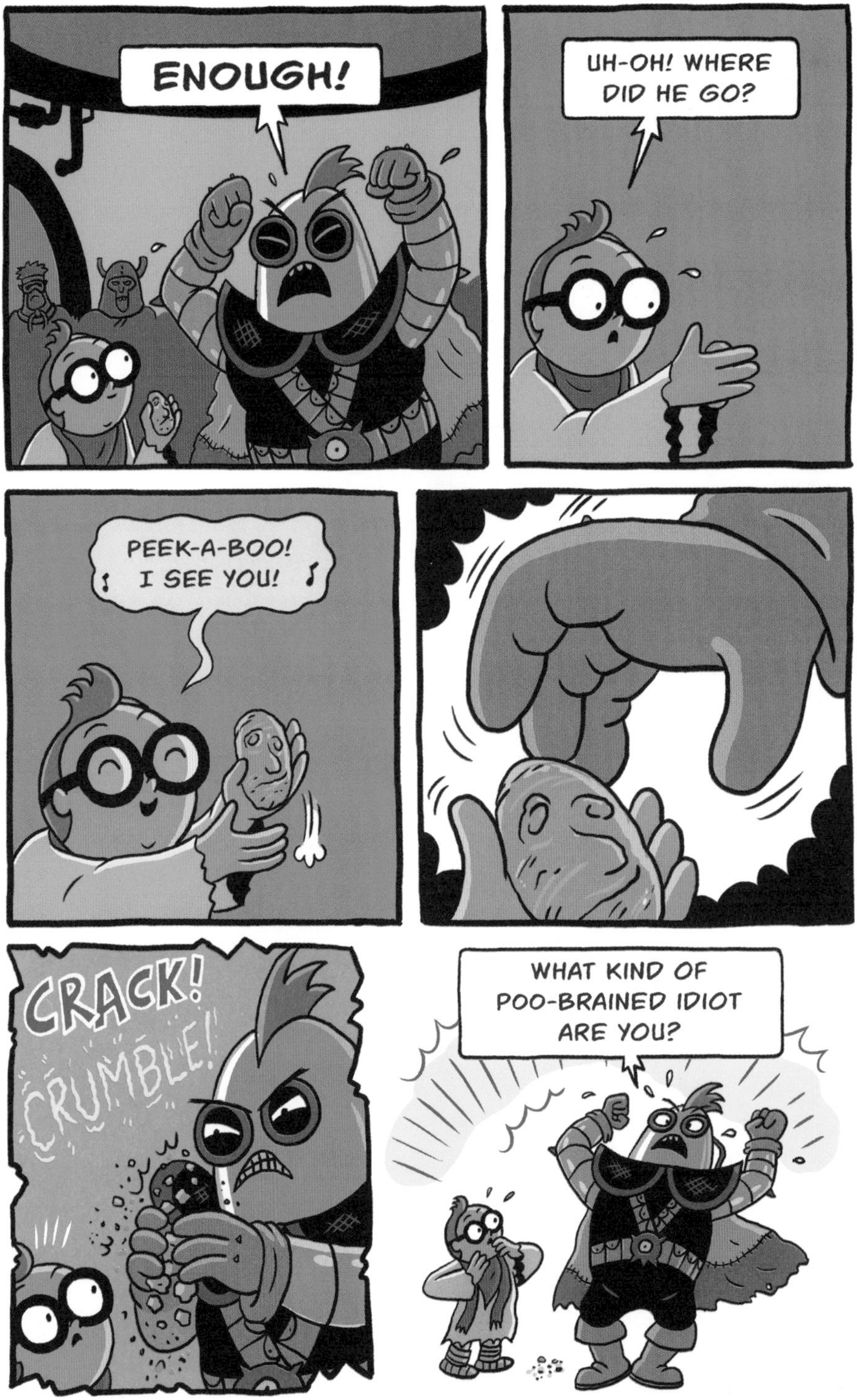

ENOUGH!
UH-OH! WHERE DID HE GO?
PEEK-A-BOO! I SEE YOU!
CRACK!
CRUMBLE!
WHAT KIND OF POO-BRAINED IDIOT ARE YOU?

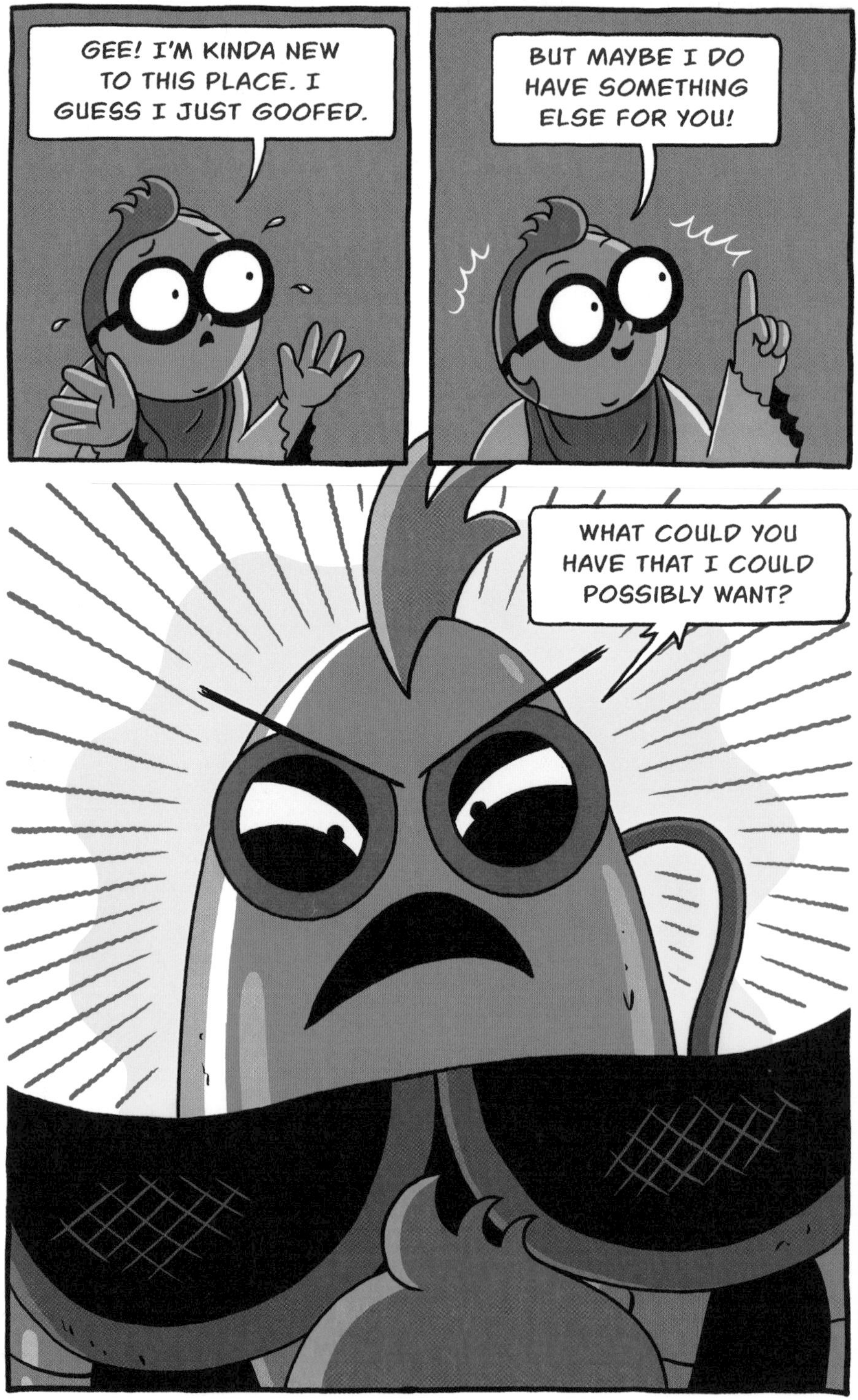
GEE! I'M KINDA NEW TO THIS PLACE. I GUESS I JUST GOOFED.
BUT MAYBE I DO HAVE SOMETHING ELSE FOR YOU!
WHAT COULD YOU HAVE THAT I COULD POSSIBLY WANT?

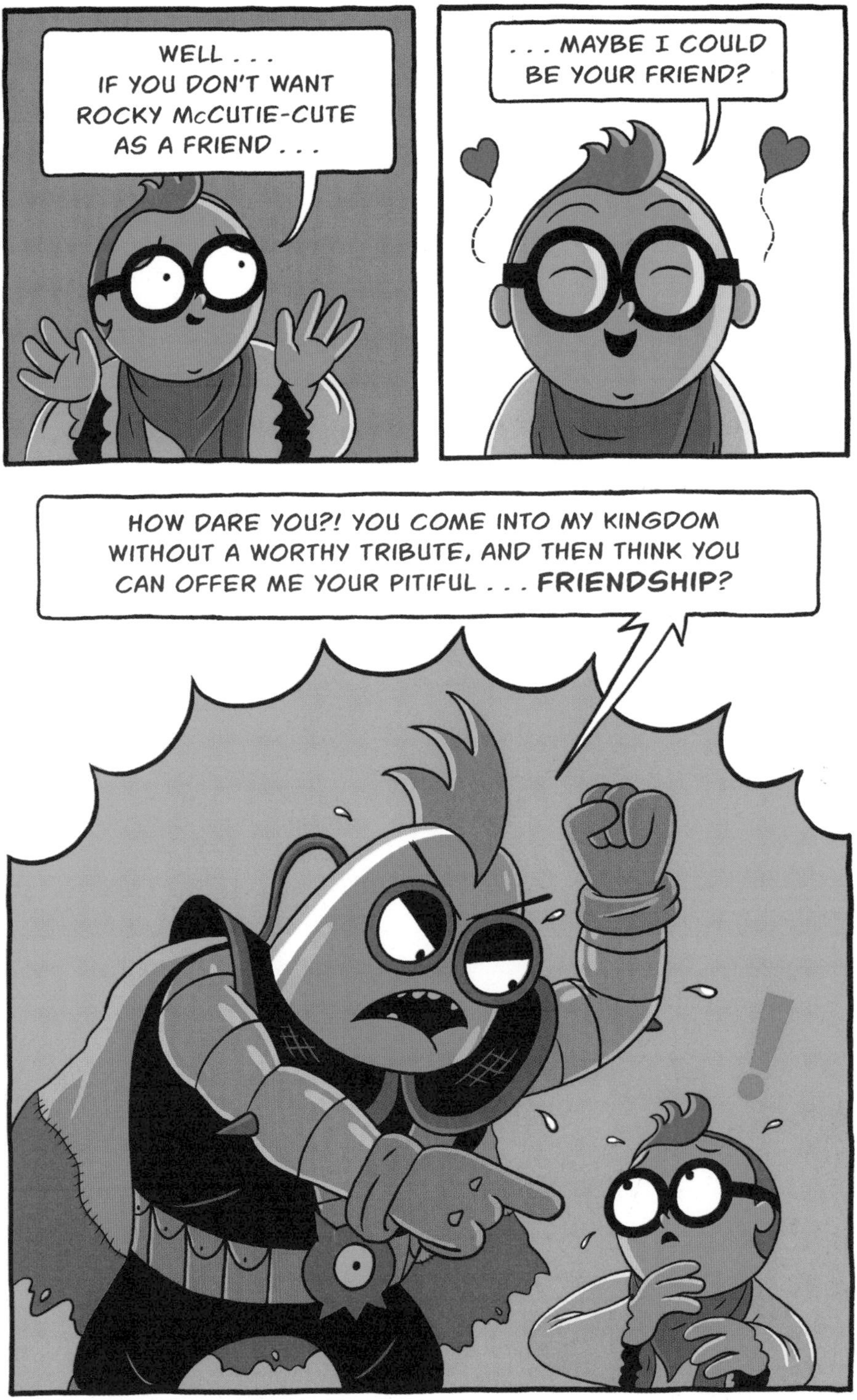
WELL . . .
IF YOU DON'T WANT ROCKY McCUTIE-CUTE AS A FRIEND . . .
. . . MAYBE I COULD BE YOUR FRIEND?
HOW DARE YOU?! YOU COME INTO MY KINGDOM WITHOUT A WORTHY TRIBUTE, AND THEN THINK YOU CAN OFFER ME YOUR PITIFUL . . . FRIENDSHIP?
!

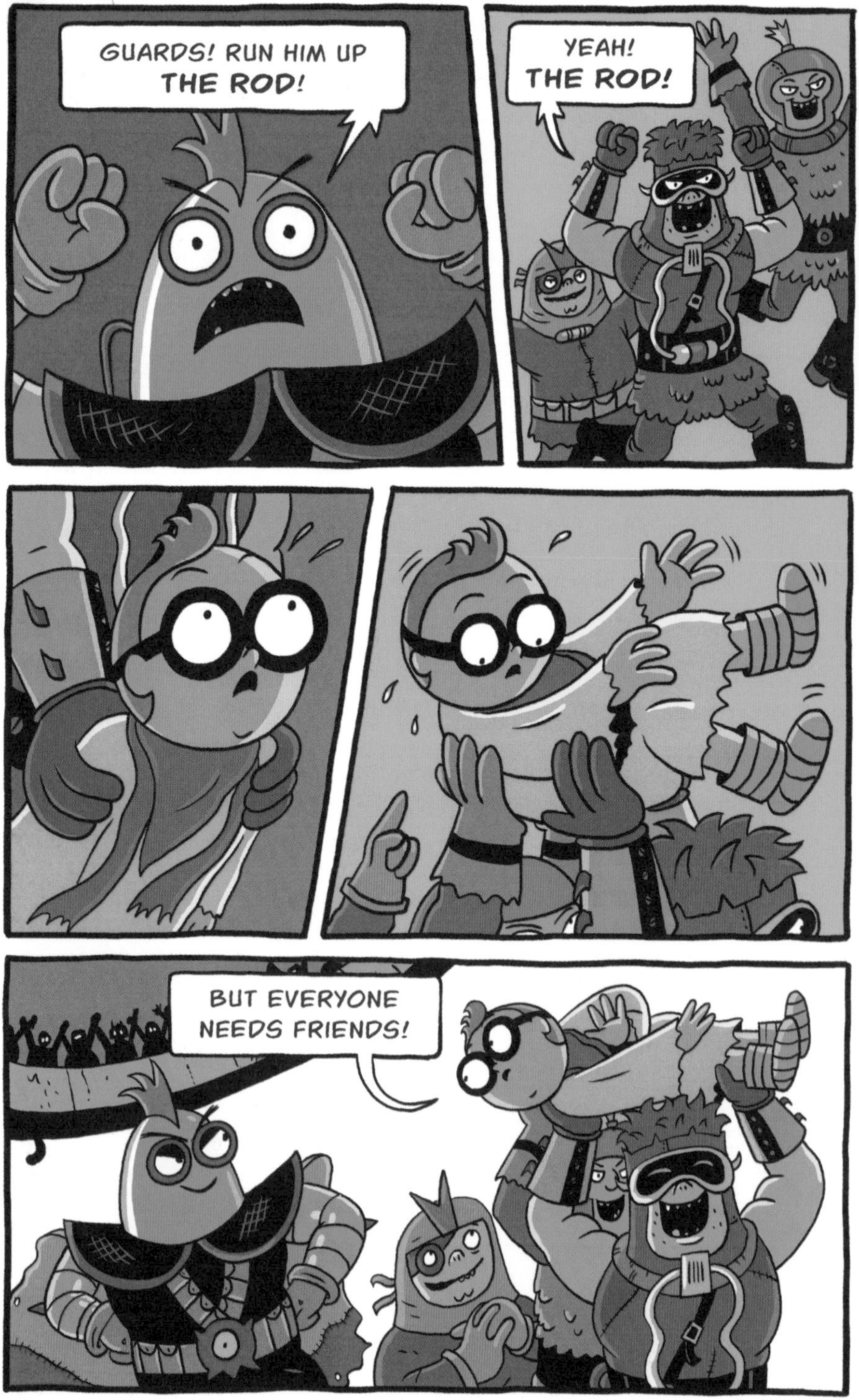
GUARDS! RUN HIM UP THE ROD!
YEAH! THE ROD!
BUT EVERYONE NEEDS FRIENDS!

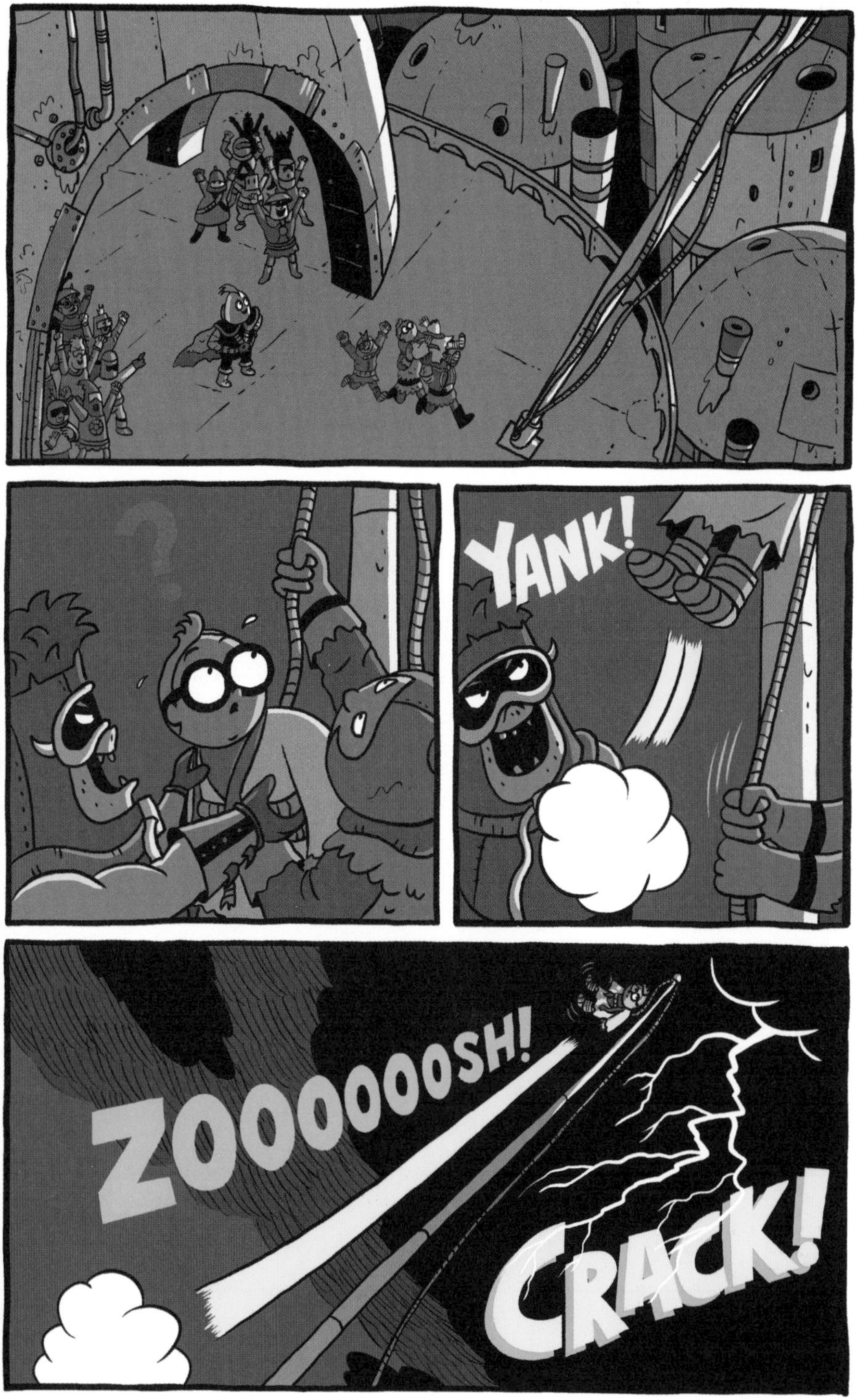
?
YANK!
ZOOOOOOOSH!
CRACK!

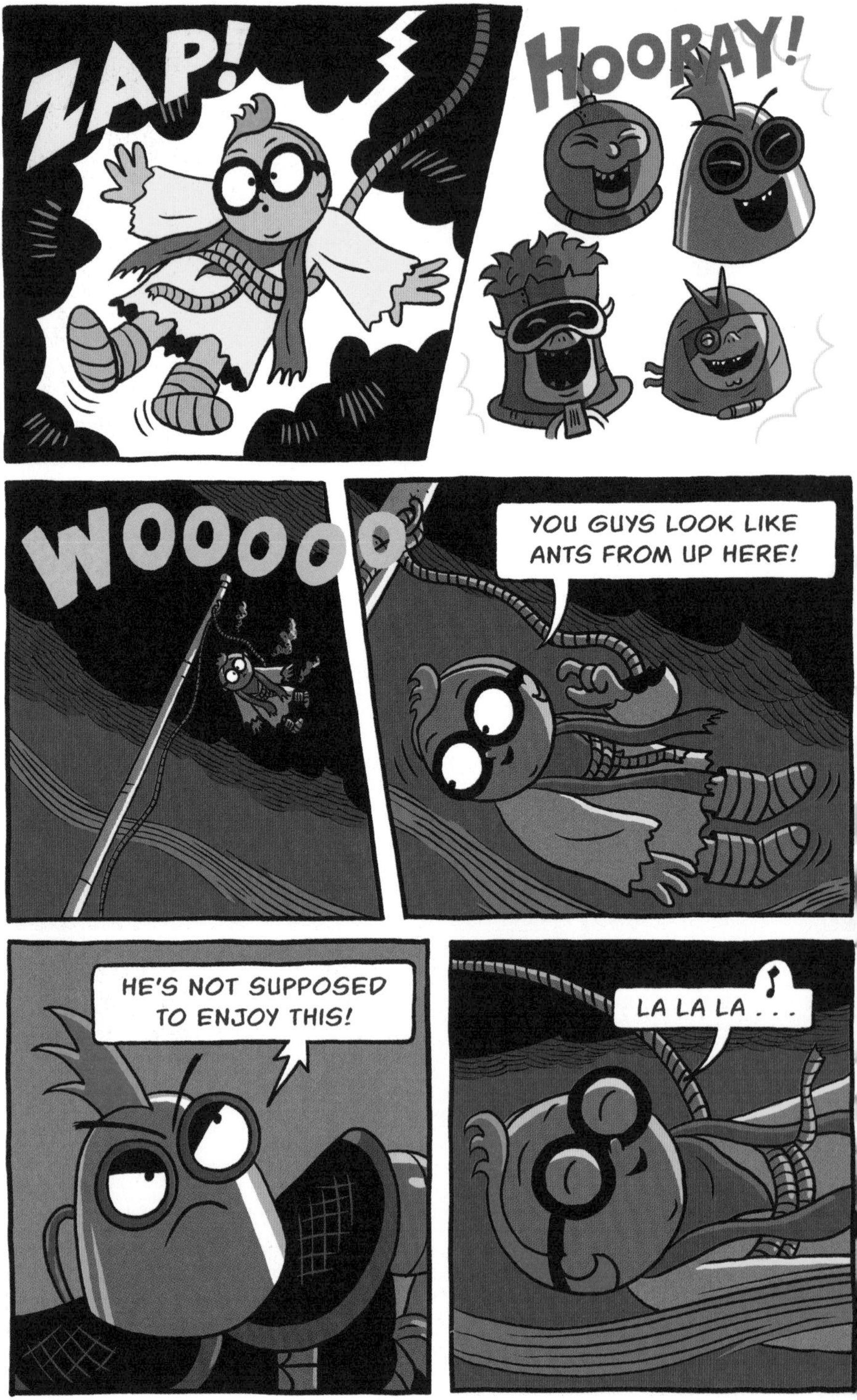
ZAP!
HOORAY!
WOOOOO
YOU GUYS LOOK LIKE ANTS FROM UP HERE!
HE'S NOT SUPPOSED TO ENJOY THIS!
LA LA LA . . .

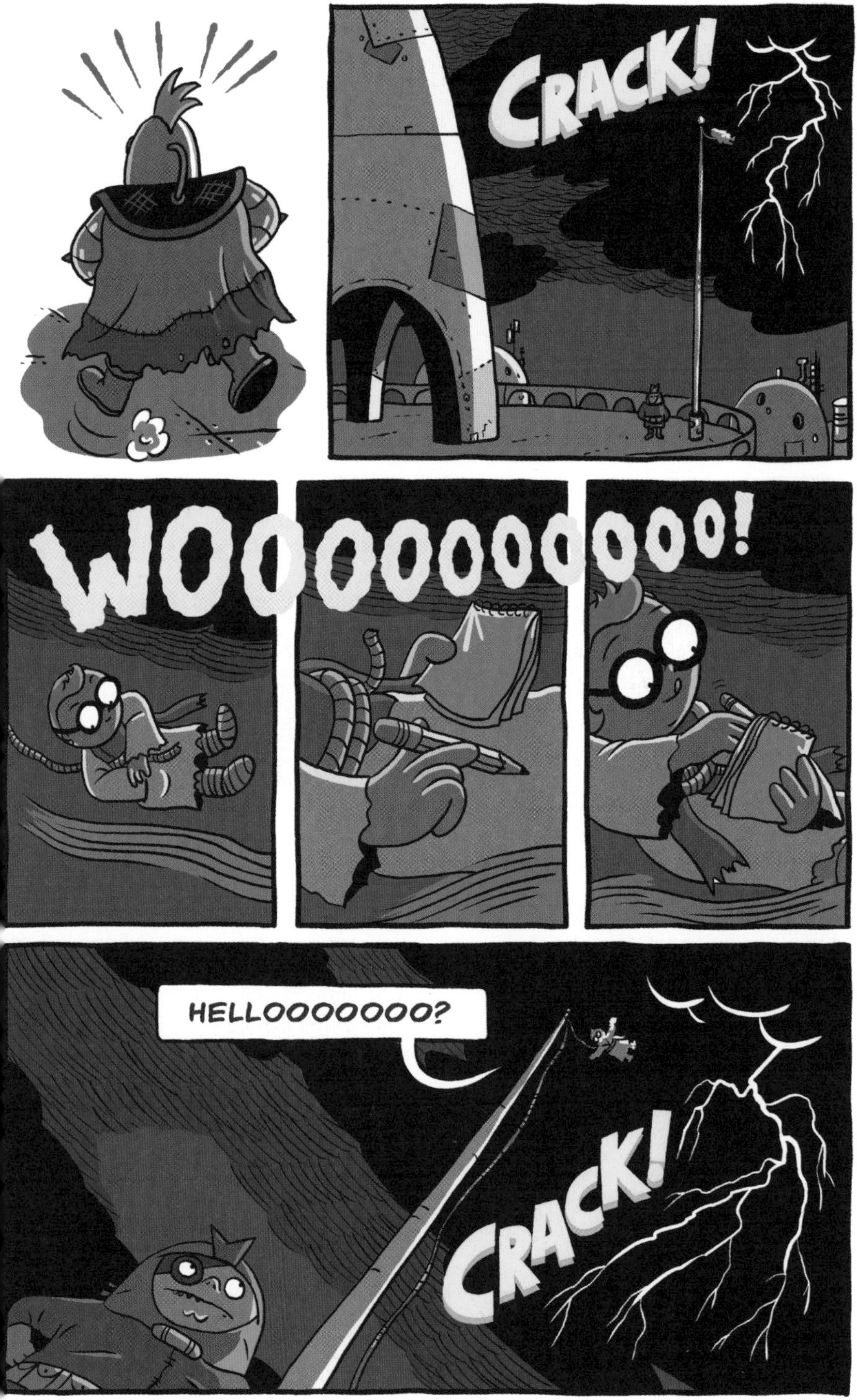

CRACK!
WOOOOOOOOOO!
HELLOOOOOOOO?
CRACK!

118

CHAPTER 10

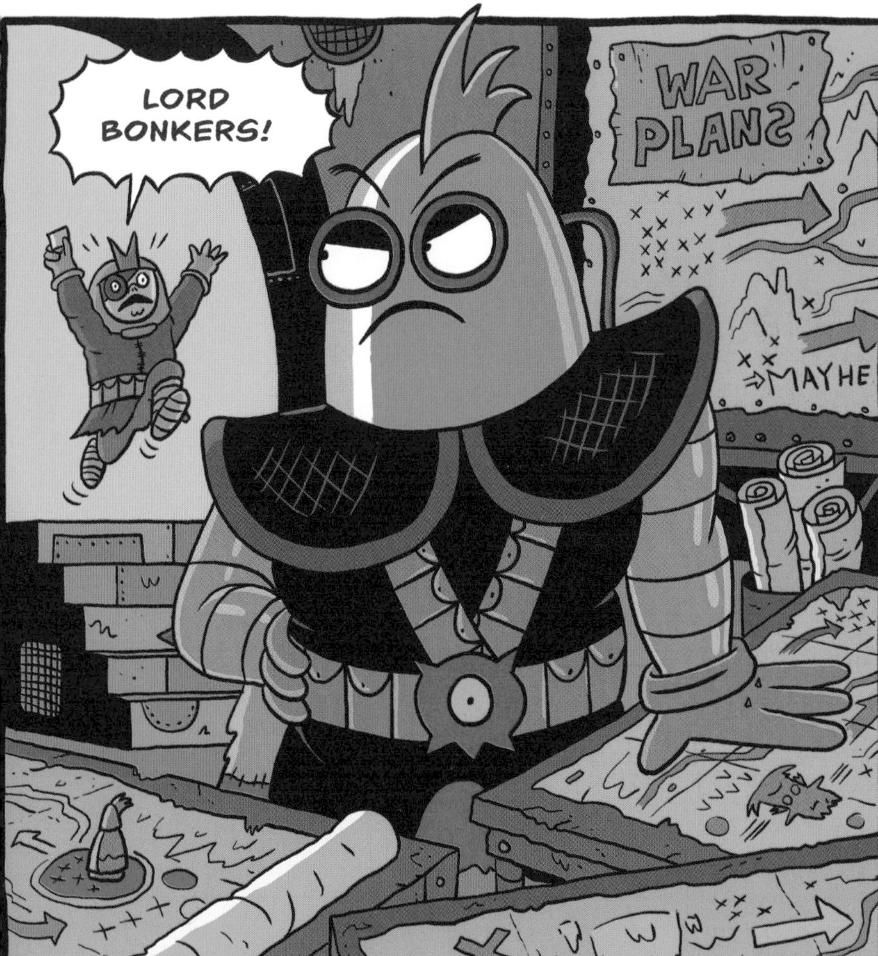
LORD BONKERS!
WAR PLANS
MAYHE

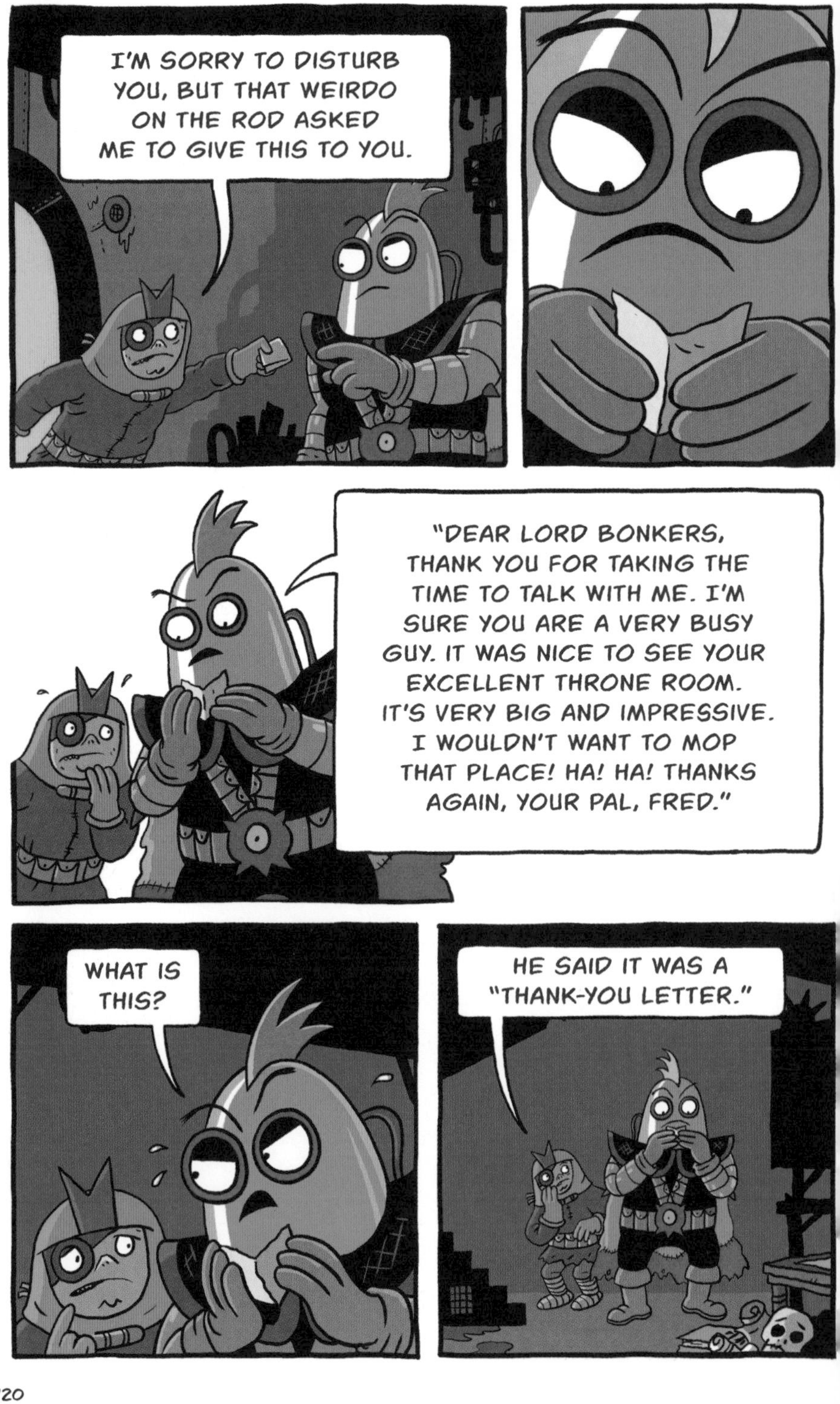
I'M SORRY TO DISTURB YOU, BUT THAT WEIRDO ON THE ROD ASKED ME TO GIVE THIS TO YOU.
"DEAR LORD BONKERS, THANK YOU FOR TAKING THE TIME TO TALK WITH ME. I'M SURE YOU ARE A VERY BUSY GUY. IT WAS NICE TO SEE YOUR EXCELLENT THRONE ROOM. IT'S VERY BIG AND IMPRESSIVE. I WOULDN'T WANT TO MOP THAT PLACE! HA! HA! THANKS AGAIN, YOUR PAL, FRED."
WHAT IS THIS?
HE SAID IT WAS A "THANK-YOU LETTER."

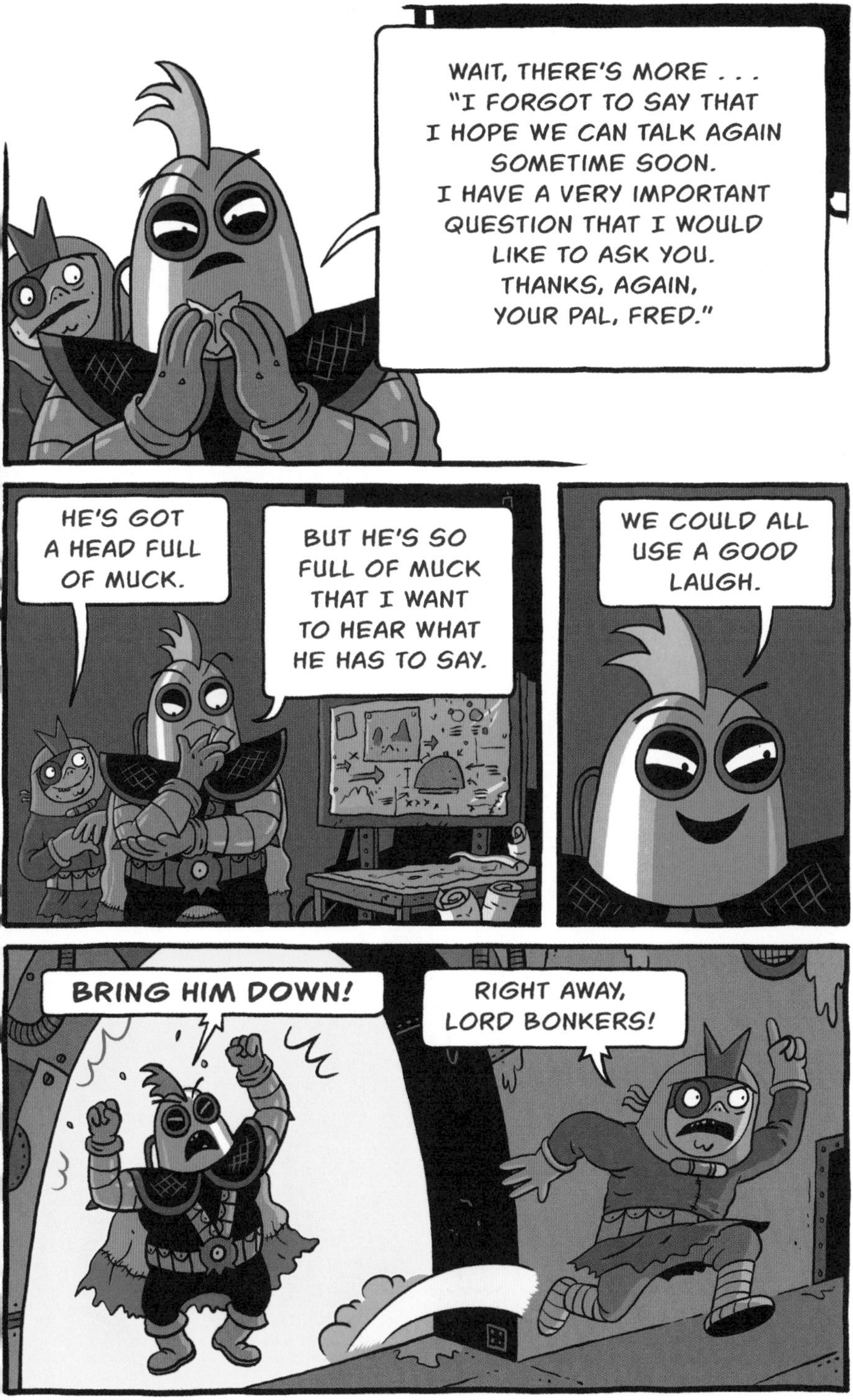
WAIT, THERE'S MORE . . .
"I FORGOT TO SAY THAT I HOPE WE CAN TALK AGAIN SOMETIME SOON. I HAVE A VERY IMPORTANT QUESTION THAT I WOULD LIKE TO ASK YOU. THANKS, AGAIN, YOUR PAL, FRED."
HE'S GOT A HEAD FULL OF MUCK.
BUT HE'S SO FULL OF MUCK THAT I WANT TO HEAR WHAT HE HAS TO SAY.
WE COULD ALL USE A GOOD LAUGH.
BRING HIM DOWN!
RIGHT AWAY, LORD BONKERS!

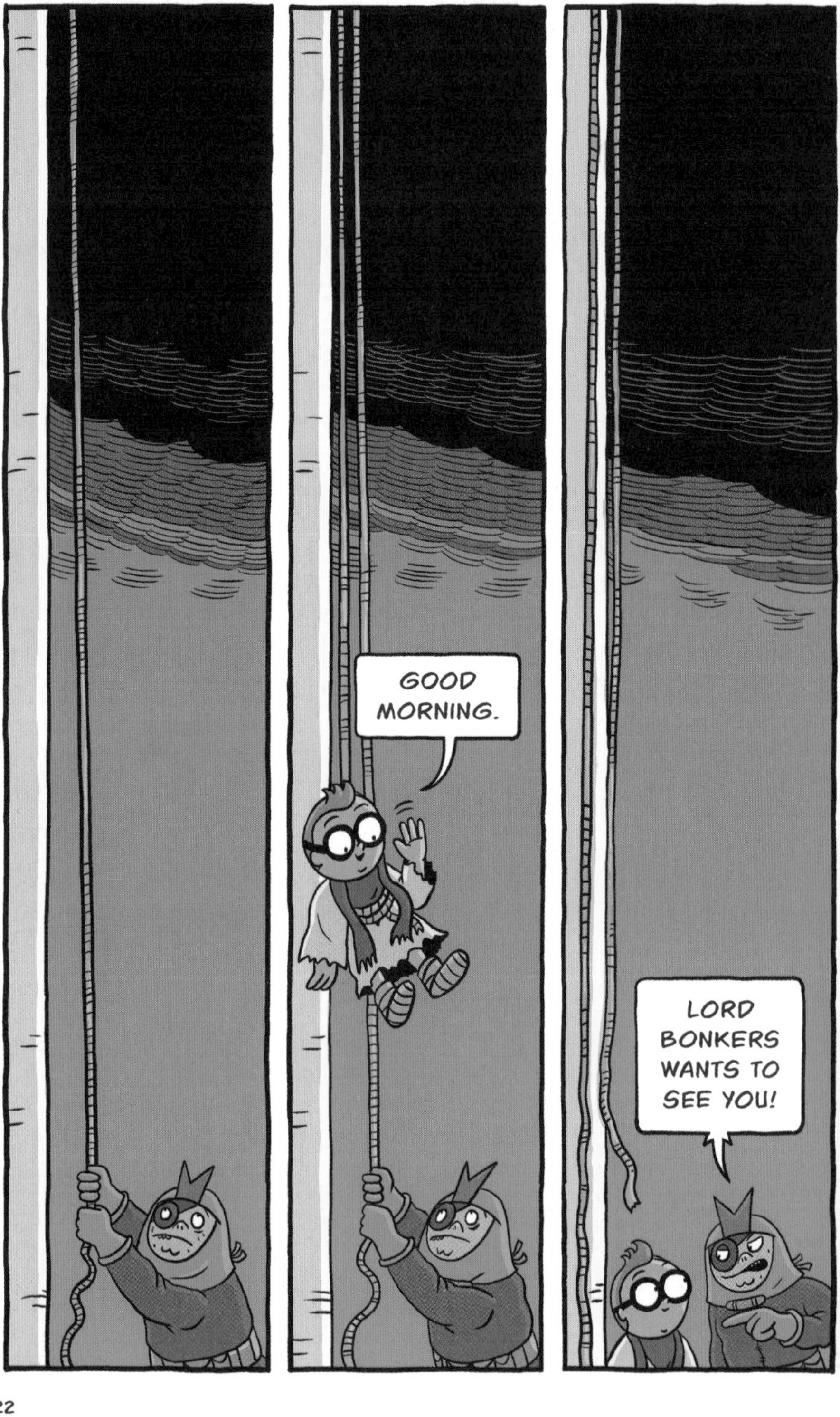
GOOD MORNING.
LORD BONKERS WANTS TO SEE YOU!

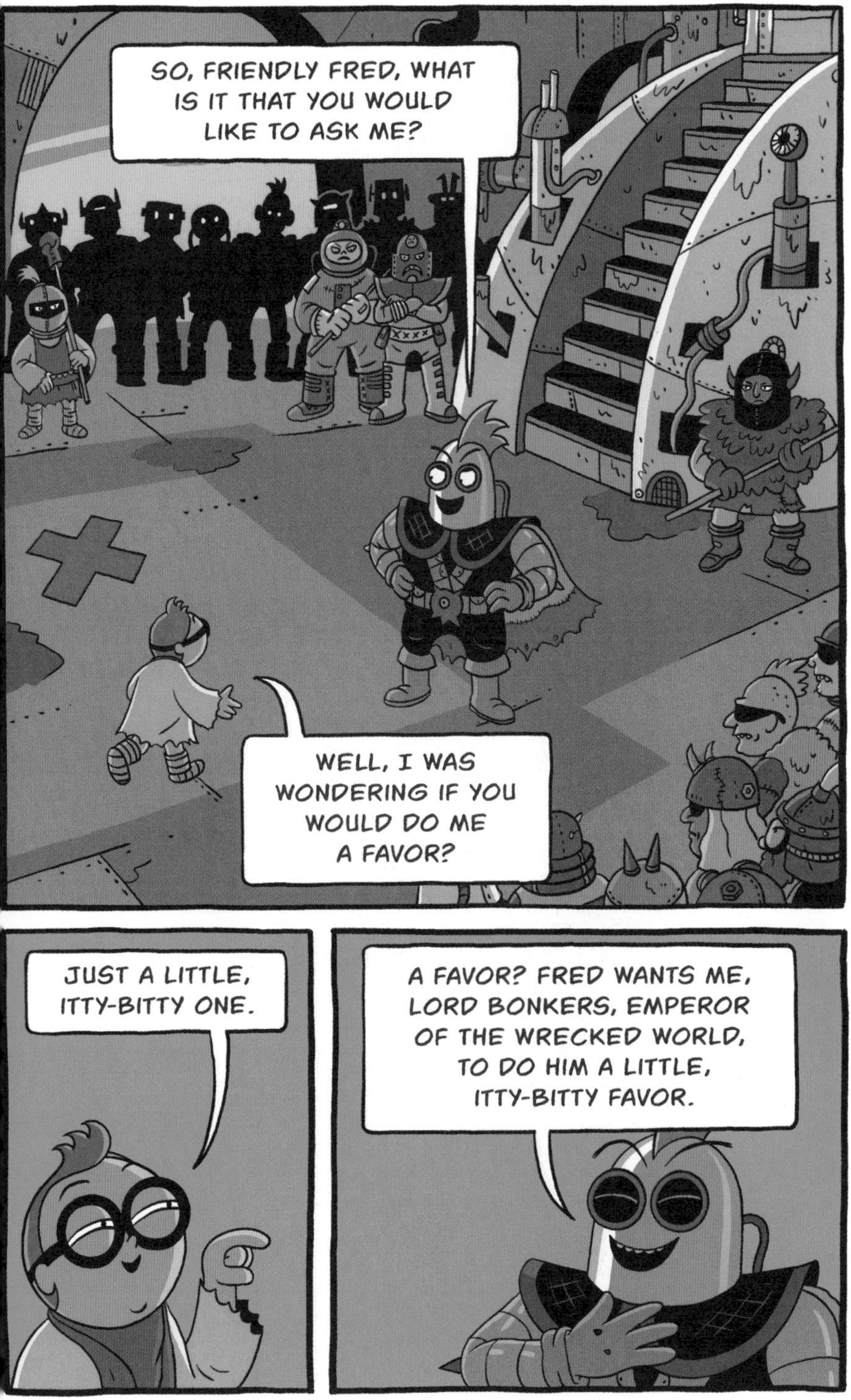
SO, FRIENDLY FRED, WHAT IS IT THAT YOU WOULD LIKE TO ASK ME?
WELL, I WAS WONDERING IF YOU WOULD DO ME A FAVOR?
JUST A LITTLE, ITTY-BITTY ONE.
A FAVOR? FRED WANTS ME, LORD BONKERS, EMPEROR OF THE WRECKED WORLD, TO DO HIM A LITTLE, ITTY-BITTY FAVOR.

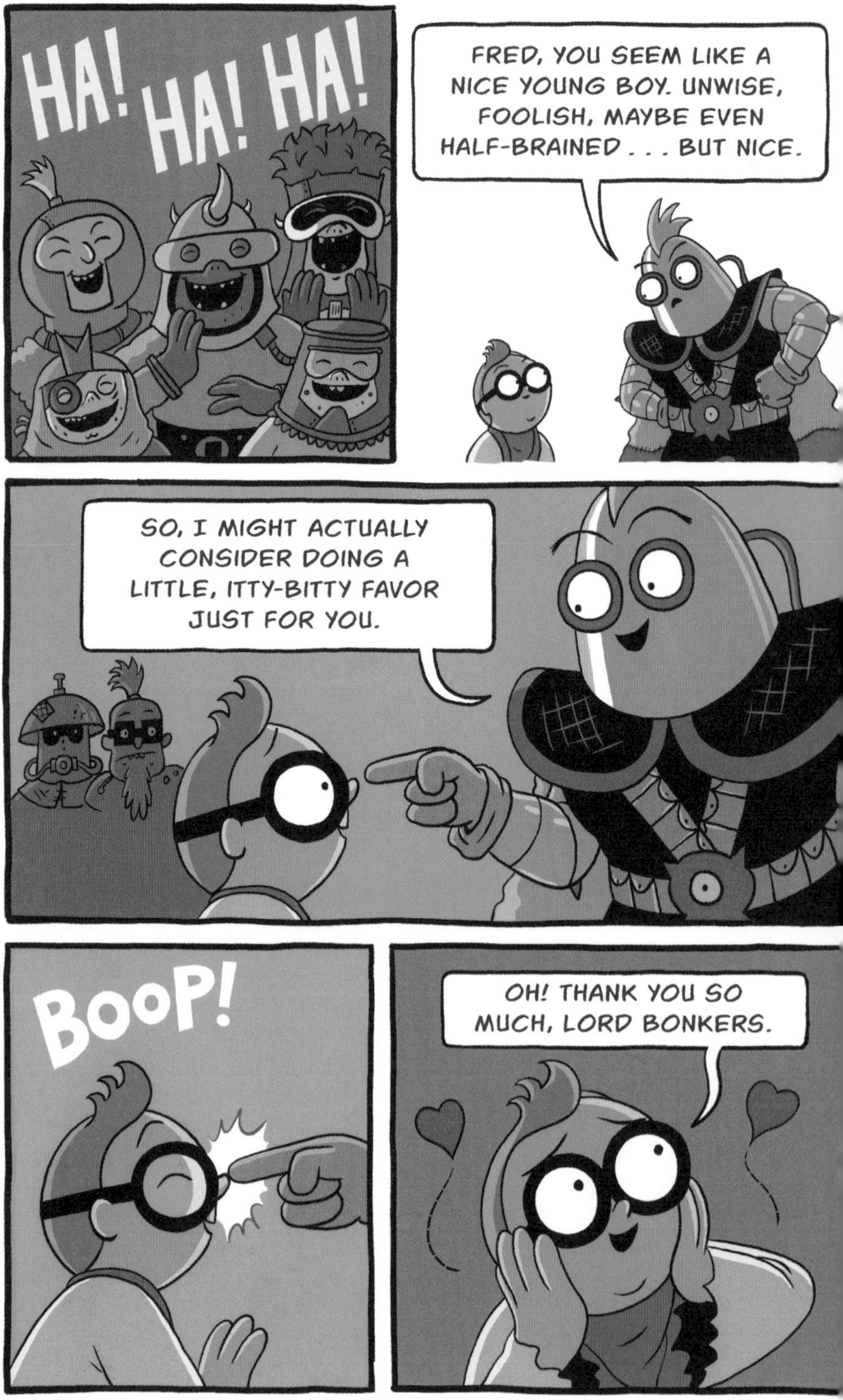
HA! HA! HA!
FRED, YOU SEEM LIKE A NICE YOUNG BOY. UNWISE, FOOLISH, MAYBE EVEN HALF-BRAINED . . . BUT NICE.
SO, I MIGHT ACTUALLY CONSIDER DOING A LITTLE, ITTY-BITTY FAVOR JUST FOR YOU.
BOOP!
OH! THANK YOU SO MUCH, LORD BONKERS.

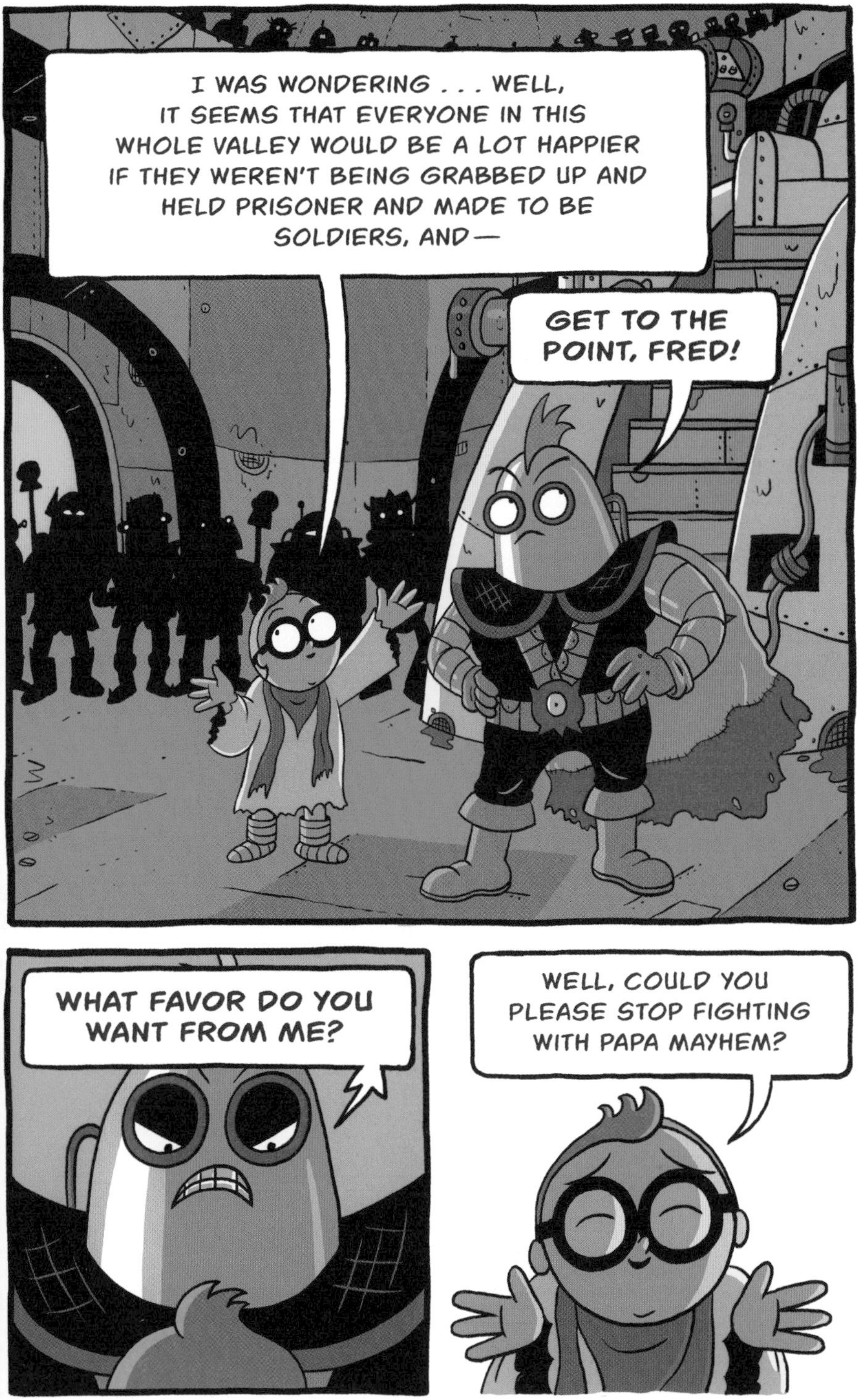
I WAS WONDERING . . . WELL, IT SEEMS THAT EVERYONE IN THIS WHOLE VALLEY WOULD BE A LOT HAPPIER IF THEY WEREN'T BEING GRABBED UP AND HELD PRISONER AND MADE TO BE SOLDIERS, AND—
GET TO THE POINT, FRED!
WHAT FAVOR DO YOU WANT FROM ME?
WELL, COULD YOU PLEASE STOP FIGHTING WITH PAPA MAYHEM?

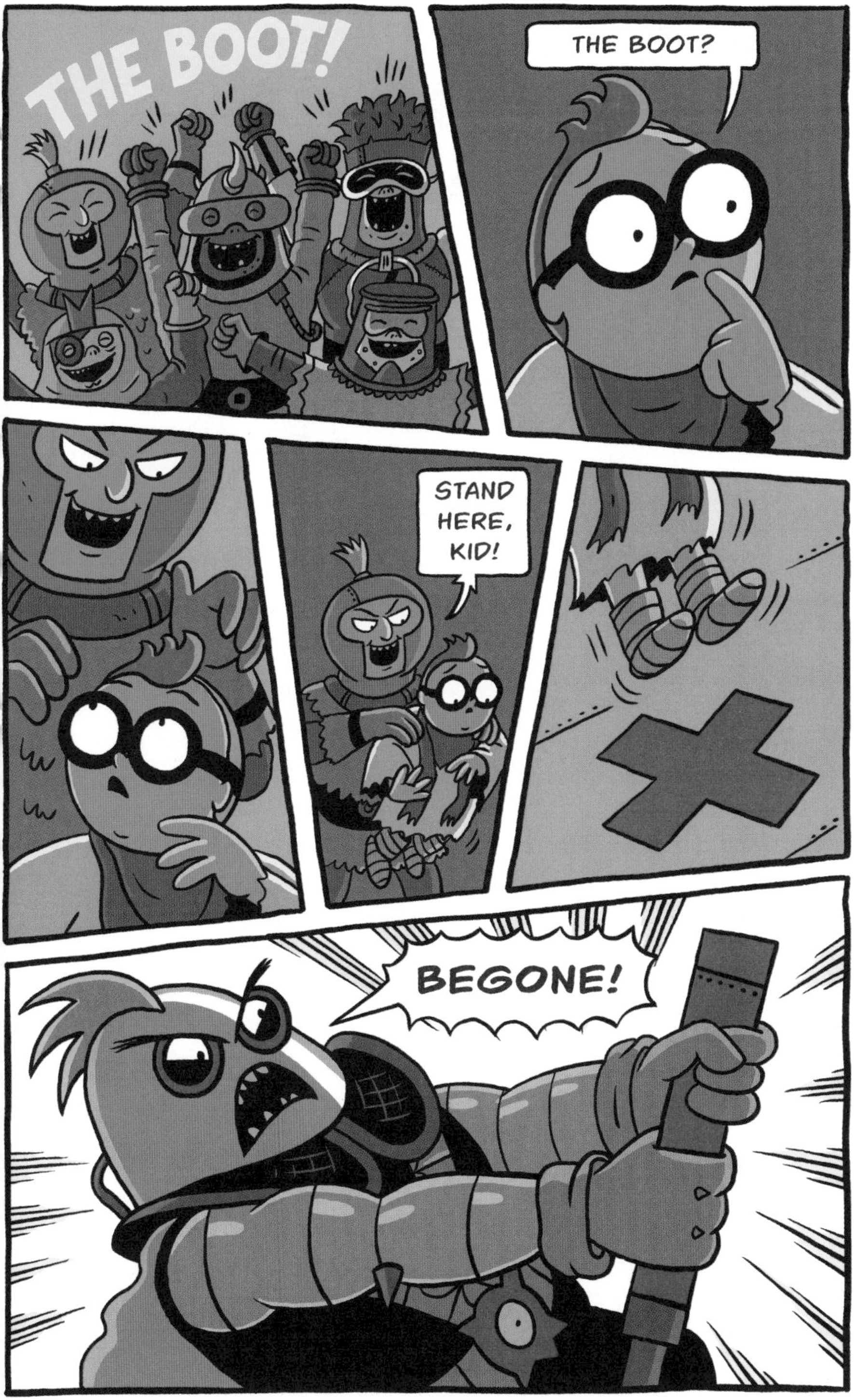
THE BOOT!
THE BOOT?
STAND HERE, KID!
BEGONE!

128

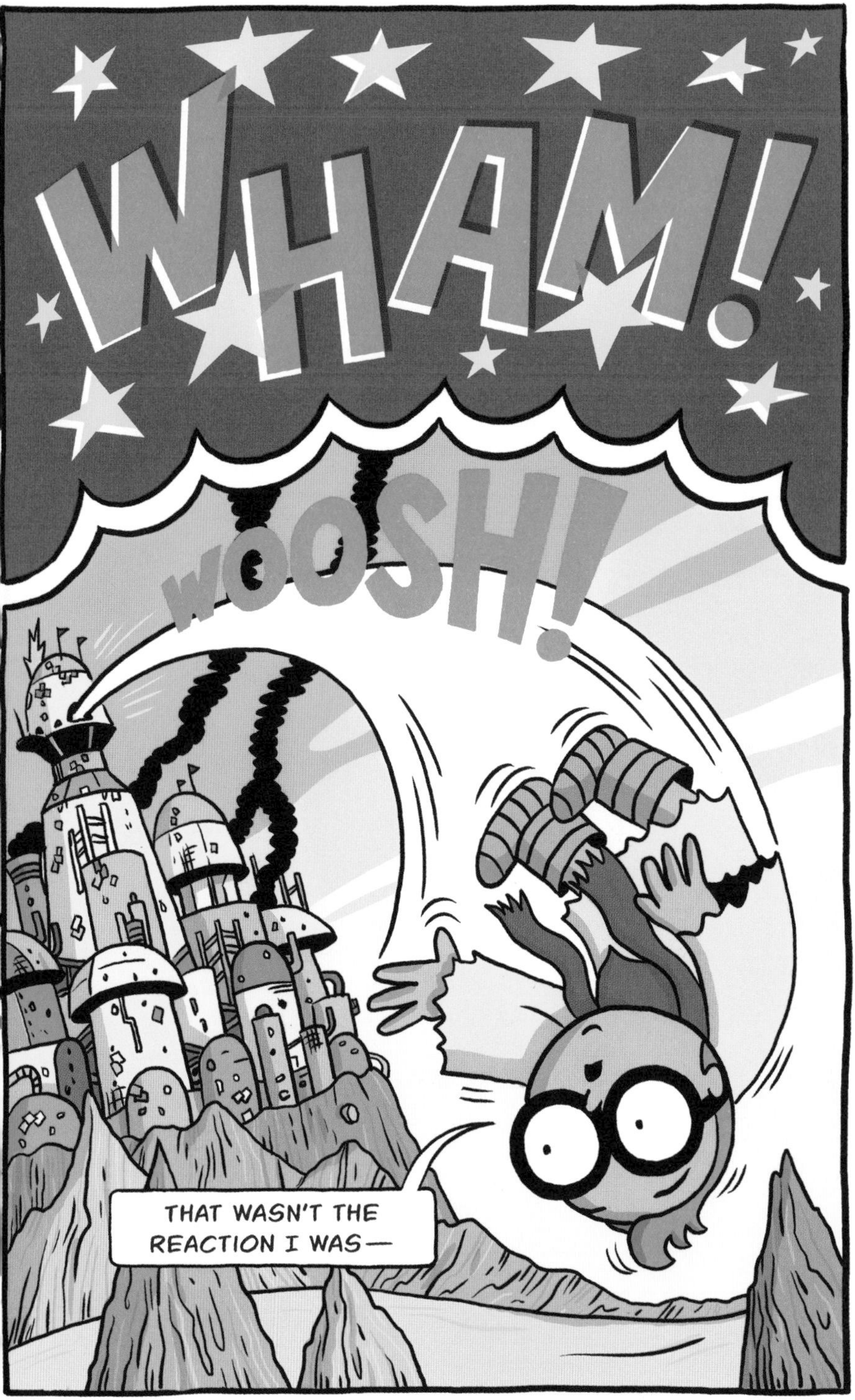
WHAM!
WOOSH!
THAT WASN'T THE REACTION I WAS—

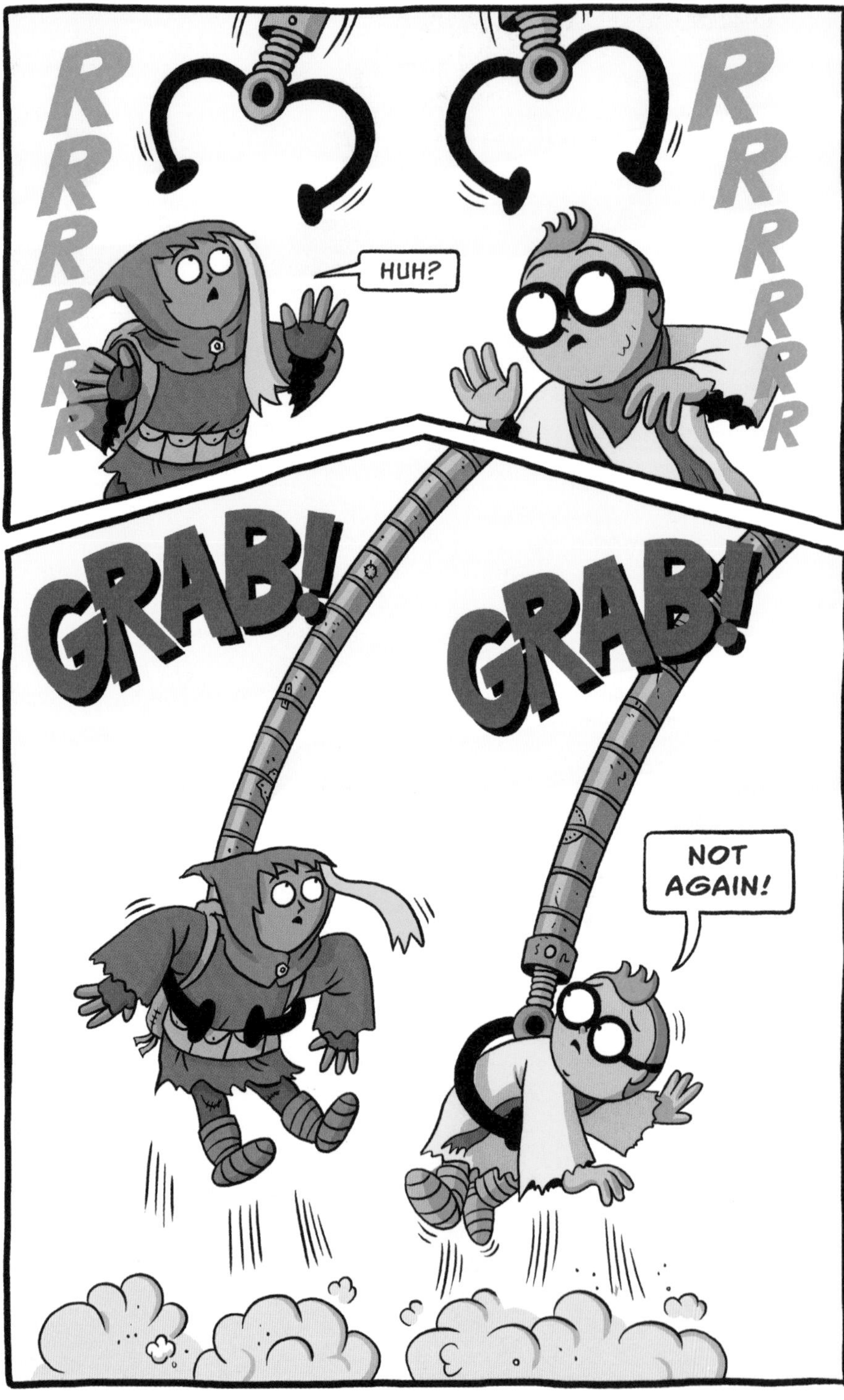
RRRRRRR
HUH?
RRRRRRR
GRAB!
GRAB!
NOT AGAIN!

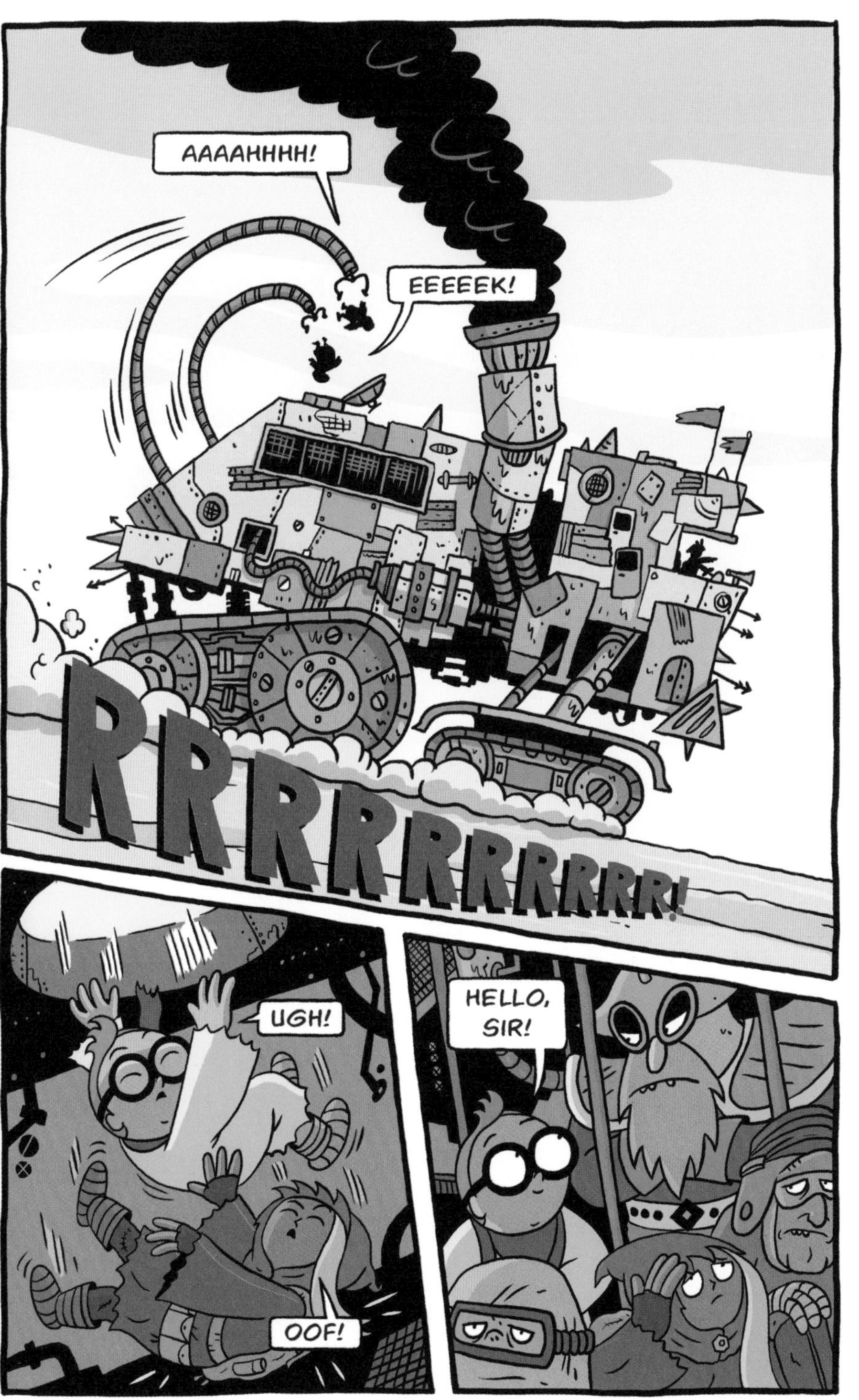
AAAAHHHH!
EEEEEK!
RRRRRRRRRRRR!
UGH!
OOF!
HELLO, SIR!

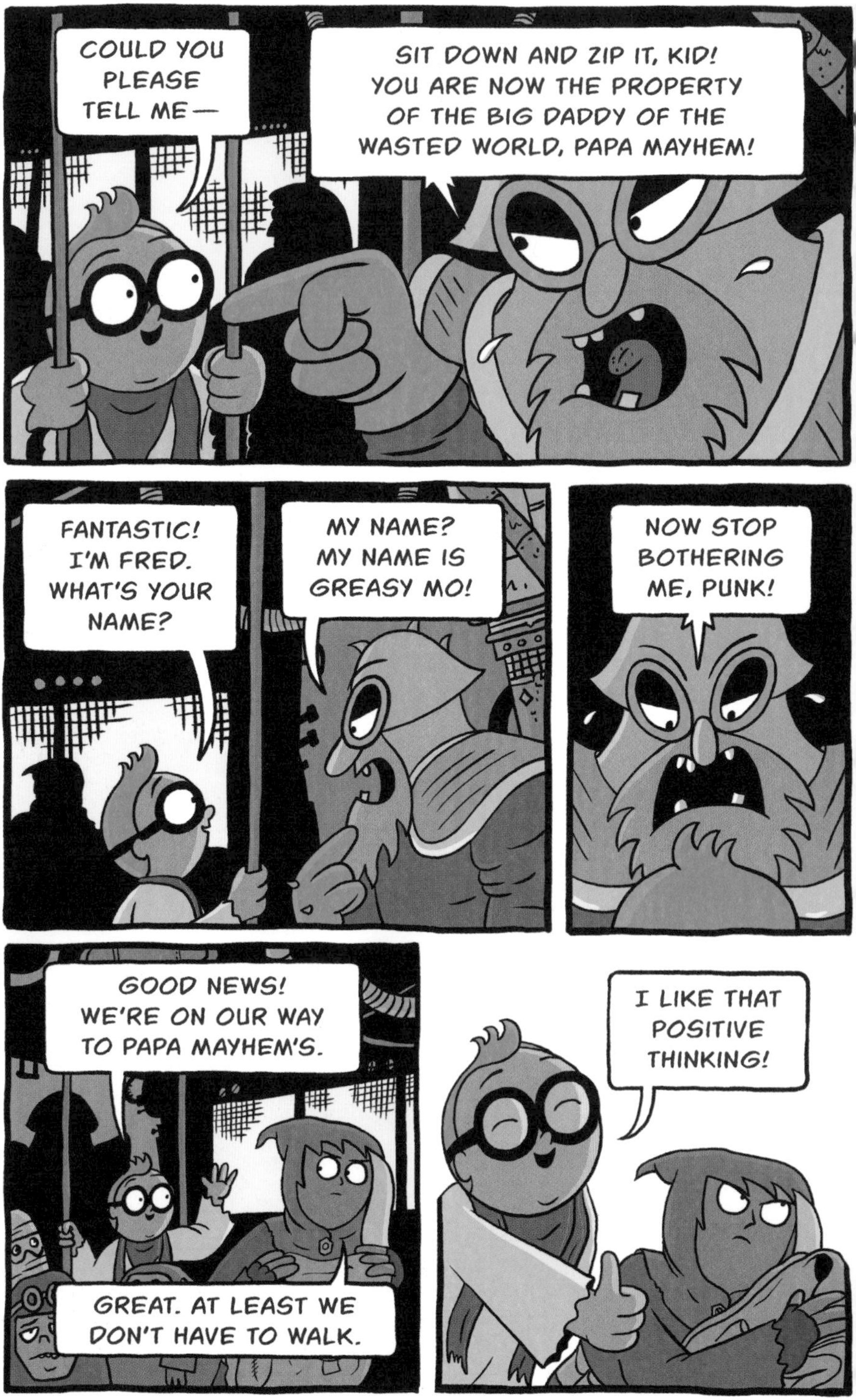
COULD YOU PLEASE TELL ME—
SIT DOWN AND ZIP IT, KID! YOU ARE NOW THE PROPERTY OF THE BIG DADDY OF THE WASTED WORLD, PAPA MAYHEM!
FANTASTIC! I'M FRED. WHAT'S YOUR NAME?
MY NAME? MY NAME IS GREASY MO!
NOW STOP BOTHERING ME, PUNK!
GOOD NEWS! WE'RE ON OUR WAY TO PAPA MAYHEM'S.
GREAT. AT LEAST WE DON'T HAVE TO WALK.
I LIKE THAT POSITIVE THINKING!

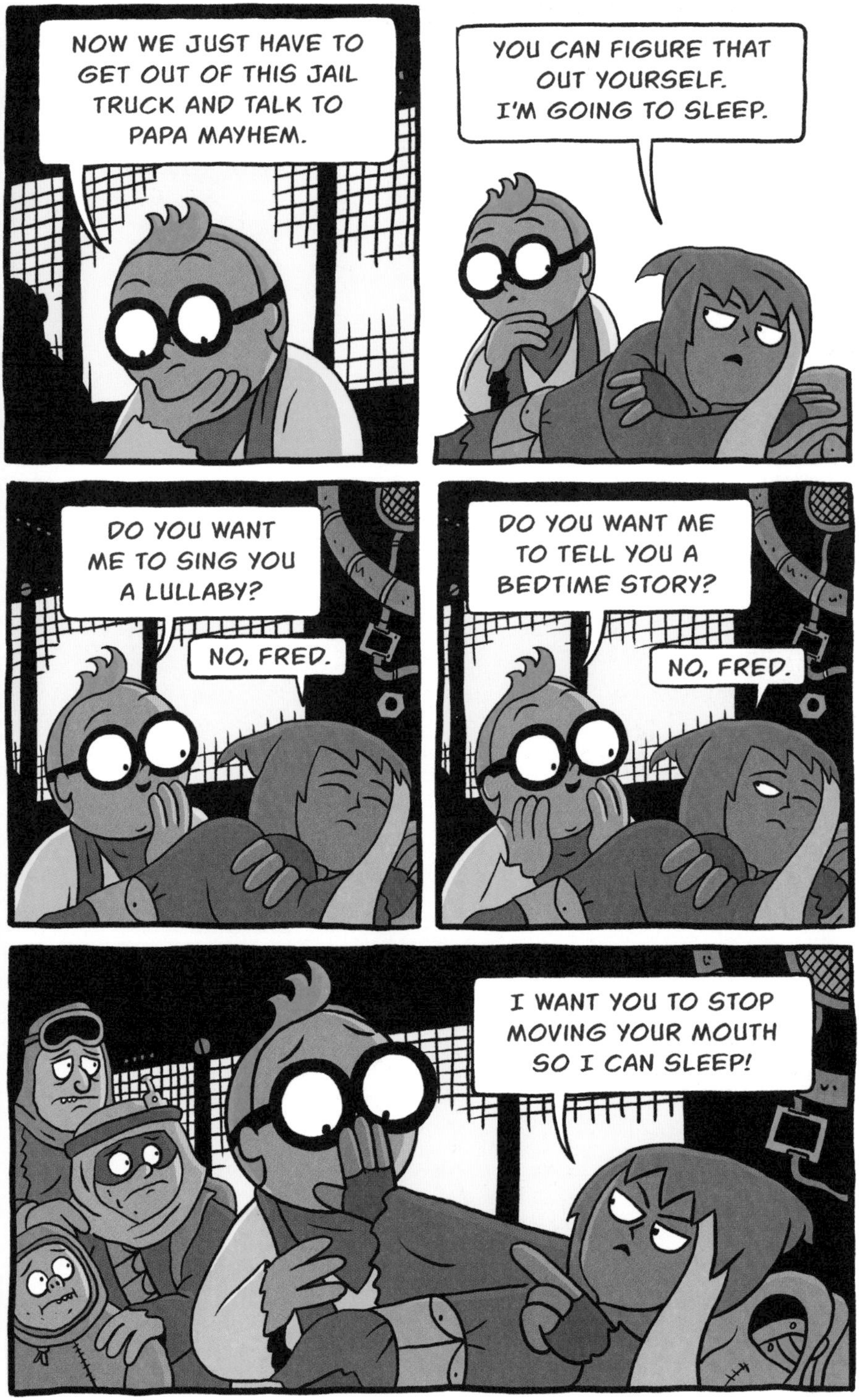
NOW WE JUST HAVE TO GET OUT OF THIS JAIL TRUCK AND TALK TO PAPA MAYHEM.
YOU CAN FIGURE THAT OUT YOURSELF. I'M GOING TO SLEEP.
DO YOU WANT ME TO SING YOU A LULLABY?
NO, FRED.
DO YOU WANT ME TO TELL YOU A BEDTIME STORY?
NO, FRED.
I WANT YOU TO STOP MOVING YOUR MOUTH SO I CAN SLEEP!

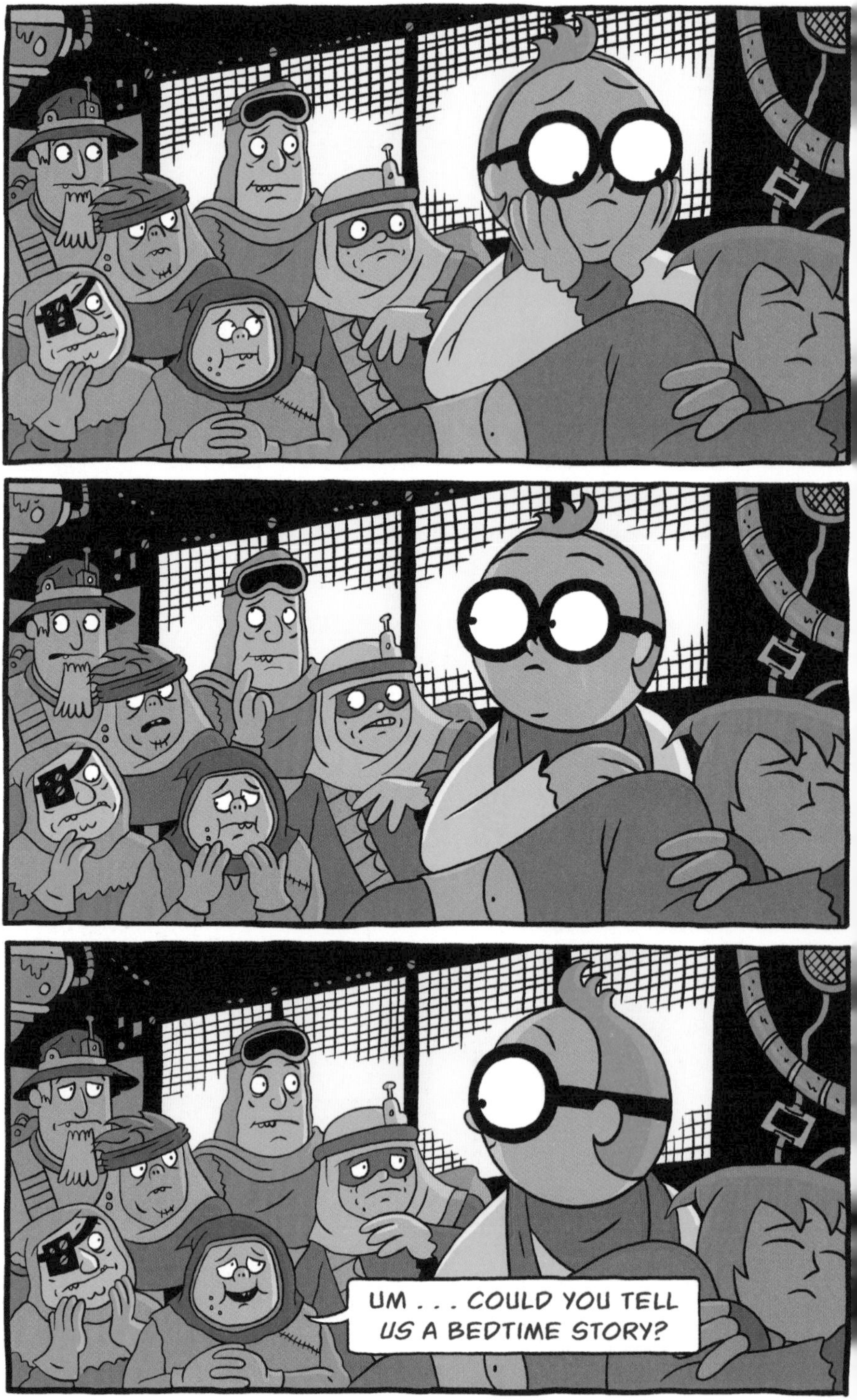
UM . . . COULD YOU TELL
US A BEDTIME STORY?

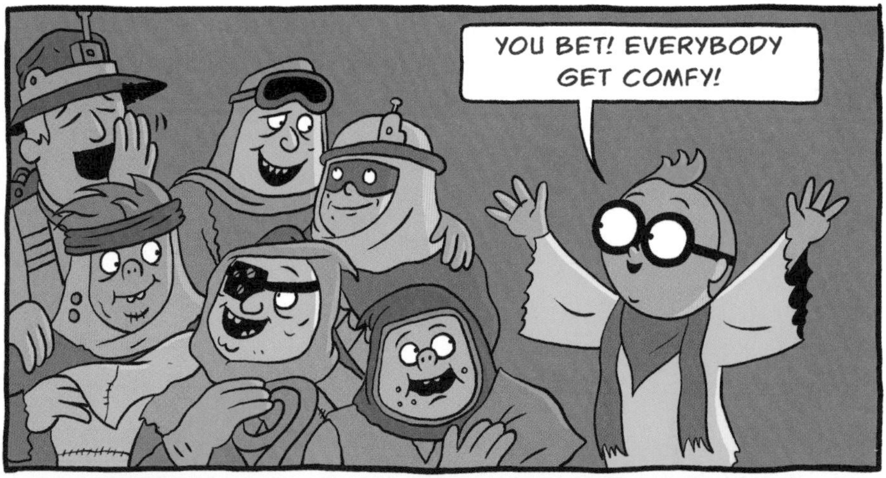
YOU BET! EVERYBODY GET COMFY!

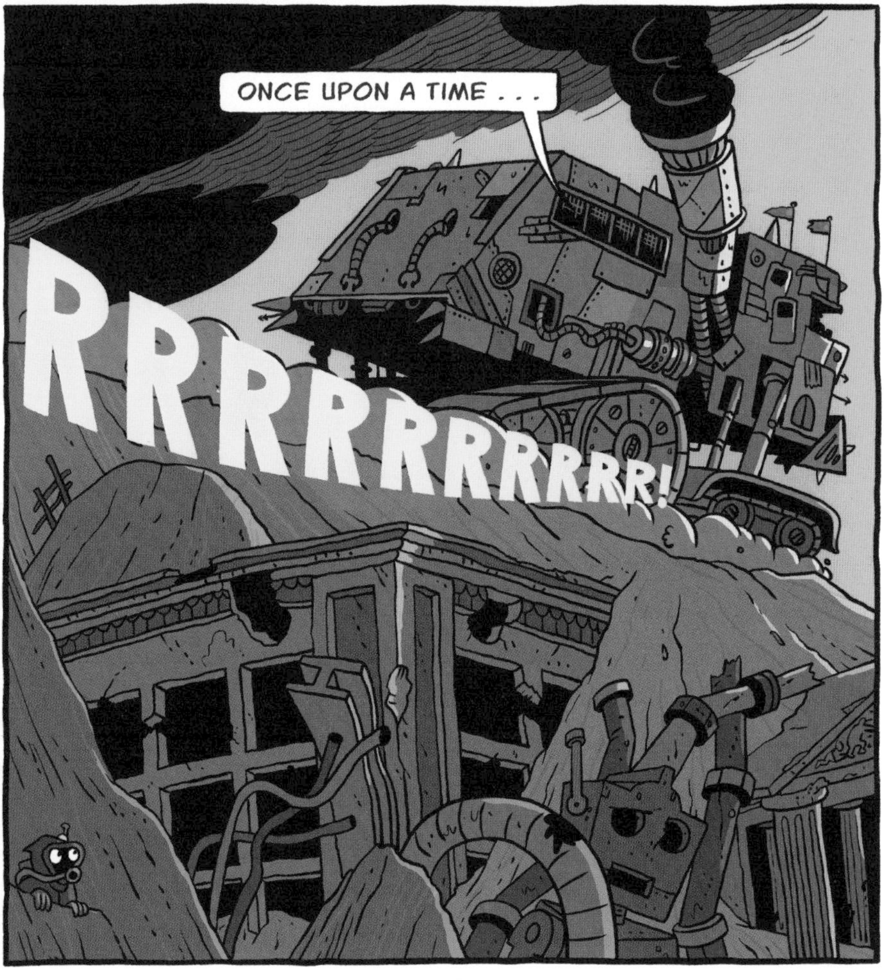
ONCE UPON A TIME . . .
RRRRRRRRRRRRR!

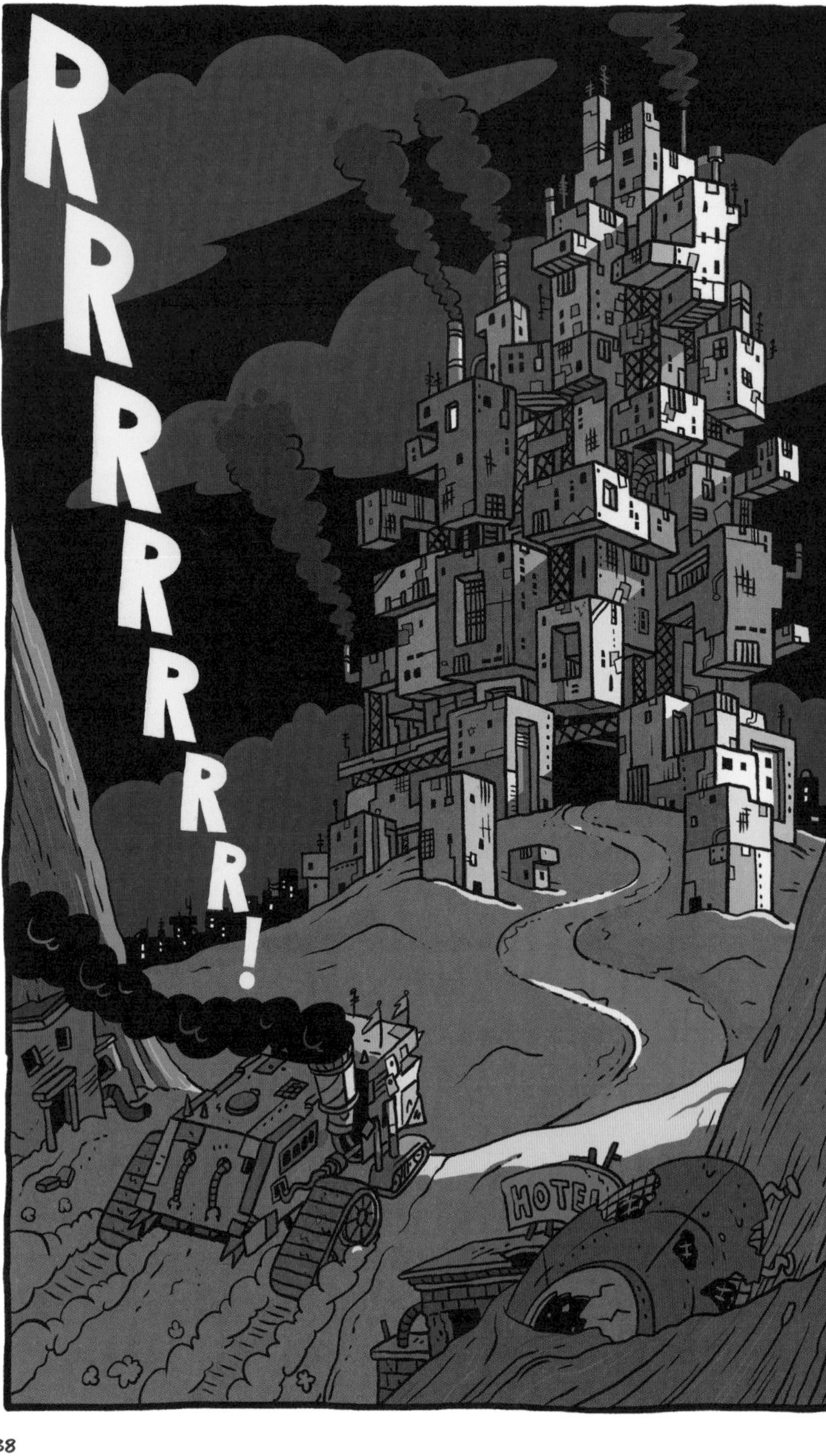
RRRRRRRR!
HOTE

CHAPTER 11

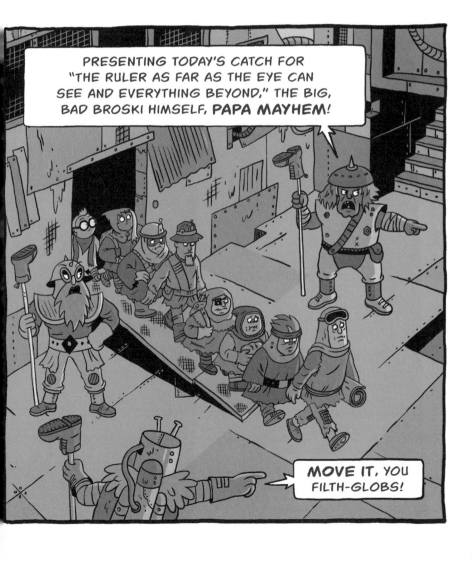

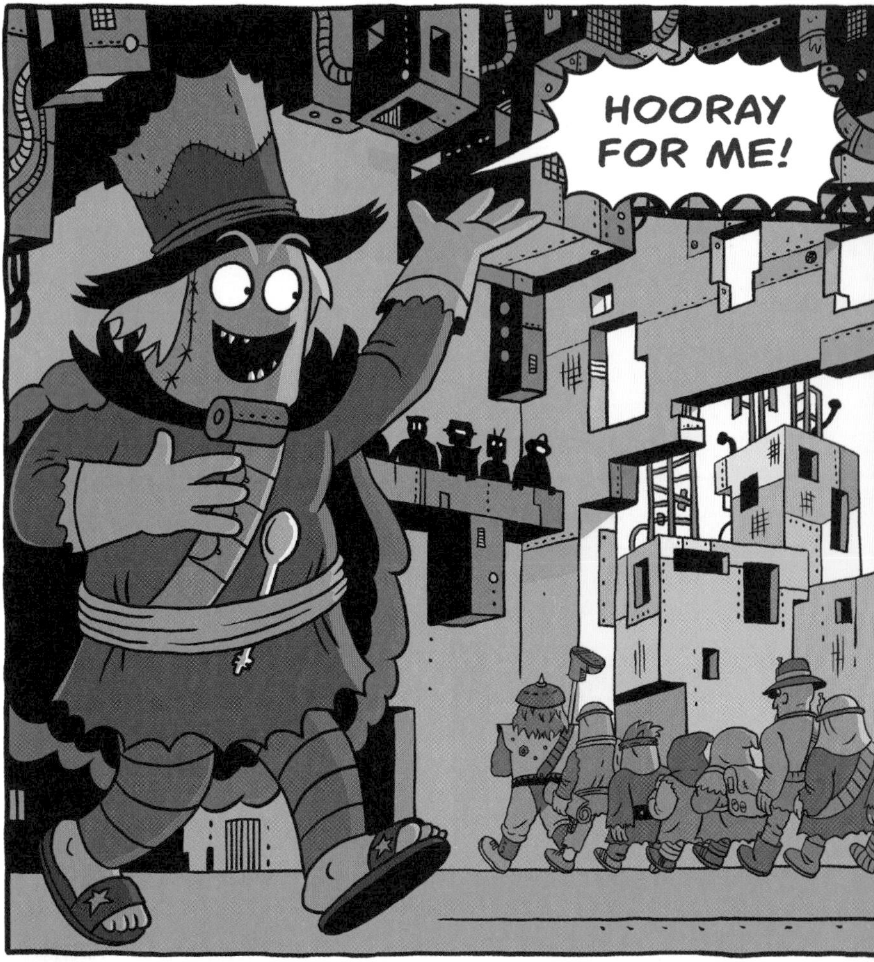
HOORAY FOR ME!

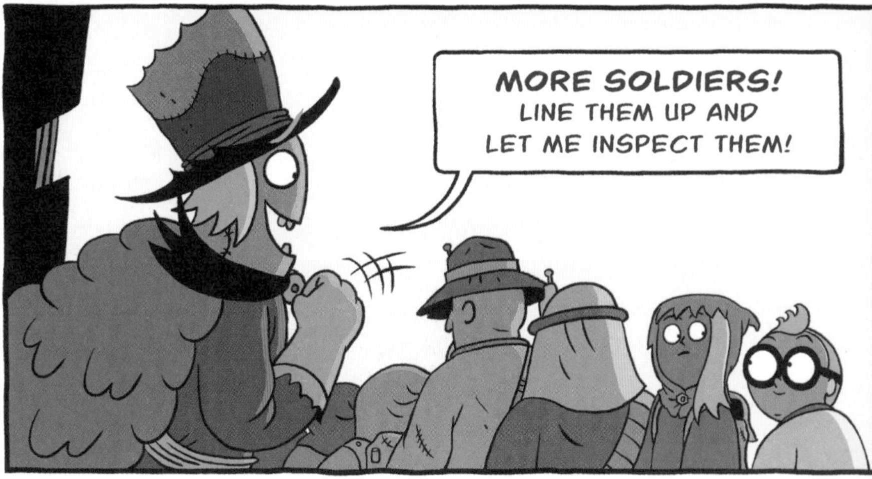
MORE SOLDIERS!
LINE THEM UP AND
LET ME INSPECT THEM!

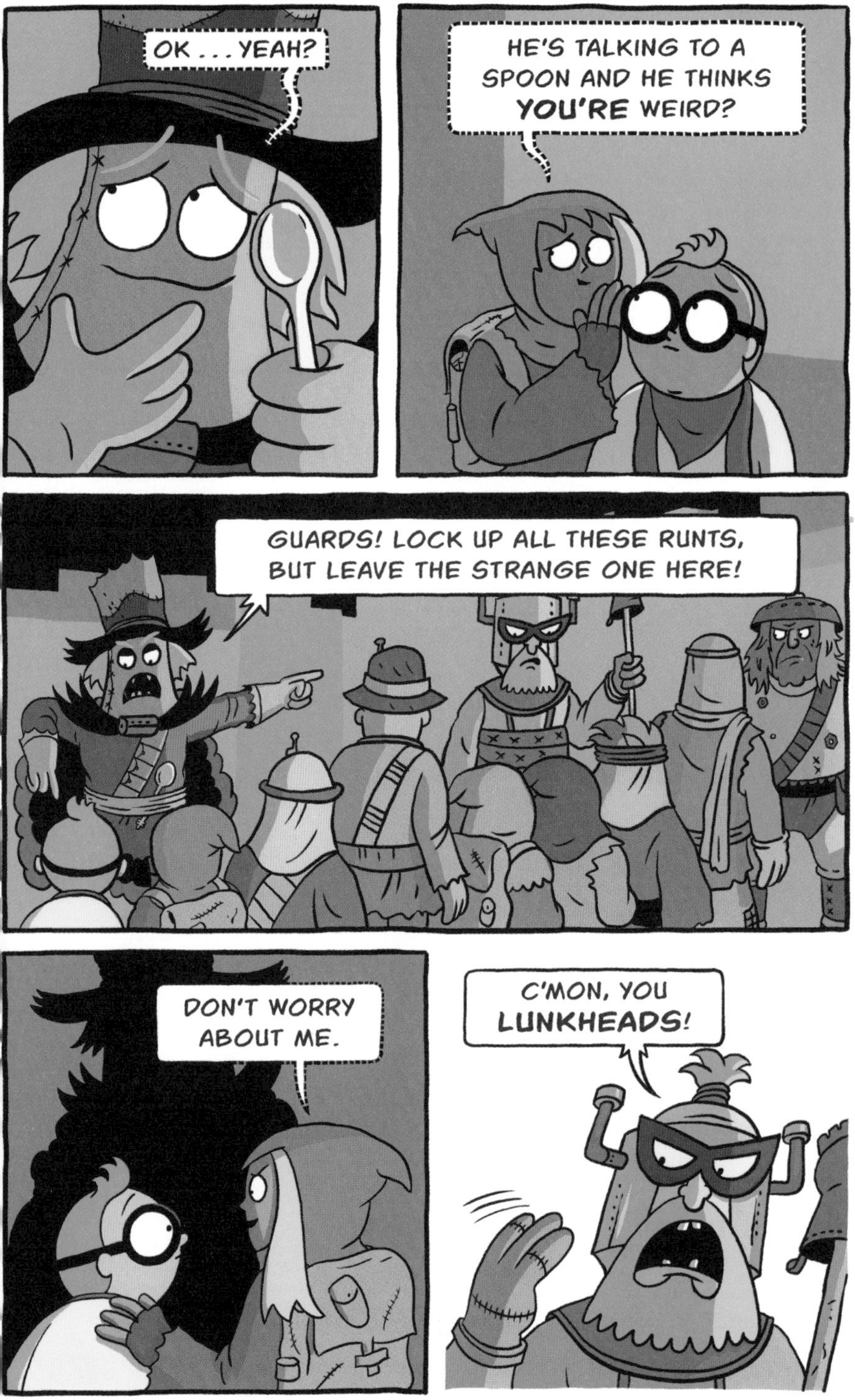
OK . . . YEAH?
HE'S TALKING TO A SPOON AND HE THINKS **YOU'RE** WEIRD?
GUARDS! LOCK UP ALL THESE RUNTS, BUT LEAVE THE STRANGE ONE HERE!
DON'T WORRY ABOUT ME.
C'MON, YOU **LUNKHEADS**!

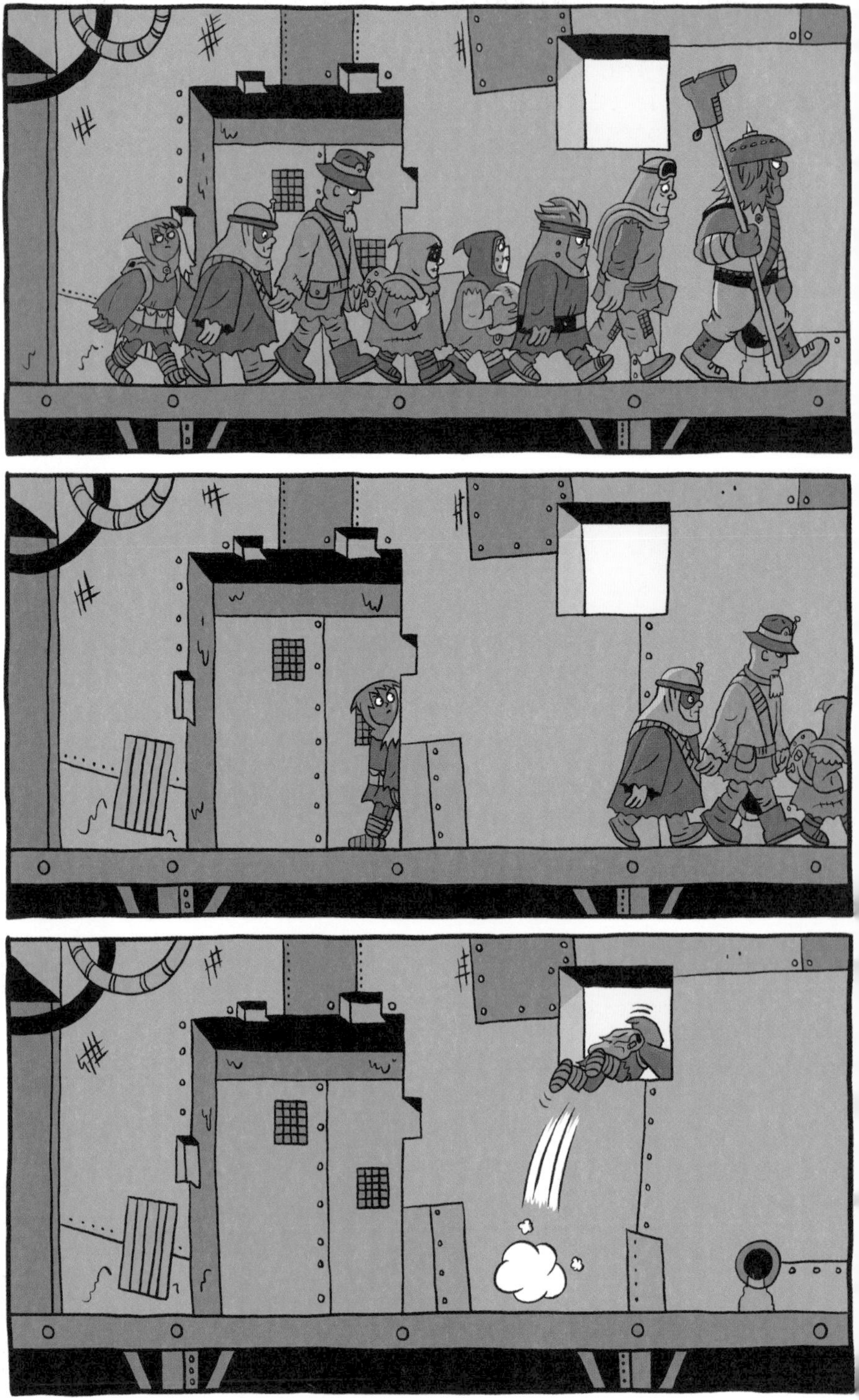

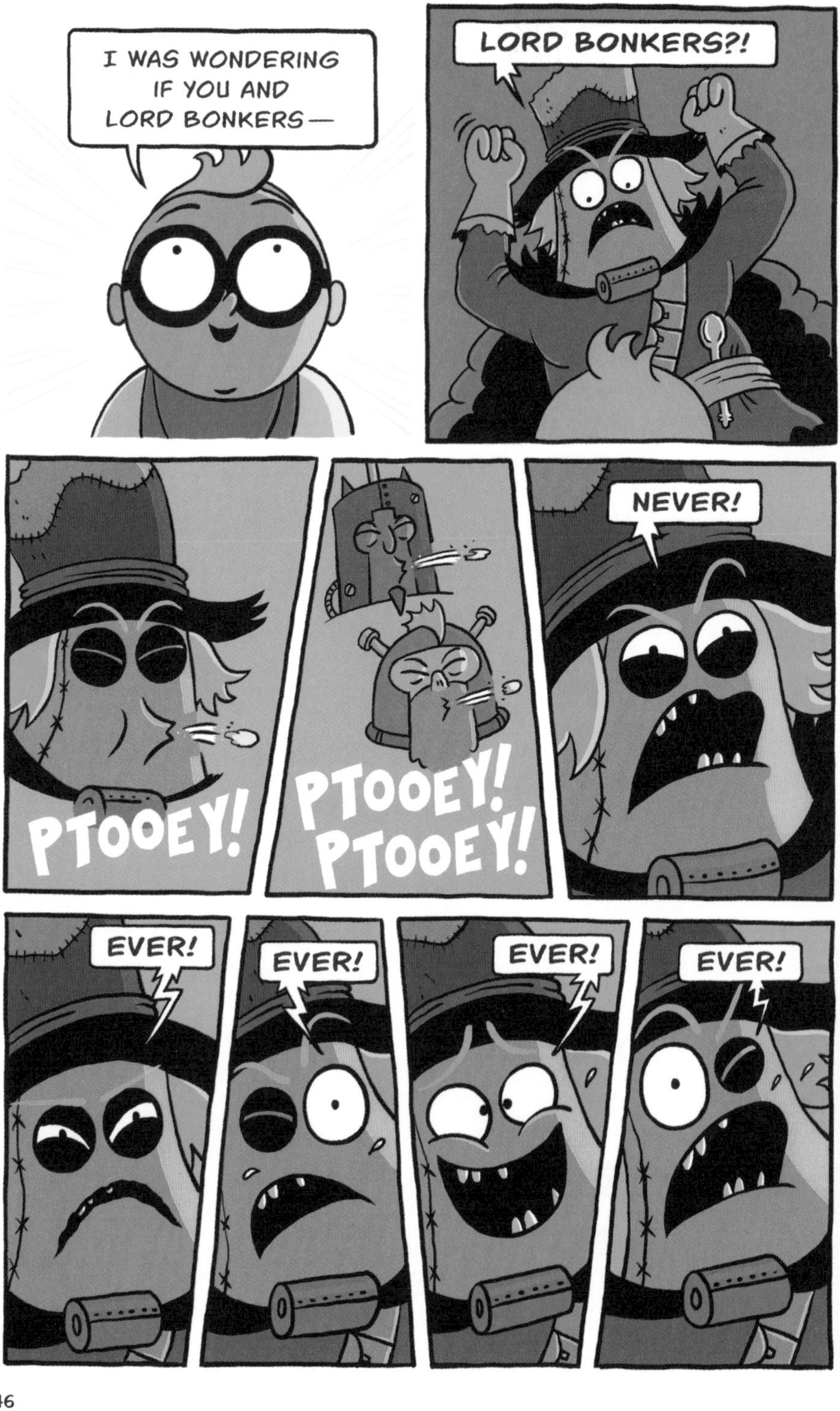
I WAS WONDERING IF YOU AND LORD BONKERS—
LORD BONKERS?!
PTOOEY!
PTOOEY! PTOOEY!
NEVER!
EVER!
EVER!
EVER!
EVER!

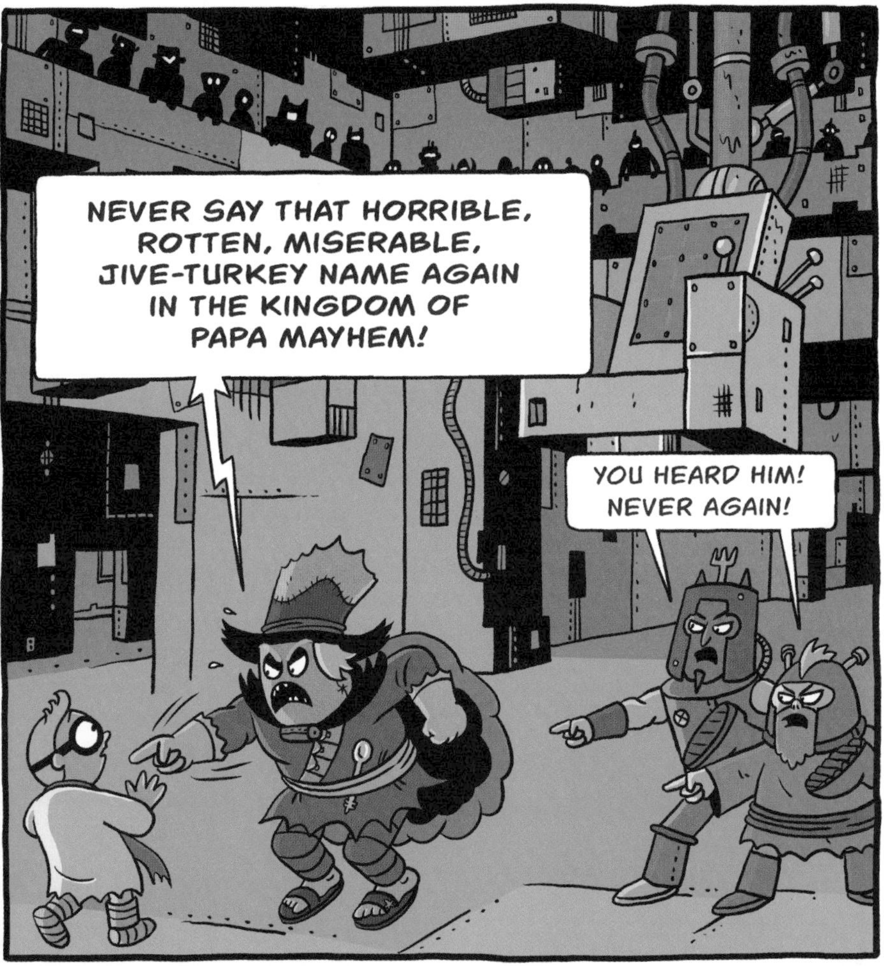
NEVER SAY THAT HORRIBLE, ROTTEN, MISERABLE, JIVE-TURKEY NAME AGAIN IN THE KINGDOM OF PAPA MAYHEM!
YOU HEARD HIM! NEVER AGAIN!

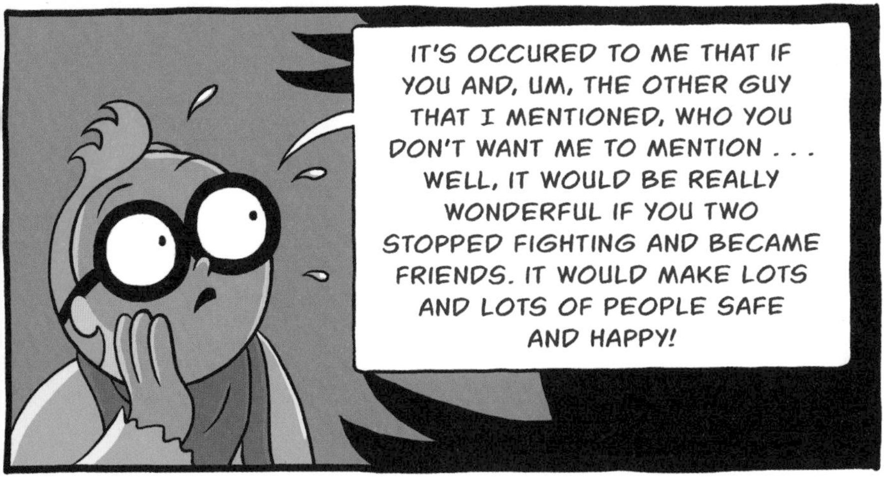
IT'S OCCURED TO ME THAT IF YOU AND, UM, THE OTHER GUY THAT I MENTIONED, WHO YOU DON'T WANT ME TO MENTION . . . WELL, IT WOULD BE REALLY WONDERFUL IF YOU TWO STOPPED FIGHTING AND BECAME FRIENDS. IT WOULD MAKE LOTS AND LOTS OF PEOPLE SAFE AND HAPPY!

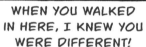

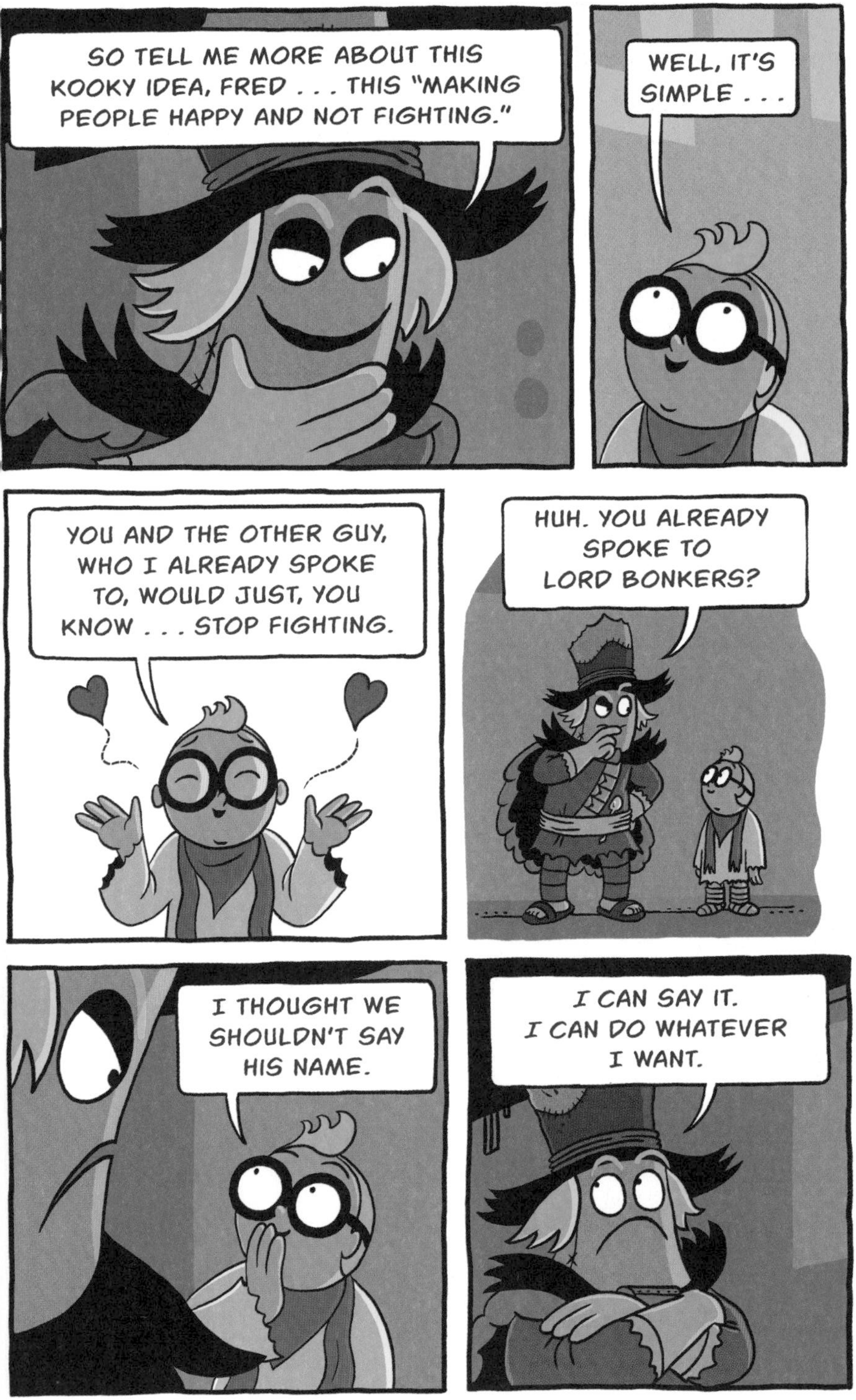
SO TELL ME MORE ABOUT THIS KOOKY IDEA, FRED . . . THIS "MAKING PEOPLE HAPPY AND NOT FIGHTING."
WELL, IT'S SIMPLE . . .
YOU AND THE OTHER GUY, WHO I ALREADY SPOKE TO, WOULD JUST, YOU KNOW . . . STOP FIGHTING.
HUH. YOU ALREADY SPOKE TO LORD BONKERS?
I THOUGHT WE SHOULDN'T SAY HIS NAME.
I CAN SAY IT. I CAN DO WHATEVER I WANT.

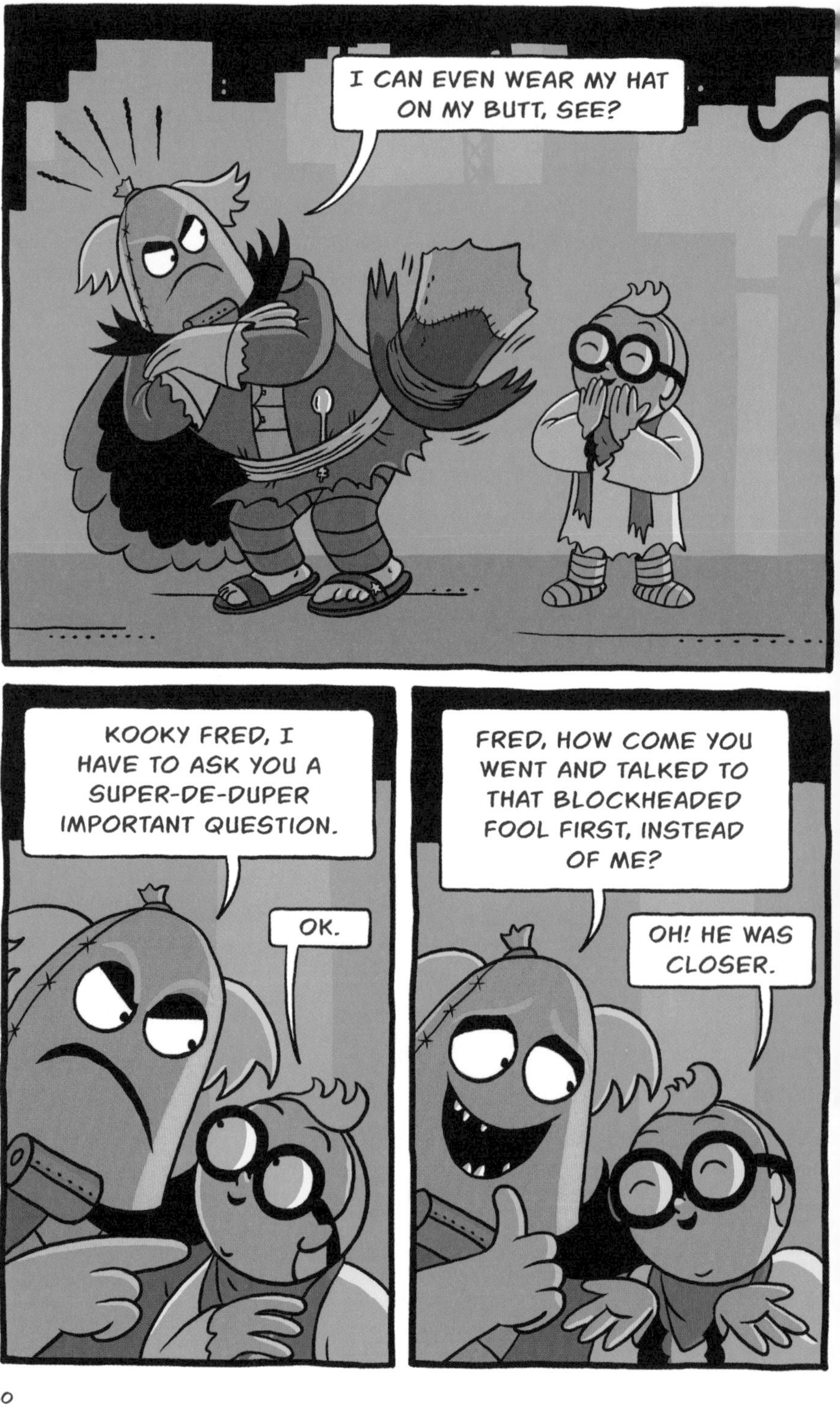
I CAN EVEN WEAR MY HAT ON MY BUTT, SEE?
KOOKY FRED, I HAVE TO ASK YOU A SUPER-DE-DUPER IMPORTANT QUESTION.
OK.
FRED, HOW COME YOU WENT AND TALKED TO THAT BLOCKHEADED FOOL FIRST, INSTEAD OF ME?
OH! HE WAS CLOSER.

CHAPTER 12

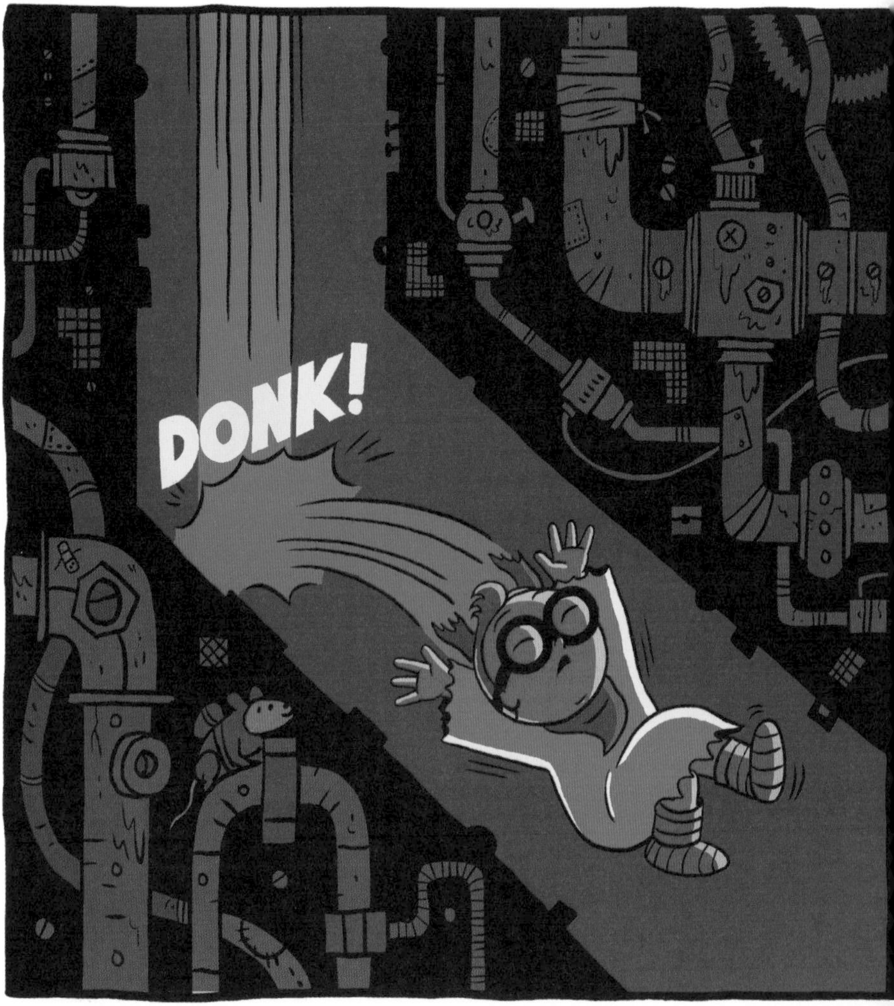
DONK!

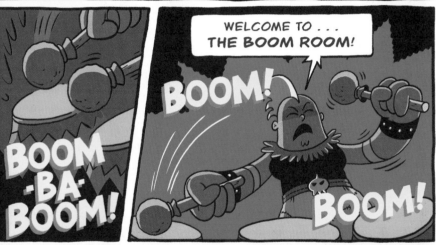

153

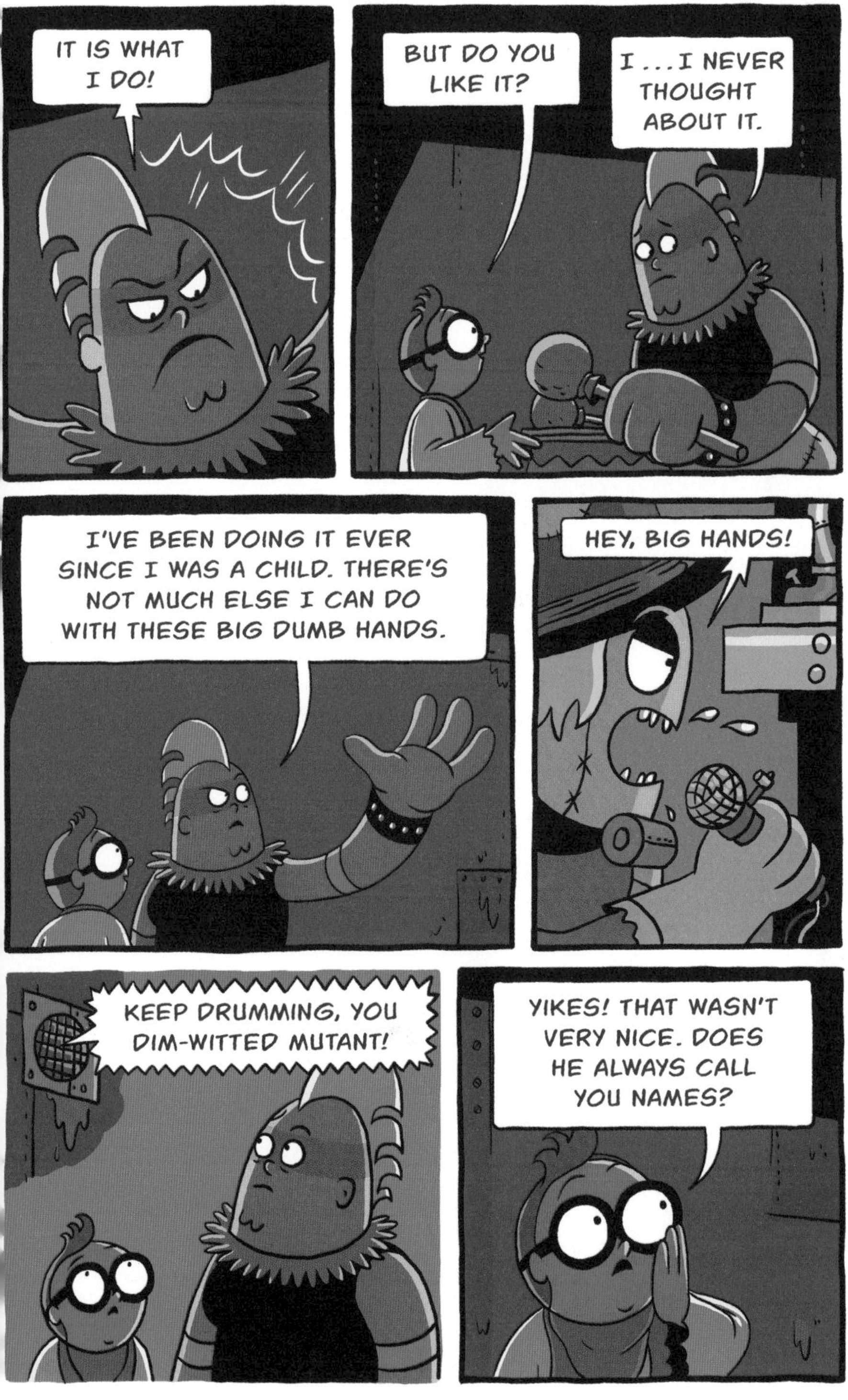
IT IS WHAT I DO!
BUT DO YOU LIKE IT?
I . . . I NEVER THOUGHT ABOUT IT.
I'VE BEEN DOING IT EVER SINCE I WAS A CHILD. THERE'S NOT MUCH ELSE I CAN DO WITH THESE BIG DUMB HANDS.
HEY, BIG HANDS!
KEEP DRUMMING, YOU DIM-WITTED MUTANT!
YIKES! THAT WASN'T VERY NICE. DOES HE ALWAYS CALL YOU NAMES?

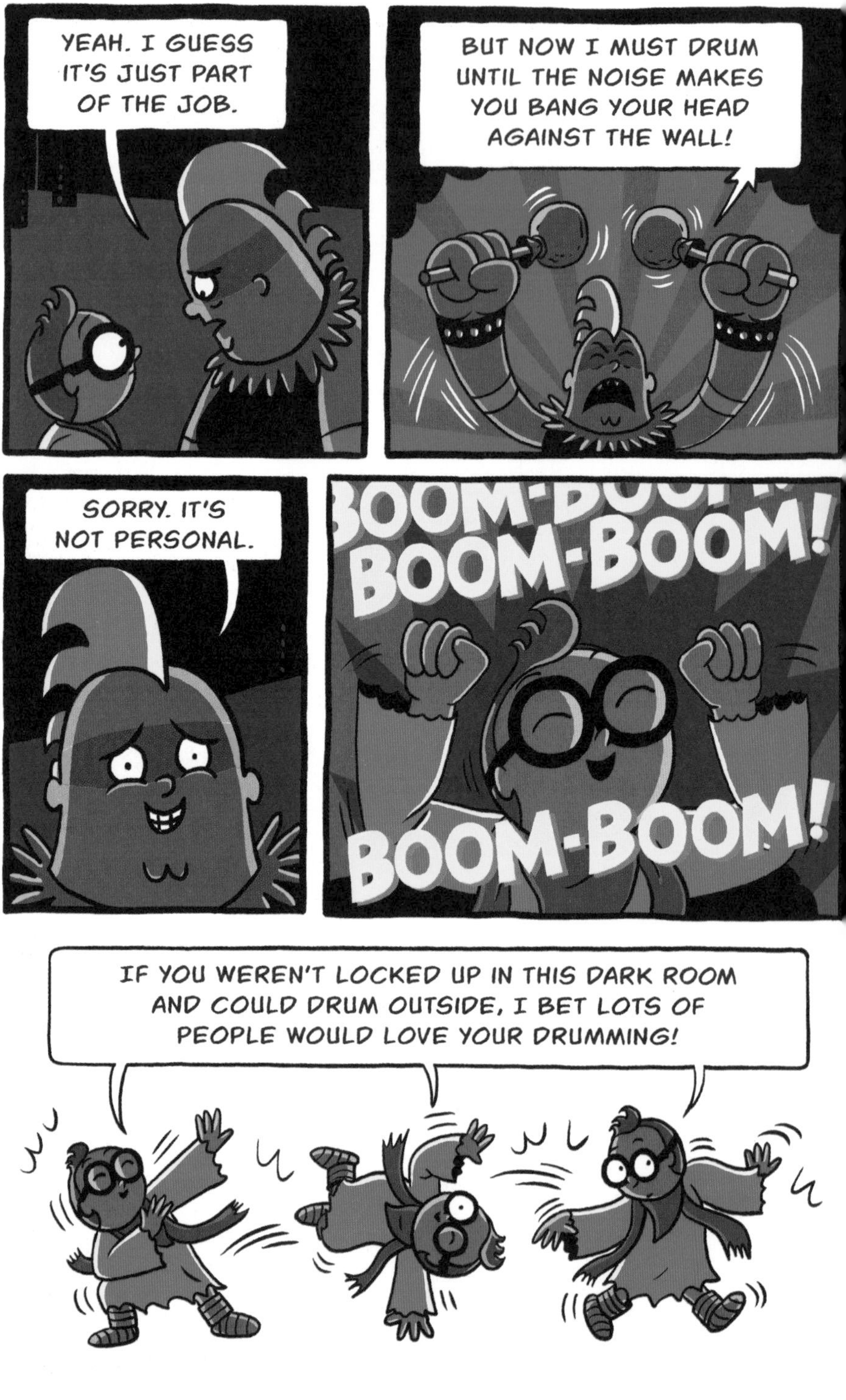
YEAH. I GUESS IT'S JUST PART OF THE JOB.
BUT NOW I MUST DRUM UNTIL THE NOISE MAKES YOU BANG YOUR HEAD AGAINST THE WALL!
SORRY. IT'S NOT PERSONAL.
BOOM-BOOM!
BOOM-BOOM!
IF YOU WEREN'T LOCKED UP IN THIS DARK ROOM AND COULD DRUM OUTSIDE, I BET LOTS OF PEOPLE WOULD LOVE YOUR DRUMMING!

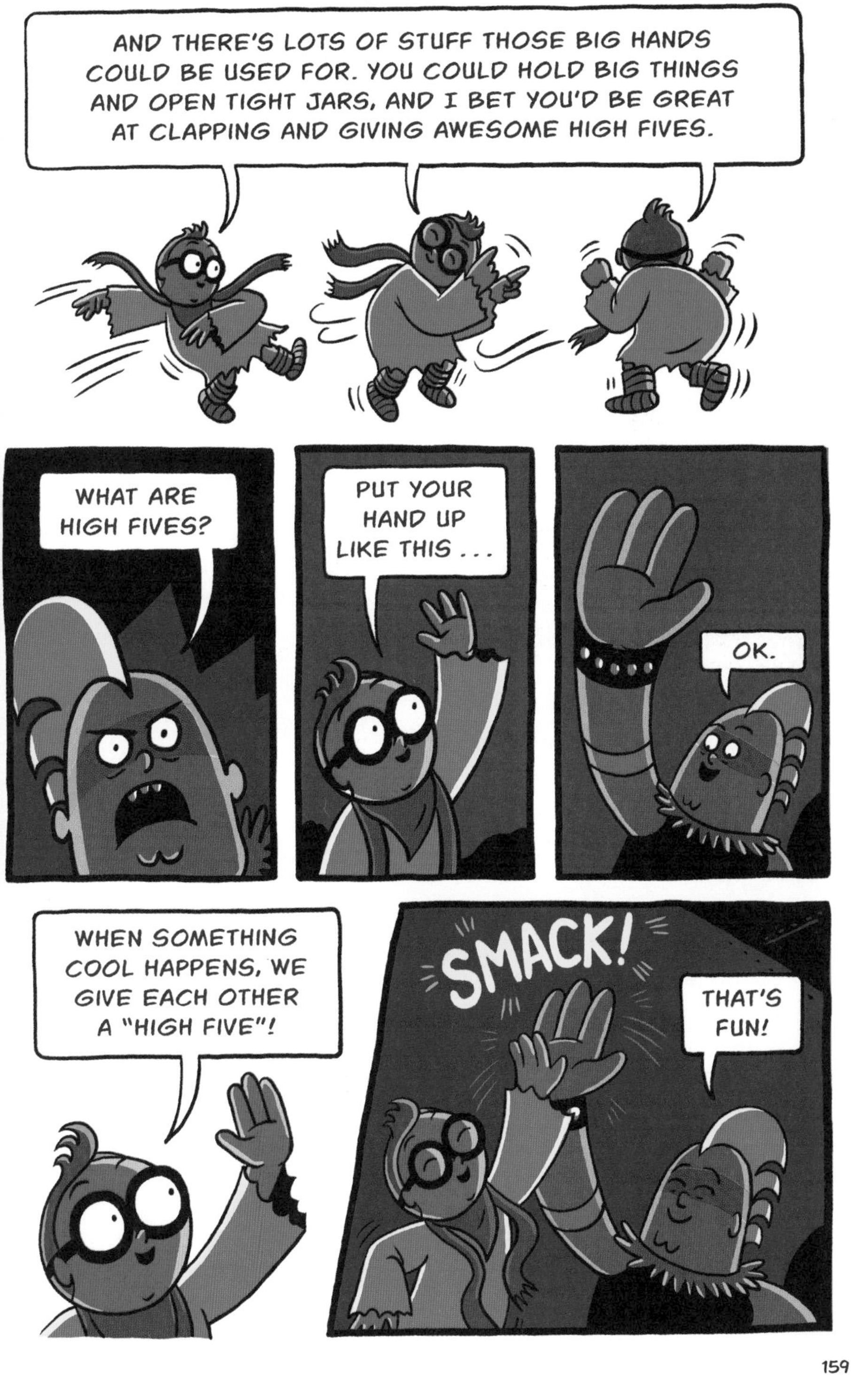
AND THERE'S LOTS OF STUFF THOSE BIG HANDS COULD BE USED FOR. YOU COULD HOLD BIG THINGS AND OPEN TIGHT JARS, AND I BET YOU'D BE GREAT AT CLAPPING AND GIVING AWESOME HIGH FIVES.
WHAT ARE HIGH FIVES?
PUT YOUR HAND UP LIKE THIS . . .
OK.
WHEN SOMETHING COOL HAPPENS, WE GIVE EACH OTHER A "HIGH FIVE"!
SMACK!
THAT'S FUN!

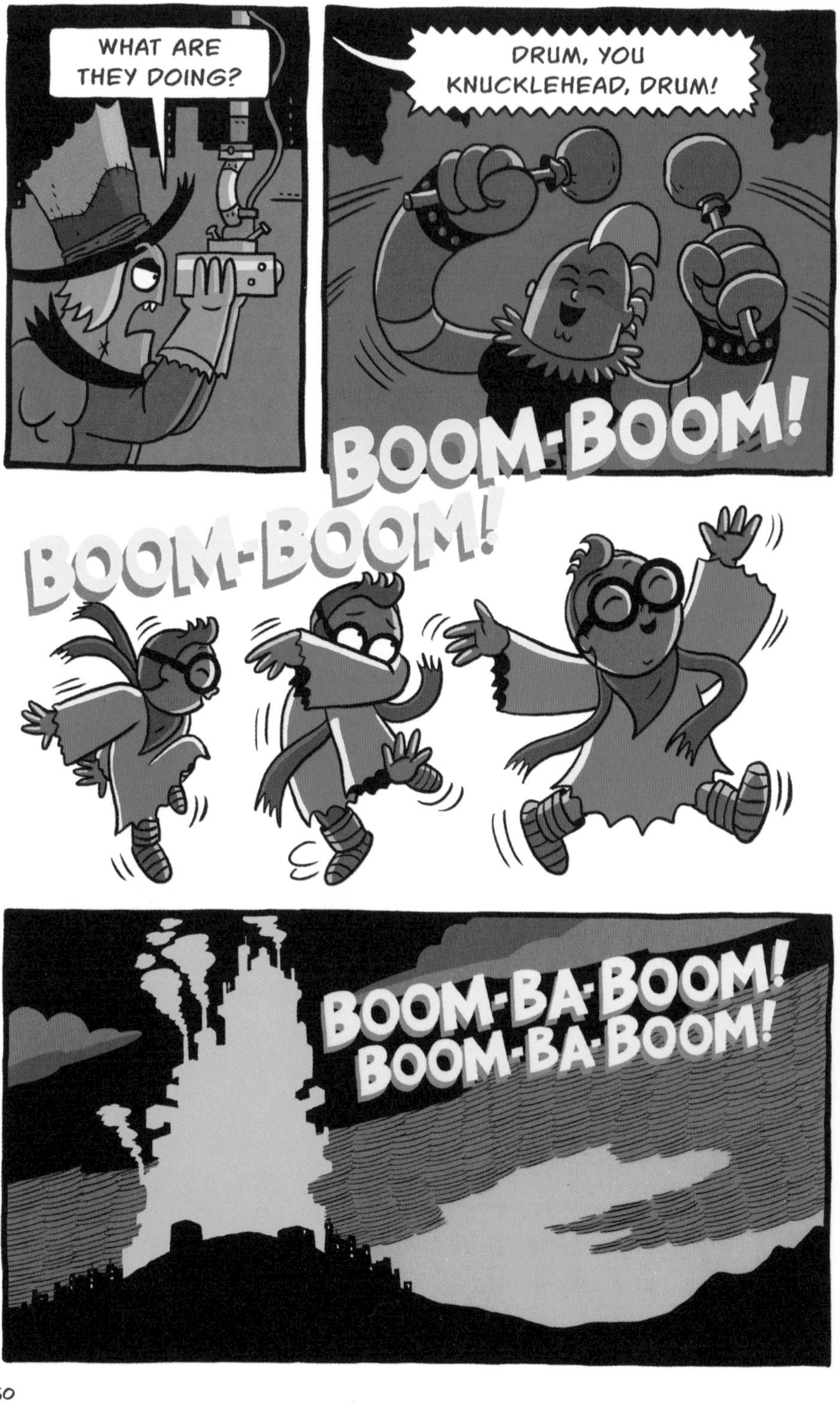
WHAT ARE THEY DOING?
DRUM, YOU KNUCKLEHEAD, DRUM!
BOOM-BOOM!
BOOM-BOOM!
BOOM-BA-BOOM!
BOOM-BA-BOOM!

CHAPTER 13

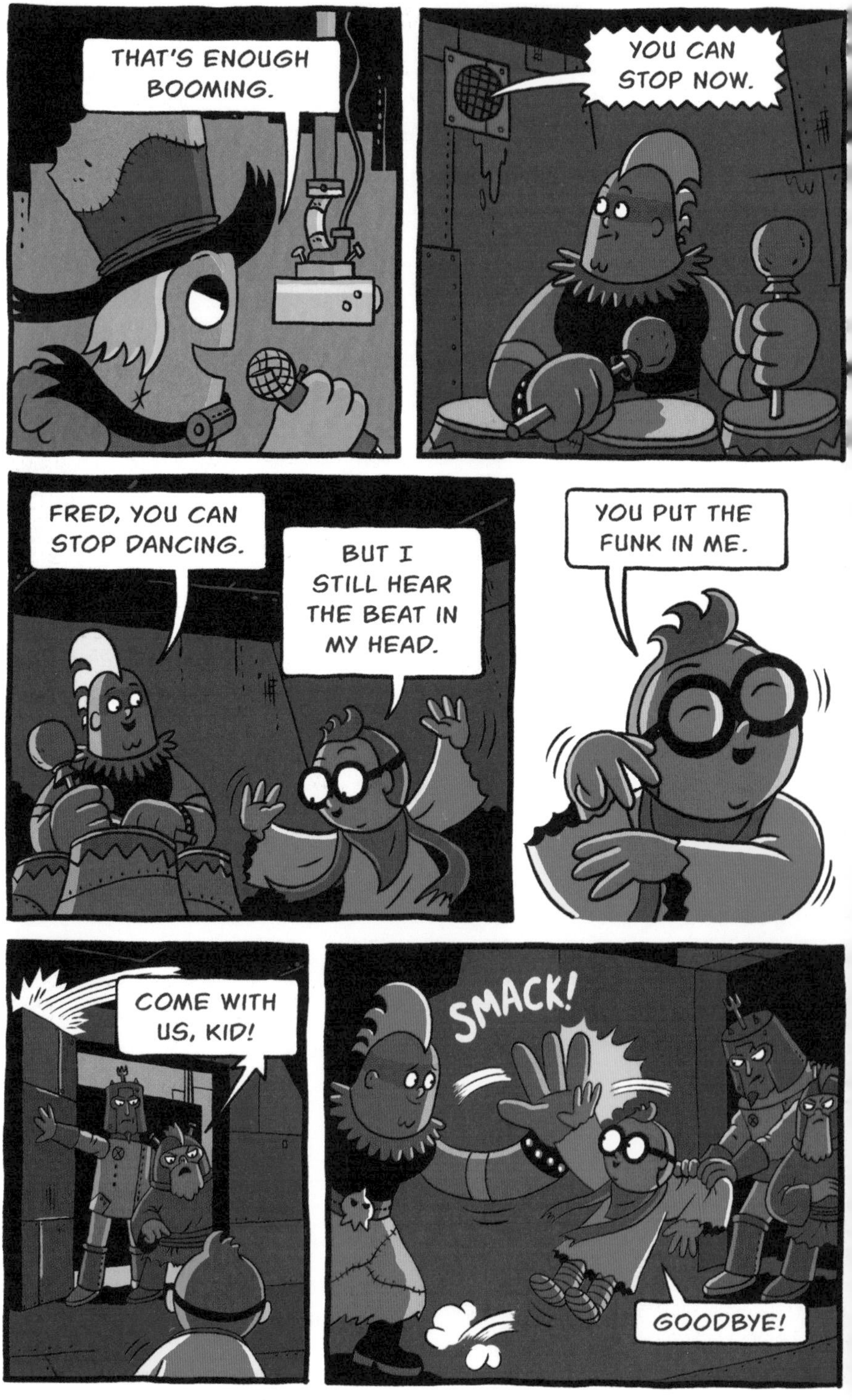
THAT'S ENOUGH BOOMING.
YOU CAN STOP NOW.
FRED, YOU CAN STOP DANCING.
BUT I STILL HEAR THE BEAT IN MY HEAD.
YOU PUT THE FUNK IN ME.
COME WITH US, KID!
SMACK!
GOODBYE!

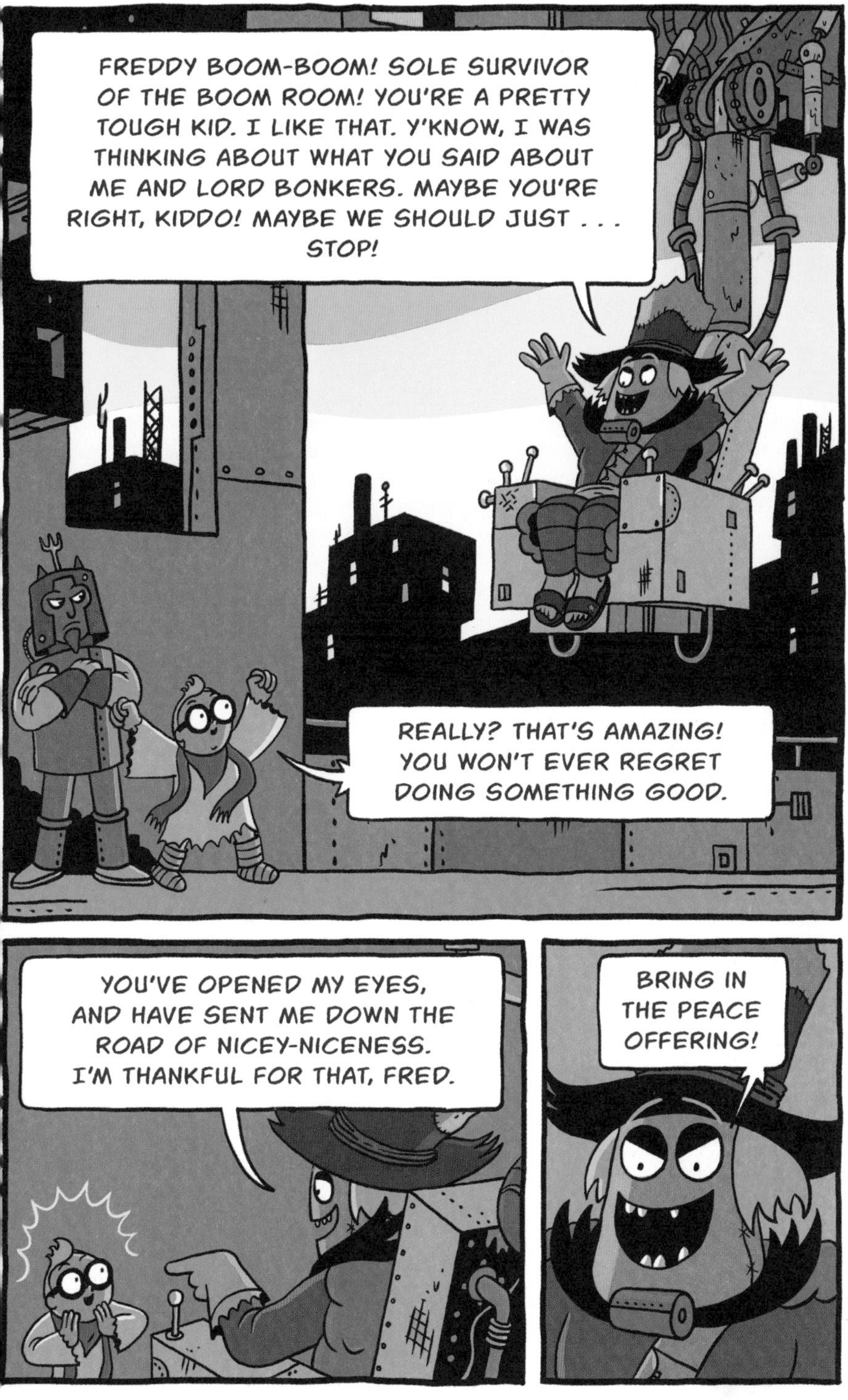
FREDDY BOOM-BOOM! SOLE SURVIVOR OF THE BOOM ROOM! YOU'RE A PRETTY TOUGH KID. I LIKE THAT. Y'KNOW, I WAS THINKING ABOUT WHAT YOU SAID ABOUT ME AND LORD BONKERS. MAYBE YOU'RE RIGHT, KIDDO! MAYBE WE SHOULD JUST . . . STOP!
REALLY? THAT'S AMAZING! YOU WON'T EVER REGRET DOING SOMETHING GOOD.
YOU'VE OPENED MY EYES, AND HAVE SENT ME DOWN THE ROAD OF NICEY-NICENESS. I'M THANKFUL FOR THAT, FRED.
BRING IN THE PEACE OFFERING!

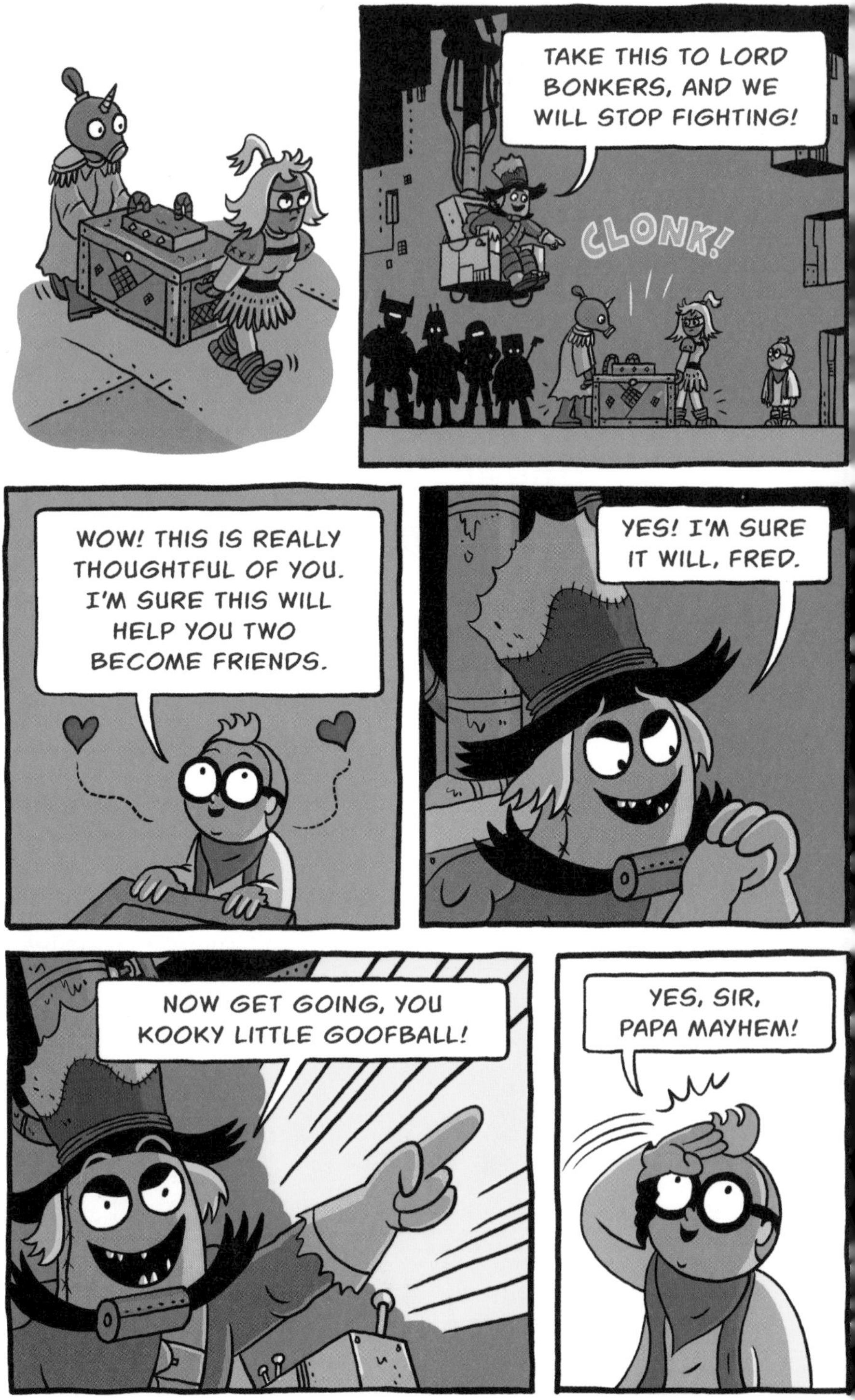
TAKE THIS TO LORD BONKERS, AND WE WILL STOP FIGHTING!
CLONK!
WOW! THIS IS REALLY THOUGHTFUL OF YOU. I'M SURE THIS WILL HELP YOU TWO BECOME FRIENDS.
YES! I'M SURE IT WILL, FRED.
NOW GET GOING, YOU KOOKY LITTLE GOOFBALL!
YES, SIR, PAPA MAYHEM!

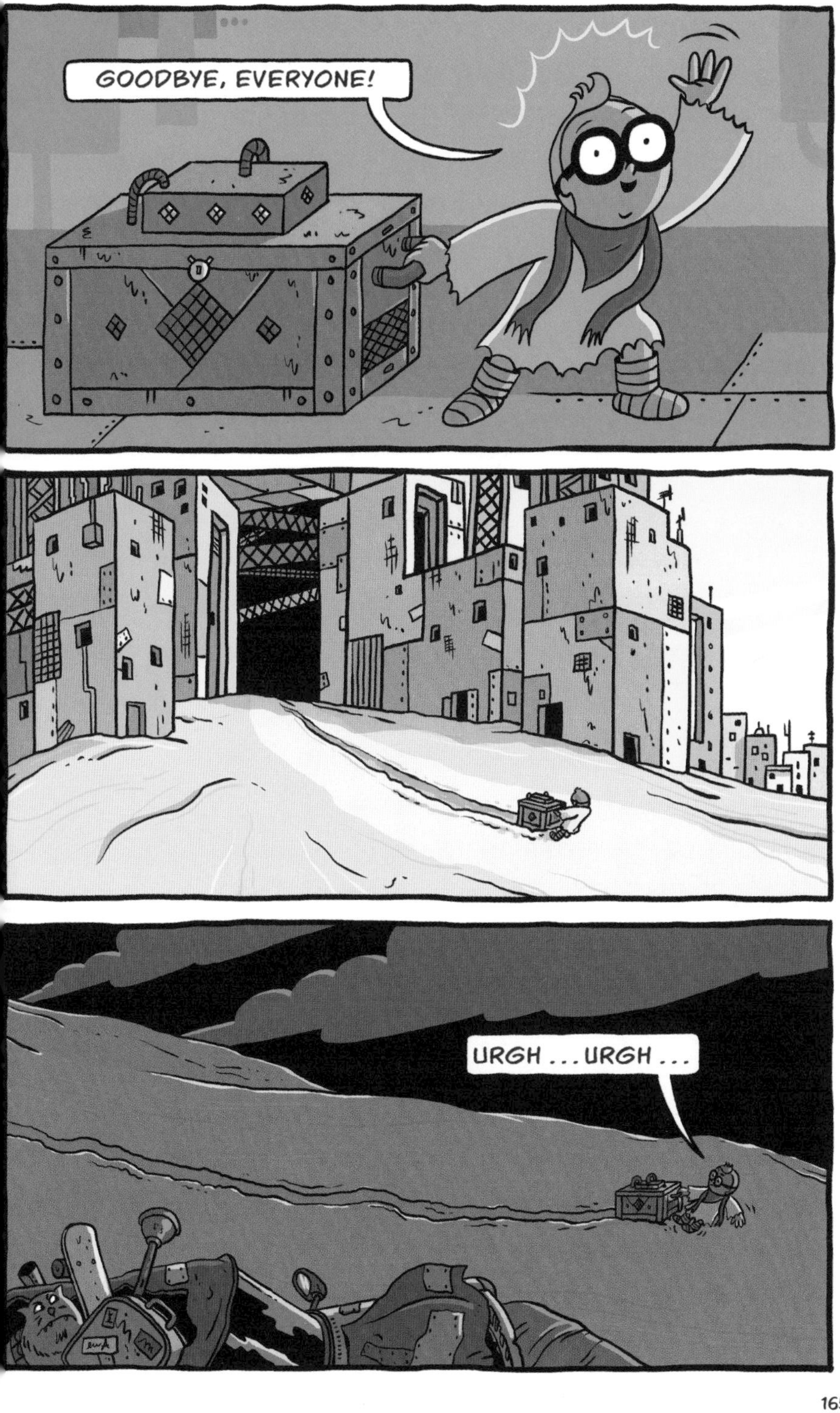
GOODBYE, EVERYONE!
URGH . . . URGH . . .

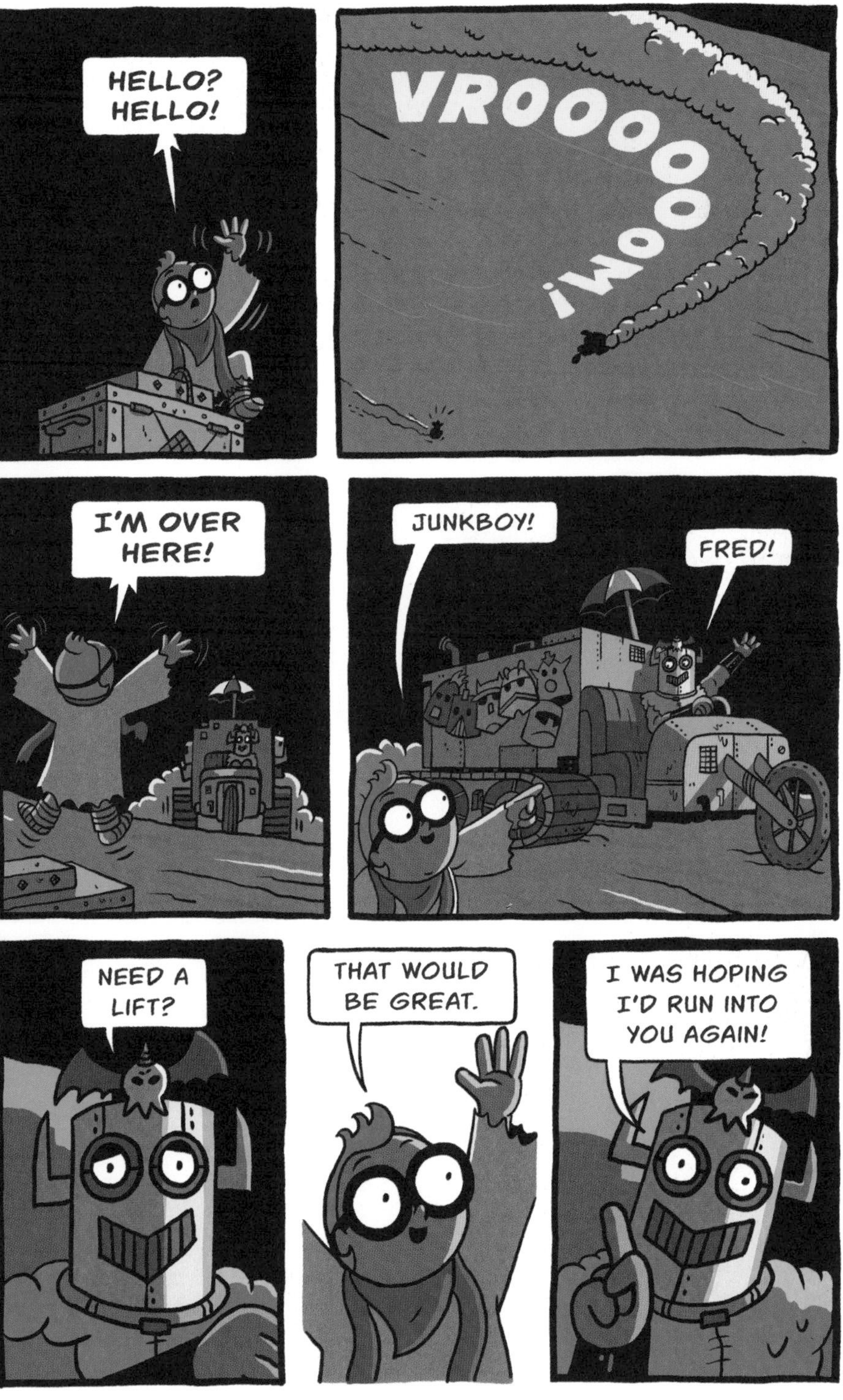
HELLO? HELLO!
VROOOOOOM!
I'M OVER HERE!
JUNKBOY!
FRED!
NEED A LIFT?
THAT WOULD BE GREAT.
I WAS HOPING I'D RUN INTO YOU AGAIN!

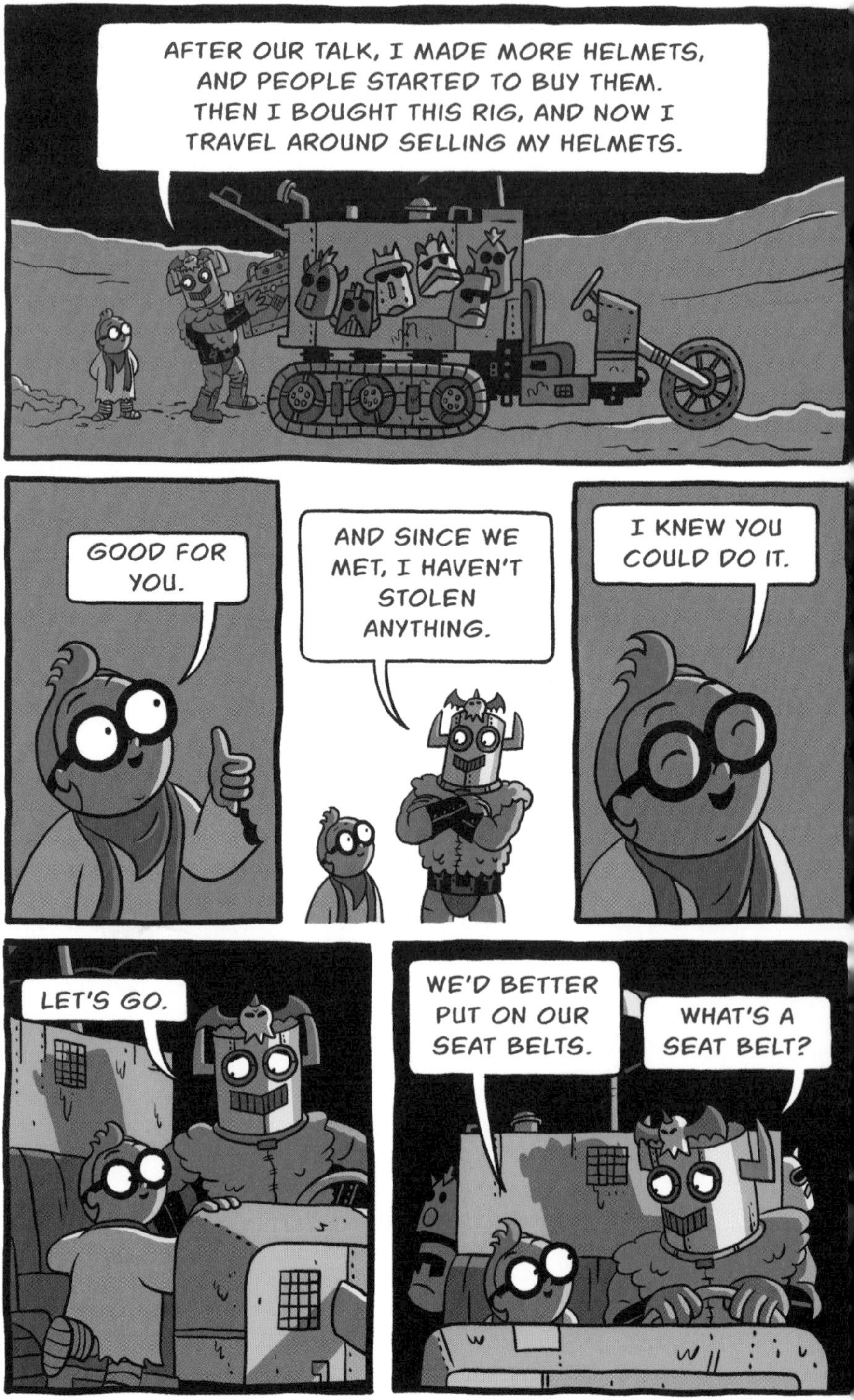
AFTER OUR TALK, I MADE MORE HELMETS, AND PEOPLE STARTED TO BUY THEM. THEN I BOUGHT THIS RIG, AND NOW I TRAVEL AROUND SELLING MY HELMETS.
GOOD FOR YOU.
AND SINCE WE MET, I HAVEN'T STOLEN ANYTHING.
I KNEW YOU COULD DO IT.
LET'S GO.
WE'D BETTER PUT ON OUR SEAT BELTS.
WHAT'S A SEAT BELT?

HEY, WHAT'S
THAT?

LET'S FIND
OUT.

CHAPTER 14

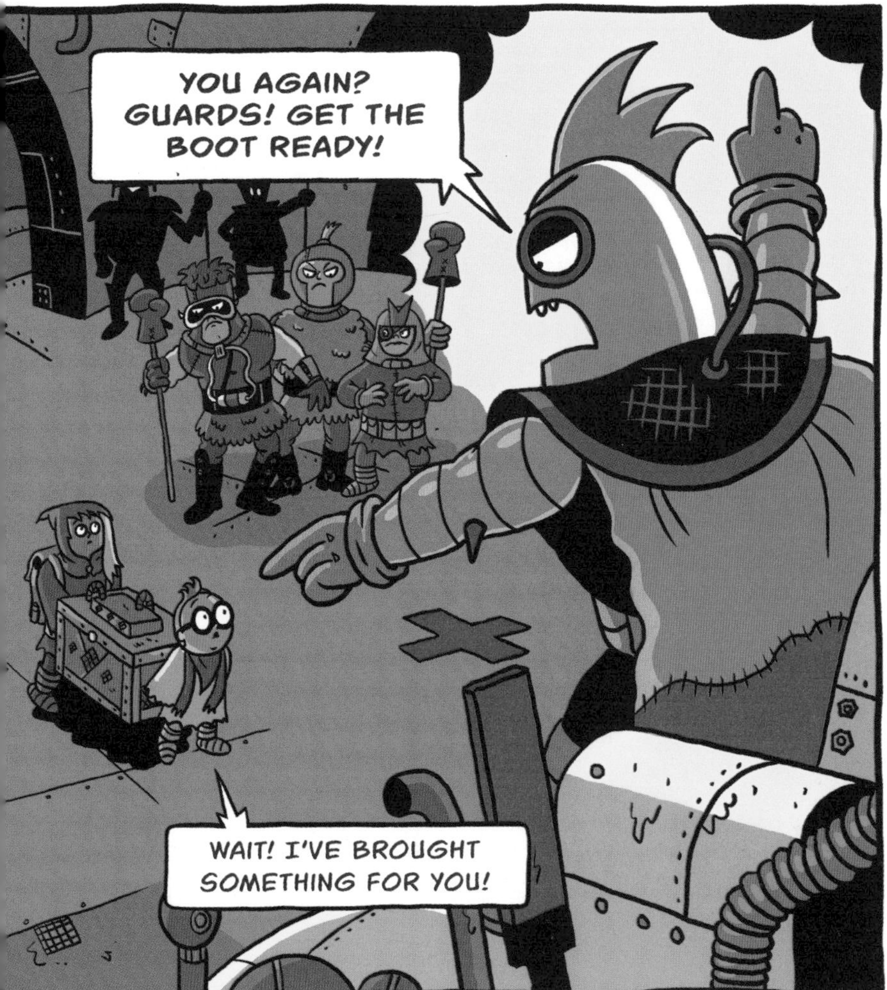
YOU AGAIN? GUARDS! GET THE BOOT READY!
WAIT! I'VE BROUGHT SOMETHING FOR YOU!

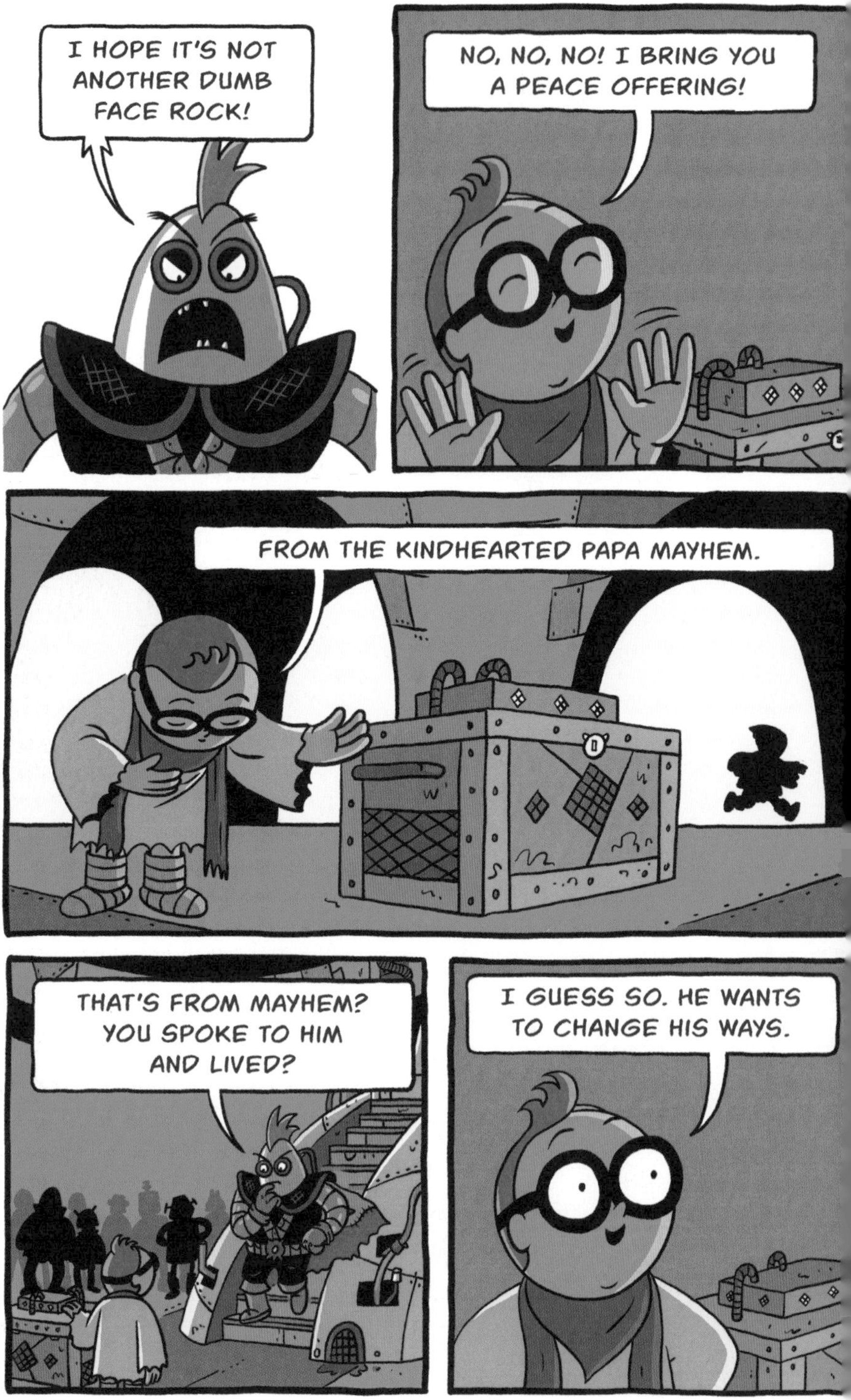
I HOPE IT'S NOT ANOTHER DUMB FACE ROCK!
NO, NO, NO! I BRING YOU A PEACE OFFERING!
FROM THE KINDHEARTED PAPA MAYHEM.
THAT'S FROM MAYHEM? YOU SPOKE TO HIM AND LIVED?
I GUESS SO. HE WANTS TO CHANGE HIS WAYS.

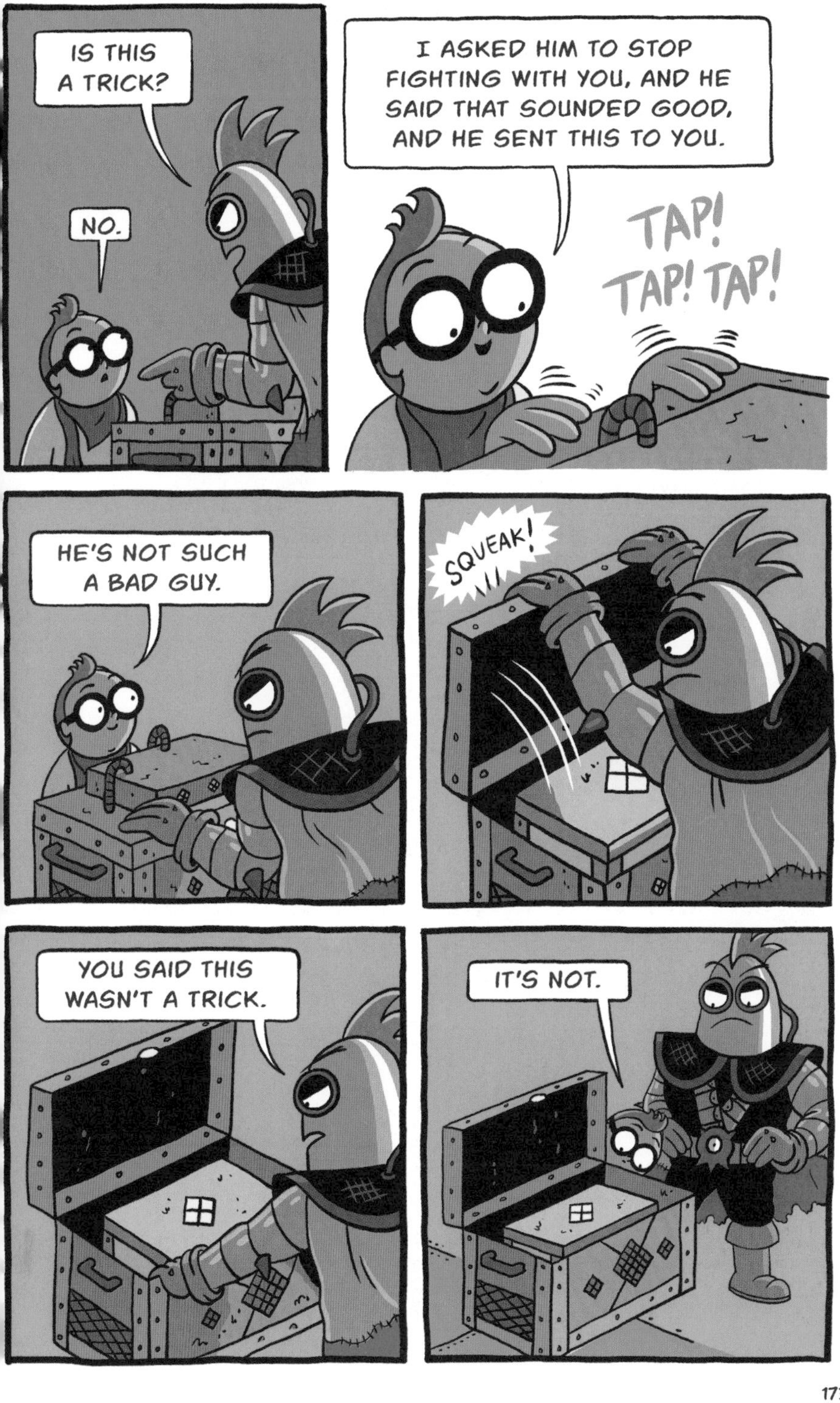
IS THIS A TRICK?
NO.
I ASKED HIM TO STOP FIGHTING WITH YOU, AND HE SAID THAT SOUNDED GOOD, AND HE SENT THIS TO YOU.
TAP! TAP! TAP!
HE'S NOT SUCH A BAD GUY.
SQUEAK!
YOU SAID THIS WASN'T A TRICK.
IT'S NOT.

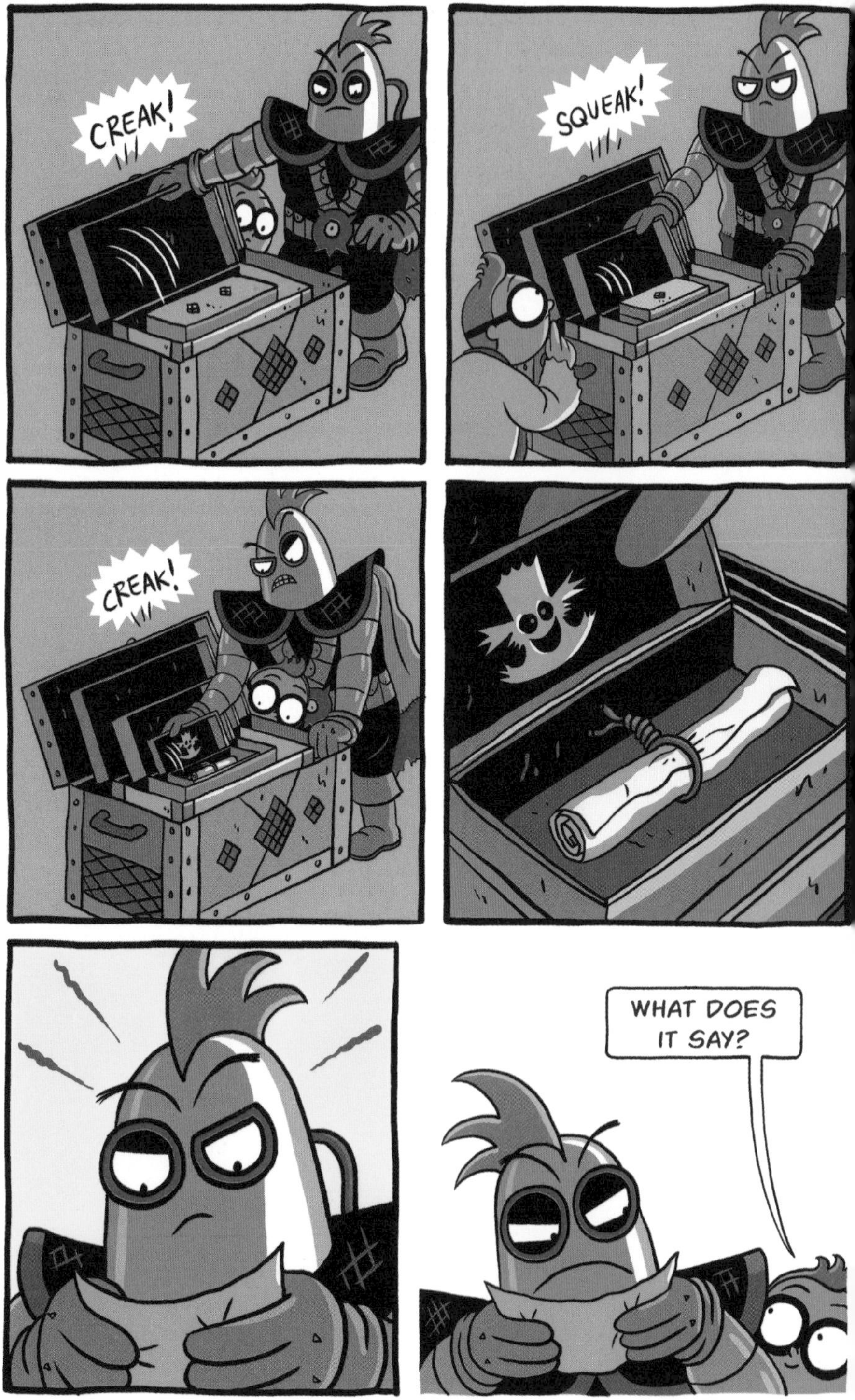
CREAK!
SQUEAK!
CREAK!
WHAT DOES IT SAY?

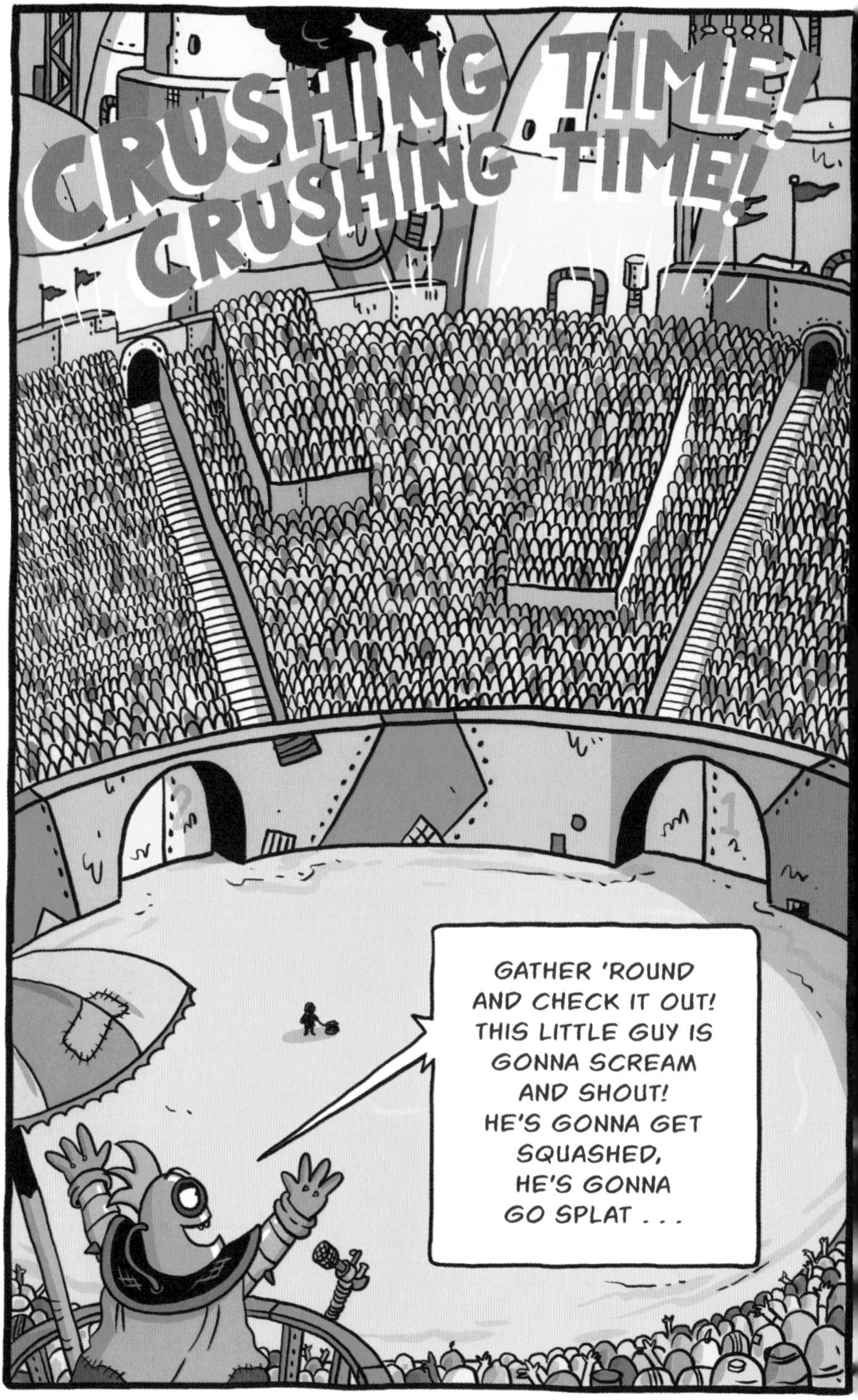
CRUSHING TIME! CRUSHING TIME!
2
1
GATHER 'ROUND AND CHECK IT OUT! THIS LITTLE GUY IS GONNA SCREAM AND SHOUT! HE'S GONNA GET SQUASHED, HE'S GONNA GO SPLAT . . .

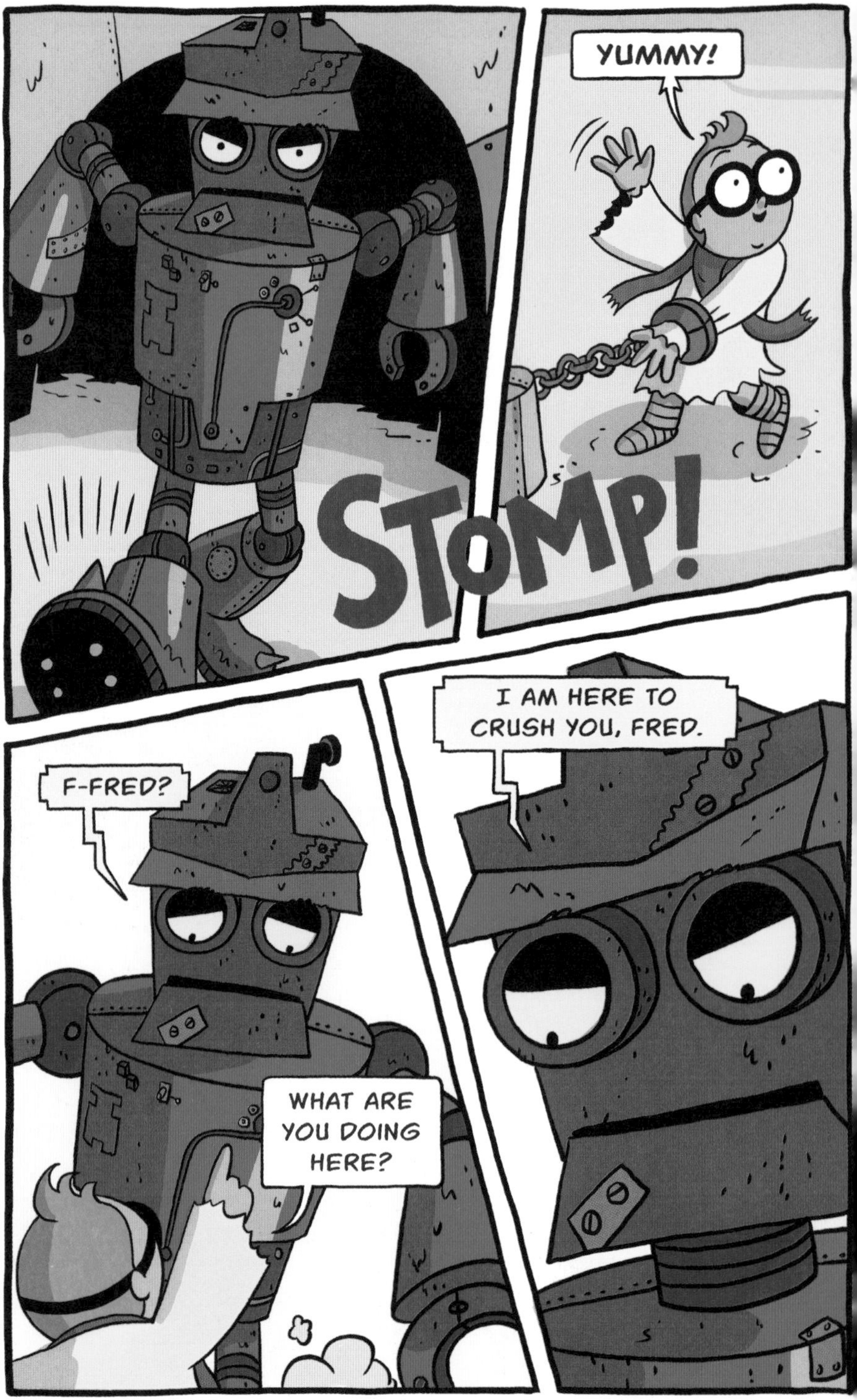
YUMMY!
STOMP!
F-FRED?
WHAT ARE YOU DOING HERE?
I AM HERE TO CRUSH YOU, FRED.

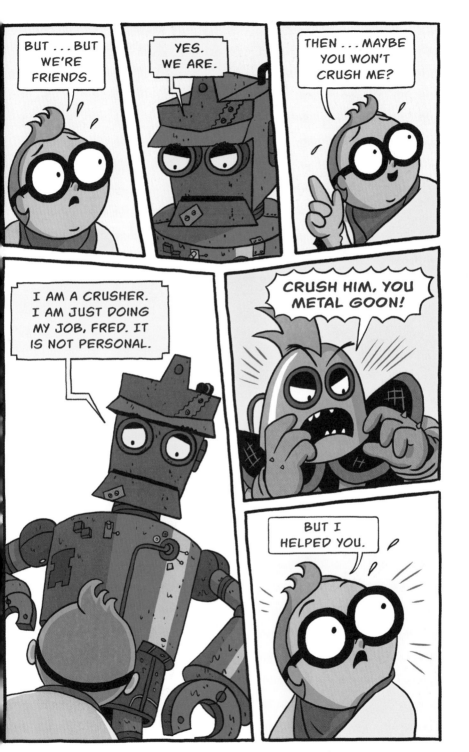

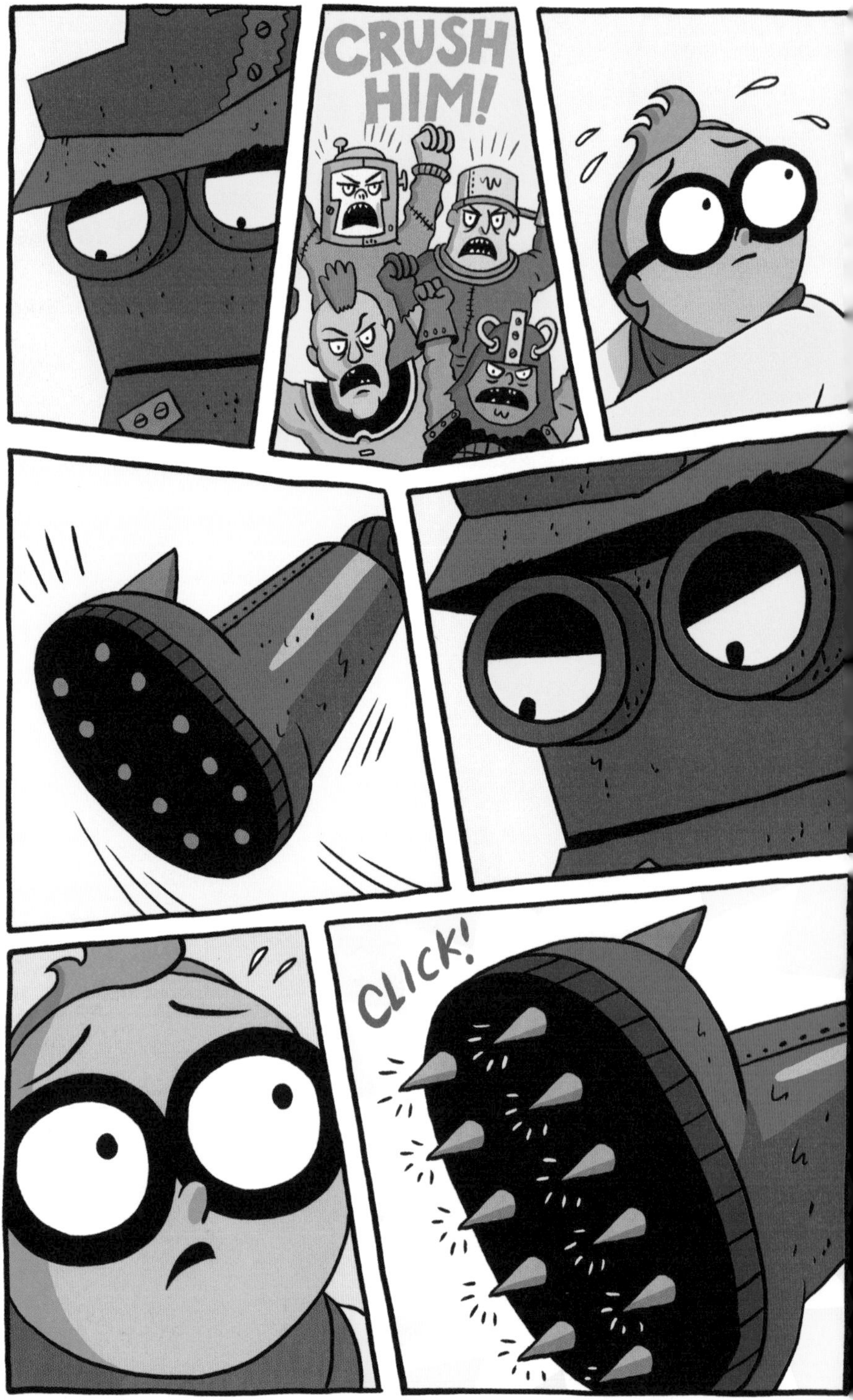
CRUSH HIM!
CLICK!

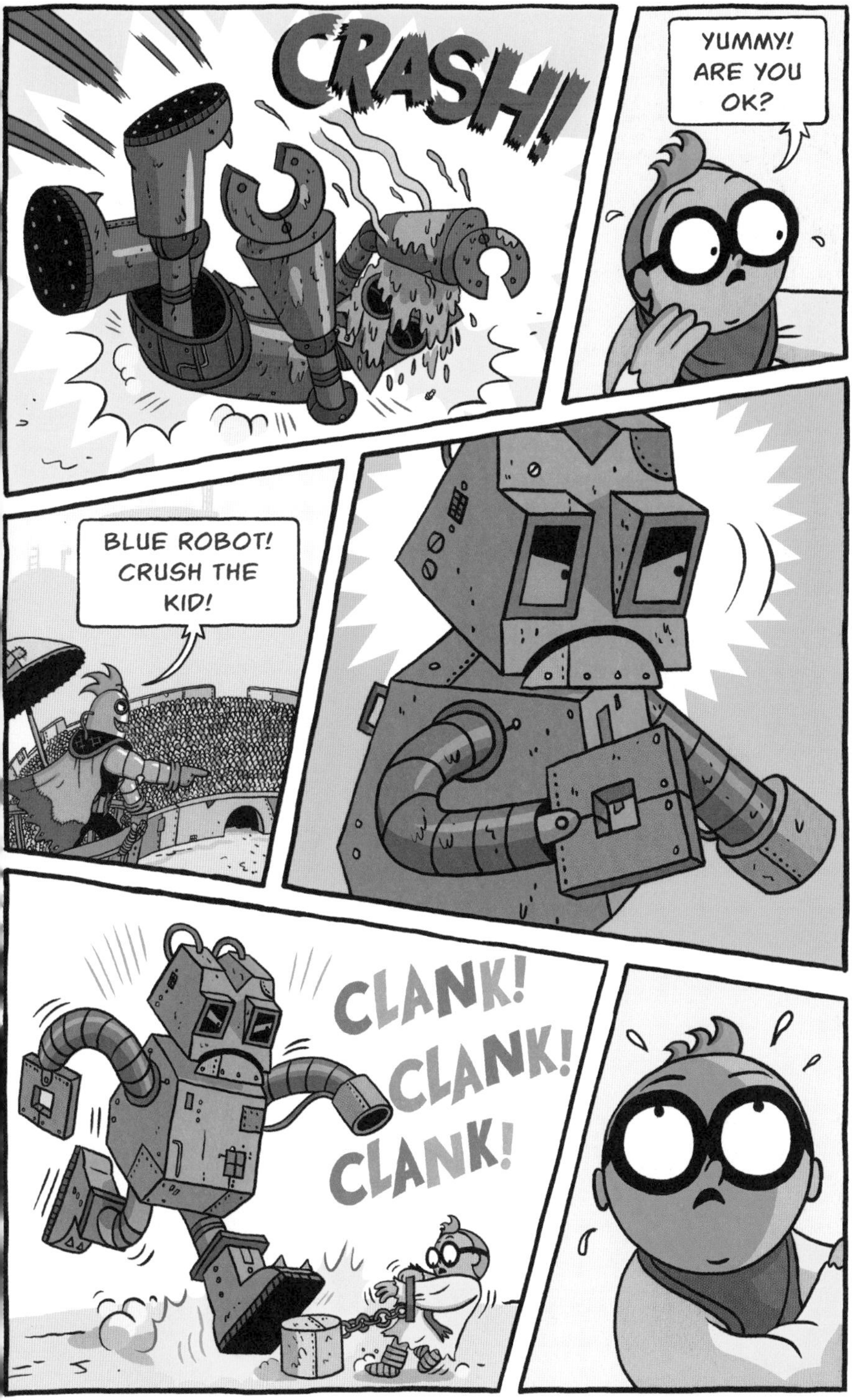
CRASH!
YUMMY! ARE YOU OK?
BLUE ROBOT! CRUSH THE KID!
CLANK!
CLANK!
CLANK!

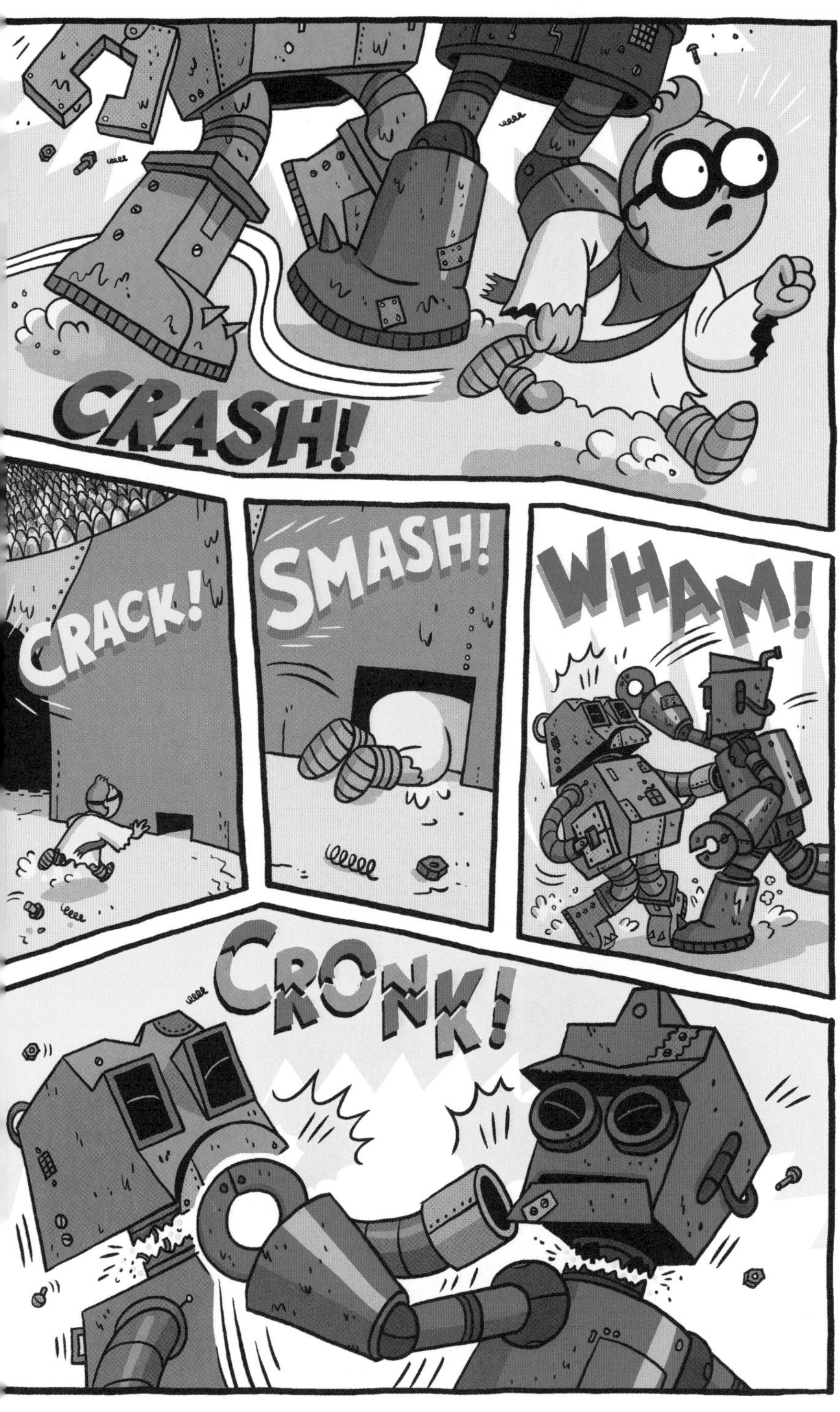
CRASH!
CRACK!
SMASH!
WHAM!
CRONK!

CHAPTER 15

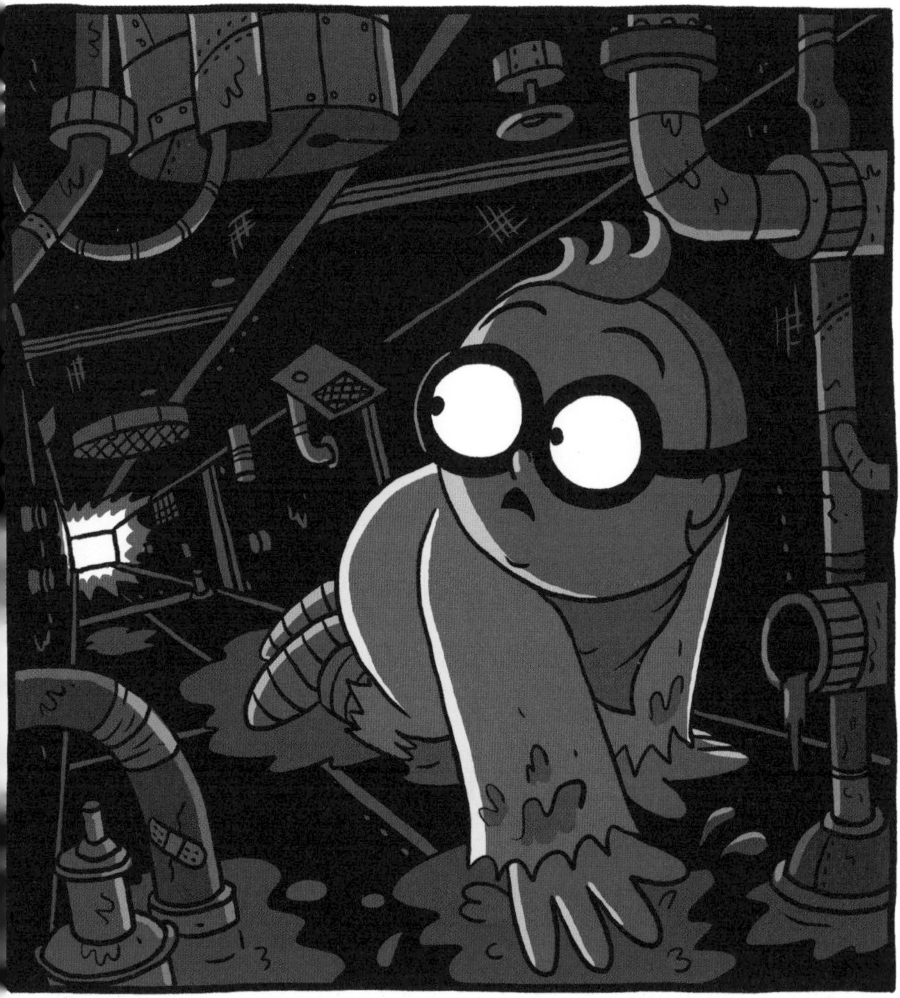

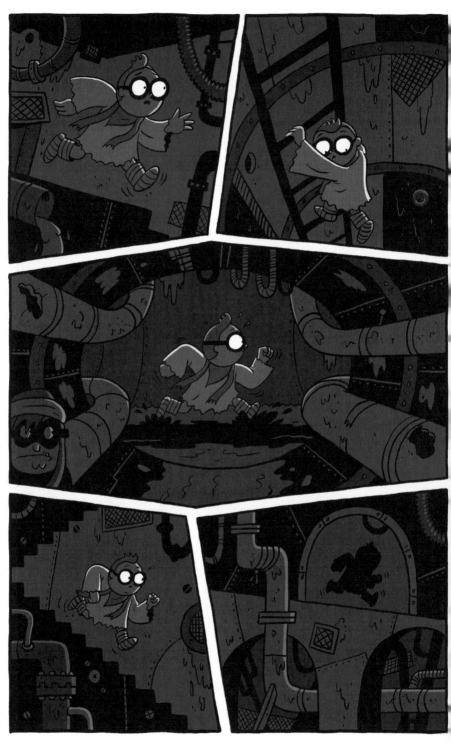

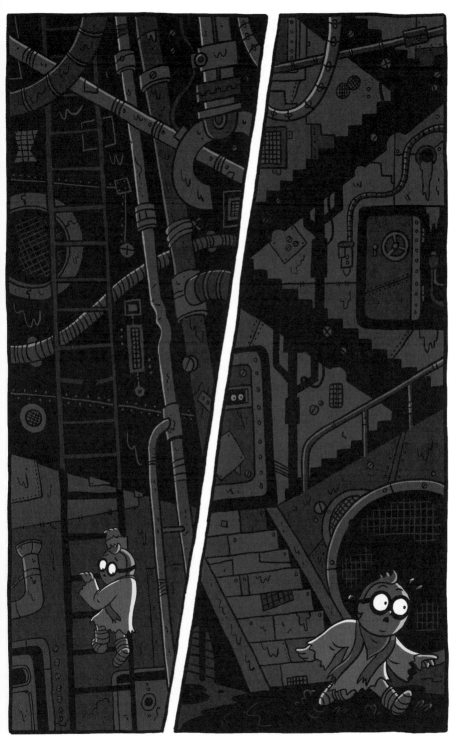

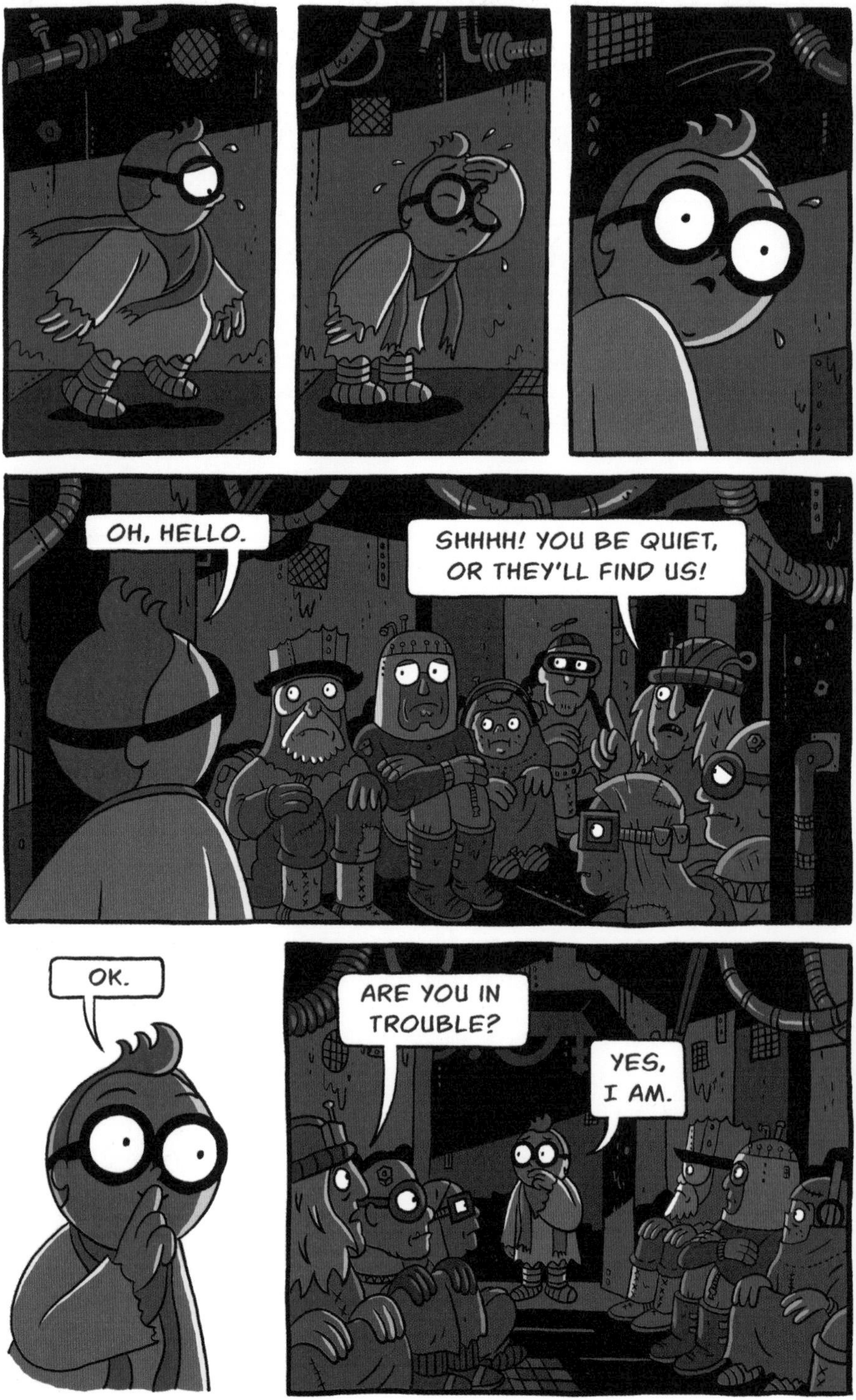
OH, HELLO.
SHHHH! YOU BE QUIET, OR THEY'LL FIND US!
OK.
ARE YOU IN TROUBLE?
YES, I AM.

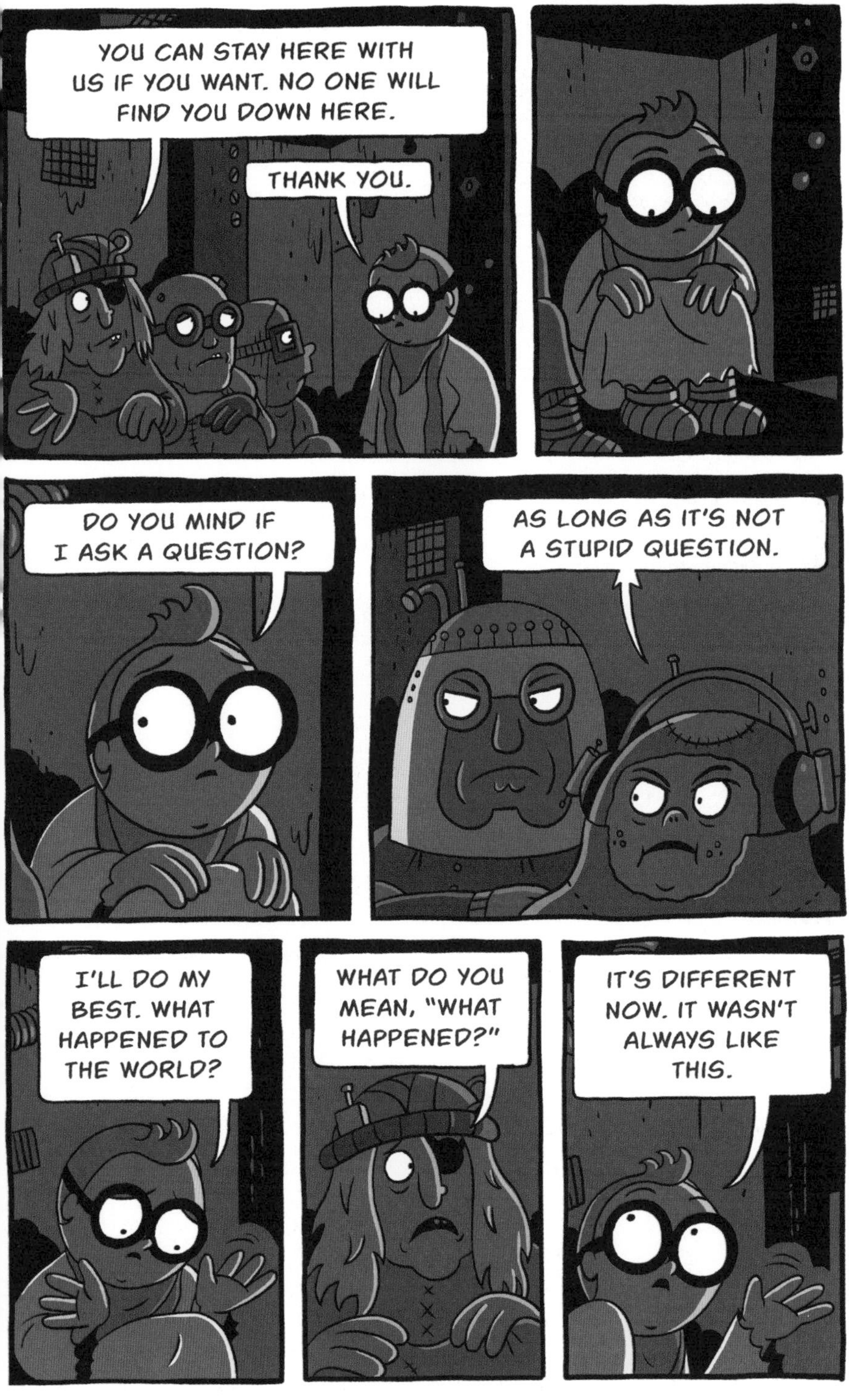

YOU CAN STAY HERE WITH US IF YOU WANT. NO ONE WILL FIND YOU DOWN HERE.
THANK YOU.
DO YOU MIND IF I ASK A QUESTION?
AS LONG AS IT'S NOT A STUPID QUESTION.
I'LL DO MY BEST. WHAT HAPPENED TO THE WORLD?
WHAT DO YOU MEAN, "WHAT HAPPENED?"
IT'S DIFFERENT NOW. IT WASN'T ALWAYS LIKE THIS.

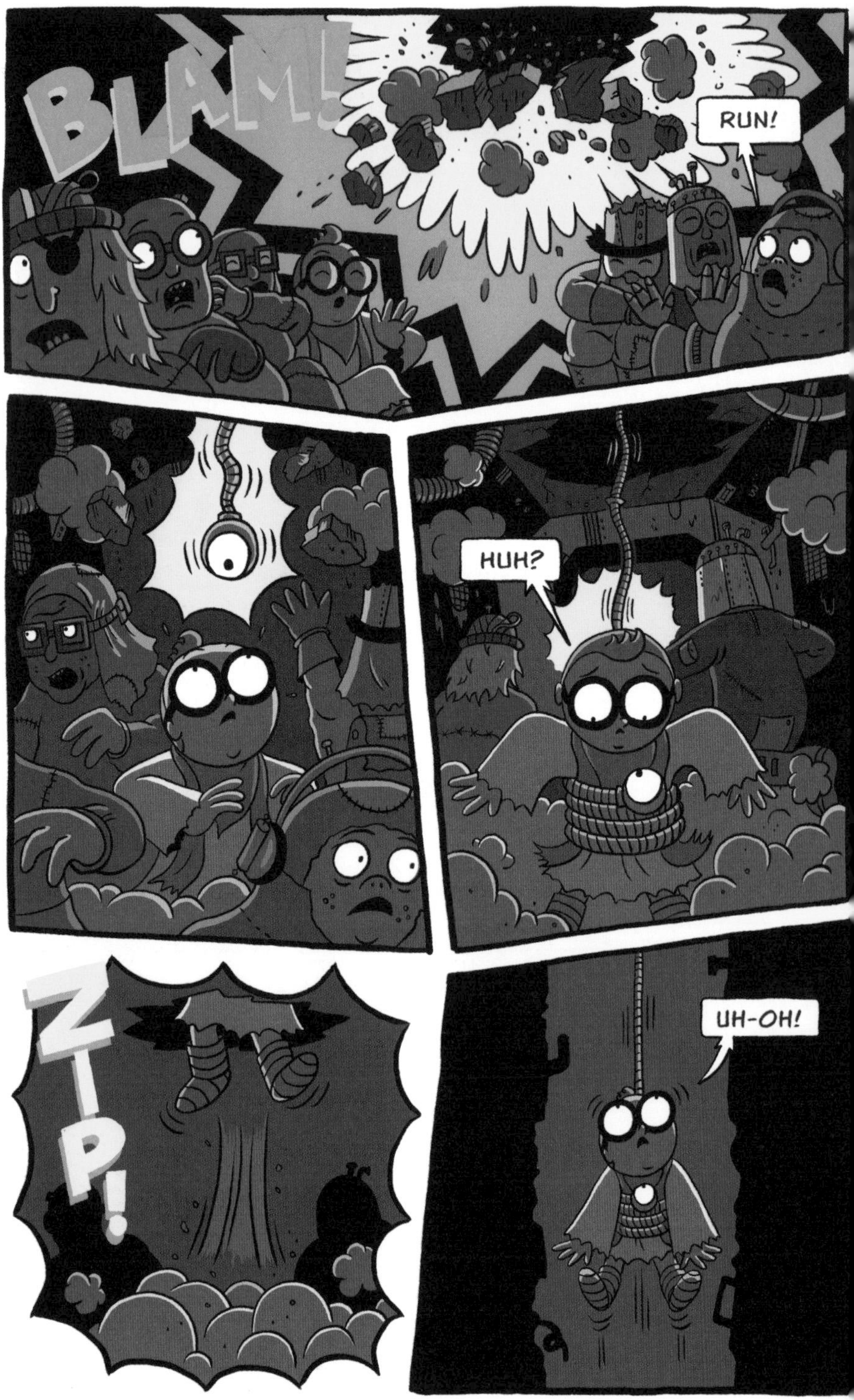
BLAM!
RUN!
HUH?
ZIP!
UH-OH!

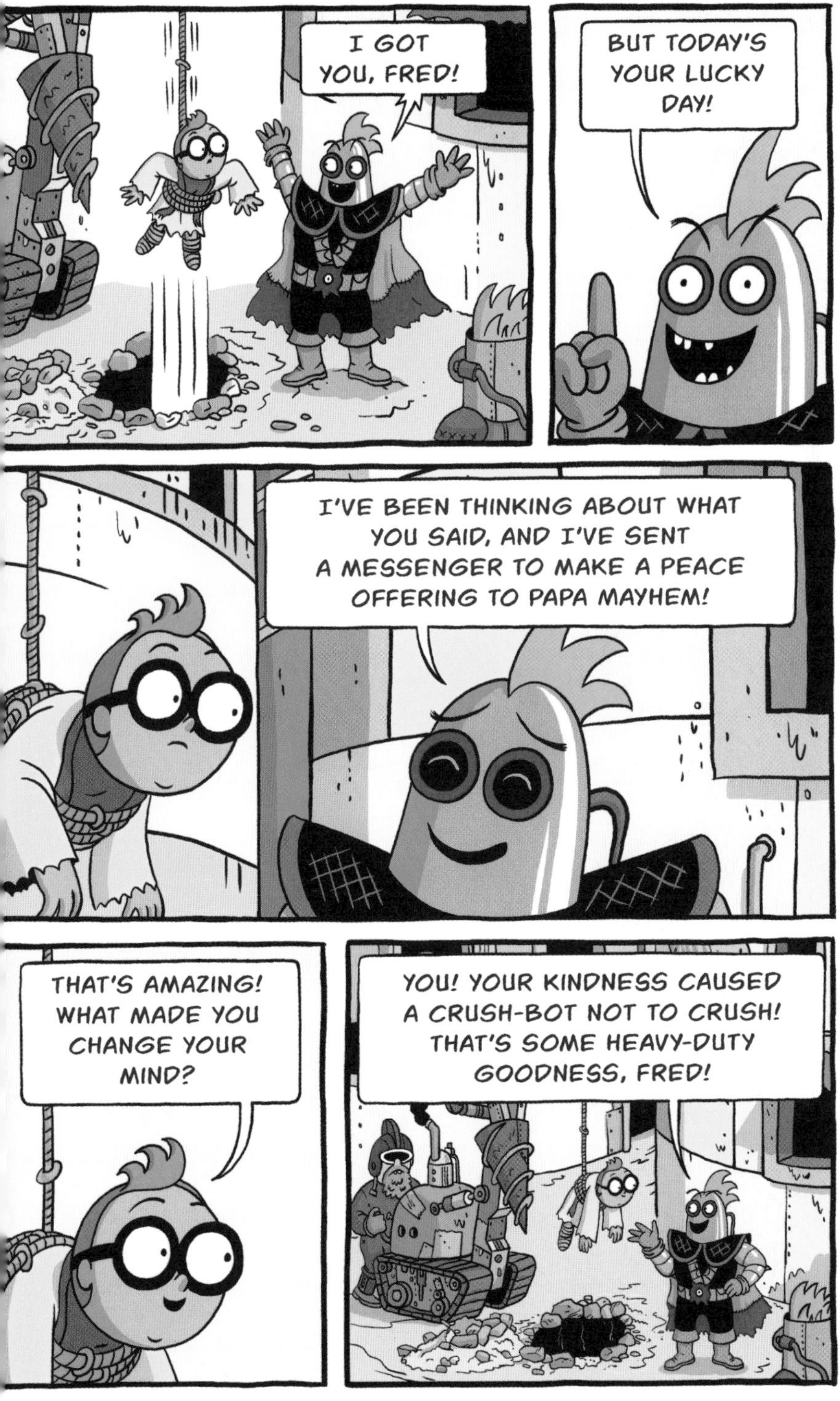

I GOT YOU, FRED!
BUT TODAY'S YOUR LUCKY DAY!
I'VE BEEN THINKING ABOUT WHAT YOU SAID, AND I'VE SENT A MESSENGER TO MAKE A PEACE OFFERING TO PAPA MAYHEM!
THAT'S AMAZING! WHAT MADE YOU CHANGE YOUR MIND?
YOU! YOUR KINDNESS CAUSED A CRUSH-BOT NOT TO CRUSH! THAT'S SOME HEAVY-DUTY GOODNESS, FRED!

198

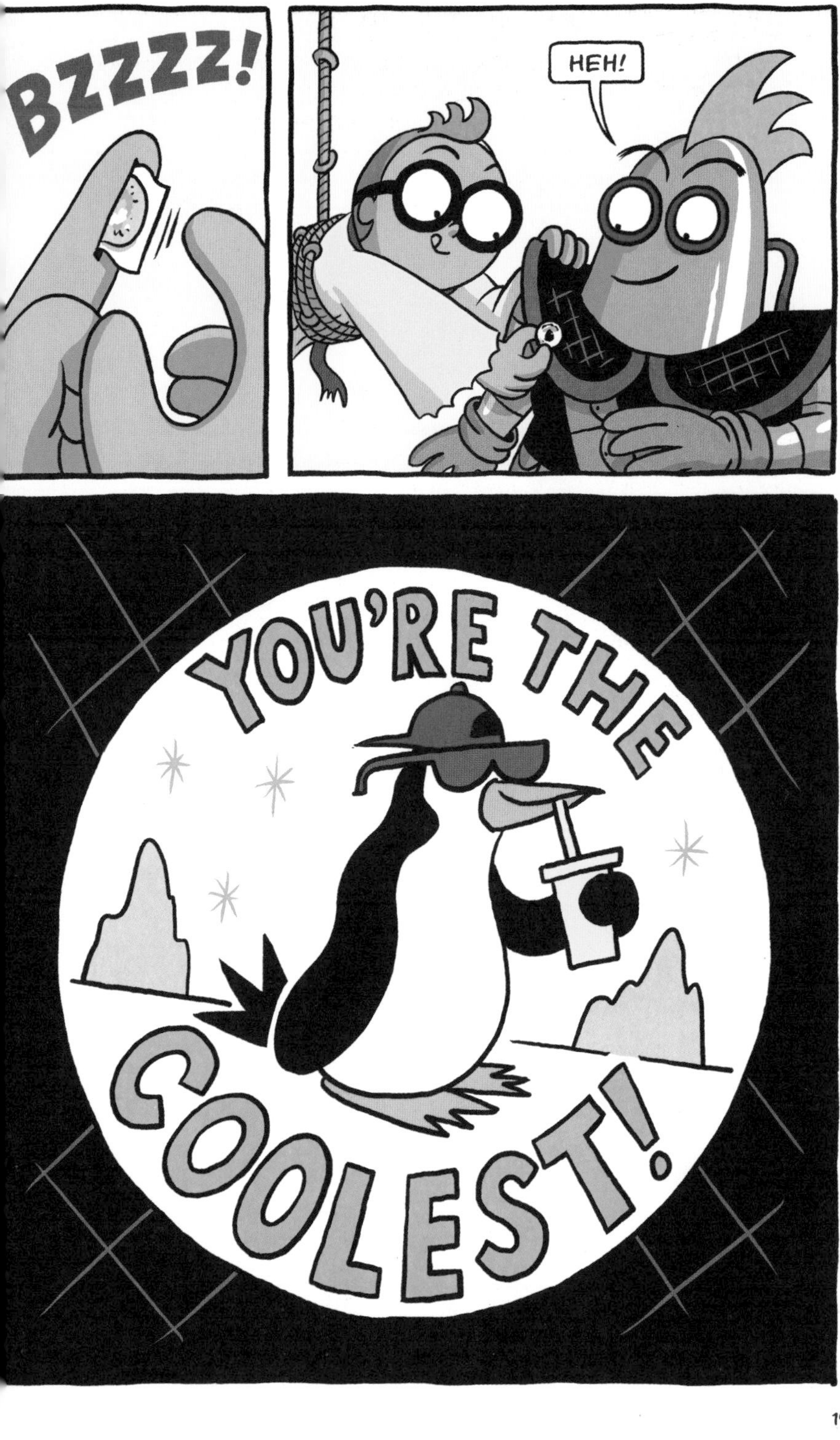
BZZZZZ!
HEH!
YOU'RE THE COOLEST!

CHAPTER 16

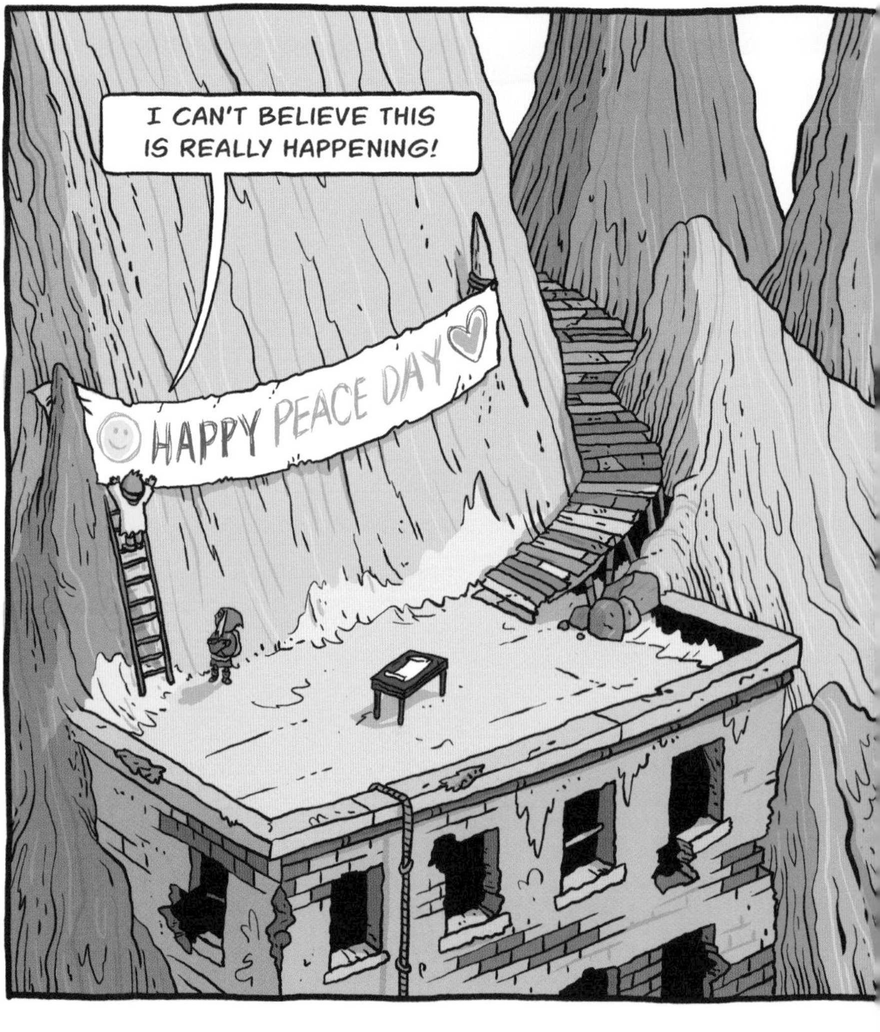
I CAN'T BELIEVE THIS IS REALLY HAPPENING!
HAPPY PEACE DAY

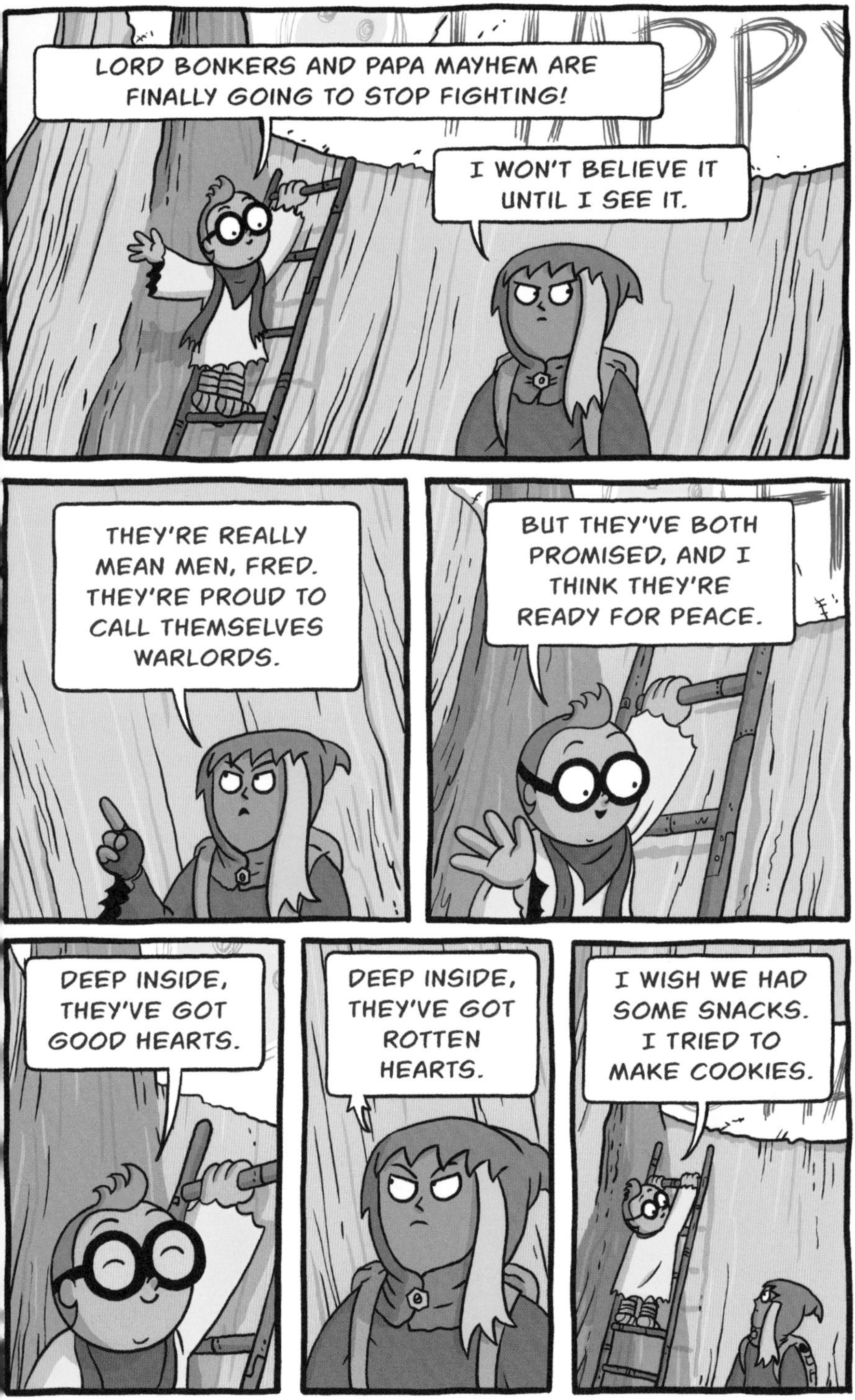
LORD BONKERS AND PAPA MAYHEM ARE FINALLY GOING TO STOP FIGHTING!
I WON'T BELIEVE IT UNTIL I SEE IT.
THEY'RE REALLY MEAN MEN, FRED. THEY'RE PROUD TO CALL THEMSELVES WARLORDS.
BUT THEY'VE BOTH PROMISED, AND I THINK THEY'RE READY FOR PEACE.
DEEP INSIDE, THEY'VE GOT GOOD HEARTS.
DEEP INSIDE, THEY'VE GOT ROTTEN HEARTS.
I WISH WE HAD SOME SNACKS. I TRIED TO MAKE COOKIES.

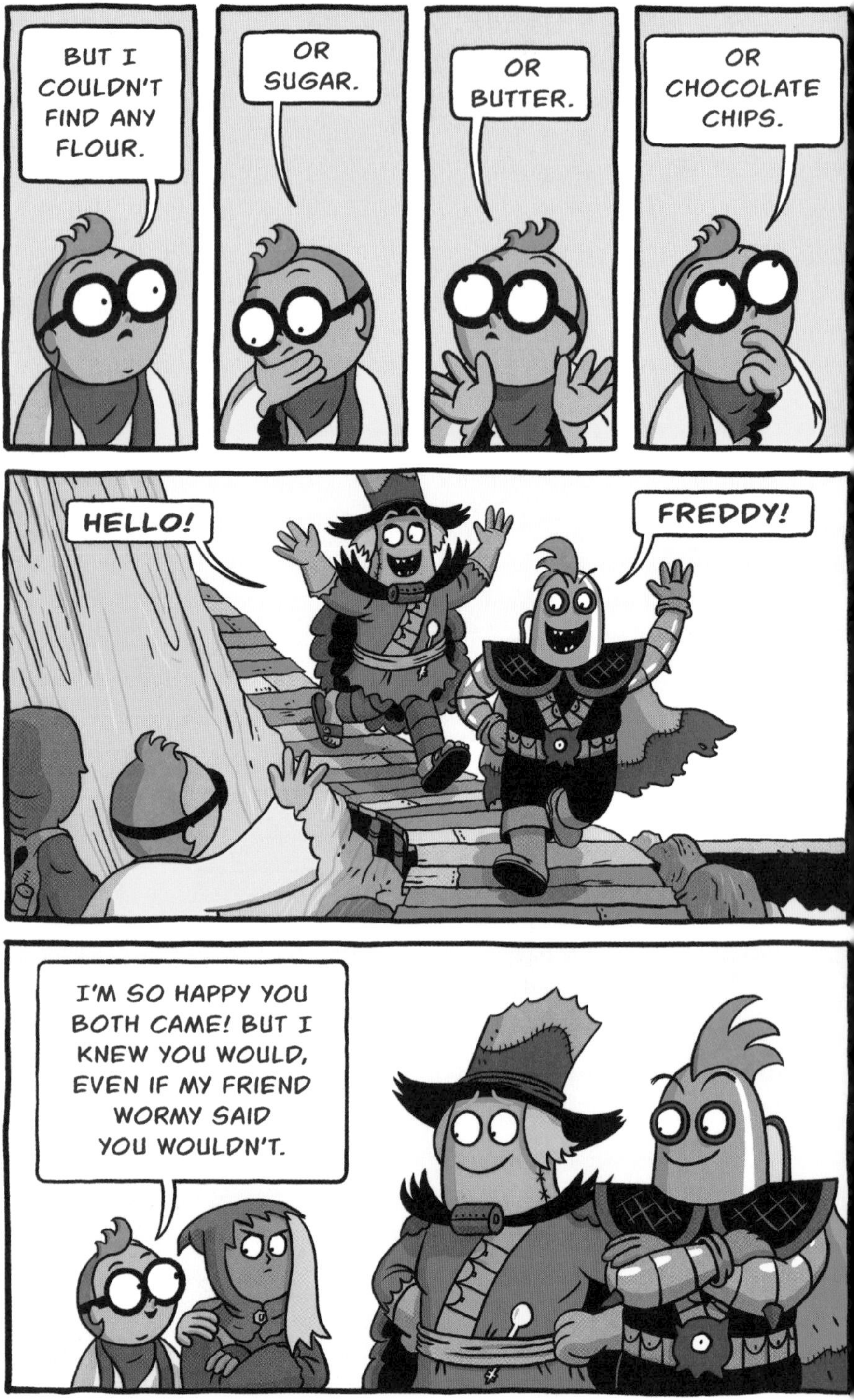
BUT I COULDN'T FIND ANY FLOUR.
OR SUGAR.
OR BUTTER.
OR CHOCOLATE CHIPS.
HELLO!
FREDDY!
I'M SO HAPPY YOU BOTH CAME! BUT I KNEW YOU WOULD, EVEN IF MY FRIEND WORMY SAID YOU WOULDN'T.

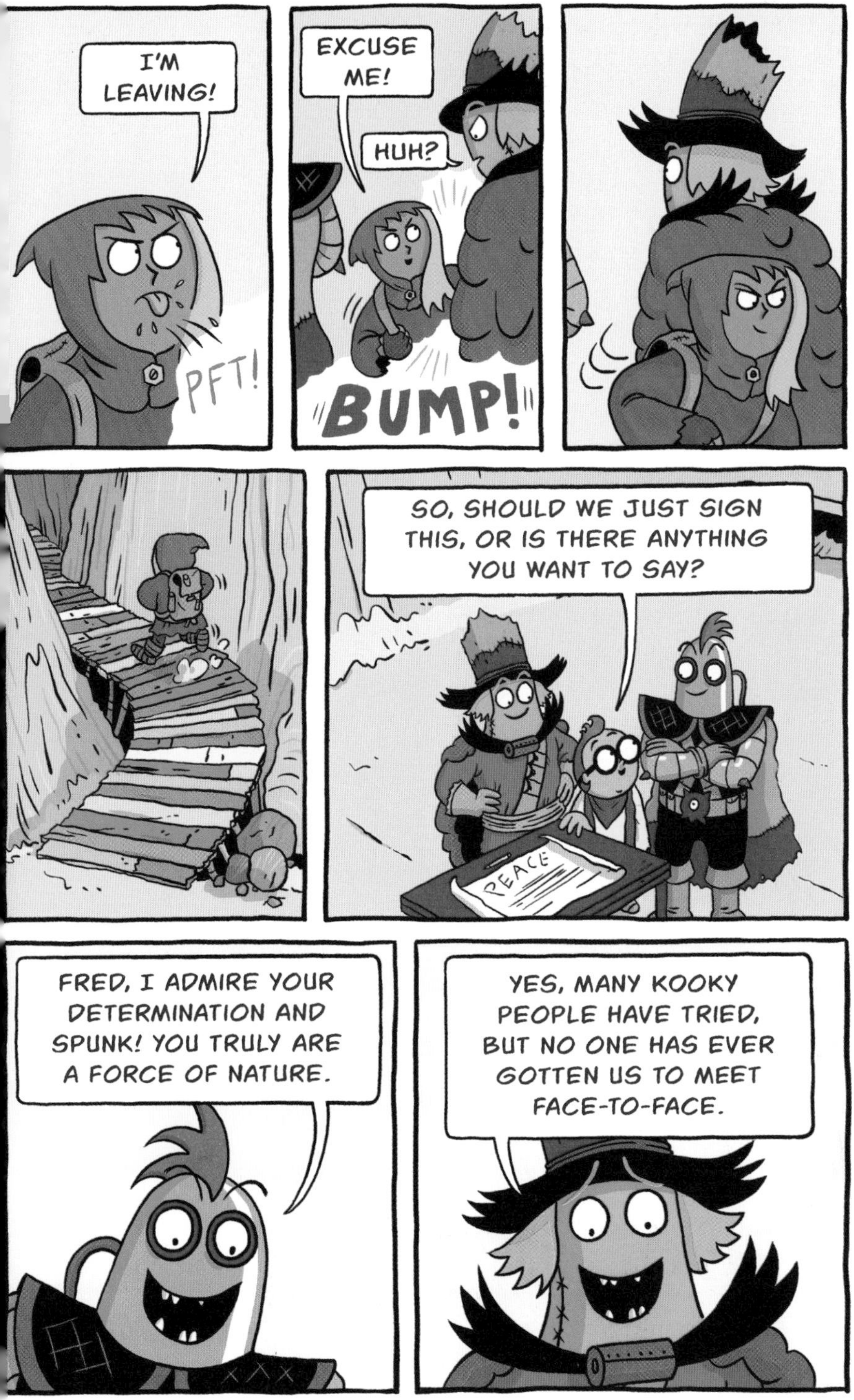
I'M LEAVING!
PFT!
EXCUSE ME!
HUH?
BUMP!
SO, SHOULD WE JUST SIGN THIS, OR IS THERE ANYTHING YOU WANT TO SAY?
PEACE
FRED, I ADMIRE YOUR DETERMINATION AND SPUNK! YOU TRULY ARE A FORCE OF NATURE.
YES, MANY KOOKY PEOPLE HAVE TRIED, BUT NO ONE HAS EVER GOTTEN US TO MEET FACE-TO-FACE.

AND NO ONE HAS EVER GOTTEN US TO AGREE TO A TREATY! TO PROVE MY DEDICATION TO LIVING IN PEACE AND HARMONY, I HAVE SOMETHING FOR PAPA MAYHEM.

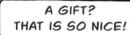

HAPPY PEACE DAY

A GIFT? THAT IS SO NICE!

BEHOLD! THE DESTRUCTO-DOME!

RUMBLE

RUMBL

RUMBLE

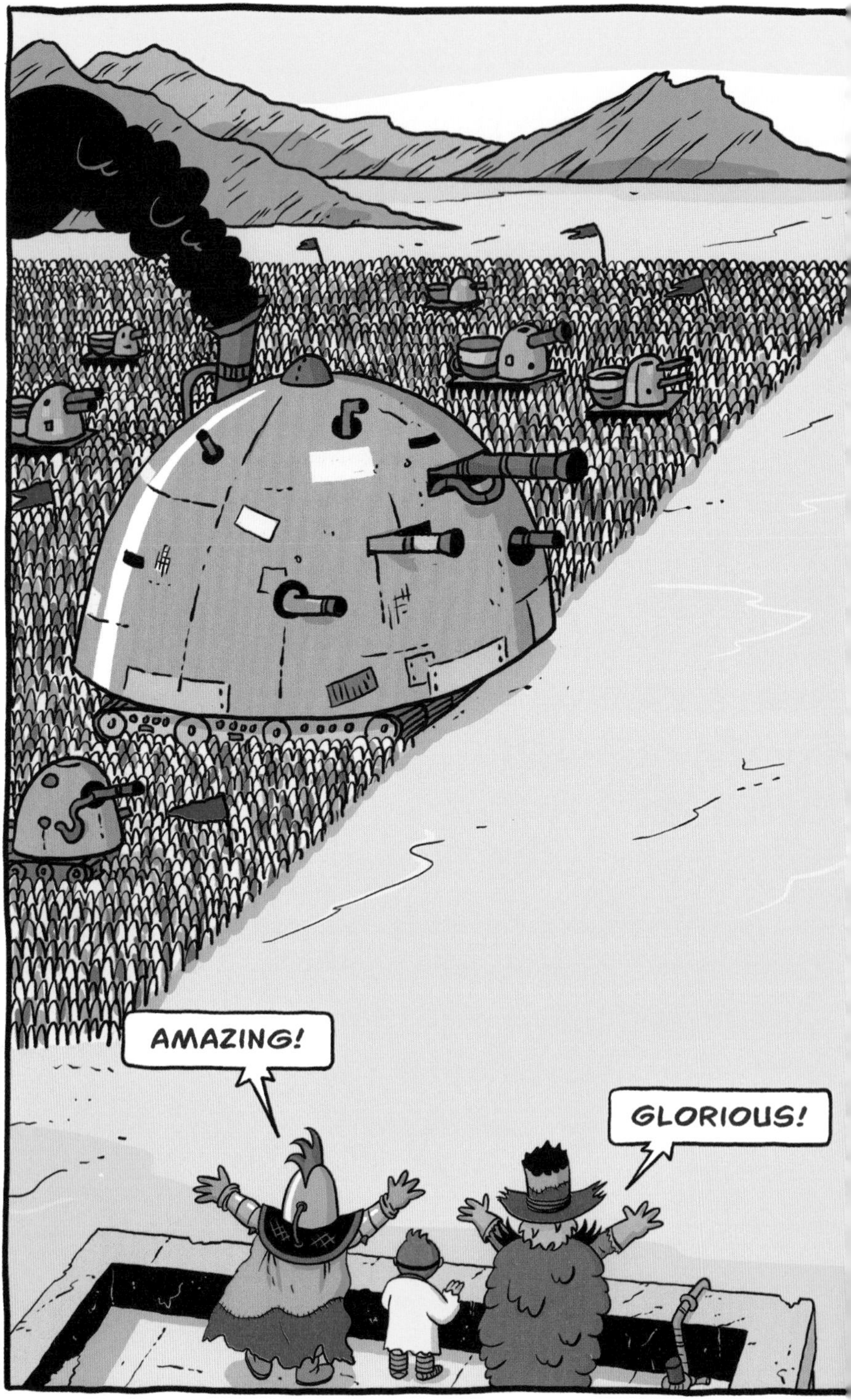
AMAZING!
GLORIOUS!

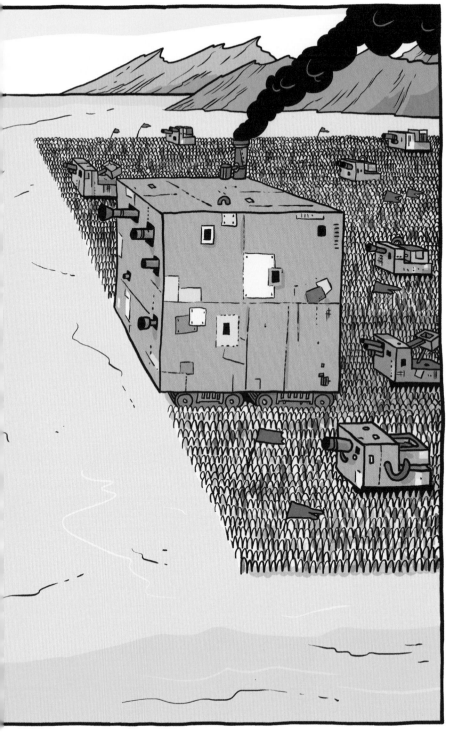

210

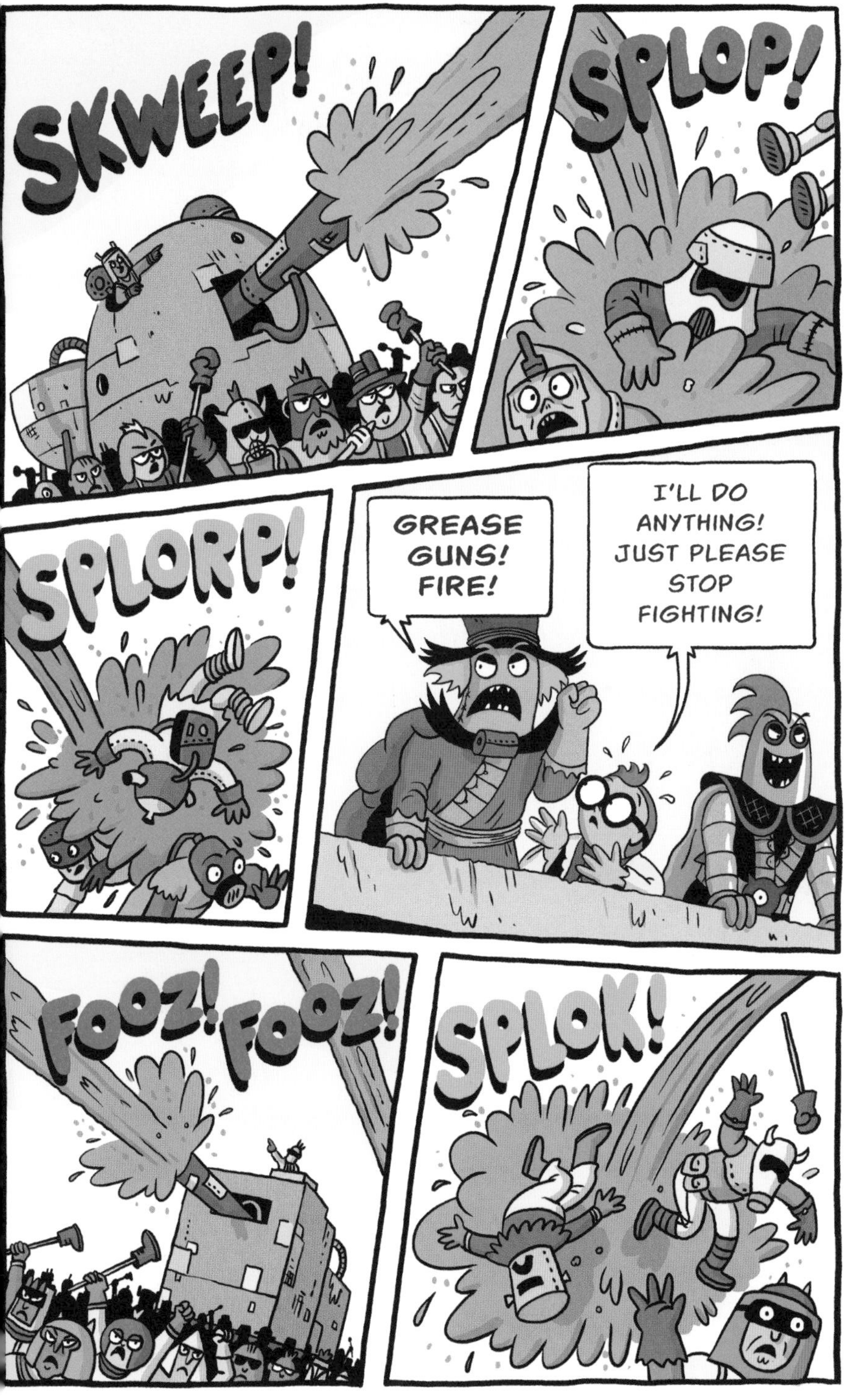
SKWEEP!
SPLOP!
SPLORP!
GREASE GUNS! FIRE!
I'LL DO ANYTHING! JUST PLEASE STOP FIGHTING!
FOOZ! FOOZ!
SPLOK!

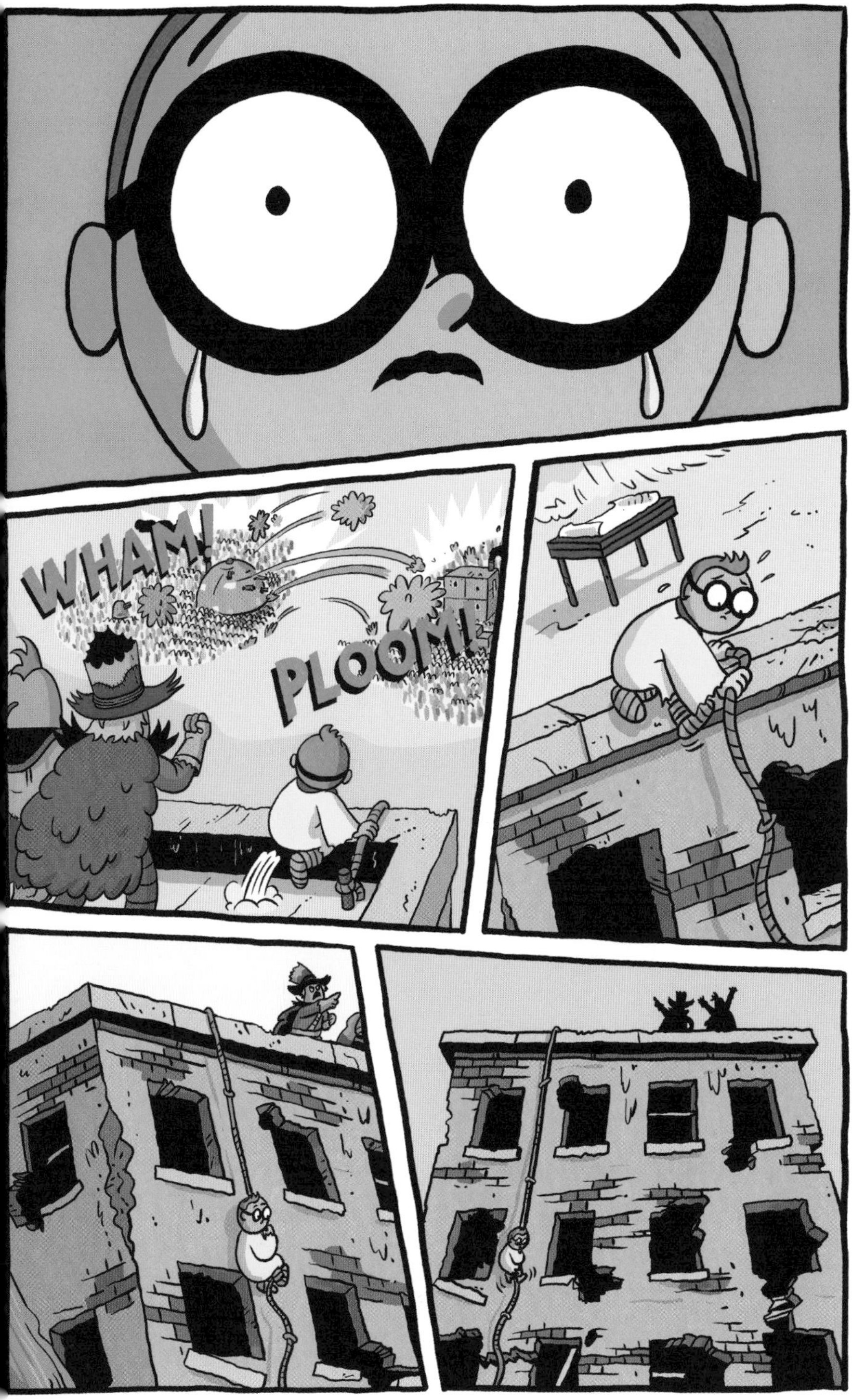
WHAM!
PLOOM!

215

216

217

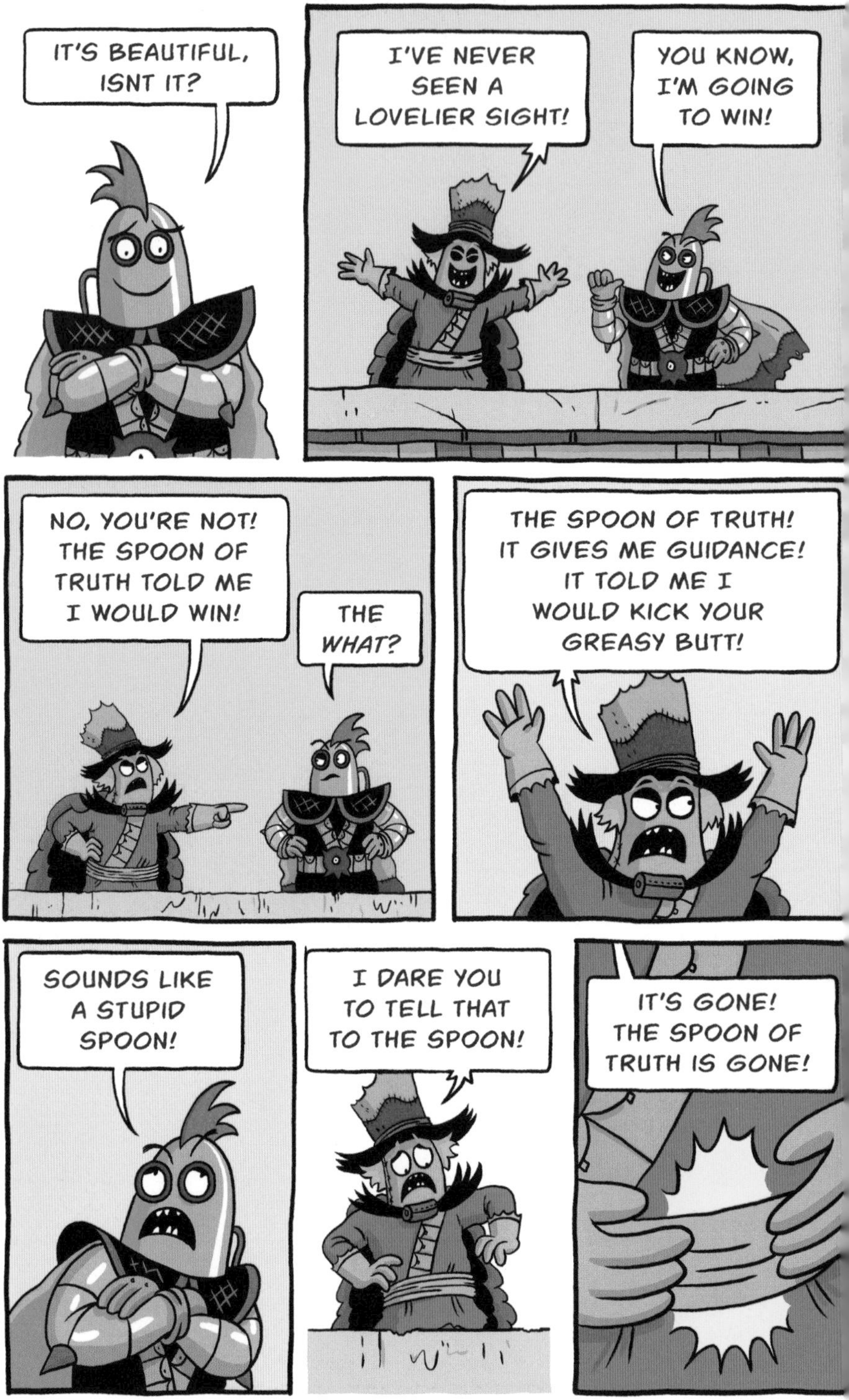
IT'S BEAUTIFUL, ISNT IT?
I'VE NEVER SEEN A LOVELIER SIGHT!
YOU KNOW, I'M GOING TO WIN!
NO, YOU'RE NOT! THE SPOON OF TRUTH TOLD ME I WOULD WIN!
THE *WHAT?*
THE SPOON OF TRUTH! IT GIVES ME GUIDANCE! IT TOLD ME I WOULD KICK YOUR GREASY BUTT!
SOUNDS LIKE A STUPID SPOON!
I DARE YOU TO TELL THAT TO THE SPOON!
IT'S GONE! THE SPOON OF TRUTH IS GONE!

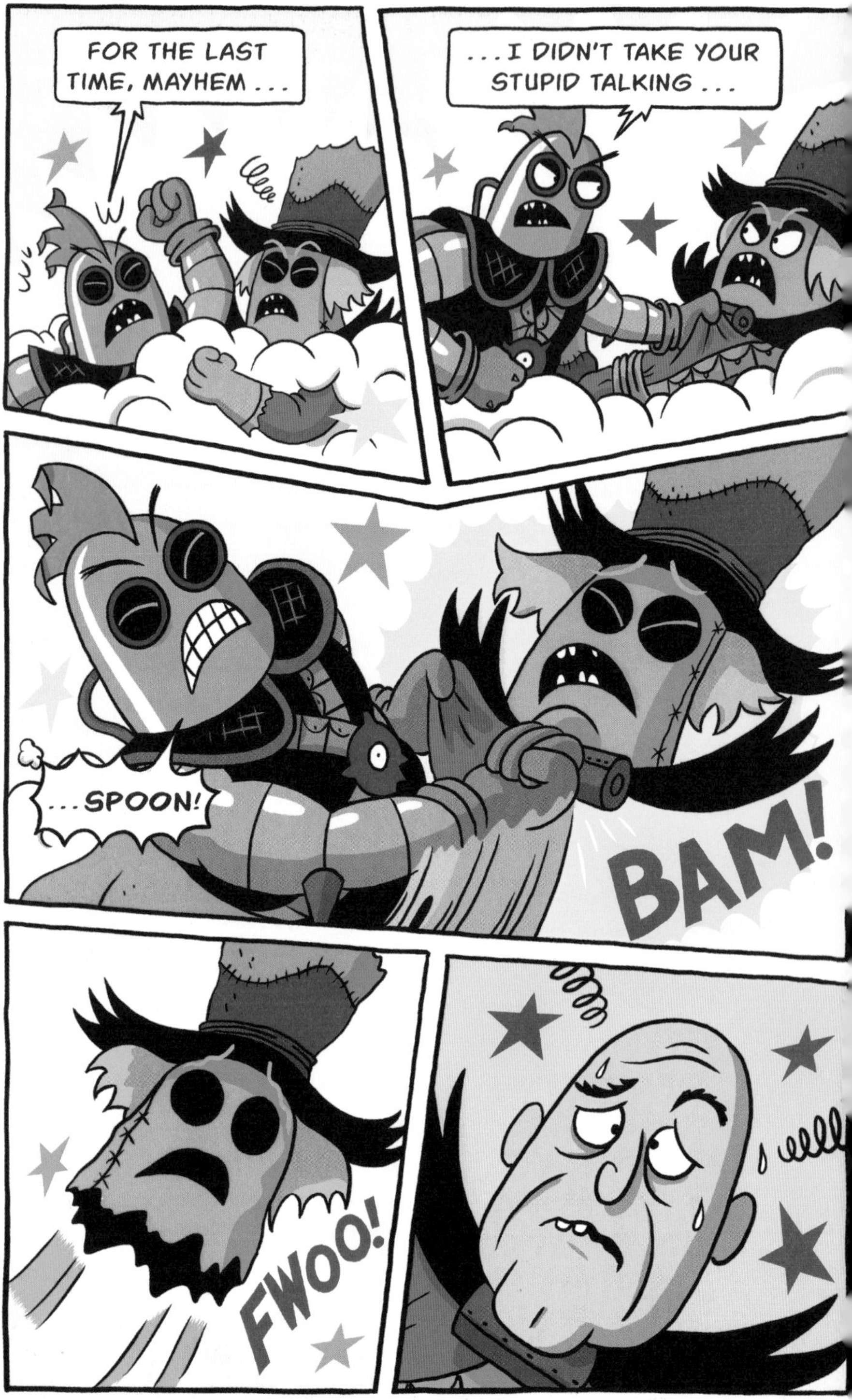
FOR THE LAST TIME, MAYHEM . . .
. . . I DIDN'T TAKE YOUR STUPID TALKING . . .
. . . SPOON!
BAM!
FWOO!

223

225

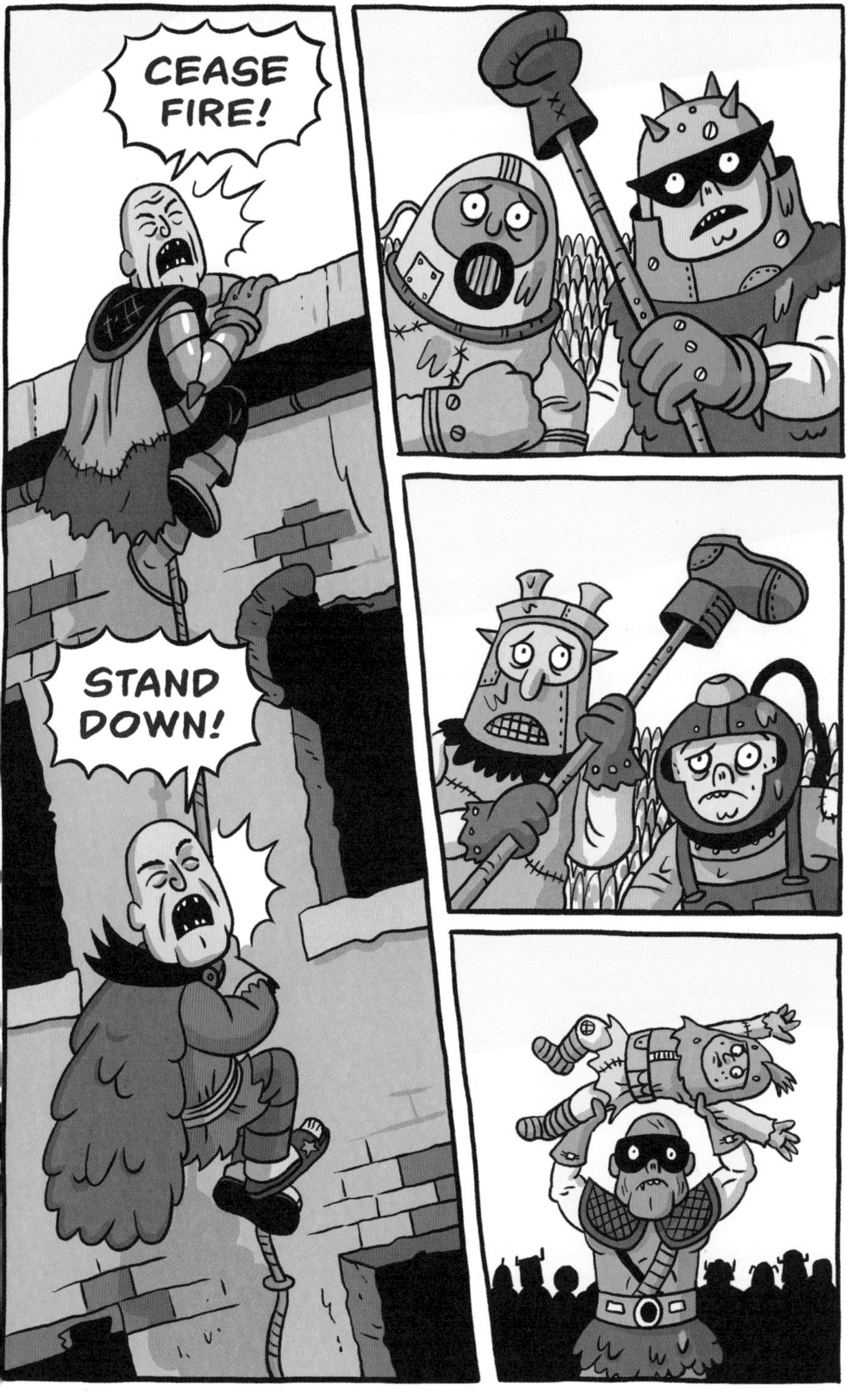

CEASE FIRE!
STAND DOWN!

CHAPTER 17

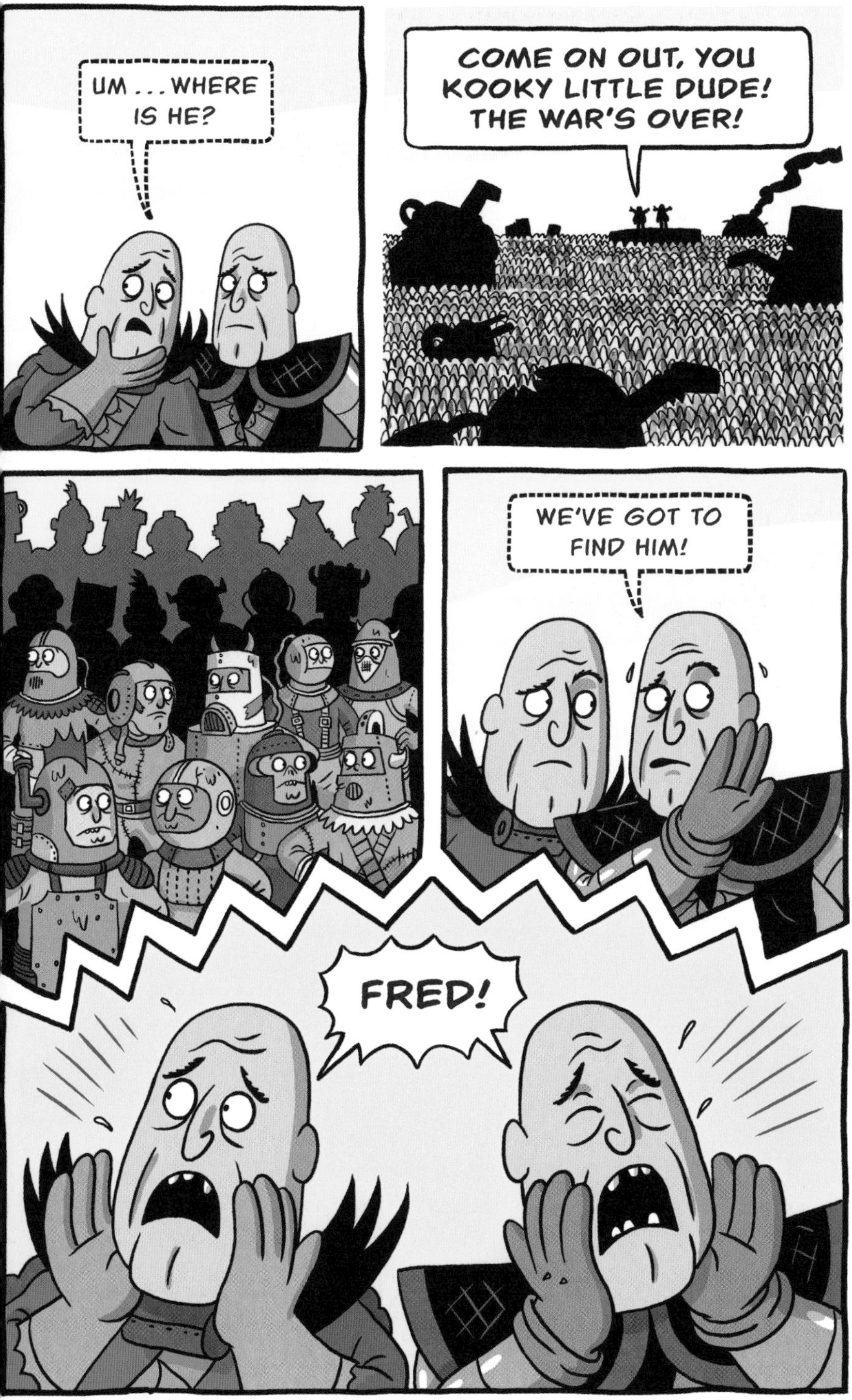
UM . . . WHERE IS HE?
COME ON OUT, YOU KOOKY LITTLE DUDE! THE WAR'S OVER!
WE'VE GOT TO FIND HIM!
FRED!

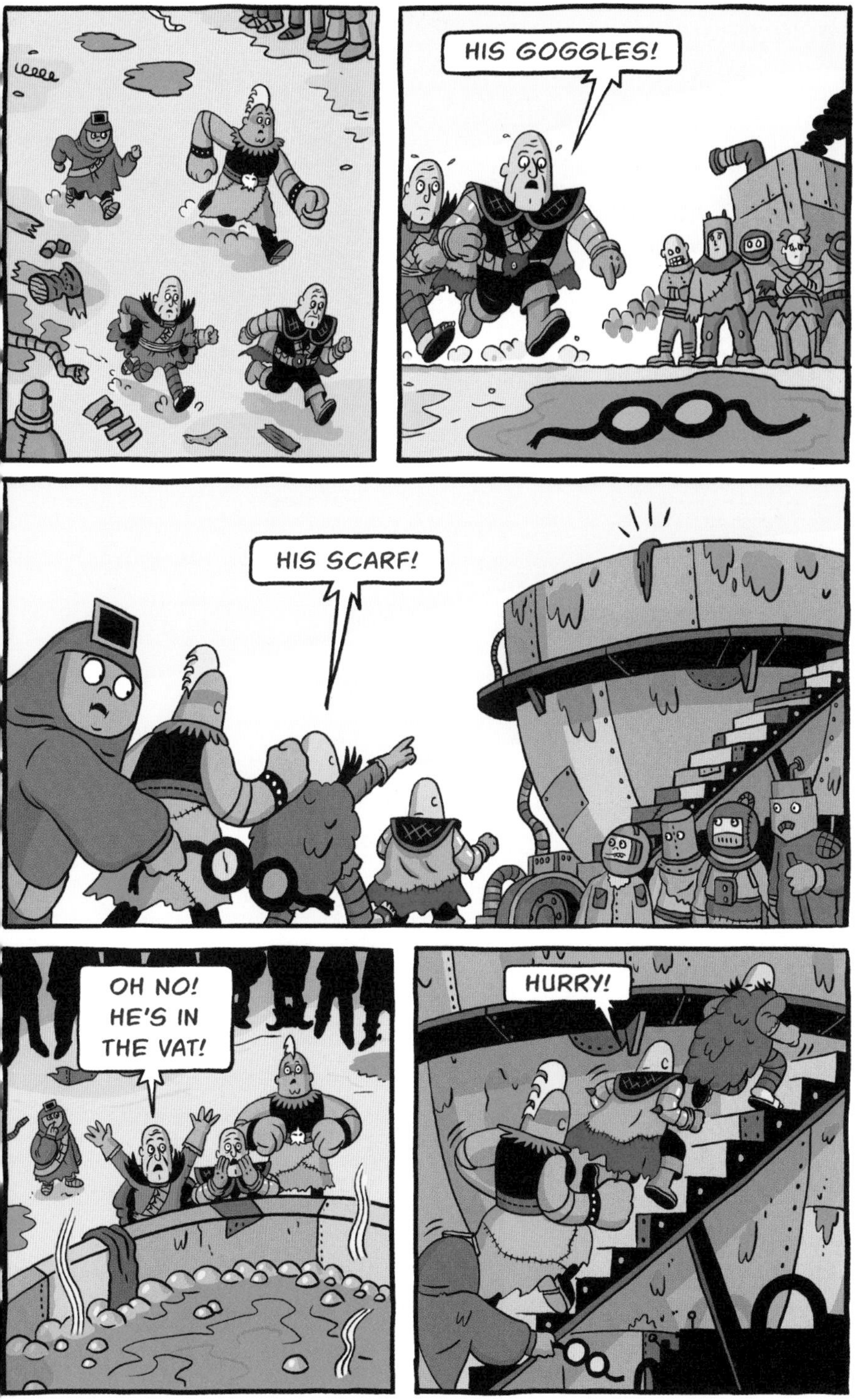
HIS GOGGLES!
HIS SCARF!
OH NO! HE'S IN THE VAT!
HURRY!

234

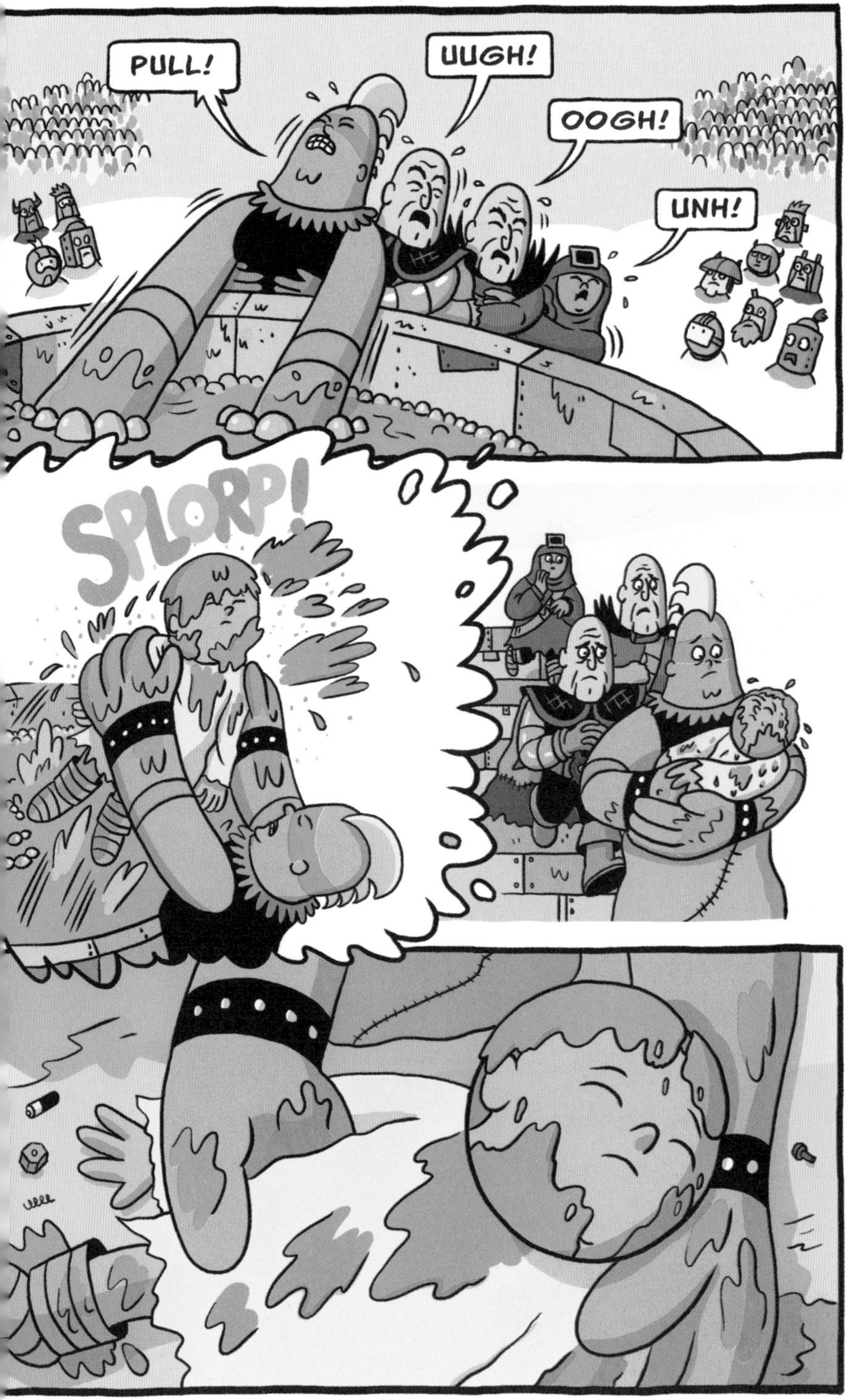
PULL!
UUGH!
OOGH!
UNH!
SPLORP!

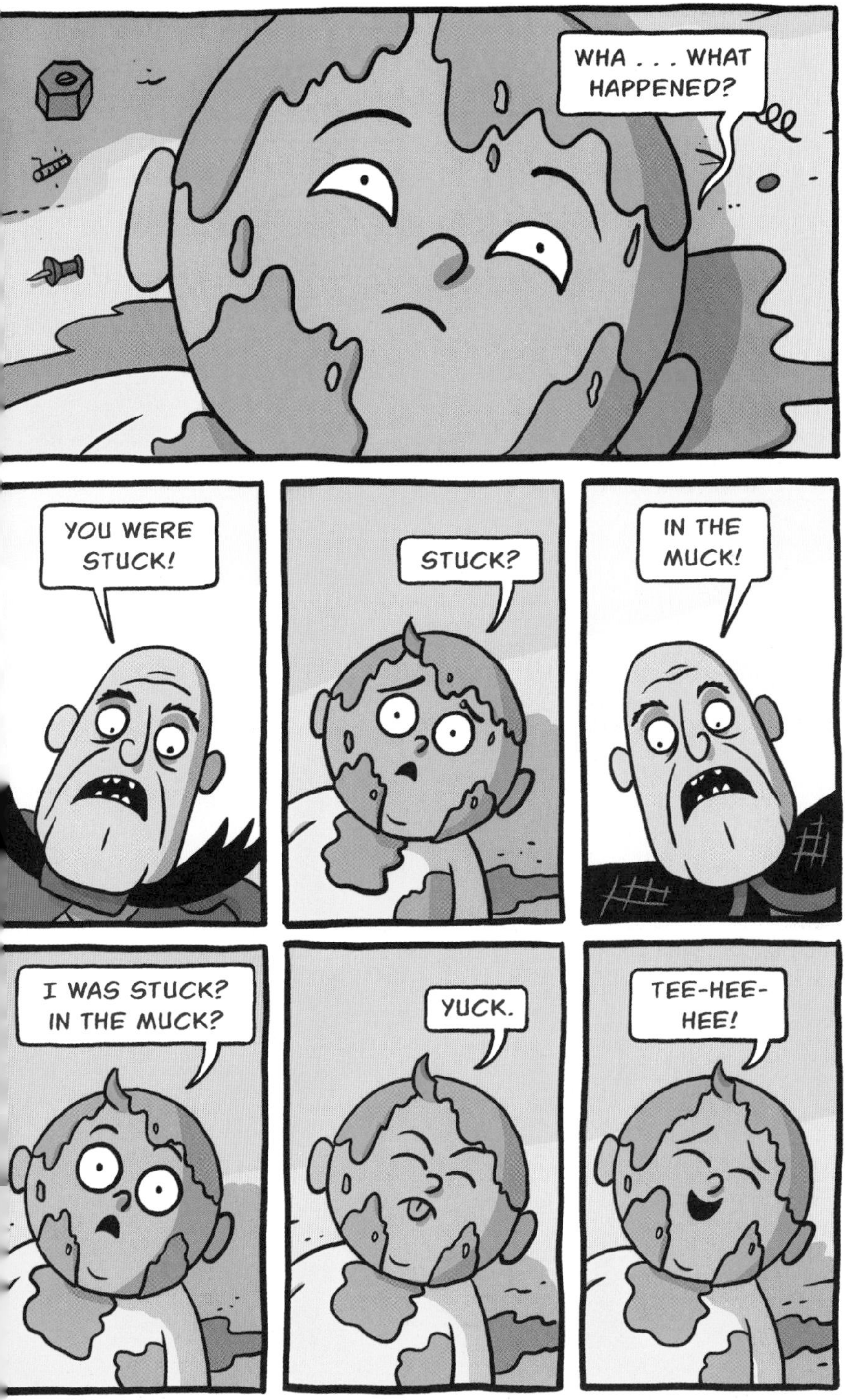
WHA . . . WHAT HAPPENED?
YOU WERE STUCK!
STUCK?
IN THE MUCK!
I WAS STUCK? IN THE MUCK?
YUCK.
TEE-HEE-HEE!

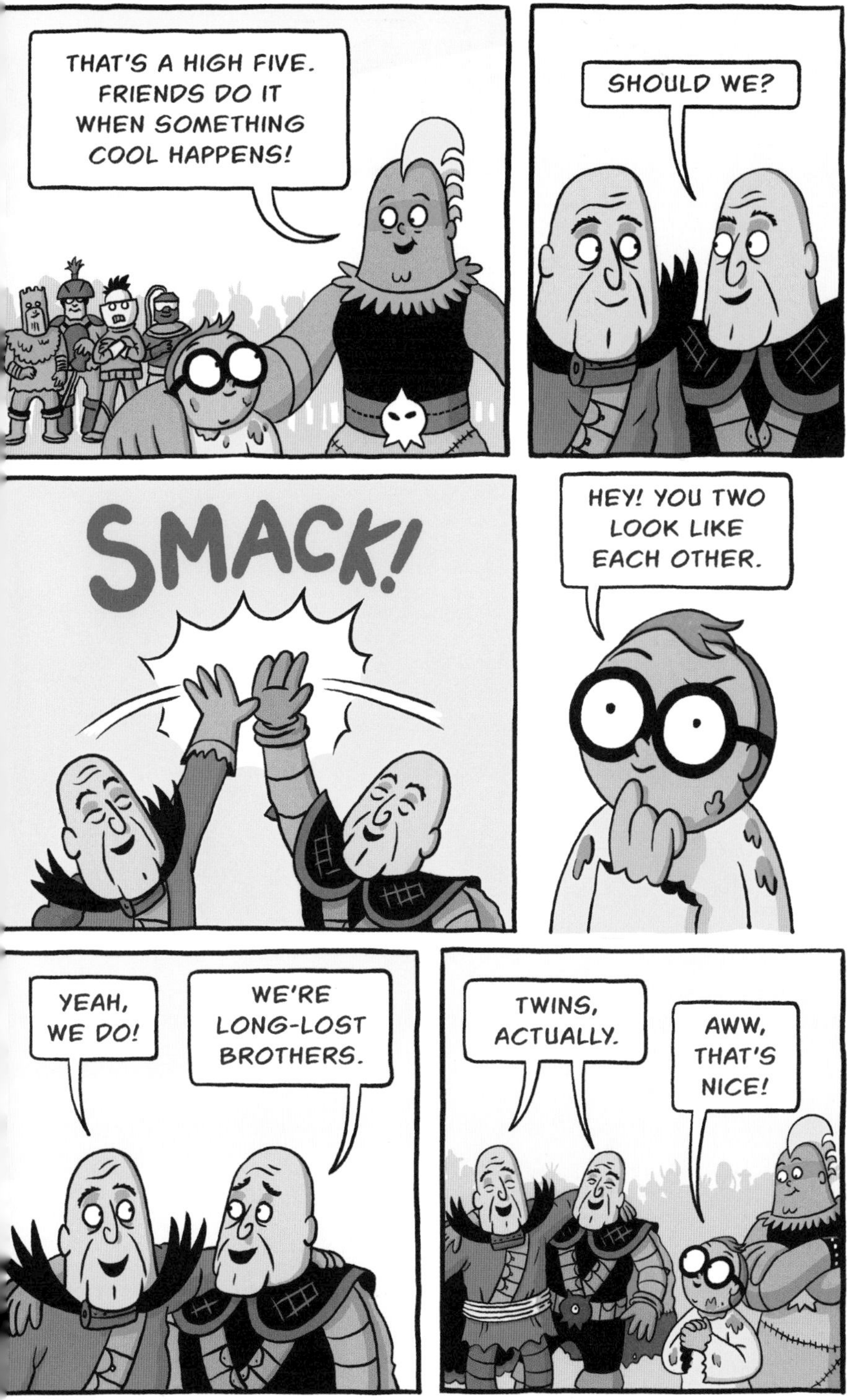
THAT'S A HIGH FIVE. FRIENDS DO IT WHEN SOMETHING COOL HAPPENS!
SHOULD WE?
SMACK!
HEY! YOU TWO LOOK LIKE EACH OTHER.
YEAH, WE DO!
WE'RE LONG-LOST BROTHERS.
TWINS, ACTUALLY.
AWW, THAT'S NICE!

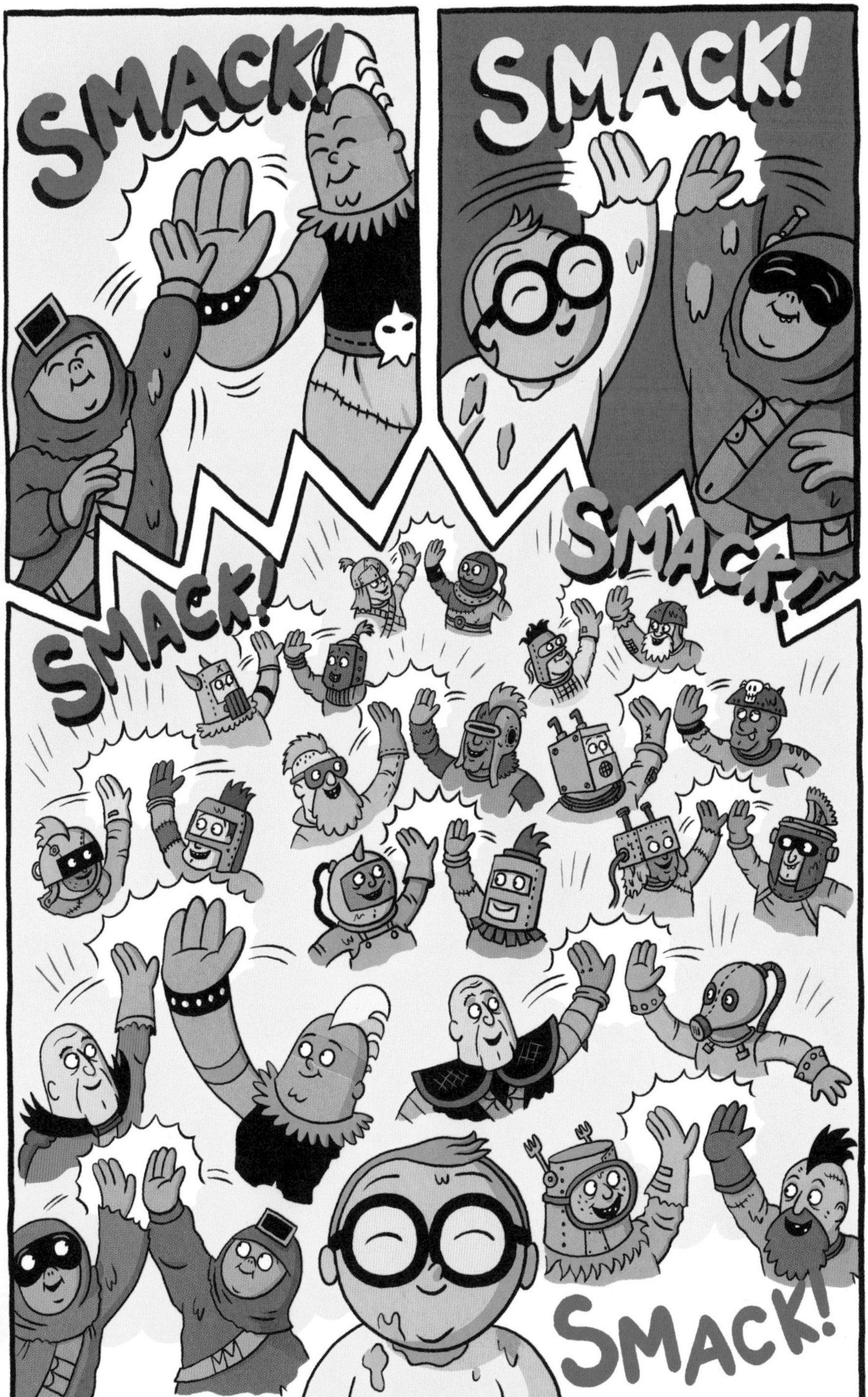
SMACK!
SMACK!
SMACK!
SMACK!
SMACK!

CHAPTER 18

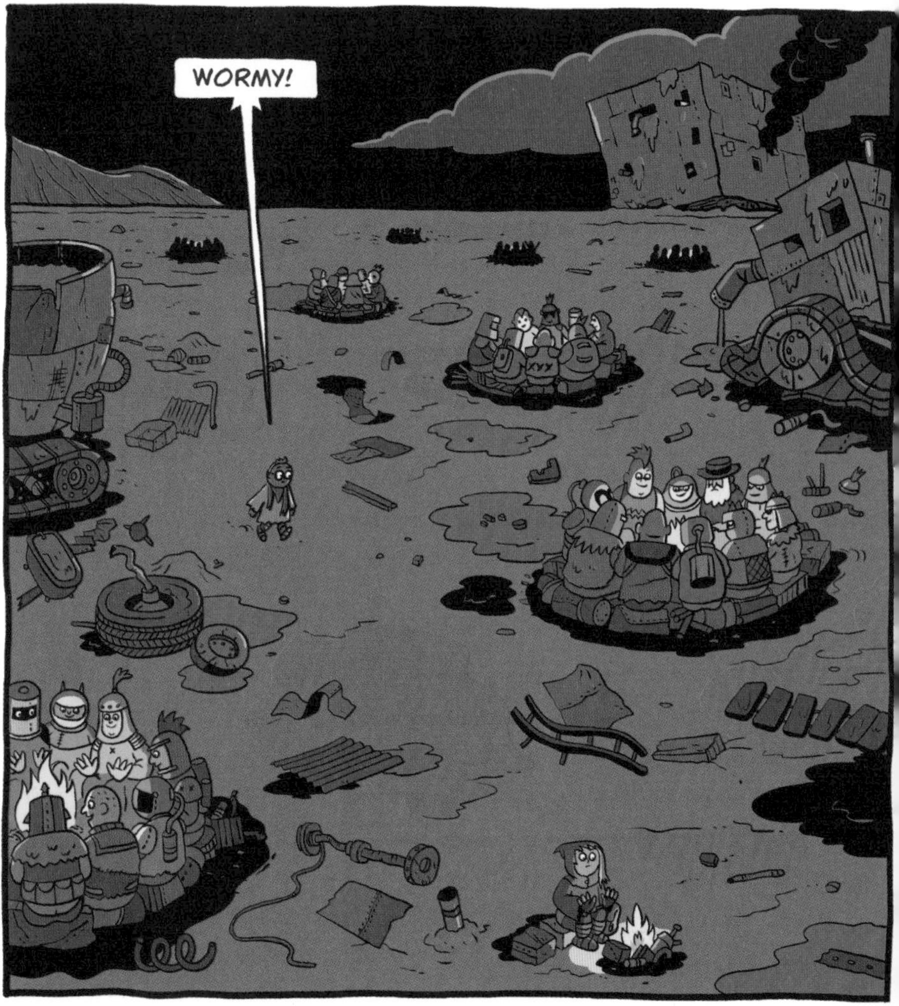

WORMY!
XYY

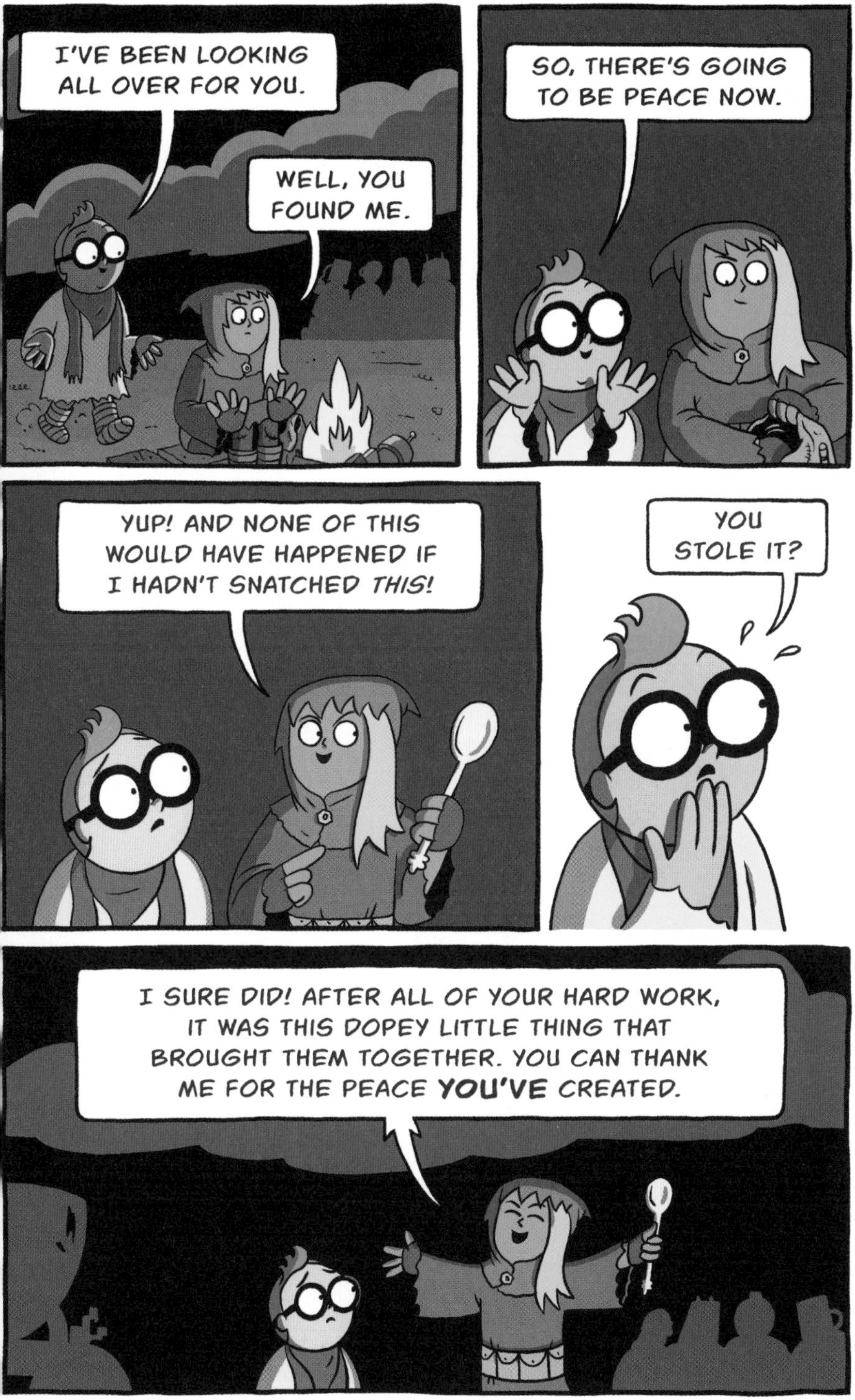
I'VE BEEN LOOKING ALL OVER FOR YOU.
WELL, YOU FOUND ME.
SO, THERE'S GOING TO BE PEACE NOW.
YUP! AND NONE OF THIS WOULD HAVE HAPPENED IF I HADN'T SNATCHED *THIS!*
YOU STOLE IT?
I SURE DID! AFTER ALL OF YOUR HARD WORK, IT WAS THIS DOPEY LITTLE THING THAT BROUGHT THEM TOGETHER. YOU CAN THANK ME FOR THE PEACE **YOU'VE** CREATED.

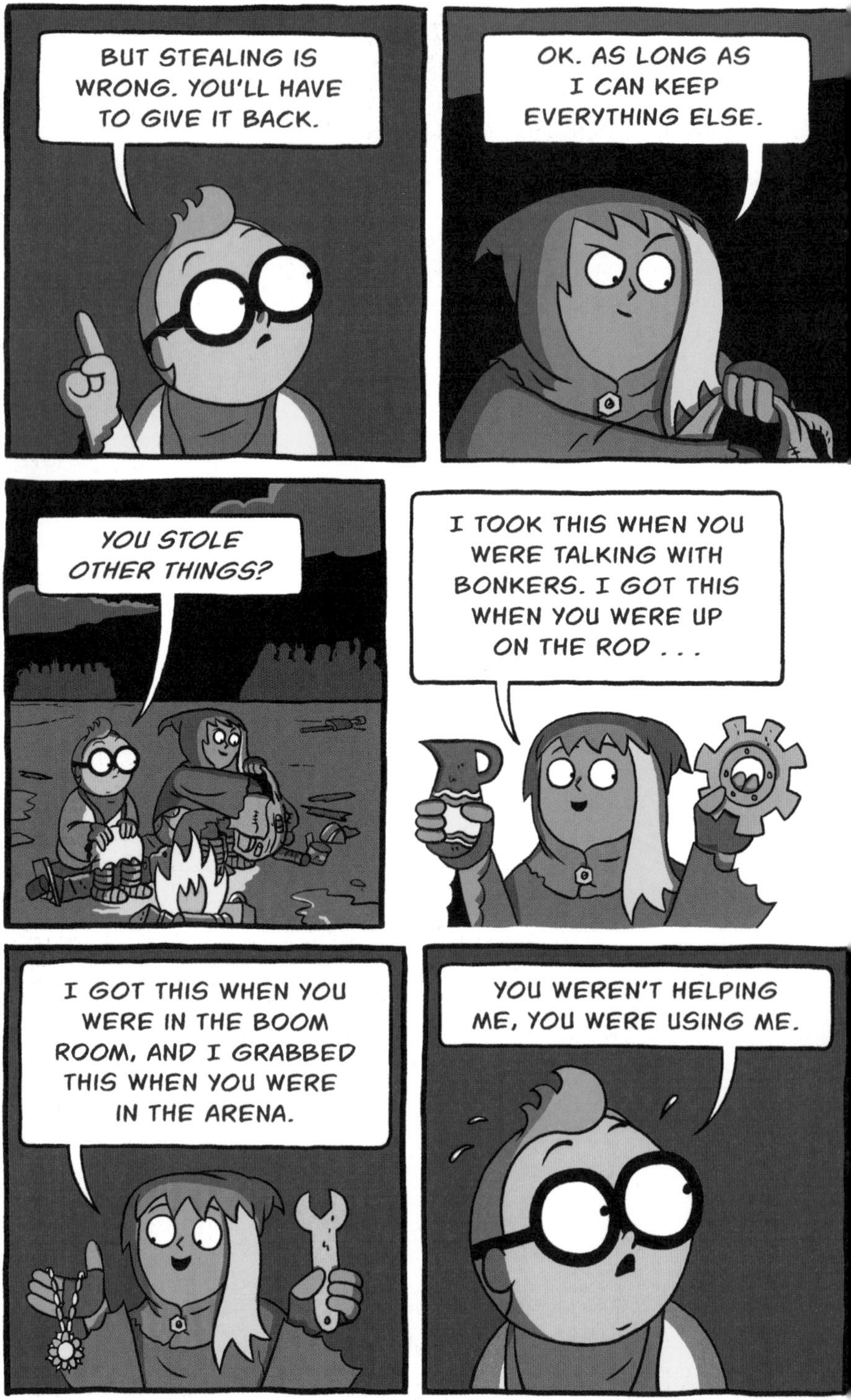
BUT STEALING IS WRONG. YOU'LL HAVE TO GIVE IT BACK.
OK. AS LONG AS I CAN KEEP EVERYTHING ELSE.
YOU STOLE OTHER THINGS?
I TOOK THIS WHEN YOU WERE TALKING WITH BONKERS. I GOT THIS WHEN YOU WERE UP ON THE ROD . . .
I GOT THIS WHEN YOU WERE IN THE BOOM ROOM, AND I GRABBED THIS WHEN YOU WERE IN THE ARENA.
YOU WEREN'T HELPING ME, YOU WERE USING ME.

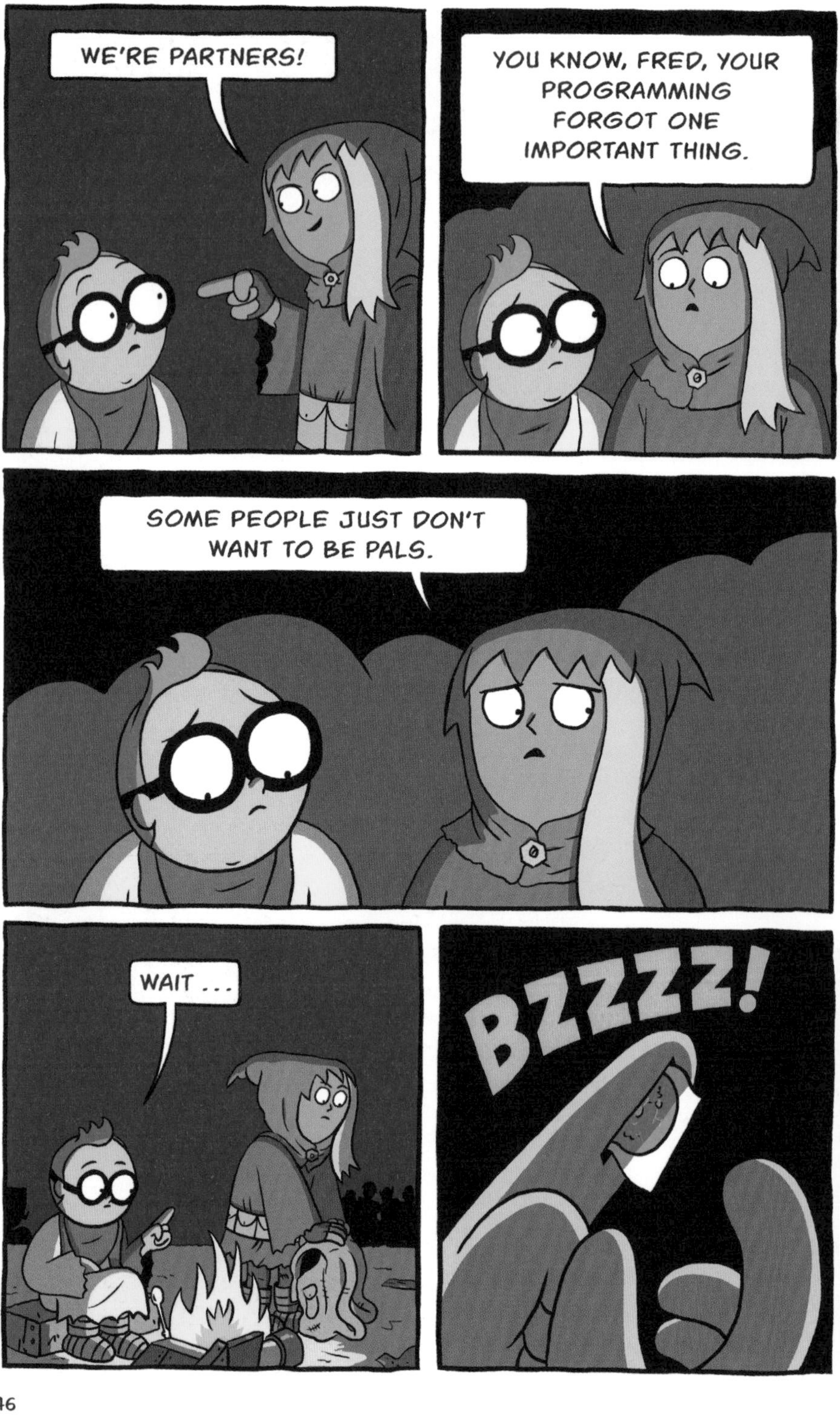
WE'RE PARTNERS!
YOU KNOW, FRED, YOUR PROGRAMMING FORGOT ONE IMPORTANT THING.
SOME PEOPLE JUST DON'T WANT TO BE PALS.
WAIT . . .
BZZZZ!

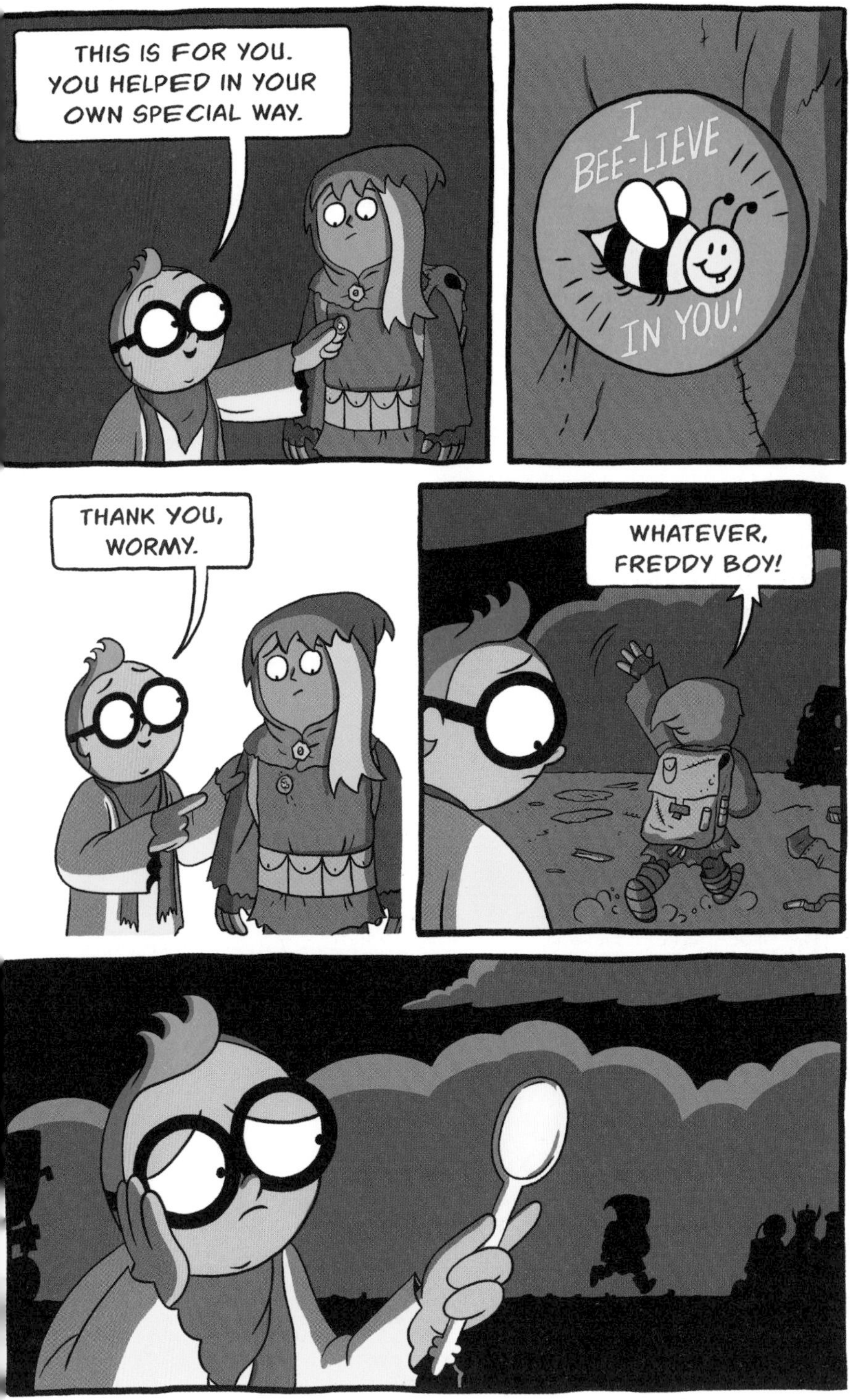
THIS IS FOR YOU. YOU HELPED IN YOUR OWN SPECIAL WAY.
I BEE-LIEVE IN YOU!
THANK YOU, WORMY.
WHATEVER, FREDDY BOY!

CHAPTER 19

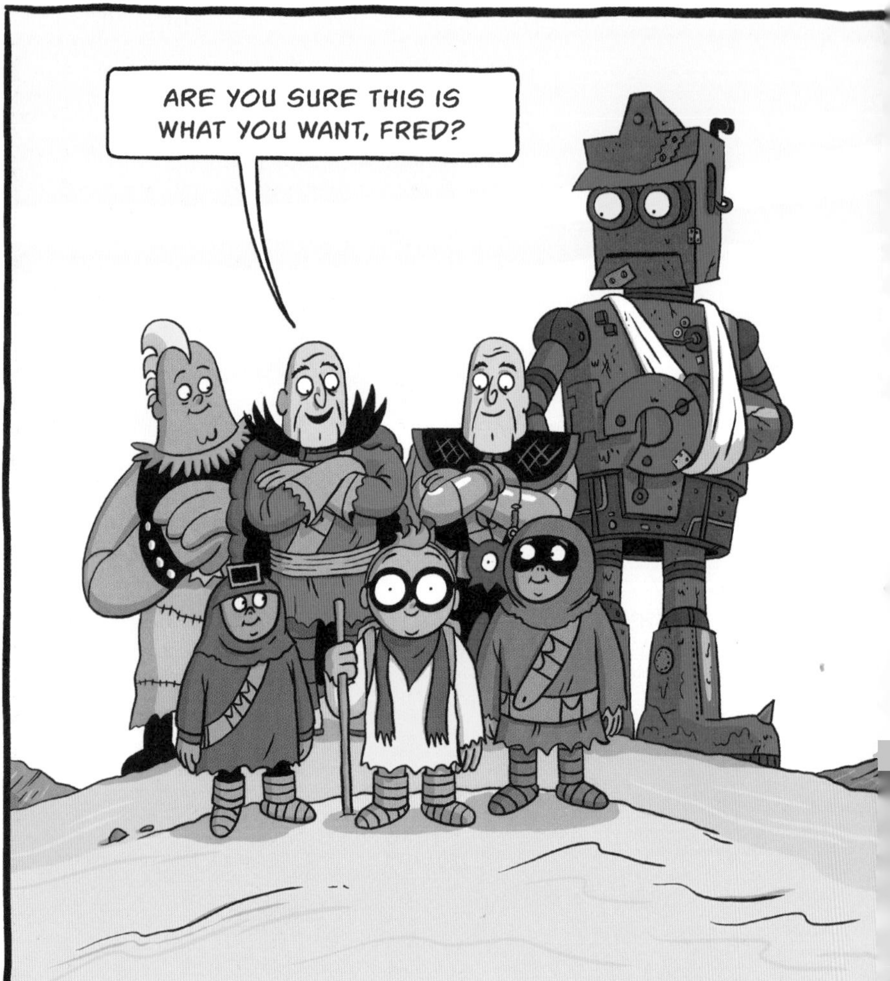
ARE YOU SURE THIS IS WHAT YOU WANT, FRED?

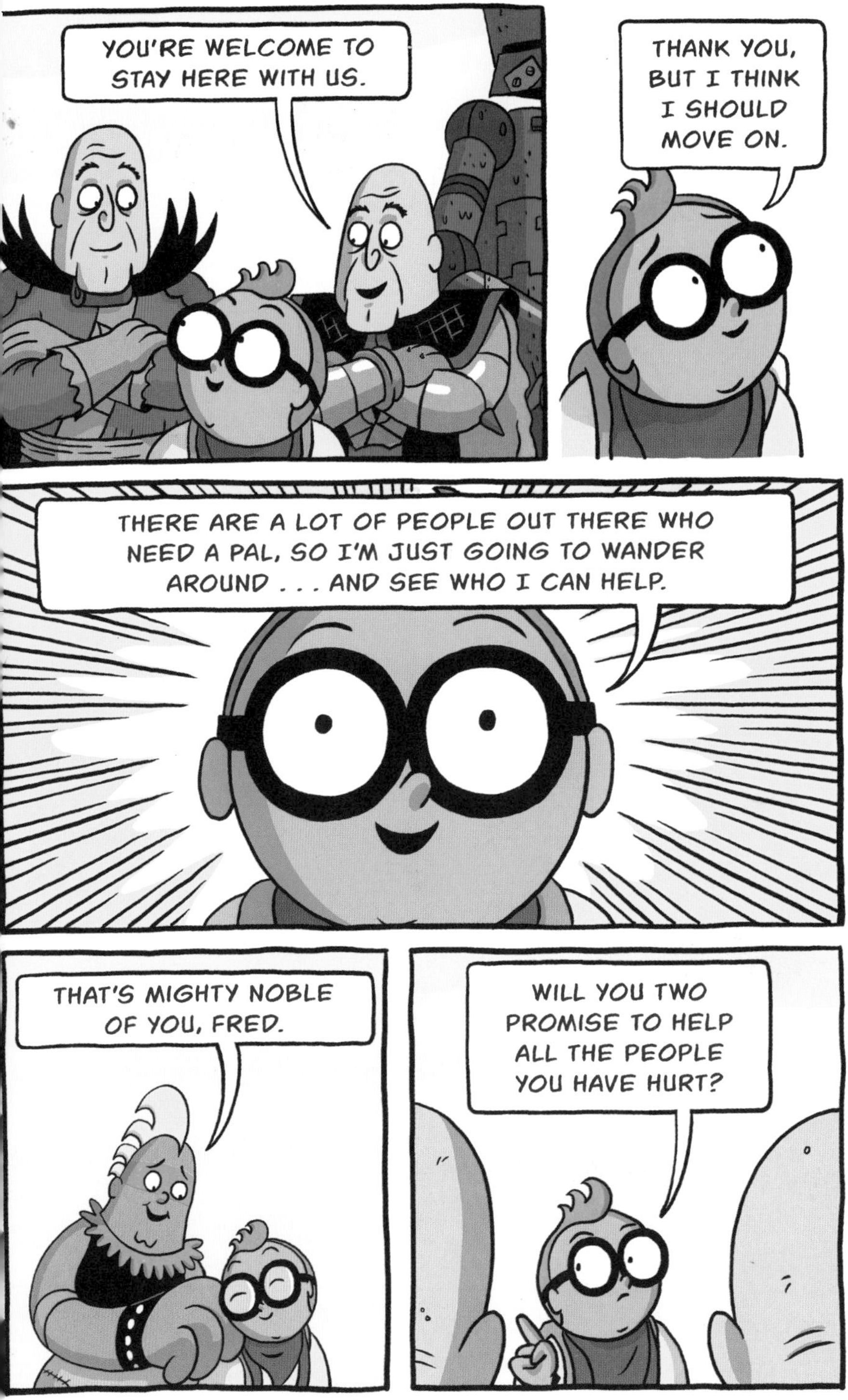
YOU'RE WELCOME TO STAY HERE WITH US.
THANK YOU, BUT I THINK I SHOULD MOVE ON.
THERE ARE A LOT OF PEOPLE OUT THERE WHO NEED A PAL, SO I'M JUST GOING TO WANDER AROUND . . . AND SEE WHO I CAN HELP.
THAT'S MIGHTY NOBLE OF YOU, FRED.
WILL YOU TWO PROMISE TO HELP ALL THE PEOPLE YOU HAVE HURT?

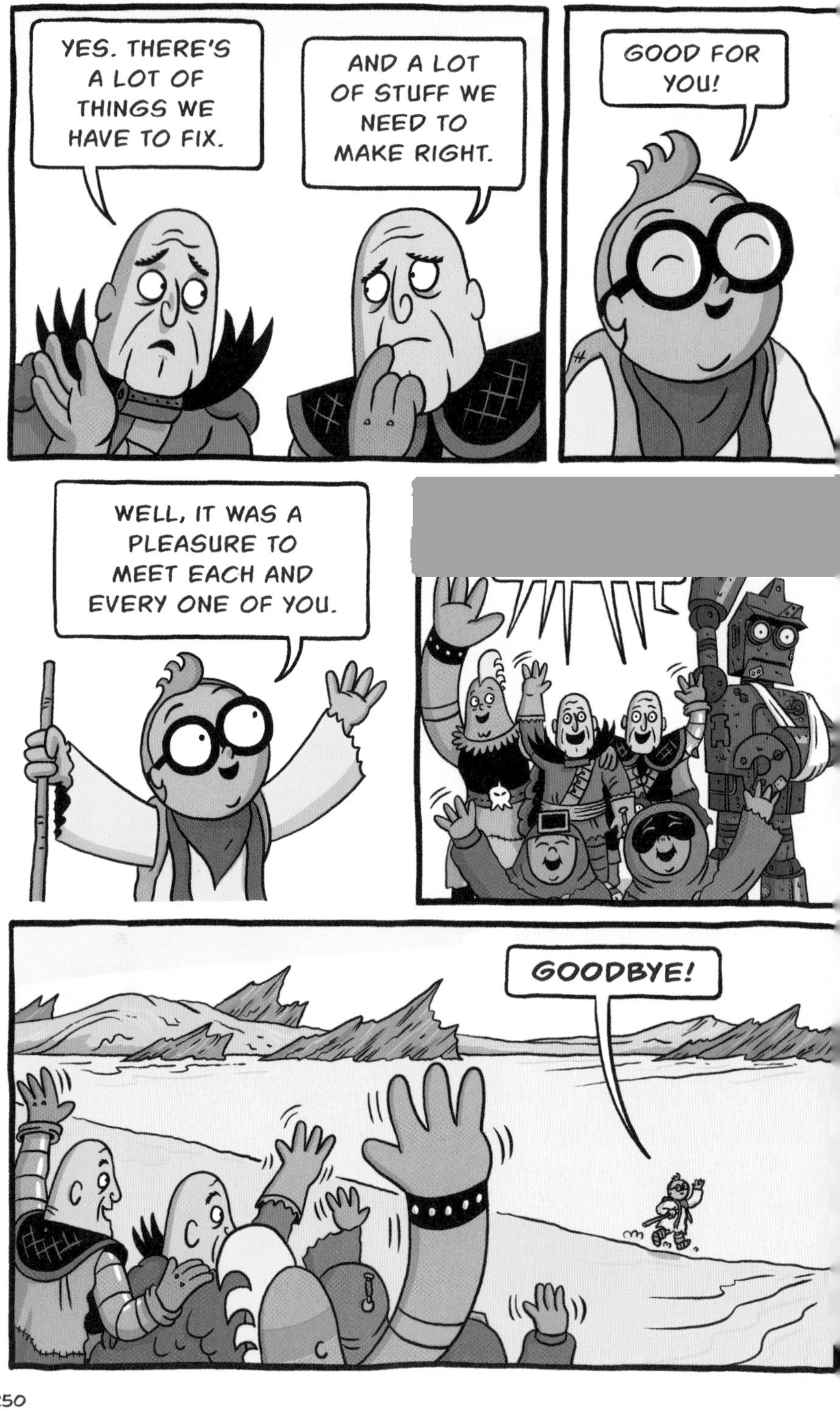
YES. THERE'S A LOT OF THINGS WE HAVE TO FIX.
AND A LOT OF STUFF WE NEED TO MAKE RIGHT.
GOOD FOR YOU!
WELL, IT WAS A PLEASURE TO MEET EACH AND EVERY ONE OF YOU.
GOODBYE!

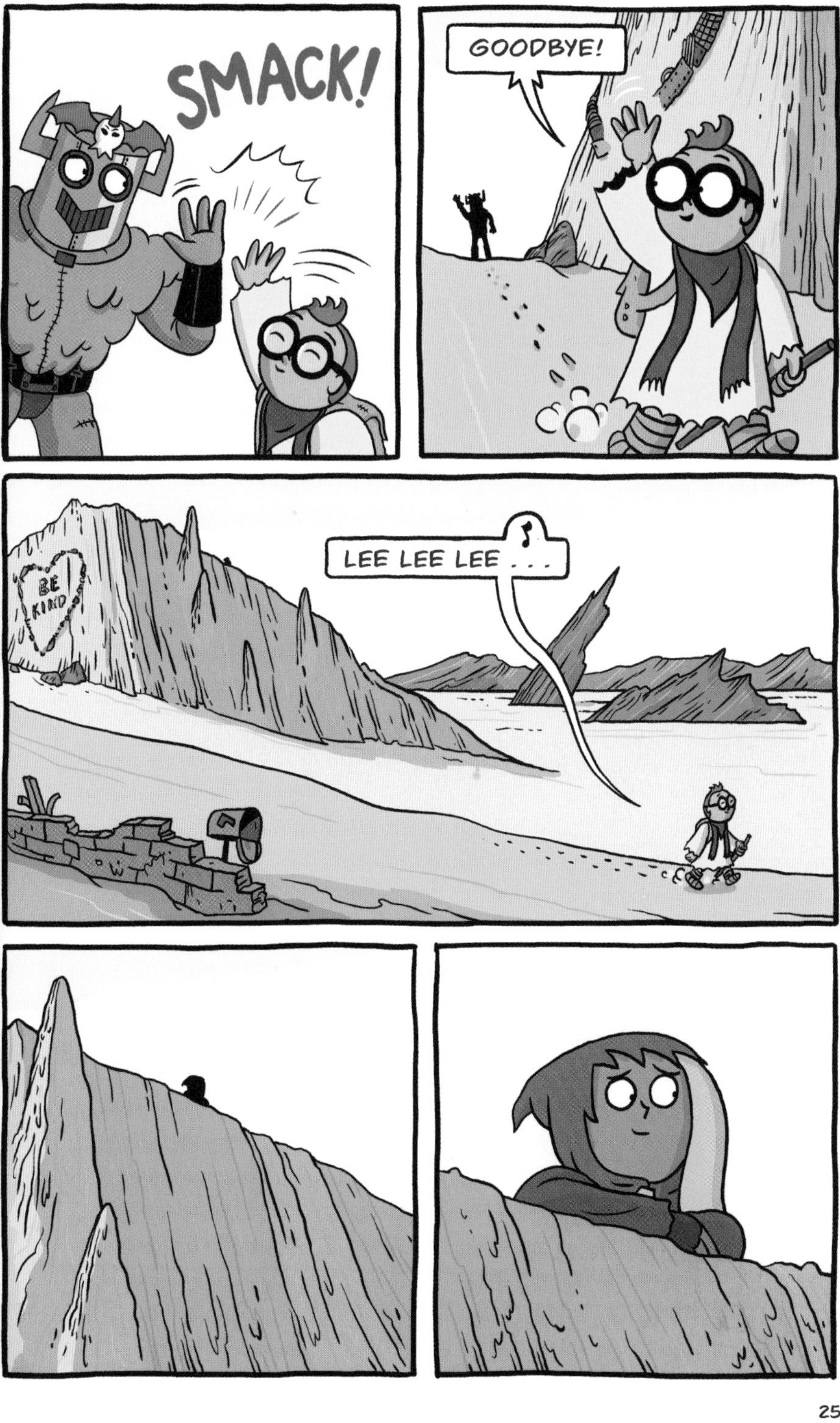

SMACK!
GOODBYE!
BE KIND
LEE LEE LEE . . .

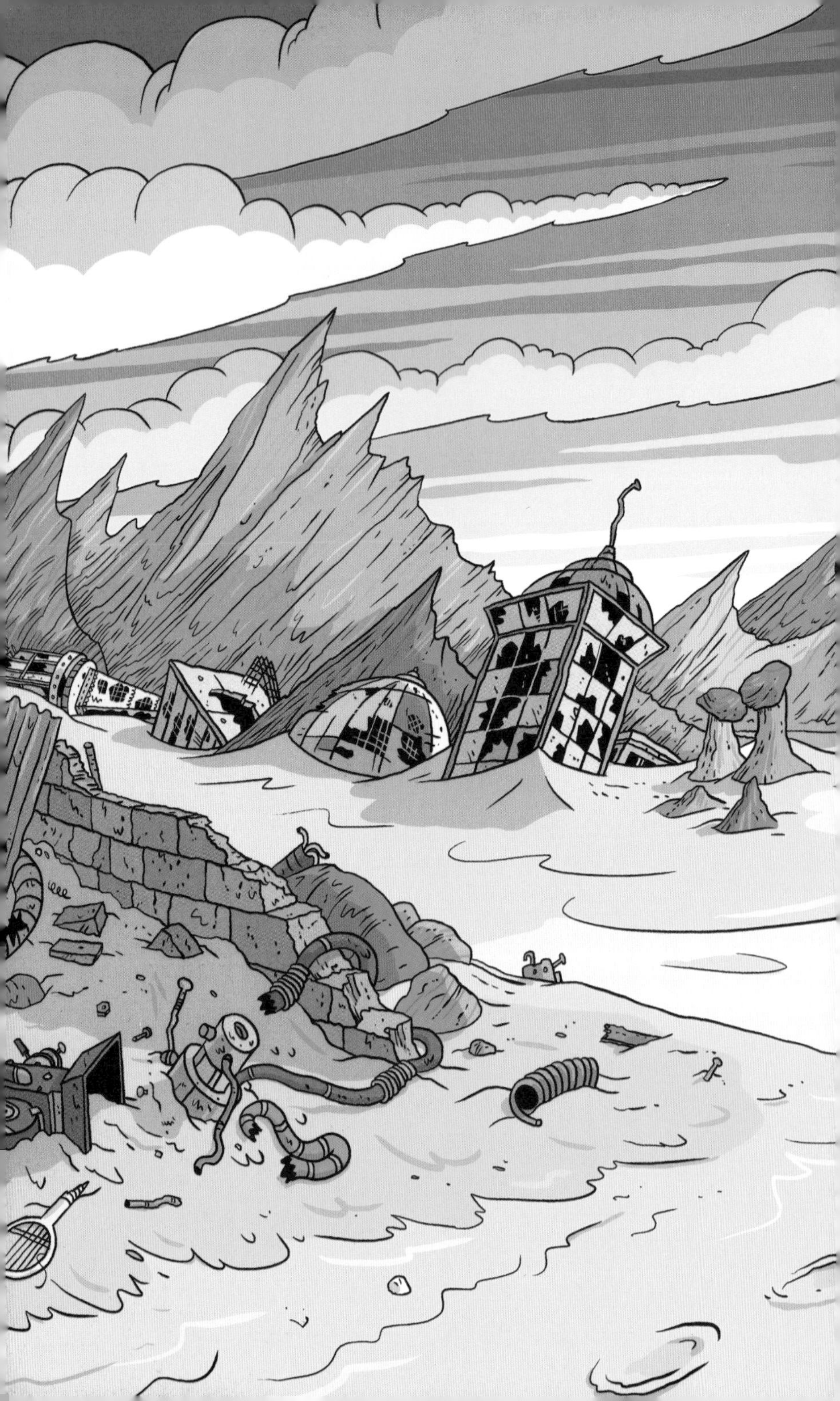

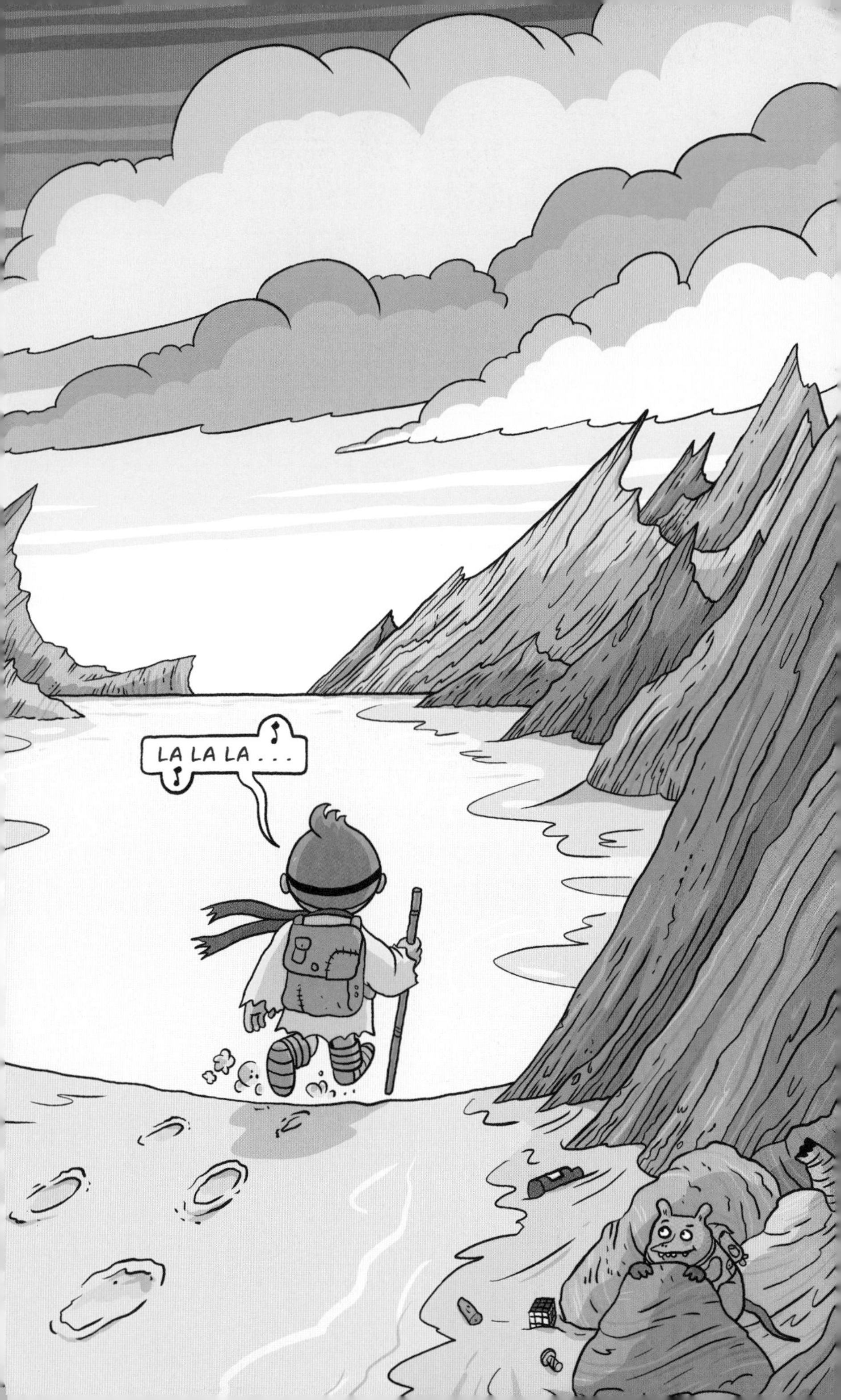
LA LA LA . . .

Mike Rex 2021

Fred's Guide to Making Friends

If you want to learn how to make friends like Fred, here are a few simple steps you can try!

STEP #1

Notice what someone is interested in.

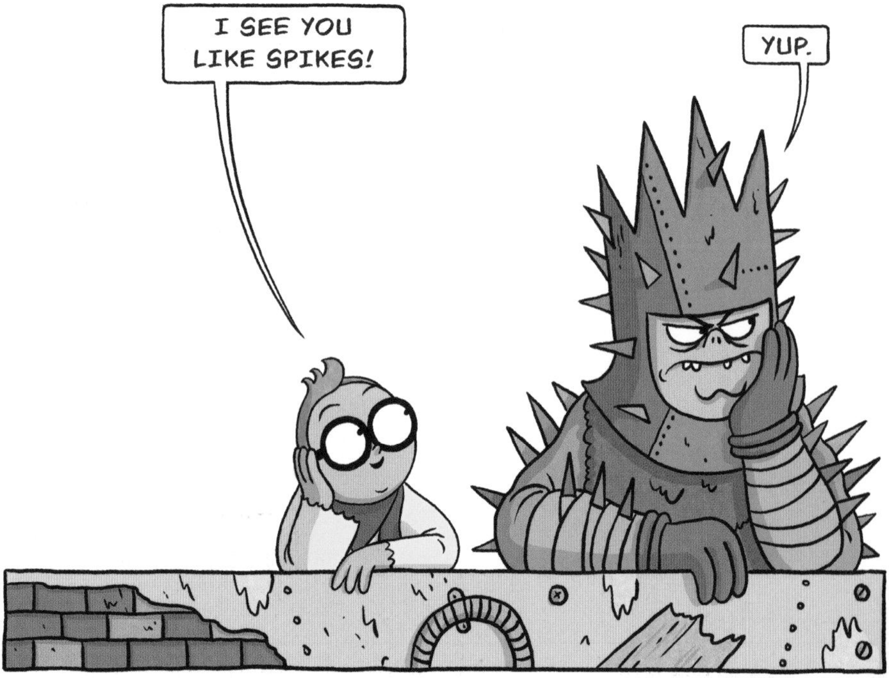

I SEE YOU LIKE SPIKES!
YUP.

STEP #2

Ask a question about that interest.

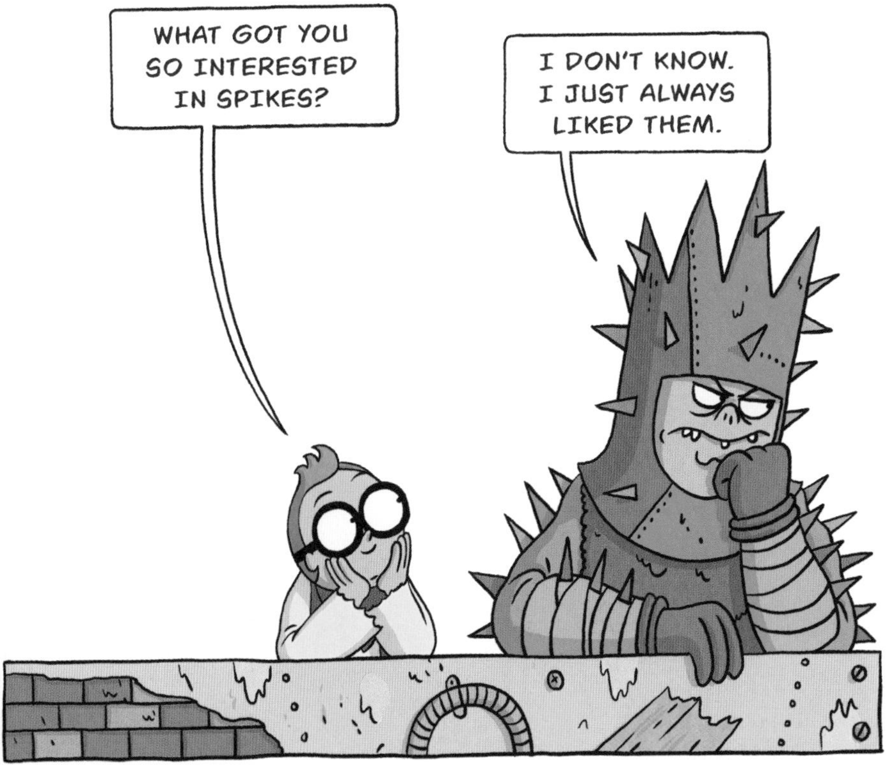
WHAT GOT YOU SO INTERESTED IN SPIKES?
I DON'T KNOW. I JUST ALWAYS LIKED THEM.

STEP #3

Compliment the person on their interest.

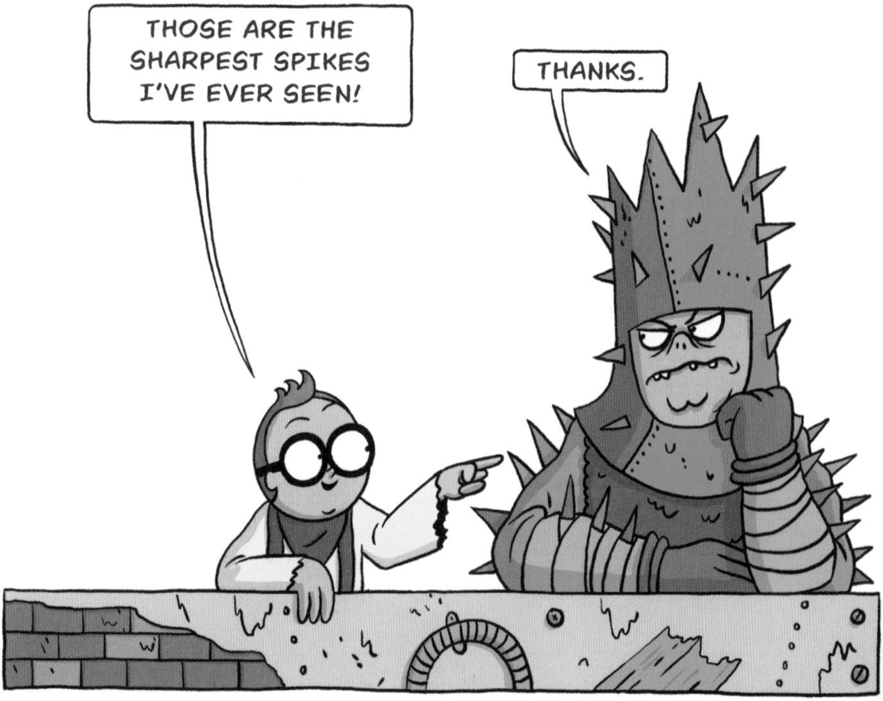
THOSE ARE THE SHARPEST SPIKES I'VE EVER SEEN!
THANKS.

STEP #4

Introduce yourself and ask the other person their name.

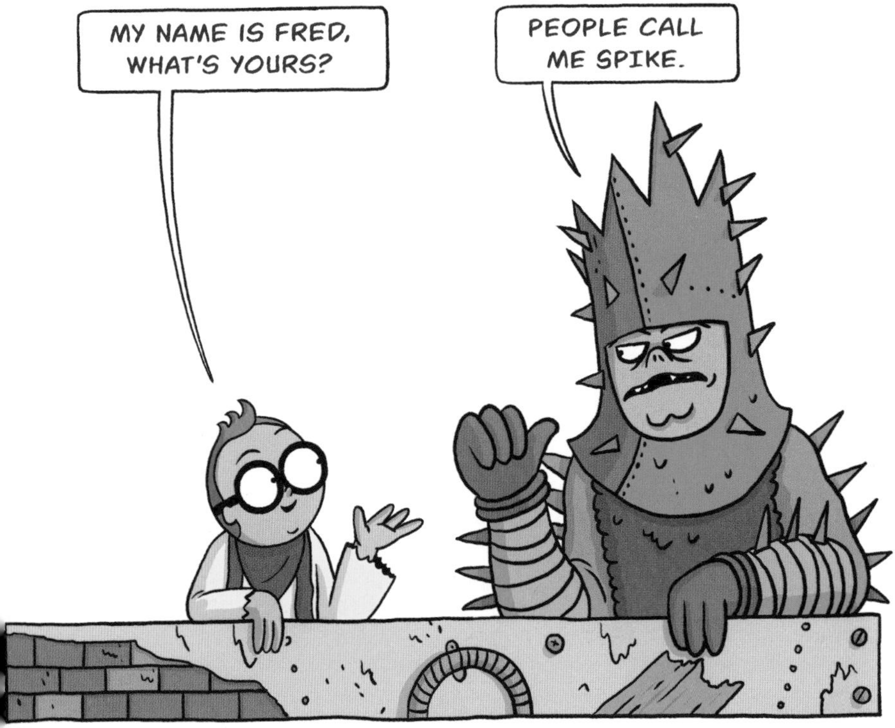
MY NAME IS FRED, WHAT'S YOURS?
PEOPLE CALL ME SPIKE.

STEP #5

Tell a joke.
(If you can make the joke related to their interest, that's even better.)

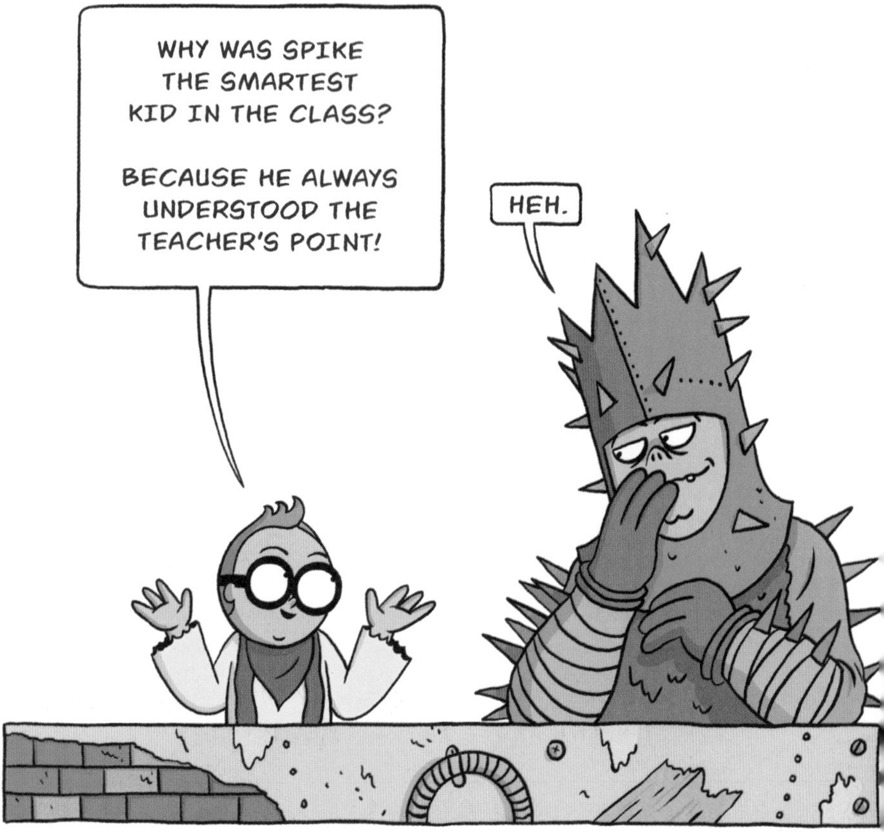
WHY WAS SPIKE THE SMARTEST KID IN THE CLASS?
BECAUSE HE ALWAYS UNDERSTOOD THE TEACHER'S POINT!
HEH.

STEP #6

Smile.
(This is the easiest step.)

MICHAEL REX has been writing and illustrating

since 1995 and has created over forty-five books for children, including the #1 bestseller and Halloween favorite *Goodnight Goon*. His Fangbone! graphic novels have been adapted into an animated TV show, and his recent picture book *Facts vs. Opinions vs. Robots* is being developed for TV as well. He's written for all ages, from simple picture books such as *Eat Pete* to the illustrated chapter book series Icky Ricky. He travels the country talking about his work with students of all ages, has a master's degree in arts education, and also taught high school art for three years in the Bronx.

He has been obsessed with postapocalyptic stories since he was young, and has wanted to tell a story like *Your Pal Fred* as long as he can remember. He lives in New Jersey with his wife, two teenage boys, and a dog named Roxy.

Visit him on Twitter @mikerexbooks, Instagram @fangbone_rex, or at mikerexbooks.blogspot.com.